I0651171

Thomas Salmon

A Short View of the Families of the Present English Nobility

Heir marriages, issue, and immediate ancestors; the posts of honour and profit

they hold in the government; their arms, mottos, and chief seats. Third Edition

Thomas Salmon

A Short View of the Families of the Present English Nobility
Heir marriages, issue, and immediate ancestors; the posts of honour and profit they hold in the government; their arms, mottos, and chief seats. Third Edition

ISBN/EAN: 9783337409920

Printed in Europe, USA, Canada, Australia, Japan

Cover: Foto ©Andreas Hilbeck / pixelio.de

More available books at **www.hansebooks.com**

A

SHORT VIEW

OF THE

FAMILIES

Of the PRESENT

ENGLISH NOBILITY;

Their MARRIAGES, ISSUE, and immediate
ANCESTORS; the POSTS of HONOUR and
PROFIT they hold in the GOVERNMENT;
their ARMS, MOTTOS, and CHIEF SEATS.

WITH

An INDEX.

Specifying the TIME of their refpective CREA-
TIONS, and SUMMONS to PARLIAMENT; the
TITLES of their Eldeft Sons; their RANK,
PRECEDENCE, &c.

By Mr. SALMON.

THE THIRD EDITION,

Enlarged and greatly correfted, fo as to exhibit a View
of the State of the PEERAGE to the Year 1761.

LONDON:

Printed for WILLIAM OWEN, near Temple-Bar.

MDCCLXI.

A
SHORT VIEW

OF THE

PEERAGE

OF

ENGLAND:

Their MARRIAGES, ISSUE, and
Immediate ANCESTORS.

---

1. HOWARD DUKE OF NORFOLK.

THE moſt noble Prince EDWARD HOWARD, Duke of NORFOLK, Earl Marſhal, and hereditary Earl Marſhal of England, Earl of Arundel, Surrey, Norfolk, and Norwich; Baron of Mowbray, Howard, &c. Premier Duke, Earl, and Baron of England next the blood royal, and chief of the family of the Howards, ſucceeded his brother Thomas, the late Duke, December 23, 1732; and married, Nov. 6, 1727, Mary, daughter of Edward Blount, of Blagdon in Devonſhire, Eſq; by whom he has no iſſue.

Thomas Duke of Norfolk, father of the preſent Duke, married Mary-Elizabeth, ſole daughter and heir of Sir John Savil, of Copley in the county of York, Bart. by whom he had iſſue five ſons; alſo a daughter, the Lady Mary, who married Walter Aſton, Baron Aſton of Forfar in Scotland.

His ſons were,

1. Thomas, late Duke of Norfolk.

B   2. Henry,

2. Henry, who died unmarried.

3. Edward, the prefent Duke.

4. Richard, who died unmarried.

5. Philip, who married to his firft wife Winifred, daughter of Thomas Stonor of Stonor, in the county of Oxford, Efq; by whom he had iffue one daughter, named Winifred, who was married to William Lord Stourton, and died July 15, 1753; and one fon named Thomas, born Feb. 4, 1727-8.

By his fecond wife, Henrietta, daughter of Edward Blount of Blagdon, in the county of Devon, Efq; and fifter to the prefent Duchefs of Norfolk, he had one fon named Edward, and a daughter named Anne. And the faid

Philip their father died Jan. 3, 1749-50.

This noble Duke is defcended from Thomas de Brotherton, Earl of Norfolk, fifth fon of King Edward I.

The Earl of Surrey, general of the Englifh army, his Grace's anceftor, obtained that decifive victory over the Scots at Flodden Field, anno 1513, wherein King James IV. of Scotland loft his life.

Arms.] Gules, in the middle of a bend between fix crofs croflets, argent; a fhield, or ; therein a demi lion rampant, pierced through the mouth with an arrow, within a double treffure counterflory, gules.

Creft.] On a chapeau, gules, turned up ermine, a lion paffant-guardant, his tail extended, gorged with a ducal coronet, argent, as defcended from Margaret, daughter and heir of Thomas de Brotherton, Earl of Norfolk, fifth fon of Edward I.

Supporters.] On the dexter fide a lion, and on the finifter a horfe, both argent ; the latter holding a flip of oak frufted, proper.

Motto.] *Sola virtus invicta.*

Chief Seats.] At Arundel-Caftle, in Suffex ; Workfop-Manor, in the county of Nottingham ; St. James's-Square, London.   2. SEY.

2. SEYMOUR, DUKE of SOMERSET.

THE moſt noble Prince EDWARD SEYMOUR, Duke of SOMERSET, Baron Seymour, and Baronet, ſucceeded his father the late Duke, who died Dec. 15, 1757.

Edward Seymour, the late Duke, married Mary, daughter and heir of Daniel Webb, of Monkton-Farley in Wiltſhire, Eſq; and niece and heir of Edward Somner, of Send in the ſame county, Eſq; by whom he had iſſue four ſons, and a daughter, viz.

1. Edward, the preſent Duke.

2. Lord Webb-Seymour, who inherits his grandfather's eſtate at Monkton-Farley.

3. Lord William, who, being entered in the Inner-Temple, was called to the bar as barriſter of law in 1744.

4. Lord Francis, appointed in July 1752, one of his Majeſty's chaplains in ordinary, and now one of the canons of Windſor; is married to Catharine, daughter of the Rev. Mr. Payne, and ſiſter to the Counteſs-Dowager of Northampton.

5. Lady Mary, married Sept. 21, 1759, to Vincent Biſcoe, Eſq;

On the death of his Grace Algernoon, Duke of Somerſet, in Feb. 1749-50, the late Duke ſucceeded to the honours of Duke of Somerſet and Baron Seymour, being lineally deſcended from Edward Duke of Somerſet, uncle of King Edward VI. and protector of the realm in the beginning of that reign.

Creations.] Baron Seymour, by letters patent, Feb. 15, 1546, (1 Edward VI.) and Duke of Somerſet the day following.

Arms.] Quarterly, firſt and fourth, or, on a pile, gules, between ſix fleur-de-Lis, azure, three lions of England; (an augmentation granted by King Henry VIII. on his marriage with the Lady Jane Seymour)

ſecond

fecond and third, the paternal coat of Seymour; gules, two wings, conjoined in lure, tips downwards, or.

Creft.] Out of a ducal coronet, or, a phœnix in flames, proper, in memory of King Edward VI.

Supporters.] On the dexter fide an unicòrn, argent, armed, crefted, and gorged, with a ducal collar, to which is affixed a chain, or. On the fir.ifter a bull, azure, collared, chained, and hoofed, as that on the dexter.

Motto.] *Foy pour devoir.*

Chief Seats.] At Maiden-Bradley in Wiltfhire, and Berry-Pomeroy in Devonfhire ; Grofvenor-ftreet, London.

---

3.   F I T Z R O Y   D U K E of C L E V E L A N D.

THE moft noble Prince WILLIAM FITZROY, Duke of CLEVELAND and SOUTHAMPTON, Earl of Southampton and Chichefter, and Baron of Non-fuch and Newbury, comptroller of the feal and green wax-office, and receiver-general and comptroller of the profits of the feals in the courts of King's-Bench and Common-Pleas, was born Feb. 19, 1697-8, fucceeded his father, the late Duke Charles, in 1730, and married, in 1731, the Lady Henrietta Finch, daughter of Daniel late Earl of Winchelfea and Nottingham ; by whom he has no iffue.

The Duchefs died in April 1742, and his Grace is yet a widower.

The late Duke Charles was the eldeft natural fon of King Charles II. by the Lady Barbara Villiers, daughter and heir of William Villiers, Vifcount Grandifon; which Lady was, on the 3d of Auguft, 22 Car. II. created Baronefs of Nonfuch, Countefs of Southampton, and Duchefs of Cleveland ; and the Duchefs dying at Chifwick, in the county of Middlefex, Oct. 9, 1709,

1709, was succeeded by her said son Charles, who was born in June 1662, and married Mary, daughter and sole heir of Sir Henry Wood, one of the clerks of the green-cloth in the reign of King Charles II. by whom he had no issue.

His Grace married again in 1694, Anne, daughter of Sir William Pultney, of Leicestershire, Knt. by whom he had three sons and three daughters, viz.

1. William, the present Duke.

2. Lord Charles Fitzroy, born Feb. 13, 1698-9, and died July 31, 1723.

3. Lord Henry Fitzroy, born August 1701, and died in 1708.

4. Lady Barbara.

5. Lady Grace, married to the Honourable Henry late Earl of Darlington.

6. Lady Anne.

Arms.] Quarterly; the first and fourth grand quarters quarterly, France and England; the second Scotland, and the third Ireland; being the arms of King Charles II. over all a baston, sinister counter-compone, ermine and azure.

Crest.] On a chapeau, gules, turned up ermine, a lion passant-guardant, or, crowned with a ducal coronet, argent, and gorged with a collar counter-compone, ermine and azure.

Supporters.] On the dexter side a lion guardant, or, crowned with a ducal coronet, azure, and gorged with a collar counter-compone, ermine and azure. On the sinister, a greyhound, argent, collared as the dexter.

Motto.} *Secundis dubiisque rectus.*

Chief Seats] At Bayles, in the county of Berks, near Windsor; at Combe Park in the county of Surrey, and St. James's-Square, London.

4. LE-

4. LENOX DUKE of RICHMOND.

THE moſt noble Prince CHARLES LENOX, Duke
of RICHMOND in South Britain, of Lenox in
North Britain, and Aubigny in France ; Earl of
March and Darnley, Baron of Settrington and Tur-
bolton, &c. colonel of the 72d regiment of foot, born
Feb. 1734-5, ſucceeded Charles the late Duke his father, in honour and eſtate, Aug. 8, 1750; and April
1, 1757, waſ married to the Lady Mary Bruce, ſiſter
to the Earl of Ayleſbury.

Charles, father of the preſent Duke, was born
May 18, 1701 ; and married in Dec. 1719, the
Lady Sarah, eldeſt daughter and coheir of William
Earl of Cadogan, who died Aug. 25, 1751; and by
whom he had iſſue,

1. Lady Georgina-Carolina, born March 27, 1723,
and married in May 1744, to the Right Hon. Henry
Fox, Eſq; now paymaſter-general of his Majeſty's
forces, and one of the lords of his Majeſty's privy-
council, only brother to Stephen Earl of Ilcheſter.

2. A ſon, who died immediately after his birth,
Sept. 3, 1724.

3. Lady Louiſa Margaret, born Nov. 15, 1725,
and died in 1728.

4. Lady Anne, born May 27, 1726, and died
the ſame year.

5. Charles Earl of March, born Sept. 9, 1730, who
died the ſame year.

6. Lady Emilia, born Oct. 6, 1731, married
Feb. 7, 1746-7, to the Earl of Kildare in Ireland.

7. Charles, now Duke of Richmond.

8. Lord George-Henry, born Nov. 27, 1737,
appointed lieutenant-colonel of the 33d regiment of
foot in May 1758, married, in 1759, to Lady ——,
daughter to the Earl of Ancram in Scotland.

9. Lady

9. Lady Margaret, born Nov. 16, 1739, and died Jan. 10, 1740-1.

10. Lady Louisa-Augusta, born Nov. 24, 1743.

11. Lady Sarah, born Feb. 14, 1744-5.

12. Lady Cecilia Margaret, born Feb. 28, 1749-50.

Charles Duke of Richmond, grandfather of the present Duke, was the only son of King Charles II. by the Lady Louisa Renée de Penencourt, of Querouelle in France; whom King Charles created Duchess of Portsmouth, Countess of Farnham, and Baroness of Petersfield, 25 Car. II. 1673; and, by the intercession of King Charles to the French King, Lewis XIV. she was created Duchess of Aubigny in France.

Charles, the said Duke, married Anne, the widow and relict of Henry Lord Belasis, eldest daughter of Francis Lord Brudnel, son and heir of Robert Earl of Cardigan, and sister to George late Earl of Cardigan, by whom he had issue,

1. Charles, late Duke of Richmond.

2. Lady Louisa, married to James, late Earl of Berkeley.

3. Lady Anne, married to William Anne, Earl of Albemarle.

Arms.] The arms of King Charles II. within a bordure-compone, argent and gules; the first charged with verdoy of roses of the second, barbed and seeded, proper.

Crest.] On a chapeau, gules, turned up ermine, a lion passant-guardant, or, crowned with a ducal coronet, gules, and gorged with a collar, gobone, counter-charged, as the bordure in the coat.

Supporters.] On the dexter side an unicorn, armed, crested, and hoofed, argent. On the sinister, an antelope, armed, crested, and hoofed, as the dexter; each supporter gorged with a collar, compone, gules and ermine.

Motto.] *En la rose je Fleurie.*

Chief Seats.] At Goodwood, in the county of Sussex; Privy-Garden, Westminster.   5. FITZ-

5. FITZROY DUKE of GRAFTON.

THÉ moſt noble Prince Augustus Henry
Fitzroy, Duke of Grafton, Earl of Euſton
and Arlington, Viſcount Thetford and Ipſwich, Baron of Arlington and Sudbury, remembrancer of
the firſt fruits, lord lieutenant and cuſtos rotulorum
of the county of Suffolk, ranger of Whitlebury-fo-
reſt in Northamptonſhire, his Majeſty's game-keeper
at Newmarket, and recorder of the city of Coventry, born in Oct. 1735, ſucceeded his grandfather,
Charles the late Duke of Grafton, May 6, 1757;
and on Jan. 29, 1756, married Anne, only daughter
of Henry Liddel, Lord Ravenſworth, who, on May
8, 1757, was brought to-bed of a daughter, named
Georgiana ; and of a ſon and heir Jan. 16, 1760.

Charles Fitzroy, the late Duke, was born Oct. 25,
1683 ; and, in 1713, married the Lady Henrietta Somerſet, daughter of Charles, Marquis of Worceſter,
eldeſt ſon of Henry, Duke of Beaufort ; by whom he
had iſſue,

1. George Earl of Euſton, who married the Lady
Dorothy Boyle, daughter of Richard Earl of Burlington ; both of them dying without iſſue.

2. Lord Auguſtus, who married ———, daughter
of colonel Coſby, by whom he left iſſue, 1. Lord Auguſtus, now Duke of Grafton ; and, 2. the Lord
Charles Fitzroy, lieutenant-colonel in the army, and
married to Miſs Warren, one of the coheireſſes of the
late Sir Peter Warren, July 27, 1758, by whom he
had a daughter born May 10, 1759. The late Lord
Auguſtus, their father, was captain of the Orford man
of war, and died at Jamaica in Feb. 1740-1.

3. Lord Charles, who died at Milan in Italy, unmarried.

4. The

4. The Lady Carolina, who married Lord Peter-fham, now Earl of Harrington; by whom fhe has iffue. *See Earl of Harrington.*

5. Lady Arabella, who married Lord Conway, now Earl of Hertford; by whom he has iffue, Francis, born 1742, &c. *See Earl of Hertford,*

Henry Fitzroy, father of the late Duke, was the fecond fon of King Charles II. by the Lady Barbara Villiers, Duchefs of Cleveland. He was born Sept. 28, 1663; created Baron of Sudbury, Vifcount Ipfwich, and Earl of Eufton, Aug. 6, 1675; and, in September following, Duke of Grafton. He received a mortal wound at the fiege of Cork in Ireland, of which he died, Oct. 9, 1690, being fucceeded in his honours and eftates by his faid fon Charles, the late Duke, whofe mother was the only daughter and heir of Henry Bennet, Earl of Arlington, by the Lady Ifabella of Naffau, fifter to Henry of Naffau, fignior D'Auverquerque.

Arms.] The arms of King Charles II, with a baton finifter-compone, argent and azure.

Creft.] On a chapeau, gules, turned up ermine, a lion paffant-guardant, or, crowned with a ducal coronet, azure, and gorged with a collar counter-compone, argent and azure.

Supporters.] On the dexter fide, a lion guardant, or, crowned with a ducal coronet, azure, and gorged with a collar counter-compone, argent and azure. On the finifter, a greyhound, argent, gorged as the lion.

Motto.] *Et decus et pretium recti.*

Chief Seats.] At Wakefield-lodge in Whitlebury-foreft, in Northamptonfhire; at Livermore-hall, and Eufton-hall, in the county of Suffolk; Old Bond-ftreet, London.

B 5 6. SOMER-

6. SOMERSET, DUKE of BEAUFORT.

THE moſt noble Prince Henry Somerset, Duke of Beaufort, Marquis and Earl of Worceſter, Earl of Glamorgan, Viſcount Groſmont, Baron Herbert, Lord of Ragland, Chepſtow, and Gower, all in the county of Monmouth; as alſo Baron Beaufort of Caldecot-caſtle, born Oct. 16, 1744, ſucceeded his father Charles, the late Duke, who died Nov. 1, 1756.

Charles, the late Duke, born Sept. 12, 1709, ſucceeded his brother Duke Henry, Feb. 24, 1745-6. His Grace married, May 1, 1740, Elizabeth, daughter of James Berkley, of Stoke in Glouceſterſhire, Eſq; by whom he had iſſue,

1. Lady Anne, born in 1741, and married, Sept. 13, 1759, to Charles, the preſent Earl of Northampton.

2. Lady Elizabeth.

3. Henry the preſent Duke.

4. Lady Rachel, who died in her infancy. And,

5. Lady Harriot, born in 1747-8; and Lady ——, born Aug. 1, 1756.

Henry, brother to the late Duke, on June 28, 1729, married Frances, only child and heir to Sir James Scudamore, of Home-Lacy in the county of Hereford, Bart. Viſcount Scudamore in Ireland, by Frances his wife, only daughter of Simon Lord Digby; by whom he had no iſſue. On June 16, 1729, his Grace was elected high-ſteward of the city of Hereford; and in 1730, an act was paſſed in parliament, for obliging his Grace and his Ducheſs, and her children, to take the additional ſurname and bear the arms of Scudamore, purſuant to a ſettlement made by her Grace's father. He was divorced from this lady, March 2, 1743-4; and dying Feb. 24, 1745 6, leaving no iſſue, was ſucceeded by the Lord Charles Noel, his brother, the late Duke.   Henry,

Henry, Duke of Beaufort, father of the two laft Dukes, was born April 2, 1684. He married, in 1702, the Lady Mary Sackville, only daughter of Charles Earl of Dorfet, who died June 18, 1705, leaving no iffue. He married to his fecond wife, in 1706, the Lady Rachel Noel, fecond daughter of Wriothefly Baptift Noel, Earl of Gainfborough ; by whom he had iffue,

1. Henry Duke of Beaufort.
2. Lord John, who died young. And,
3. The Lord Charles Noel, the late Duke, of whom the Duchefs died in childbed.

His Grace married to his third wife, the Lady Mary Ofborne, youngeft daughter of Peregrine Duke of Leeds; by whom he had no iffue.

This noble Duke is lineally defcended from John of Gaunt, Duke of Lancafter, fourth fon of King Edward III.

Arms.] Quarterly, France and England, within a bordure-compone, argent and azure.

Creft.] A portcullis, or, nailed, azure; chains of the firft.

Supporters.] On the dexter fide a panther, argent, fpotted with various colours, fire iffuing out of his mouth and ears, proper, gorged with a collar, and chain pendant, or. On the finifter, a wyverne, vert, holding in his mouth a finifter-hand couped at the wrift, proper.

Motto.] *Mutare vel timere fperno.*

Chief Seats.] At Badminton in Gloucefterfhire ; Chepftow-caftle in Monmouthfhire; at Netherhaven in the county of Wilts ; and Upper Grofvenor-ftreet, London.

2 A SHORT VIEW of THE

7. BEAUCLERK, DUKE of
St. ALBANS.

THE moſt noble Prince GEORGE BEAUCLERK, Duke of St. ALBANS, Earl of Burford, and Baron of Heddington, was born June 25, 1730, is hereditary grand falconer, regiſter of the court of Chancery, and lord lieutenant and cuſtos rotulorum of the county of Berks, and high-ſteward of the corporation of Windſor. He ſucceeded his father Charles the late Duke, on his deceaſe July 27, 1751. He married, Oct. 23, 1752, Jane, ſole daughter and heir of Sir Walter Roberts, of Glaſſenbury in Kent, Bart.

His Grace Charles Duke of St. Albans, grandfather of the preſent Duke, was a natural ſon of King Charles II. by Mrs. Eleanor Gwin (on whom his Majeſty conferred the ſirname of Beauclerk) born May 8, 1670; and Dec. 26, 1676, was created Baron of Heddington, in the county of Oxford, and Earl of Burford; and 35 Car. II. 1683, created Duke of St. Albans. His Grace, April 17, 1694, married the Lady Diana Vere, eldeſt daughter and coheir to the Right Hon. Aubrey de Vere, laſt Earl of Oxford of that noble family; by whom he had iſſue,

1. Charles, the late Duke, born April 6, 1696, ſucceeded his father May 11, 1726, and married, Dec. 13, 1722, Lucy, daughter of Sir John Werdon, of Hollyport in the county of Berks, Bart. by whom he had iſſue George the preſent Duke, and a daughter, Diana, born Oct. 23, 1725.

2. Lord William, born May 22, 1698; who, in 1722, married Charlotte, daughter and coheir of Sir John Worden, Bart. by whom he had iſſue, 1. William, who died at Eaton-ſchool. 2. Charles Beauclerk, Eſq; 3. Charlotte; and, 4. Caroline.

3. Lord Vere, born July 14, 1699, who married, in April 1736, Mary, eldeſt daughter, and one of the coheirs of the late Sir Thomas Chambers, of Hanworth in the county of Middleſex, Bart. by whom.

whom he had iffue, 1. Chambers Beauclerk, Efq; fince dead. 2. Aubrey. 3. Vere, who died an infant; and 4. a daughter.

4. Lord Henry, born Auguft 11, 1701; who married, in December 1738, Mary, fifter and heir of Nevil Lord Lovèlace; by whom he has iffue living, a fon, and feveral daughters.

5. Lord Sidney, born February 27, 1702; married, Dec. 9, 1736, Mary, daughter of Thomas Norris, of Speak in the county of Lancafter, Efq; His Lordfhip died Nov. 23, 1744.

6. Lord George, major-general of his Majefty's forces.

7. Lord James, bifhop of Hereford, unmarried.

8. Lord Aubrey, born in 1711; killed on board the Prince Frederick man of war at Carthagena.

Arms.] The arms of King Charles II. with a baton finifter, gules; charged with three rofes, argent, feeded and barbed, proper.

Creft.] On a chapeau, gules, turned up ermine, a lion paffant-guardant, or, crowned with a ducal coronet party per pale, argent and gules, and gorged with a collar, gules, charged with three rofes, argent, feeded and barbed, proper.

Supporters.] On the dexter fide, an antelope, argent, armed and unguled, or. On the finifter, a greyhound, argent, gorged and unguled, as the other.

Motto.] *Aufpicium melioris ævi.*

Chief Seats.] At Windfor in Berkfhire; at Crawley in Hampfhire; and St. James's-Place, London.

8. POWLET, DUKE of BOLTON.

THE moft noble Prince CHARLES POWLET, Duke of BOLTON, Marquis of Winchefter, Earl of Wiltfhire, Baron St. John of Bafing, premier Marquis of England, a knight of the Bath, lord lieutenant and cuftos rotulorum of the county and town of
Southampton,

Southampton, and one of his Majesty's most honourable privy-council, succeeded his father Harry, the late Duke, upon his death, which happened Oct. 9, 1759.

Harry the late Duke of Bolton, succeeded his brother Charles, Aug. 26, 1754.

The said Charles Duke of Bolton, married the Lady Anne Vaughan, daughter and sole heir to John Lord Vaughan, Earl of Carbery in Ireland, and Baron of Emlyn in England ; but not cohabiting with her, had no children by her : and the Duchess dying Sept. 20, 1751, he married Mrs. Lavinia Fenton, the famous Polly Peachum, by whom he had no legitimate issue, tho' he had several children by her before he married her.   Her Grace died Jan. 17, 1760.

Charles Marquis of Winchester, eldest son of John Marquis of Winchester, was created Duke of Bolton r William and. Mary, 1689 : besides the late Duke Charles, his Grace's other sons were,

1. Lord Nassau, married, in 1731, to Lady Isabella, daughter and coheir of John Earl of Thanet, and had two sons, viz. 1. Nassau, who died in 1741. 2. Charles ; and two daughters.   His Lordship died in Aug. 1741 ; and his lady is since married to Francis Blake Delaval, of Seaton-Delaval in Northumberland, Esq; member of parliament for Andover.

2. Harry the late Duke, who married Catharine, daughter of Charles Parry, of Oakfield in Berkshire, Esq; by whom he hath issue two sons, and two daughters, viz.

1. Charles, now Duke of Bolton.

2. Lord Harry, vice-admiral of the White, and member of parliament for Lymington ; married, May 13, 1752, Miss Nunn, of Eltham in Kent, and has issue.

3. Lady Henrietta, married, July 12, 1741, to Robert Colebrooke, of Chilham-castle in Kent, Esq;: member of parliament for Malden ; and is deceased.

4. Lady

4. Lady Catharine, married firſt, June 4, 1749, to William Aſhe, Eſq; and, ſecondly, in Feb. 1755, to Adam Drummond, Eſq;

This noble Duke is deſcended from Hercules Lord of Tournon in Picardy, who came over to England with Jeffrey Plantagenet, Earl of Anjou, third ſon of King Henry II. and among other lands, had the lord-ſhip of Paulet in Somerſetſhire conferred upon him. It has been a moſt loyal family : John Marquis of Wincheſter fortified his houſe at Baſing, and, intro-ducing a brave garriſon into it, defended it for King Charles I. for two years, againſt all the power of his enemies, refuſing to ſurrender until the place was taken by ſtorm.

Arms.] Sable, three ſwords in pile, their points to-wards the baſe, argent, the pomels and hilts, or, a creſcent for difference.

Creſt.] On a wreath a mount, vert, from whence a falcon, riſing, or, gorged with a ducal coronet, gules, the creſt of Lord St. John of Baſing, as a deſ-cendant of an heir female of that family.

Supporters.] Two hinds, purpure, ſemi of Eſtoils, argent, gorged with a ducal coronet, or

Motto.] *Aymez loyaulte.*

Chief Seats.] At Hackwood-park, and Abbotſtone, in Hampſhire ; at Golden-grove in the county of Caer-marthen ; Bolton-hall in Yorkſhire ; and at Hook-park in the county of Dorſet ; Downing-ſtreet, London.

---

9. OSBORNE, DUKE of LEEDS.

THE moſt noble Prince THOMAS OSBORNE, Duke of Leeds, Marquis of Caermarthen, Earl of Danby, Viſcount Latimer and Dumblain, Baron Oſborne of Kiveton, one of the lords of his Majeſty's privy-council, cofferer of his Majeſty's houſhold, and knight of the moſt noble order of the garter, ſuc-ceeded his father the late Duke Peregrine, May 9, 1731;

1731; and, on June 6, 1740, married the Lady Mary, youngeft daughter of Francis Farl of Godolphin, and grand-daughter of John late Duke of Marlborouglr; by whom he has iffue living, a fon, Thomas Marquis of Caermartlien, born Oct. 5, 1747, and Lord Francis, born Jan. 29, 1750-1.

The late Duke Peregrine, father of the prefent Duke, married the Lady Elizabeth, daughter to Edward Harley, Earl of Oxford, lord high-treafurer of England; by whom he had iffue, Thomas, the prefent Duke. This Lady dying, Nov. 20, 1713, his Grace married the Lady Anne Seymour, third daughter of Charles Duke of Somerfet; and after her death, in April 1725, his Grace married to his third wife Juliana, daughter and coheir to Roger Hole, Efq; by whom he had no iffue.

Sir Thomas Ofborne, the grandfather of the prefent Duke, was conftituted lord high-treafurer of England by King Charles II. about 1673; and, in 25 Car. II. he was created a Baron, by the title of Baron Kiveton, and Vifcount Latimer; and the 27 Car. II. he was created Earl of Danby, and Vifcount Dumblain in Scotland. In May 1689 he was, by King William, created Marquis of Caermarthen; and, on May 4, 1694, he was, by the fame King, created Duke of Leeds.

This noble Duke is defcended from the honourable family of the Ofbornes, of Afhford in the county of Kent.

Arms.] Quarterly, ermine and azure, a crofs, or.

Creft.] On a wreath of his colours, a tyger paffant, argent.

Supporters.] On the dexter fide, a griphon, or. On the finifter, a tyger, argent; each gorged with a ducal coronet, azure.

Motto.] *Pax in bello.*

Chief Seats.] At North-Myms in Hertfordfhire; at Kiveton, Harthill-hall, Thorp-hall, and Waller-hall, all in the county of York. St. James's-fquare, London.

10. RUSSEL, DUKE of BEDFORD.

THE moſt noble Prince JOHN RUSSEL, Duke of
BEDFORD, Marquis of Taviſtock, Earl of Bedford, Baron Ruſſel of Cheneys-Thornaugh, and Baron Howland of Stretham, lord lieutenant of the
counties of Bedford and Devon, high-ſteward of the
corporation of Huntingdon, lieutenant-general of
his Majeſty's forces, lieutenant-general and governor
of Ireland, knight of the moſt noble order of the
garter, one of the lords of his Majeſty's moſt honourable privy-council, maſter of the Trinity-Houſe, preſident of the Foundling-Hoſpital, one of the governors of the Charter-Houſe, and warden and keeper
of New Foreſt, was born Sept. 30, 1710, and married, in Oct. 1731, to the Lady Diana Spencer, youngeſt
daughter of Charles Earl of Sunderland, by the Lady
Anne, daughter of John Duke of Marlborough ; by
whom he had iſſue one ſon, who died the day he was
born ; and her Grace dying, Sept. 27, 1735, his
Grace married again, in April 1737, Gertrude, eldeſt
daughter of John Lord Gower ; by whom he hath iſſue,

1. Francis Marquis of Taviſtock, born Sept. 26, 1739.

2. Lady Carolina, born in Jan. 1742-3.

Wriotheſley Duke of Bedford, father of the late and
preſent Duke, was born Nov. 1, 1680, and married,
May 23, 1695, Elizabeth, daughter and heireſs of
John Howland, of Stretham, Eſq; and was thereupon
created Baron Howland of Stretham, the 13th of June
following. His Grace died, May 26, 1711, leaving
iſſue two ſons and two daughters, viz.

1. Wriotheſley, the late Duke; and,

2. Lord John, the preſent Duke.

Wriotheſley, the late Duke, ſucceeded his father
in 1711; and, in 1725, married the Lady Anne
Egerton, only daughter of Scroop, late Duke of
Bridgwater, by whom he had no iſſue ; and dying,
October

October 23, 1732, was succeeded in honour and estate by his only brother, the said Lord John Ruffel, now Duke of Bedford.

The fisters of the late and present Dukes are,

1. Lady Rachel, who married his Grace Scroop Egerton, late Duke of Bridgwater, and is since married to Sir Richard Lyttleton, knight of the Bath.

2. Lady Elizabeth, married, in 1726, to William Earl of Effex.

William Earl of Bedford, father of the late famous Lord William Ruffel, was created Marquis of Taviftock, and Duke of Bedford, 6 Wm. and Mary, 1694. The preamble to his patent recites, That it was not the least inducement to the conferring these honours upon him, that he was father to the late Lord Ruffel, the ornament of his age. His Grace died Sept. 7, 1700, in the 87th year of his age, having had issue, among other children,

1. Lord Francis, who died in 1679, unmarried.

2. Lord William, who married the Lady Rachel, fecond daughter and heir of Thomas Wriothefley Earl of Southampton, and lord high-treasurer of England; and by her left issue one son, named Wriothefley, born May 1, 1688, who succeeded his grandfather in his honours and estates, Sept. 7, 1700. He left also two daughters: 1. Lady Rachel, born 1674, married to his Grace William Cavendish, late Duke of Devonshire. 2. The Lady Catharine, born Aug. 23, 1676, married to John Manners, late Marquis of Granby, afterwards Duke of Rutland.

This noble Duke is of Norman extraction, and his ancestors appear to have been poffeffed of a confiderable estate in the county of Dorset in the year 1202.

Arms.] Argent; a lion rampant, gules; on a chief, fable, three escallops of the first.

Creft.] On a wreath, a goat paffant, argent, armed, or.

Supporters.]

Supporters.] On the dexter fide a lion; on the finifter an antelope, both gules; the latter gorged with
a ducal collar, chained, armed, crefted, tufted, and
hoofed, or.

Motto.] *Che Sara, Sara.*

Chief Seats.] At Woburn-abbey in Bedfordfhire;
Thornhaugh in Northamptonfhire; Cheneys in Bucks;
and at Bedford-houfe in Bloomsbury-fquare, London.

---

11. CAVENDISH, DUKE of DEVONSHIRE.

THE moft noble Prince WILLIAM CAVENDISH,
Duke of DEVONSHIRE, Marquis of Hartington,
Earl of Devonfhire, and Baron Cavendifh of Hardwick, lord-chamberlain of his Majefty's houfhold,
knight of the moft noble order of the garter, lord
lieutenant and cuftos rotulorum of the county of
Derby, lord high-treafurer of Ireland, governor of the
county of Cork in that kingdom, and governor of
the Charter-houfe, one of the lords of his Majefty's
privy-council, fucceeded his father in his honours
and eftates on the 5th of Dec. 1755.

His Grace married, in March 1748, the Lady
Charlotta Boyle, youngeft daughter of the late Earl
of Burlington, by which lady, who died in December
1754, he had iffue,

1. William Marquis of Hartington, born in Dec.
1748.

2. Lord Richard, born June 19, 1752.

3. Lord George Henry, born in March 1754.

4. Lady Dorothy, born Aug. 17 :750.

William the late Duke, on March 27, 1718, married Catharine, the daughter and fole heir of John
Hofkins, Efq; by whom he had iffue,

1. William, the prefent Duke.

2. Lord

2. Lord George Cavendiſh.

3. Lord Frederick Cavendiſh, appointed colonel of a regiment of foot, and aid de camp to his Majeſty in May 1758, and, in Nov. 1759, appointed colonel of the 64th regiment of foot, in the room of Brigadier Townſhend.

4. Lord John Cavendiſh; all three unmarried. The ſaid Duke's daughters were,

1. Lady Carolina, who married, in 1739, to William Ponſonby, Lord Viſcount Duncannon, now Earl of Beſsborough of the kingdom of Ireland, and died Jan. 20, 1760.

2. Lady Elizabeth, married, in 1743, to the Hon. John Ponſonby, Eſq; brother to the Earl of Beſborough.

3. Lady Rachel, who married, in 1748, to Horace Lord Walpole of Woolterton.

His Grace William Duke of Devonſhire, grandfather of the preſent Duke, married the Lady Rachel, daughter of William Lord Ruſſel, and ſiſter to Wriotheſley, father of the late and preſent Dukes of Bedford, and by her had iſſue,

1. William the late Duke of Devonſhire.

2. Lord James, colonel of a regiment of foot, died in 1741.

3. Lord Charles, who married, Jan. 9, 1728-9, the Lady Anne Grey, third daughter of his Grace Henry Duke of Kent; and by her had iſſue two ſons.

4. Lord John, who died May 10, 1720.-

5. Lady Mary, died June 15, 1719, unmarried.

6. Lady Rachel, married to Sir William Morgan of Tredegar in the county of Monmouth, Knight.

7. Lady Elizabeth, married to Sir Thomas Lowther, of Hooker in the county of Lancaſter, Bart. and died in 1737.

8. Lady Catharine.

9. Lady Anne; and,

10. Lady

10. Lady Diana; all three died unmarried.

This noble Duke is defcended from Robert de Gernon, a Norman commander, who attended William Duke of Normandy, in his invafion of England, in the year 1066.

Arms.] Sable ; three harts heads cabofhed, argent, attired, or.

Creft.] On a wreath, a fnake noue, proper,

Supporters.] Two harts, each gorged with a garland or fprig of rofes, proper ; attired, or.

Motto.] *Cavendo tutus.*

Chief Seats.] At Chatfworth and Hardwick, in Derbyfhire ; and Devonfhire-houfe in Piccadily, London.

---

12. SPENCER, DUKE of MARLBOROUGH.

THE moft noble Prince GEORGE SPENCER, Duke of MARLBOROUOH, Marquis of Blandford, Earl of Sunderland and Marlborough, Baron Spencer of Wormleighton, and Baron Churchill of Sandridge, prefident of the Small-pox-hofpital, born Jan. 26, 1738, fucceeded his father Charles in Oct. 1758.

Charles, the late Duke, was born Nov. 22, 1706 ; and, in 1731, on the death of William Marquis of Blandford, fon and heir of Francis Earl of Godolphin and Henrietta Duchefs of Marlborough, he fucceeded to that title, and to 8000 *l. per ann.* of the late Duke of Marlborough's eftate ; and on the death of the faid Henrietta Duchefs of Marlborough, in 1733, he fucceeded to the title of Duke of Marlborough, as heir to the Lady Anne Churchill, his mother, fecond daughter and coheir of John Duke of Marlborough. His Grace when he died was general over all and fingular the foot forces, employed, or to be employed, in his Majefty's fervice, and commander in chief of

all

all the British forces upon the Rhine, under Prince Ferdinand of Brunfwick : he was mafter of the ordnance, lord lieutenant and cuftos rotulorum of the county of Oxford, knight of the moft noble order of the garter, and one of his Majefty's privy-council. His Grace was married, on May 23, 1732, to Elizabeth, daughter of Thomas Lord Trevor ; by whom he had iffue,

1. The Lady Diana, born March 24, 1734; and married, Sept. 9, 1757, to Lord Vifcount Bolingbroke.
2. Lady Elizabeth, born Dec. 29, 1737, married, March 13, 1756, to Henry Earl of Pembroke.
3. George, the prefent Duke.
4. Lord Charles, born in 1740.
5. Lord Robert, born May 8, 1747.

The late Duke (by the mother) was defcended from Roger de Courcil, of the family of Leon in France ; who came over with William the Conqueror in 1066, and had a confiderable eftate in lands conferred on him, for his fervices in that expedition ; and particularly, the lordfhip of Churchill in the county of Somerfet, which became the principal feat of the family, and from whence he took his furname.

Sir Winfton Churchill, father of John, firft Duke of Marlborough, had feven fons, viz.
1. Winfton.
2. John.
3. George.
4. Charles.
5. Montjoy.
6. Jafper.
7. Theobald.

And four daughters, of which

Arabella (the eldeft) had by King James II. James Fitzjames Duke of Berwick ; and a daughter Henrietta, married to Henry Lord Waldgrave.

Winfton, Montjoy, and Jafper, died young ; Theobald entered into holy orders, and died in 1685.

Charles,

Charles, the fourth fon, was brigadier-general at the battle of Steinkirk, 1691; and, in 1693, at the battle of Landen, took the Duke of Berwick prifoner: he was general of foot at the battle of Hockftet in 1704, to which victory he contributed confiderably. He married Mary, daughter of James Gould of Dorchefter, Efq; by whom he had no iffue, and died in 1716 : George, the third fon, was made admiral of the Blue, in the reign of Queen Anne, but died on May 8, 1710, unmarried.

John, the eldeft furviving fon, was born on May 24, 1650 : he was firft page of honour to James Duke of York ; then had a pair of colours in the foot-guards, in Sir Charles Lyttleton's regiment, and ferved abroad, in Tangier, when that town was befieged by the Moors : he ferved afterwards under the Duke of Monmouth, who commanded that body of Englifh which joined the French, in the invafion of the United Provinces, in 1672; he was captain of the Englifh grenadiers at the attack of the counterfcarp of Maeftricht, where he was wounded ; and was thereupon made lieutenant-colonel, and afterwards colonel of dragoons ; and in 1682 he was created Baron of Aymouth in Scotland, and made colonel of the third troop of horfe-guards: in 1685, 1 Jac. II. he was created Baron of Sandridge in the county of Hertford, and being made brigadier-general, fignalized himfelf in the battle fought with the Duke of Monmouth, at Sedgmore in Somerfetfhire : he abandoned King James, at the revolution, and joined the Prince of Orange, who made him lieutenant-general; and on April 9, 1689, King William created him Earl of Marlborough ; in 1690, he was made general of the forces fent to Ireland, where he reduced the towns of Cork and Kinfale, making the garrifons prifoners of war ; and in the year 1691, made a campaign in Flanders; however, the year following he was difmiffed from all his employments, on a prefumption that he

and his Countefs were too zealoufly attached to the
fervice of the Princefs Anne, particularly in pro-
moting a bill in parliament for fettling a revenue on
that Princefs. The Earl remained unemployed until
after the peace of Ryfwick; but in 1698 he was called
to council again, and made governor to his Royal
Highnefs the Duke of Gloucefter; in the year 1701,
King William conftituted the Earl general of foot,
and commander in chief of the Englifh forces in the
Netherlands, as alfo ambaffador-extraordinary and
plenipotentiary in Holland.

On the acceffion of Queen Anne to the throne, he
was immediately declared captain general of all her
forces in England, or which were employed abroad in
conjunction with the troops of her Majefty's allies, as
alfo mafter-general of the ordnance.

In the year 1701 he took the towns of Venlow,
Ruremond, Stevenfwaert, and Liege; whereupon the
States-General made him generaliffimo of their forces.
In 1702 he was created Duke of Marlborough by Q.
Anne, and 5000*l. per ann.* fettled upon him for life.
In 1704 he led the confederate army from the Netherlands to the Danube, and obtained that memorable victory at Hockftet, over the united forces of
the French and Bavarians, when he took the French
general, marfhal Tallard, prifoner, with upwards of
13000 French and Bavarians, twenty thoufand of the
enemy being killed, or drowned in the Danube; there
were taken alfo one hundred pieces of cannon, twen-
ty-four mortars, one hundred and twenty-nine colours, one hundred and feventy-one ftandards, with
the enemy's tents, treafure, baggage, and ammuni-
tion: upon which victory, the emperor Leopold
created him Prince of Mindelheim in Swabia; and
the commons of England addreffed her Majefty Queen
Anne, to grant him the manor and honor of Woodftock, which were fettled on his Grace and his heirs by
act of parliament, in March 1704-5.

On May 23, 1706, N. S. his Grace obtained that memorable victory of Ramillies, and reduced moſt of the Spaniſh Netherlands, the ſame campaign.

In July 1708, his Grace obtained the victory of Oudenard, took Liſle, and recovered the cities of Ghent and Bruges, which had been ſurpriſed by the French in the beginning of the year.

In 1709, he obtained that ſignal victory of Blaregnies, or Malplaquet, near Mons ; and the ſame campaign, and the following, took Mons, Doway, and ſeveral other ſtrong towns on the frontiers of the French Netherlands.

The ſaid Duke of Marlborough, great-grand-father of the preſent Duke, married Sarah, daughter of Richard Jennings of Sandridge, in the county of Hertford, Eſq; by whom he had iſſue one ſon, named John, who died at Cambridge, anno 1705, and four daughters, viz.

1. Lady Henrietta (married to Francis Earl of Godolphin) who dying in Oct. 1733, left no iſſue male.

2. Lady Anne, the ſecond daughter, married Charles Spencer Earl of Sunderland ; by whom ſhe had iſſue, Charles the late Duke.

3. Lady Elizabeth, who married Scroop Egerton, late Duke of Bridgwater.

4. Lady Mary, who married his Grace John the late Duke of Montague, who left no iſſue by her.

His Grace John Duke of Marlborough, died on June 16, 1722, in the 73d year of his age.

Charles Earl of Sunderland, father of the late Duke of Marlborough, married to his firſt lady, Arabella Cavendiſh, youngeſt daughter and coheir of his Grace Henry late Duke of Newcaſtle ; and dying in June 1698, left Frances, his only daughter, who was married to Henry, late Earl of Carliſle. The ſaid Charles Earl of Sunderland married to his ſecond

his Grace John Duke of Marlborough ; and by her
he had issue four sons and two daughters, viz.

1. Robert Lord Spencer, born December 9, 1700,
who died in his infancy.

2. Robert late Earl of Sunderland.

3. Charles, the late Duke of Marlborough, and
Earl of Sunderland.

4. John, born May 13, 1708, was married, Feb.
14, 1733-4, to the Lady Georgina-Carolina, third
daughter to the present Earl of Granville, and
by her had issue, John, born Dec. 6, 1734, and a
daughter, who died young. The Hon. John Spencer, dying anno ————, his widow and relict married, in 1750, William Lord Cowper. The Lady
Anne Spencer, the only surviving daughter of the
said Charles late Earl of Sunderland, married William Lord Viscount Bateman, by whom she had issue
two sons.

The Right Hon. Robert Earl of Sunderland, great-
grandfather of the present Duke of Marlborough, was
secretary of state in the reign of King Charles II. president of the council in the reign of King James II.
and afterwards lord chamberlain, in the reign of King
William III.

This family derive their pedigree from a younger
branch of the ancient barons Spencer, among whom
were the two Hugh de Spencers, father and son, fa-
vourites of King Edward II.

Arms.] Quarterly, argent and gules, in the second
and third, a fret, or ; over all, on a bend, sable, three
escallops of the first.

Crest.] In a ducal coronet, or, a gryphon's head
between two wings erected, argent, gorged with a plain
collar, gules, beaked, or.

Supporters.] The dexter a gryphon, party per fess,
argent and or, sinister, a wyvern, argent, wings expanded, each collared and chained, sable ; each collar charged with three escallops, argent.

2   *Motto.*]

Motto.] *Dieu defend le droit.*

Chief Seats.] At Blenheim, and Cornbury, in Ox-fordshire; Langley-Park in Bucks; Pall-mall, London.

---

13. MANNERS, DUKE of RUTLAND.

THE most noble Prince JOHN MANNERS, Duke of RUTLAND, Marquis of Granby, Baron Roos of Hamlake, Trusbut and Belvoir, and Baron Manners of Haddon, lord steward of his Majesty's household, lord lieutenant and custos rotulorum of the county of Leicester, knight of the most noble order of the garter, and one of the lords of his Majesty's privy-council, succeeded his father in honours and estate in 1720 : his Grace was born Oct. 21, 1696 ; and on Aug. 27, 1717, married Bridget, only daughter and heir of Robert Sutton Lord Lexington, by whom he had issue seven sons and six daughters, of which are living,

1. John Marquis of Granby, lieutenant-general of the ordnance, and lieutenant-general of his Majesty's forces, colonel of the royal regiment of horse-guards, was, Aug. 25, 1759, appointed commander in chief of the English forces under Duke Ferdinand of Brunswick in Germany : he was born in January 1720-21, married, in September 1750, to the Lady Frances Seymour, eldest daughter of the late Charles Duke of Somerset; by which Lady, who died Jan. 25, 1760, he had issue two sons, John Lord Roos, born Aug. 22, 1751, died June 3, 1760; Charles, born March 15, 1754; and three daughters, Frances, born March 24, 1753; Catharine, born March 28, 1755; and another daughter born Aug. 22, 1756, but died in January following; also another son born Feb. 6, 1758.

2. Lord Robert Sutton, born Feb. 2, 1721-2.

3. Lord George, born March 8, 1722-3, married, Dec. 1749, to Diana, daughter of Thomas Chaplain, of Blankley in the county of Lancafter, Efq; by whom he hath iffue,

   1. George, born Aug. 1, 1751.
   2. John, born July 12, 1752.
   3. Robert, born Jan. 5, 1754.
   4. Charles, born Feb. 14, 1755.

The daughters died unmarried, and the Duchefs, their mother, died in June 1734.

The late Duke, John, father of the prefent Duke, was born in Sept. 1676 : he married his firft wife, Catharine, fecond daughter of William Lord Ruffel, and fifter of Wriothefley, father of the Duke of Bedford, in 1693; by whom he had iffue,

   1. John, the prefent Duke.
   2. Lord William Manners.
   3. Lord Thomas, who died unmarried, 1723.
   4. Lord Edward, who died young.
   5. Lady Catharine, married, in 1726, to the late Right Hon. Henry Pelham, Efq; brother to the Duke of Newcaftle.
   6. Lady Rachel, who died young.
   7. Lady Frances, married, in 1732, to Richard Arundel, Efq;
   8. Lady Elizabeth, married to John Monkton, Vifcount Galway of the kingdom of Ireland.

His Grace married to his fecond wife the Lady Lucy, fifter to Bennet Sherrard, late Earl of Harborough, in 1712; by whom he had iffue,

   1. Lord Sherrard Manners, who died in 1742.
   2. Lord Robert Manners, colonel of the 36th regiment of foot, and lieutenant-general of his Majefty's forces. He married, Jan. 1, 1756, Mifs Digges, of Grofvenor-fquare, by whom he had a daughter, born Nov. 20, 1756, and another daughter, born Jan. 2, 1758.
   3. Lord Henry, who died in 1745.

4. Lord Charles, colonel of the 56th regiment of foot, and major-general of his Majesty's forces.

5. Lord James.

6. Lady Carolina, married first, in 1734, to Sir Henry Harpur, Bart. 2dly, July 18, 1753, to Sir Robert Burdett, Bart.

7. Lady Lucy, married anno 1742, to his Grace William Graham, Duke of Montrose.

This noble family derive their pedigree from Sir Robert Manners, of Hethall in the county of Northumberland, who flourished in the reign of King Henry III.

Arms.] Or, two bars, azure, a chief, quarterly of the second, and gules, the first charged with two fleurs de lis, of the first, and the last with a lion of the same, which chief was anciently gules, and the charge thereon is an honorary augmentation, shewing his descent from the blood royal of king Edward IV.

Crest.] On a chapeau, gules, turned up with ermine, a peacock in pride, proper.

Supporters.] Two unicorns, argent; their horns, crests, tufts, and hoofs, or.

Motto.] *Pour y parvenir.*

Chief Seats.] At Haddon-Hall in Derbyshire; Belvoir-castle in Lincolnshire; and Averham-park in Nottinghamshire; Albemarle street, London.

14. D O U G L A S, D U K E of D O V E R.

THE most noble Prince Charles Douglas, Duke of Dover and Queensberry, Marquis of Beverley and Solloway, Viscount Drumlanrig, and Baron of Rippon, was born at Edinburgh, in Nov. 1698. His Grace, in March 1719-20, married the Lady Catharine Hyde, second daughter of Henry Hyde Earl of Rochester; by whom he had issue two sons, and a daughter who died young.

1. Henry Marquis of Beverley, born Oct. 30, 1722, married in 1754, the Lady Elizabeth Hope, eldest daughter of John Earl of Hopetoun; and coming from Scotland to London, with his father and mother the Duke and Duchess, as he was riding over a ploughed field, drew a pistol and shot himself, whether designedly or by accident is uncertain; whereupon the family returned to Scotland, and buried him. His lady died in April 1756, without issue.

2. Lord Charles, born in July 1726, died in Oct. 1756.

James Duke of Queensberry, father of the present Duke, was born Dec. 18, 1662; and in the year 1708 was created, by Queen Anne, a peer of this realm, by the title of Duke of Dover, Marquis of Beverley, and Baron of Rippon. His Grace married, on Dec. 1, 1685, the Hon. Mary Boyle, second daughter of Charles Lord Clifford, eldest son of Richard Earl of Burlington; by whom he had issue, besides the present Duke, two daughters.

1, Jane, married, in 1720, to the Earl of Dalkeith, (*See Doncaster Earl.*)

2. Anne, married, in 1732, to the Hon. William Finch, Esq; and died without issue.

Besides which, he had other children, who died unmarried.

[*For a more ample account of this family, we refer the reader to the title of Duke of Queensberry in the second volume of this work, containing a View of the Families of the Scottish Nobility.*]

Arms.] Quarterly, first and fourth, argent, a heart, gules, crowned with an imperial crown, or, on a chief, azure, three mullets of the field, for Douglas; second and third, azure, a bend between six cross croslets, fitche, or, for the earldom of Mar; the whole within a bordure, or, charged within a double treffure fleury and counter-fleury of the second, being an augmentation, as is also the heart in the first quarter, used in

memory

memory of the pilgrimage made by Sir James Douglas, anceftor of his Grace, to the Holy Land, with the
heart of King Robert Bruce, in the year 1330, which
was there interred according to that King's defire :
and the double treffure was added by King Charles
II. when he honoured the family with the marquifate
of Queenfberry, the bordure before that time being
borne only plain.

Creft.] On a wreath, a heart between two wings,
gules, crowned with an imperial crown, or.

Supporters.] Two pegafuffes, argent, wings, crefts,
tails, and hoofs, or.

Motto.] *Forward.*

Chief Seats.] At Drumlanrig in the county of Dum-
fries; Amefbury in the county of Wilts; and Bur-
lington-gardens, London.

---

15. HAMILTON, DUKE of BRANDON.

THE moft noble Prince JAMES HAMILTON, Duke
of BRANDON and HAMILTON, Marquis of Hamilton, and Baron of Dutton, born Feb. 18, 1755, fucceeded his father James, the late Duke, Jan. 17, 1758.

James the late Duke, fucceeded James his father
in March, 1742-3. He married, Feb. 14, 1752, Elizabeth, fecond daughter of John Gunning, Efq; by
his wife Bridget, daughter of John Lord Vifcount
Mayo of the kingdom of Ireland; by which Lady,
(who married, fecondly, March 3, 1759, colonel John
Campbell, eldeft fon of lieutenant-general John
Campbell, by whom fhe had a fon and heir, born
March 31, 1760) he left iffue the prefent Duke, and a
fecond fon, born July 24, 1756, and two daughters.

James Duke of Hamilton and Brandon, grandfather of the prefent Duke, married to his firft wife a
daughter of John Cochran Earl of Dundonald; by
whom he had only one fon, James the late Duke;

C 4   and

and she dying in Aug. 1724, his Grace married in
1727, his second wife, Elizabeth, daughter and coheir of Thomas Strangeways, of Dorsetshire, Esq;
who dying in Nov. 1729, without issue, his Grace
married his third wife, Elizabeth, the daughter and
heir of Edward Spencer, Esq; by whom he had a son,
born in 1740.

James Duke of Hamilton, great-grandfather of the
present Duke, was, by Queen Anne, created a peer
of Great Britain, by the title of Duke of Brandon
and Baron of Dutton, Sept. 10, 1711. His Grace
married his first wife, the Lady Anne Spencer,
daughter of Robert Earl of Sunderland ; by whom
he had two daughters that died young; and this
lady dying, he married his second wife, Elizabeth,
daughter and sole heiress of Digby Lord Gerrard;
by whom he had issue,

1. James, the late Duke's father.

2. Lady Elizabeth, and Lady Catharine, who died
young.

4. Lady Charlotte.

5. Lord William, who married, in 1732, Anne,
daughter of Francis Hawes, Esq;

His Grace was made a knight of the order of
the garter, as well as of the thistle, by Queen Anne,
who declared she would wear both orders herself: and
on the conclusion of the peace of Utrecht, 1714, she
appointed him her ambassador-extraordinary to the
court of France: but as he was about to set out for
that kingdom, he fought a duel with Lord Mohun,
wherein they were both killed. Some suspected the
Duke was killed unfairly by Gen. Maccartney, Lord
Mohun's second; but he took his trial after the accession of King George, and was acquitted.

*[For a more particular account of this family consult
the second volume of this work, containing an account of
the Peerage of Scotland, under the title of Duke of Hamilton.]*

Arms.] Quarterly, 1ſt and 4th, gules, three cinq-foils, ermine 2d and 3d, argent; a ſhip having her ſails furled, ſable.

Creſt.] Or, an oak fructed, proper, having a frame-ſaw, tranſverſly fixed in the body of the firſt.

Supporters.] Two antelopes, argent, armed and gorged, with ducal coronets, or, chains affixed to the coronets, and their hoofs of the ſecond.

Motto.] *Through.*

Chief Seats.] At Hamilton in the county of Lanerk; and Kennel in the county of Stirling.

---

16. BERTIE, DUKE of ANCASTER.

THE moſt noble Prince Peregrine Bertie, Duke of Ancaster and Kesteven, Marquis and Earl of Lindſey, Baron Willoughby of Eresby; lord great chamberlain of England; by inheritance, a lord of the bed-chamber to his Majeſty, lord lieutenant and cuſtos rotulorum of the county of Lincoln, one of the lords of his Majeſty's privy-council, lieutenant-general of his Majeſty's forces, recorder of Boſton, and keeper of Waltham-foreſt in the ſaid county, ſucceeded his father Peregrine, the late Duke, Jan. 1, 1742. He married, May 22, 1735, Elizabeth, daughter and ſole heir to William Blundell of Baſing-ſtoke in the county of Southampton, Eſq; and relict of Sir Charles Gunter Nichol, by whom he had no iſſue. Upon her deceaſe he married to his ſecond wife, Nov. 27, 1750, Mary, daughter of Thomas Panton, Eſq; maſter of the King's running-horſes; by whom he has one daughter, born April 15, 1754, and a ſon named Peregrine, born May 21, 1755, who died Dec. 12, 1758; alſo another ſon, born in Nov. 1756, and a third ſon, born Sept. 14, 1759, who is ſince dead.

His Grace Peregrine Duke of Ancaster, father of the present Duke, was born April 29, 1686. He married Jane, one of the daughters and coheirs to Sir John Brownlow, of Belton, Bart. by whom he had issue, besides the present Duke,

1. Lord Albemarle.

2. Lord Brownlow; both unmarried.

His daughters were,

1. Lady Mary, married to Samuel Greathead, Esq;

2. Lady Albina, married to John Beckford, Esq; on March 8, 1744; and died in March 1754.

3. Lady Jane, married to Capt. Matthews.

4. Lady Carolina, married, March 31, 1753, to George Dawar, Esq;

5. Lady Anne, died in Aug. 1735.

This noble family came into England with the Saxons, who made a conquest of South Britain, in the 5th century; and had a castle conferred on them by one of the Saxon kings, from them denominated Bertiestad, now Bersted, near Maidstone in Kent.

Arms.] Argent, three battering rams, barways, armed and garnished, azure.

Crest.] On a wreath, the busto of a king (named Barbicon) couped at the breast, proper, crowned ducally, or, being the crest of the Barons Willoughby. Their crest, as Bertie, is a pine-tree, proper.

Supporters.] On the dexter side, a pilgrim, or fryar, vested in russet, with his staff and pater-noster, or. On the sinister, a savage wreathed about the temples and middle, with ivy, all proper.

Motto.] *Loyaulte me oblige.*

Chief Seats.] At Grimsthorpe in the county of Lincoln; and Berkley-square, London.

17. PIER

17. PIERREPONT, DUKE of KINGSTON.

THE moſt noble Prince EVELYN PIERREPONT, Duke of KINGSTON, Marquis of Dorcheſter, Earl of Kingſton, Viſcount Newark, and Baron Pierre-pont, lieutenant-general of his Majeſty's forces, and knight of the moſt noble order of the garter, ſuc-ceeded his grandfather, Evelyn Duke of Kingſton, March 5, 1725-6; William, father of the preſent Duke, dying in the life-time of his grandfather. His Grace is yet unmarried.

William Pierrepont, father of the preſent Duke, was born Oct. 21, 1692; and died in the one and twen--tieth year of his age, on July 1, 1713, leaving iſſue by Rachel his wife, daughter of Thomas Baynton, Eſq;

Evelyn, the preſent Duke of Kingſton; and

An only daughter, Lady Frances, married to Phi-lip Meadows, Knt. by whom ſhe had iſſue five ſons and one daughter, viz.

1. Evelyn.
2. Charles.
3. William.
4. Edward.
5. Thomas.
6. Frances.

This Duke's grandfather was the fifth Earl of Kingſton, the ſecond Marquis of Dorcheſter, and was created Duke, July 20, 1715, 1 Geo. I.

This noble family derive their pedigree from Ro-bert de Pierrepont, of Norman extraction, who at-tended William the Conqueror in his invaſion of Eng-land, in the year 1066.

Arms.] Argent, ſemé of cinqfoils, gules; a lion rampant, ſable.

Creſt.] On a wreath, a lion rampant, ſable; between two wings erect, argent.

Supporters.] Two lions, ſable, armed and languid, gules. C 6 *Motto.*]

Motto.] *Pie repone te.*

Chief Seats.] Holme-Pierrepont, Thoresby-park in Nottinghamſhire ; Tong-caſtle in the county of Salop ; Bradford in the county of Wilts ; and at Hanſlope in Bucks ; and Arlington-ſtreet, London.

18. PELLAM HOLLES, DUKE of NEWCASTLE.

THE moſt noble Prince THOMAS PELHAM HOL-LES, Duke of NEWCASTLE, and Duke of Newcaſtle-Under-Line in the County of Stafford, Marquis and Earl of Clare, Viſcount Haughton, and Baron Pelham of Laughton, and Baronet ; lord lieutenant and cuſtos rotulorum of the county of Middleſex, and city and liberty of Weſtminſter, and county of Nottingham ; ſteward, keeper, and warden of the foreſt of Sherwood, and park of Folewood, in the county of Nottingham ; firſt lord commiſſioner of the Treaſury, one of the governors of the Charterhouſe, knight of the moſt noble order of the garter, chancellor of the univerſity of Cambridge, and fellow of the Royal Society.

His Grace was born July 21, 1694 ; and by the laſt will and teſtament of his uncle John Holles, Duke of Newcaſtle, who died July 15, 1711, was adopted his heir, and authoriſed to bear the name and arms of Holles.

On Oct. 26, 1714, King George I. created him Earl of Clare in the county of Suffolk, and Viſcount Haughton in Nottinghamſhire, with remainder to the Hon. Henry Pelham his brother, and his male heirs ; and in 1715, he was created Marquis and Duke of Newcaſtle, with the remainder to the Hon. Henry Pelham, his brother.

His Grace was married, April 2, 1717, to the Lady Harriot Godolphin, daughter of the Right Hon.

Francis Earl of Godolphin, by the Lady Henrietta his wife, eldeſt daughter and coheir of his Grace John late Duke of Marlborough ; and on the 13th of April following, was declared lord chamberlain of his Majeſty's houſhold, and ſworn of the privy-council the 16th of April ; alſo at a chapter held at St. James's the 31ſt of March, 1718, was elected one of the knights of the garter, and inſtalled at Windſor the 30th of April following.

On April 2, 1724, his Grace reſigning his poſt of lord chamberlain, was declared one of his Majeſty's principal ſecretaries of ſtate.

Henry Pelham, his only brother, married, Oct. 29, 1726, the Lady Catharine Manners, ſiſter of John late Duke of Rutland ; by whom he had iſſue two ſons, viz.

1. Thomas, who died young.

2. Henry, who alſo died young.

And ſix daughters, viz.

3 Catharine, born July 24, 1727, married in 1744, to Henry Earl of Lincoln, and died July 27, 1760.

4. Frances, born Aug. 18, 1728, married in Oct. 1752, to Lewis Watſon, Eſq; brother to the Lord Monſon, now Lord Sondes.

5. Grace, born in Jan. 1734-5.

6. Mary, born in Sept. 1739.

7. Lucy. And

8. Dorothy ; both deceaſed.

The Right Hon. Henry Pelham, Eſq; only brother to his Grace the Duke of Newcaſtle, firſt lord com-miſſioner of the Treaſury, and prime miniſter, died March 6, 1754.

His Grace, beſides his ſaid brother, had five ſiſters.

1. Grace, who married George Naylor, Eſq; died in 1710.

2. Frances, married, in 1715, to Chriſtopher Lord Viſcount Caſtlecomer of the kingdom of Ireland.

3. Gertrude, married to David Polhill, Eſq; ſince

4. Lucy, married to the Right Hon. Henry Clinton Earl of Lincoln.

5. Margaret, married to Sir John Shelly, Bart. and died Nov. 23, 1758.

The anceftors of this noble Duke took their name from the lordfhip of Pelham in Hertfordfhire, of which they appear to have been poffeffed in the reign of Henry III.

Arms.] Quarterly, in the firft and fourth, three pelicans, argent (the arms of Pelham) ; and in the fecond and third, ermine, two piles, in point, fable, the arms of Holles.

Creft.] On a wreath, a peacock in his pride, argent; and fometimes a buckle, argent; in memory of Sir John Pelham's taking King John of France prifoner.

Supporters.] On the dexter fide, a bay horfe ; on the finifter, a bear, proper ; each collared or gorged with a belt, argent ; buckle and ftuds, or.

Motto.] *Vincit amor patriæ.*

Chief Seats.] At Claremont in Surrey ; at Nottingham-caftle, and Haughton, in Nottinghamfhire; at Bifhopftone in the county of Suffex ; and Lincoln's-Inn-Fields, London.

19.   B E N T I N C K,   D U K E OF P O R T L A N D.

THE moft noble Prince WILLIAM BENTINCK, Duke of PORTLAND, Marquis of Tichfield, Vifcount Woodftock, and Baron of Cirencefter, and knight of the moft noble order of the garter, prefident of the Lying-in-Hofpital for married women in Brownlow-ftreet, Long-Acre, London, and fellow of the Royal Society, born in March 1708-9, fucceeded Henry, the late Duke, July 4, 1726, and married, only daughter and heir of Edward Earl of Oxford, by whom he had issue,

1. Lady Elizabeth married, May 22, 1759, to Thomas the present Viscount Weymouth.

2. Lady Henrietta.

3. William-Henry, Marquis of Tichfield, born April 14, 1738.

4. Lady Margaret, who died April 28, 1756.

5. Lady Frances, who died in March 1742. And,

6. Lord Edward-Charles, born March 3, 1744.

William Earl of Portland, grandfather of the present Duke, was page of honour to the Prince of Orange (William III. King of Great Britain.) He was afterwards gentleman of the bedchamber to that Prince, who sent him into England to negotiate a marriage between his Royal Highness and the Princess Mary, eldest daughter of the then Duke of York, in 1677. He attended the Prince into England in his expedition of 1688; and, it is said, was principally relied on in that enterprize. Soon after his master ascended the British throne, viz. on April 19, 1689, he was created Baron of Cirencester, Viscount Woodstock, and Earl of Portland. He also received a grant of the lordships of Denbigh, Bromfield, and Yale, and other lands, comprehending the best part of one of the counties of Wales; but that grant was resumed, on an address of the house of commons for that purpose. He negotiated the peace of Ryswick with Marshal Boufflers between the two armies, in 1697, and on the conclusion of that peace was sent ambassador to France. One hundred and thirty-five thousand acres of the forfeited estates in Ireland were granted to the Earl of Portland; but resumed by the British parliament, anno 1699.

This William Earl of Portland, grandfather of the present Earl, married, to his first wife, Anne, daughter of Sir Edward Villiers, knight, and sister to Edward Earl of Jerfey, by whom he had iffue three fons and five daughters, viz.

1. William, who died in his infancy.

2. Henry, fecond fon, afterwards Earl and Duke of Portland.

3. Alfo another William, who died young in Holland.

4. Lady Mary, eldeft daughter, married to Algernoon Earl of Effex, and fince his deceafe to the Hon. Conyers D'arcy, Efq; only brother to Robert late Earl of Holdernefs.

5. Lady Anna Margaretta, fecond daughter, married to Monf. Duyvenvorde, one of the principal nobles of Holland.

6. Lady Frances Williamyna, third daughter, married to William Lord Byron, and died March 31, 1712.

7. Lady Eleanora, fourth daughter, died unmarried.

8. Lady Ifabella, youngeft daughter, married to Evelyn Pierrepont, Duke of Kingfton, and died on Feb. 23, 1727-8.

His Lordfhip, on May 16, 1700, married his fecond wife, Jane, fixth daughter of Sir John Temple, of Eaft-Sheen in the county of Surrey, Bart. fifter to Henry Lord Vifcount Palmerfton, and widow of John Lord Berkeley, of Stratton; and by her (who died March 26, 1751) had two fons and four daughters.

1. William, now one of the nobles of Holland.

2. Charles-John, an officer in the army of the States-General.

3. Lady Sophia, married, March 24, 1738-9, to his Grace Henry de Grey, late Duke of Kent.

4. Lady Elizabeth, married to Dr. Henry Egerton, bifhop of Hereford, brother to his Grace Scroop Duke of Bridgewater.

5. Lady Harriot, married to James Hamilton, Vifcount Limerick, of the kingdom of Ireland.

6. Lady

6. Lady Barbara, married to William Godolphin, Efq; and died April 15, 1736.

The eldeſt ſon Henry Earl of Portland, father of the preſent Duke, married, June 9, 1704, the Lady Elizabeth Noel, eldeſt daughter and coheir of Wrio-theſley Baptiſt, Earl of Gainſborough. · He was created, by his late Majeſty, Marquis of Tichfield, Hampſhire, and Duke of Portland, by letters patent, bearing date July 6, 1716. On Sept. 29, 1721, he was appointed captain-general, and governor of the iſland of Jamaica ; where he died, July 4, 1726, in the 45th year of his age. Her Grace accompanied him to Jamaica, and came over with his remains. They had ſeveral children, of which two ſons and three daughters ſurvived them.

1. William, now Duke of Portland; and

2. Lord George, a colonel of foot, who died March 2, 1759.

3. Lady Anne, married to lieutenant-colonel Daniel Paul, died in Jan. 1748-9.

4. Lady Iſabella, married, Nov. 8, 1739, to Henry Monk, Efq; of the kingdom of Ireland.

5. Lady Amelia, married to Jacob Arran Van Waſ-ſenar, one of the nobles of Holland, died in Jan. 1756.

Arms.] Azure, a croſs moline, argent.

Creſt.] Out of a marquis's coronet, proper, two arms counter, embowed and veſted, gules ; gloved, or; and holding each an oſtrich-feather, argent.

Supporters.] Two lions double queveé ; the dexter, proper ; the other, ſable.

Motto.] *Craignez boute.*

Chief Seats.] At Bulſtrode in Buckinghamſhire ; Welbeck in Nottinghamſhire ; and Privy-Gardens, Weſtminſter.

20. MONTAGU, DUKE of MANCHESTER.

THE moſt noble ROBERT MONTAGU, Duke and Earl of MANCHESTER, Viſcount Mandeville, Baron Montagu of Kimbolton, one of the lords of his Majeſty's bedchamber, and lord lieutenant and cuſtos rotulorum of the county of Huntingdon, ſucceeded his brother, the late Duke William, in Oct. 1739. He was married on April 3, 1735, to Harriot, daughter of Edmund Dunch, Eſq: who dying in Feb. 1755, left iſſue,

1. George Lord Viſc. Mandeville, born Ap. 6, 1737.
2. Lord Charles, born May 29, 1741.
3. Lady Caroline, born Feb. 19, 1735-6.
4. Lady Louiſa, born in July 1740, and died unmarried.

Charles Earl of Mancheſter, father of the preſent and late Dukes, was, on April 30, 1719, created Duke of Mancheſter. His Grace married Dodington, the youngeſt of the two daughters and coheirs of Robert Greville, Lord Brooke; by whom he had iſſue, beſides the late and preſent Dukes,

1. Lady Anne, who died unmarried.
2. Lady Dodington; and,
3. Lady Elizabeth, both unmarried.
4. Lady Charlotte, married to Pattee Byng, late Lord Viſcount Torrington, by whom ſhe had no iſſue.

Arms.] Quarterly, firſt and fourth, argent, three lozenges, conjoined in feſs, gules, within a border, ſable, with a creſcent, for difference, for Montagu; ſecond and third, or, an eagle diſplayed, vert; beaked and membered, gules, for Montheriner.

Creſt.] On a wreath, a gryphon's head, couped, or; wings indorſed, ſable; gorged with a collar, argent, charged with three lozenges, gules.

Supporters.] On the dexter fide, an antelope, or ; armed, crefted, and hoofed, argent. On the finifter, a gryphon of the firft, gorged, with a collar, argent ; charged with three fufils, gules.

Motto.] *Difponendo me non mutando me.*

Chief Seats.] At Kimbolton-caftle, in the county of Huntingdon ; and Berkley-fquare, London.

21. BRYDGES, DUKE of CHANDOS.

THE moft noble Prince HENRY BRYDGES, Duke of CHANDOS, Marquis and Earl of Carnarvon, Vifcount Wilton, and Baron Chandos of Sudley, baronet and knight of the Bath, clerk of the hanaper, and high-fteward of the city of Winchefter, fucceeded his father James, the late Duke, Aug. 9, 1744 ; and Dec. 21, 1728, married Mary, eldeft daughter of Charles Lord Bruce, by whom he had iffue one fon and a daughter, viz. James Marquis of Carnarvon, born Dec. 27, 1731, and married March 22, 1753, to Margaret, daughter and heir of John Nichol, of Southgate in the county of Middlefex ; and Lady Caroline, born March 29, 1729-30, and married, March 17, 1755, to John Leigh, Efq; of Addlefthrape in Gloucefterfhire. The Duchefs dying in 1738, his Grace married for his fecond wife, in 1745, Mrs. Anne Wells, by which lady, who died Aug. 12, 1759, he hath iffue Lady Augufta, born Oct. 6, 1748.

James, the father of the prefent Duke, was created Vifcount Wilton, and Earl of Carnarvon, Oct. 19, 1714; and Marquis of Carnarvon, and Duke of Chandos, April 30, 1719. He married Mary, the daughter of Sir Thomas Lake, of Cannons in the county of Middlefex, Knt. in 1696, by whom he had feveral fons and daughters; but Henry, the prefent Duke, only furvived him. He married to his fecond wife

Caſſandra Willoughby, ſiſter of the Lord Middleton, by whom he had no iſſue ; after whoſe death he married to his third wife Lydia-Catharine, widow of Sir Thomas Davel, by whom he left no iſſue.

The anceſtors of this noble family took their name from the city of Bruges, or Brugge, in Flanders ; and one of them came over with William the Conqueror, and had a conſiderable ſhare in the victory obtained near Haſtings in Suſſex, 1066.

Arms.] Argent, on a croſs, a leopard's head, or.

Creſt.] On a wreath, the buſt of an old man, ſidefaced, proper, wreathed about the temples, argent and azure, veſted paly of the firſt, and gules and ſemi of roundles counterchanged, the cape ermine ; and on his head is a cap, or, lined with white fur.

Supporters.] Two otters, argent.

Motto.] *Main tein la droit.*

Chief Seats.] At Wilton-caſtle in Herefordſhire, and Aconbury in the ſame county ; at Biddeſden near Luggerſhell in Wiltſhire ; and Upper Brook-ſtreet, London.

22. SACKVILLE, DUKE of DORSET.

THE moſt noble Prince Lionel Cranfield Sackville, Duke of the county of Dorset, Earl of Dorſet and Middleſex, Baron Buckhurſt, and Baron Cranfield, lord warden and admiral of the cinque-ports, governor of Dover-caſtle, lord lieutenant and cuſtos rotulorum of the county of Kent, and of the city of Canterbury, and vice-admiral of the ſaid county of Kent, high-ſteward of Stratford-upon-Avon, and the borough of Tamworth, a go-vernor of the Charter-houſe, one of his Majeſty's moſt honourable privy-council, and knight of the moſt noble order of the garter, ſucceeded his father, the late Earl Charles, in 1705-6. His Grace was born January 18, 1687-8, and created Duke of

Dorſet, January 13, 1720. He married in January 1708-9, Elizabeth, daughter of lieutenant-general Philip Colyear, by whom he had iſſue,

1. Lady Anne, who died in the eleventh year of her age.

2. Charles Earl of Middleſex, born in Feb. 1710-11; who married Grace, daughter and ſole heir of Richard Boyle, Lord Viſcount Shannon of the kingdom of Ireland.

3. Lady Elizabeth, married, in 1726, to Thomas Lord Viſcount Weymouth; but died before they cohabited.

4. Lord John-Philip, born in 1713, married to Lady Frances, fourth daughter to Earl Gower.

5. Lord George, born Jan. 26, 1715-16, married, in Sept. 1754, to Diana, ſecond daughter and coheir of John Sambroke, Eſq;

6. Lady Caroline, married to Joſeph Damer, Eſq; now Low Lord Milton in Ireland, July 27, 1742.

Charles Earl of Dorſet, father to the preſent Duke, was born Jan. 24, 1637. He married the Lady Elizabeth, daughter of Harvey Bagot, and widow of Charles Berkley, Earl of Falmouth; who dying without iſſue, he married, March 7, 1684-5, the Lady Mary, daughter of James Compton, Earl of Northampton, by whom he had iſſue,

1. Lionel, the preſent Duke; and,

2. The Lady Mary, married, in 1702, to Henry Somerſet, Duke of Beaufort, and died in child-bed in 1705, leaving no iſſue.

The anceſtors of this family were lords of the town and ſeigniory of Sackville in Normandy, and came over with the Conqueror, when he invaded England, 1066.

Arms.] Quarterly, or and gules, a bend over all, vaire.

Creſt.]

Creſt.] Out of a ducal coronet, or, an eſtoile of ?
eight points, argent.

Supporters.] Two leopards, argent; ſpotted, ſable.

Motto.] *Aut nunquam tentes, aut perfice.*

Chief Seats.] At Knowle in Kent; at Buckhurſt in
Suſſex; at Croxhall in Derbyſhire; and the Cockpit,
Whitehall, Weſtminſter.

23. EGERTON, DUKE of BRIDGWATER.

THE moſt noble Francis Egerton, Duke of
Bridgwater, and Marquis of Brackley, Earl
of Bridgwater, Viſcount Brackley, and Baron of El-
leſmĕre, was born in May 1736, ſucceeded the late
Duke John his brother in 1747-8; and is unmarried.

Scroop, the father of the late and preſent Dukes,
married the Lady Elizabeth Churchill, third daughter
of John Duke of Marlborough, by whom he had iſſue,

1. John Lord Viſcount Brackley, who died at Eaton-ſchool.

2. Another ſon, who died ſoon after he was born.
And one daughter, viz.

3. Lady Anne, who, on April 22, 1725, married
Wriotheſley Ruſſel, late Duke of Bedford; after
whoſe death ſhe married William now Earl of Jerſey,
and has iſſue. [*See Jerſey Earl.*]

Scroop, the late Duke of Bridgwater, having buried his firſt wife, married the Lady Rachel Ruſſel,
daughter to Wriotheſley late Duke of Bedford, by
whom he had iſſue,

1. Lady Louiſa, born in 1723; married, in 1748,
to Lord Trentham, now Earl Gower, being his ſecond
wife, by whom ſhe has iſſue a daughter, named
Louiſa.

2. Lady

2. Lady Caroline, born in 1724.

3. Charles Marquis of Brackley, born in 1725; who died in 1731.

4. John Marquis of Brackley, born April 29, 1727, who succeeded his father in Jan. 1744-5, and died in 1747-8.

5. Lord William who died soon after he was born.

6. Lord Thomas, who died soon after he was born.

7. Lady Diana, born in 1731; married, in 1753, to Frederick Lord Baltimore, and died July 18, 1758.

8. Lord Francis, the present Duke.

This family derive their pedigree from the ancient family of Egerton, descended from the Barons of Malpas in Cheshire.

The present Duke is lineally descended from Lord Ellesmere, lord high-chancellor of England in the reign of King James I.

Arms.] Argent, a lion rampant, gules, between three pheons heads, sable.

Crest.] On a chapeau, gules, turned up, ermine, a lion rampant of the first, holding a pheon, or; headed and feathered, argent.

Supporters.] On the dexter side, an horse, argent, gorged with a ducal coronet, or. On the sinister, a gryphon segreant, or, gorged with a plain collar and chain, azure.

Motto.] *Sic donec.*

Chief Seats.] At Ashridge, in the county of Bucks; and Cleveland-row, St. James's.

A SHORT

A

SHORT VIEW

OF THE

PEERAGE

OF

ENGLAND.

I. WENTORTH, MARQUIS of ROCKINGHAM.

THE moft noble Prince CHARLES-WATSON
WENTWORTH, Marquis of ROCKINGHAM, Earl
of Malton, Vifcount Higham of Higham-Ferrers,
Baron Rockingham of Rockingham, Baron of Malton, Waith, and Harrowden, lord lieutenant and cuftos rotulorum of the weft-riding of the county of
York, and cuftos rotulorum of the north-riding of the
faid county, vice-admiral of the whole county of York,
and the maritime parts thereof, lord of the bed-chamber to his Majefty, and knight of the moft noble order of the garter.

He was born May 13, 1730, and, on the death of
his father, fucceeded to his honours. He married, on
Feb. 26, 1752, Mary, daughter and heir of Thomas
Bright, of Badfworth in the county of York, Efq;

Thomas, the late Marquis, father of the prefent
Marquis of Rockingham, was created Baron of Malton in May 1728; and, in Nov. 1734, was created
Earl of Malton, Vifcount Higham of Higham Ferrers,
and Baron of Waith and Harrowden; and by the
death of Thomas Earl of Rockingham, in Feb. 1745-6,
the honour of Baron of Rockingham-caftle devolved

2   on

on him; whereupon he was created Marquis of Rockingham in April 1746. His lordſhip married the Lady Mary Finch, daughter to Daniel late Earl of Winchelſea and Nottingham, by whom he had iſſue, beſides the preſent Marquis, four daughters, viz.

1. Lady Anne, eldeſt daughter, married, June 22,
1744, to the Right Hon. William Earl of Fitz-Williams, &c.

2. Lady Mary, born July 18, 1727.

3. Lady Charlotte, born Feb. 11, 1732; and,

4. Lady Henrietta-Alicia, born Dec. 7, 1737.

The Hon. Thomas Watſon, ſon of Edward Lord
Rockingham, by the Lady Anne Wentworth, daughter of Thomas late Earl of Strafford, was grandfather of the preſent Marquis, and took upon him the
firname of Wentworth.

The Watſon and Wentworth families were united in
his lordſhip's great-grandfather Thomas. The noble
family of Watſon are deſcended from Edward Watſon,
of Lydington in the county of Rutland, who flouriſhed
in the reign of King Edward IV.

The Wentworths are of Saxon original, deſcended
from Reginald de Wentworth, or Wintewade, ſo called
from their manor of Wentworth, in the county of
York, where the ſaid Reginald reſided at the time of
the conqueſt. The Earl of Strafford, prime miniſter
to King Charles I. one of the anceſtors of this noble
Marquis, is ſaid to be deſcended from John of Gaunt,
fourth ſon of King Edward III. in the patent whereby
he was created Earl of Strafford.

Arms.] Quarterly, firſt and fourth, argent, on a
chevron ingrailed, azure, between three martlets, ſable, as many creſcents, or, for Watſon; ſecond and
third, ſable, a chevron between three leopards faces,
or, for Wentworth.

Creſt.] A gryphon's head eraſed, argent, gorged with
a ducal coronet, or, for Watſon. A gryphon paſſant,

D wings

wings expanded, argent, gorged with a ducal coronet, or, for Wentworth.

Supporters.] On the dexter fide a gryphon, argent, gorged with a ducal coronet, or, for Watfon. On the finifter fide, a lion of the fecond, for Wentworth.

Mottos.] *Mea gloria fides.* And, *En Dieu est tout.*

Chief Seats.] At Wentworth-houfe in the county of York ; at Malton in the fame county ; at Great Harrowden in Northamptonfhire ; and in Grofvenor-fquare, London.

A SHORT

A
SHORT VIEW
OF THE
PEERAGE
OF
ENGLAND.

1. TALBOT, EARL OF SHREWSBURY.

THE Right Hon. GEORGE TALBOT, Earl of Shrewsbury in England, Wexford and Waterford in Ireland, and Baron Talbot, born Dec. 11, 1719, fucceeded George the late Earl his father, in 1733; and married, Nov. 21, 1753, Elizabeth, daughter of the Hon. John Dormer, of Peterley in Buckinghamfhire.

George, late Earl of Shrewfbury, father of the prefent Earl, married, March 11, 1718-19, Mary, daughter to Thomas Fitz-Williams, Vifcount Fitz-Williams, of Merion in Ireland, by whom he left iffue fix fons and three daughters, viz.

1. George, the prefent Earl.

2. The Hon. Charles Talbot, married to Mary, daughter and coheir of Robert Allwyn of Traford, in the county of Suffex, Efq; which Lady died in childbed of a daughter, Mary, June 2, 1750; and he married, fecondly, April 2, 1752, Mary, daughter of Sir Pierce Moyfton, of Talacre in Flintfhire, Bart. by whom he has a fon Charles, born March 8, 1753, and a daughter Anne, born March 9, 1754.

3. John.
4. James.
5. Thomas.
6. Francis. And,
7. Gilbert, who died an infant.

8. Lady

8. Lady Barbara, his eldeſt daughter, married, June 30, 1744, to James Lord Aſton, and died at Paris in Nov. 1759.

9. Lady Mary, married, in July 1749, to Charles Dormer, Eſq; ſon and heir to the Hon. John Dormer, of Peterly in Buckingſhire.   And,

10. Lady Lucy, who is unmarried.

His Grace Charles, late Duke of Shrewſbury, dying without iſſue in 1717, the titles of Duke and Marquis, which were only granted to him and his heirs male, ceaſed with him; but the Earldom of Shrewſbury devolved on Gilbert Talbot, the eldeſt ſurviving ſon of Thomas Talbot, of Longford, only ſon of John, the tenth Earl of Shrewſbury, by Frances, his ſecond wife, daughter to Thomas Lord Arundel of Wardour; upon whoſe death ſucceeded George the late Earl, his brother.

This family of Talbot, or Talebot, appear to have been poſſeſſed of a large eſtate in England, in the reign of William the Conqueror.   In the third of Edward III. Gilbert Talbot, with his eldeſt ſon Richard Talbot, embarked with the King for France.   The deſcendants of theſe Talbots had a great ſhare in the victories obtained by the Engliſh in France and Scotland. Sir John Talbot particularly attended King Henry V. in his triumphant entry into Paris; and Sir John Talbot was created Earl of Shrewſbury, 20 Hen. VI. 1442.

Charles, the late Duke of Shrewsbury, was, at the death of Q. Anne, lord lieutenant of Ireland, lord high-treaſurer of Great Britain, and lord chamberlain of her Majeſty's houſhold, at one and the ſame time.

Arms.] Gules, a lion rampant, within a border engrailed, or.

Creſt.] On a chapeau, gules, turned up, ermine, a lion, or, his lail extended.

Supporters.] Two talbots, argent.

Motto.] *Preſt d'accomplir.*

Chief Seats.] At Ifleworth in Middlefex; at Alton-caftle in Staffordfhire; at Heathorpe, near Woodftock, in Oxfordfhire; and Hill-ftreet, London.

---

2. STANLEY, EARL of DERBY.

THE Right Hon. EDWARD STANLEY, Earl of DERBY, Lord and Baron Stanley of Latham, and Baronet, lord lieutenant of the county of Lancafter, was born Sept. 17, 1689. On the death of James, the tenth Earl of Derby, the Earldom devolved on the faid Sir Edward Stanley, of Bickerftaff, Bart. in the year 1735-6. His lordfhip married, in 1714, Elizabeth, only daughter and heir of Robert Hefketh of Rufford in Lancafhire, Efq; by whom he had iffue,

1. James Lord Strange, born in Jan. 1716-17, married, March 17, 1746-7, to Lucy, one of the daughters and coheirs of Hugh Smith, of Weald-hall in Effex, Efq; and by her, who died Feb. 7, 1759, has iffue.

2. Edward Stanley, born in June 1732.

And fix daughters, viz.

1. Lady Elizabeth, married, in March 1746, to Sir Peter Warburton, Bart.

2. Lady Mary.
3. Lady Ifabella.
4. Lady Margaret
5. Lady Jane. And,

6. Lady Charlotte, married to John Bourgoine, Efq; Sir Thomas Stanley, Bart. father of the prefent Earl, was born Sept. 27, 1670. He married to his firft wife, Elizabeth, only daughter and heir to Thomas Patten, of Prefton in the county of Lancafter, Efq; by whom he had iffue four fons, of which Edward, the prefent Earl of Derby, and John the fecond fon, only are living. He married, fecondly, Margaret, daughter of Thomas Holcroft, in Lancafhire, Efq; relict of Sir Richard Standifh, of Duxbury, in the fame county, Bart. by whom he had no iffue.

The Earls of Derby are defcended from Thomas Lord Stanley, who married the Lady Margaret, widow of Edmund Earl of Richmond, and mother of King Henry VII. and joining the Earl of Richmond his son at the battle of Bosworth, obtained a compleat victory over King Richard III. who being killed in the field of battle, the Lord Stanley set the crown on the head of the Earl of Richmond, and proclaimed him King of England, France, &c. and he succeeded King Richard III. by the name of Henry VII.

Arms.] Argent, on a bend, azure, three bucks heads cabossed, or.

Crest.] On a chapeau, gules, turned up, ermine, an eagle with wings expanded, or, preying upon an infant in its cradle, proper.

Supporters.] On the dexter side, a griffin ; on the sinister, a buck, both or, ducally collared, and chained, azure.

Motto.] *Sans Changer.*

Chief Seats.] At Knowesly and Bickerstaff, both in the county of Lancaster ; and Clifford-street, London.

3. HASTINGS, EARL of HUNTINGDON.

THE Right Hon. Francis Hastings, Earl of Huntingdon, and Baron Hastings, Hungerford, Botreaux, Molins, Newmark, and Moles, and master of the horse to the Prince of Wales, was born March 13, 1728, and succeeded his father Theophilus, the late Earl, in his honours and estate, Oct. 13, 1746.

Theophilus Hastings, Earl of Huntingdon, father of the present Earl, was born in 1700 ; married, June 3, 1728, the Lady Selina Shirley, second daughter and coheir of Washington Earl Ferrers, by whom he had issue four sons and three daughters, viz.

1. Francis, the present Earl.

2. George, born March 29, 1730, who died aged 14.

3. Ferdinando, born Jan. 23, 1732, who died in

4. Henry, born Dec. 12, 1739, died Sept. 12, 1758.

5. Lady Elizabeth, the eldeſt daughter, born March 23, 1731, married, Feb. 26, 1752, to John Lord Rawdon of the kingdom of Ireland.

6. Lady Selina, born in June 1735, who died an infant.

7. Lady Selina, the third daughter, born Dec. 3, 1737.

This noble Earl is deſcended from Hugh de Haſtings, a younger ſon of the ancient and noble family of the Haſtings Earl of Pembroke, of which family was William de Haſtings, ſteward to King Henry I.

Arms.] Argent, a maunch, ſable.

Creſt.] On a wreath a buffalo's head eraſed, ſable, gorged with a ducal coronet, and armed, or.

Supporters.] Two man-tygers affrontée, or, their viſage like the human, proper.

Motto.] *In veritate victoria.*

Chief Seats.] At Aſhby-de-la-Zouch, and at Donnington, both in the county of Leiceſter.

4. HERBERT, EARL of PEMBROKE.

THE Right Hon. HENRY HERBERT, Earl of PEMBROKE, and Montgomery, Baron Herbert of Caerdiff, Rofs of Kendal, Parr, Fitz-Hugh, Marmion, St. Quintin, and Herbert of Shurland, colonel of a company in the firſt regiment of guards, and aide de camp to his Majeſty, lord lieutenant and cuſtos rotulorum of the county of Wilts, and a lord of the bedchamber to the Prince of Wales, was born July 3, 1734, and ſucceeded Henry, the late Earl, his father, Jan. 9, 1749-50. His lordſhip married, March 13, 1756, Lady Elizabeth Spencer, ſecond daughter to Charles the late Duke of Marlborough, who was brought to-bed of a ſon and heir, Sept. 11, 1759.

Henry Earl of Pembroke, father of the preſent Earl, married, Aug. 28, 1733, Mary, eldeſt daughter of Richard, Vifcount Fitz-Williams, of the kingdom of Ireland, by whom he had iffue,

Henry, the prefent Earl, his only fon.

This noble family are defcended from Henry Fitz-Roy, natural fon to King Henry I. And the firft of this family that had the title of Earl, was William Herbert, Lord of Ragland, in the county of Monmouth; which William was alfo chief juftice and chamberlain of South Wales, and knight of the garter; but was afterwards beheaded at Northampton, by the command of the Duke of Clarence and the Earl of Warwick, for oppofing the Lancaftrian party in behalf of the King.

Sir William Herbert, one of the anceftors of the prefent Earl, was mafter of the horfe to King Henry VIII. lord prefident of the marches of Wales, and knight of the garter. He was alfo, by that King, advanced to the dignity of Baron Herbert of Caerdiff, and the very next day created Earl of Pembroke, anno 1551. He was general of the forces to Queen Mary, againft the Kentifh rebels; one of the privy-council to Queen Elizabeth, and mafter of her houfhold.

Arms.] Party-per-pale, azure and gules, three lions rampant, argent.

Creft.] On a wreath, a wyvern, with wings elevated, vert, holding in its mouth a finifter hand, couped at the wrift, gules.

Supporters.] On the dexter fide, a panther guardant, argent, fpotted of various colours, with fire iffuing out of his mouth and ears, his ducal collar, azure. On the finifter, a lion, argent, gorged with a ducal coronet, gules.

Motto.] Ung je ferviray.

Chief Seats] At Wilton, in the county of Wilts; and Whitehall, Privy-Garden.

5. CLIN.

5. CLINTON, EARL OF LINCOLN.

THE Right Hon. HENRY CLINTON, Earl of LIN-
COLN, Baron Say, one of the lords of his Majefty's bedchamber, auditor of the receipt of his Majefty's exchequer for life, comptroller of the cuftoms
in the port of London, mafter of Geddington-Chace,
Northamptonfhire, high fteward of Weftminfter,
knight of the moft noble order of the garter, F. R. S.
and L. L. D. born April 20, 1720, fucceeded George
the late Earl, his brother, April 30, 1730. His lordfhip married, Oct. 3, 1744, Catharine, eldeft daughter
to Henry Pelham, late brother to the Duke of Newcaftle, by which lady, who died July 27, 1760, he had
iffue,

1. George Lord Clinton, born Oct. 2, 1745, and
died in Auguft 1751.

2. Henry Lord Clinton, born Nov. 5, 1750.

3. Thomas, born July 2, 1752.

4. John, born Oct. 13, 1755.

Henry, Earl of Lincoln, father of the prefent
and late Earls, married the Lady Lucy, fifter to
Thomas Pelham Holles, Duke of Newcaftle. His
lordfhip dying Sept. 7, 1728, in the 44th year of his
age, left iffue by her two fons,

1. George, his fucceffor ; and,

2. Henry, the prefent Earl.

As alfo three daughters, of which

3. Lady Lucy only is living, and unmarried ; and
the Countefs, their mother, died July 20, 1736.

This noble family are defcended from Jeffrey de
Clinton, lord chamberlain and treafurer to King
Henry I. grandfon to William de Tankerville, chamberlain of Normandy; from whom defcended William de Clinton, chief juftice of Chefter, governor of
Dover-caftle, lord-warden of the cinque-ports, and
lord-warden of the King's forefts fouth of Trent.

Edward Lord Clinton, another of the Earl's ancef-

life in the reign of Queen Elizabeth, who created him
Earl of Lincoln.

Arms.] Argent, fix crofs croflets fitchy, 3, 2, and
1, fable; on a chief, azure, two mullets pierced, or.

Creft.] In a ducal coronet, gules, five oftrich-fea-
thers, argent, banded, azure.

Supporters.] Two greyhounds, argent, their plain
collars and lines gules.

Motto.] *Loyalte na bonte.*

Chief Seats.] At Oatland in Surry; and Palace-yard,
Weftminfter.

---

6. HOWARD, EARL OF SUFFOLK AND BERKSHIRE.

THE Right Hon. HENRY BOWES HOWARD, Earl
of SUFFOLK and BERKSHIRE, Vifcount Andover, and Baron Howard of Charlton, fucceeded his
grandfather Henry, the late Earl, March 21, 1757.
The faid late Earl fucceeded to the titles of Earl of
Berkfhire, Vifcount Andover, and Baron Howard of
Charlton, in 1706, and fucceeded to the titles of Earl
of Suffolk and Bindon, Baron Howard of Waldon, and
Baron of Chefterford, April 23, 1745, on the death of
the Right Hon. Henry Bowes Howard, Earl of Suffolk. He married, March 5, 1708, Catherine, daughter of James Graham, Efq; of Levens, and by her had
iffue,

1. Lady Diana, born Jan. 13, 1709-10, who died
in Jan. 1712-13.

2. Henry Lord Vifcount Andover, born Dec. 31,
1710; and,

3. James: both died in their minority.

4. William, Lord Vifcount Andover, who died in
July 1756, by a fall from his horfe, was born Dec.
23, 1714; and married to the Lady Mary Finch, fecond daughter of Heneage Finch, Earl of Aylesford,

Nov. 6, 1736, by whom he hath had iffue Henry, now Earl of Suffolk, born May 10, 1739. Catharine, born July 6, 1741. Elizabeth, born May 14, 1744, fince dead. And, Frances, born Feb. 27, 1746.

5. Lady Catharine, born Jan. 29, 1715, died unmarried.

6. Charles, born Oct. 13, 1717.

7. Thomas, born June 11, 1721, married, April 13, 1747, to Mifs —— Kingfcott.

8. Graham, born Oct. 27, 1722, fince dead. And,

9. Lady Frances, born June 17, 1725, died unmarried.

Craven, great grandfather of the prefent Earl, married, to his firft wife, Anne, daughter to Thomas Ogle, of Pinchbeck in Lincolnfhire, Efq; and had iffue one daughter, Anne, who died unmarried. He afterwards married Mary, daughter and fole heir of the Hon. George Bowes, of Elford in Staffordfhire, by whom he had iffue,

1. Henry, his only fon, late Earl of Suffolk and Berkfhire; and two daughters, viz.

2. Mary, and,

3. Dorothy, both deceafed.

The faid Craven was only fon and heir of the Hon. William Howard, fourth fon of Thomas, the firft Earl of Berkfhire, fecond fon of Thomas Howard, created Earl of Suffolk, July 21, 1603, who was fecond fon of Thomas, the fecond Duke of Norfolk, of the family of Howard.

The late Thomas, Earl of Berkfhire, was introduced into the houfe of peers on April 17, 1679. He married two wives, viz. Frances, daughter of Sir Richard Harrifon, of Hurft in Berkfhire, Bart. by whom he had iffue two daughters.

1. Frances, married to Sir Henry Winchcombe, of Bucklebury in the county of Berks, Bart. And,

2. Mary, who died unmarried.

His second wife was Margaret, daughter of Sir Thomas Parker, of Batten in the county of Suffex, knight, by whom he had no iffue, whereupon the honour devolved on the late earl at his death, in 1706.

This noble family are defcended from Thomas de Brotherton, Earl of Norfolk, fifth fon of King Edward I. from whom defcended Thomas Howard, a younger fon of Thomas the fecond Duke of Norfolk, by Margaret, his fecond wife, daughter and fole heir of Thomas Lord Audley of Walden. Which Thomas was, by King James I. created Earl of Suffolk, conftituted lord chamberlain of his Majefty's houfhold, lord treafurer of England, and knight of the moft noble order of the garter.

Suffolk Arms.] Gules, a bend between fix crofs croflets fitche, argent, with an augmentation in the midft of the bend on an efcutcheon, or, a demi-lion rampant, pierced through the mouth with an arrow, within a double treffure counterflory, gules.

Creft.] On a chapeau, gules, turned up, ermine, a lion guardant, his tail extended, or, gorged with a ducal coronet, argent.

Supporters.] On the dexter fide, a lion guardant, or, gorged ducally, argent. On the finifter, a lion, argent.

Motto.] *Non quo fed quomodo.*

Chief Seats.] At Charlton in Wilts; at Levenz in Weftmoreland; at Elford in Staffordfhire; and at Oxford.

·7. CECIL, EARL of SALISBURY.

THE Right Hon. James Cecil, Earl of Salisbury, Vifcount Cranburn, and Baron Cecil of Effingdon, was born in 1713, and fucceeded James, his father, late Earl of Salifbury, Oct. 9, 1728. His lordfhip married, in 1743, Mifs Elizabeth Keet, eldeft daughter of Mr. Edward Keet of Canterbury,

by

by whom he hath iffue James Lord Vifcount Cranburn, born in Sept. 1748; Lady Anne, born in March 1745-6; and Lady Bennet, born in April 1747.

The faid James Cecil, late Earl of Salisbury, father of the prefent Earl, married in Feb. 1708-9, the Lady Anne Tufton, fecond daughter and coheir of James late Earl of Thanet, who died April 22, 1757, and by whom he had iffue,

1. James, the prefent Earl.

2. William, who died unmarried, in 1740.

3. Lady Anne, married to William Stroud, of Punf-burn, in the county of Hertford, Efq; died in July 1752.

4. Lady Catharine, married, in 1736-7, to John now Earl of Egmont, in Ireland, by whom fhe has had iffue five fons and two daughters, and died in Aug. 1752.

5. Lady Margaret.

This noble Earl is defcended from William Cecil, Lord Burleigh, fecretary of ftate, and afterwards lord-treafurer of England, in the reign of Queen Elizabeth, the moft celebrated ftatefman of that age; whofe younger fon, Robert, anceftor of the prefent noble Lord, was conftituted fecretary of ftate, and mafter of the court of Wards, by Queen Elizabeth; and in the fucceeding reign of King James I. was conftituted lord high-treafurer of England; created Baron Cecil, of Effindon in the county of Rutland, in 1603, and Vifcount Cranburn, in the county of Dorfet, Auguft 20, 1604, and Earl of Salisbury, May 4, 1605.

Arms.] Barry of ten, argent and azure, over all fix efcutcheons, 3, 2, and 1, fable, each charged with a lion rampant of the field, a crefcent for difference.

Creft.] On a wreath, fix arrows, or, heads and fea-thers, argent, girt together with a bandage, or belt, azure, garnifhed, or; and over thofe feathers a mo-tion-cap, proper.

Supporters.] Two lions, ermine.

5   *Motto.*

Motto.] *Sero, fed ferio.*

Chief Seats.] At Hatfield in Hertfordſhire ; Cran-
burn-houſe in Dorſetſhire ; Quickſwood in the county
of Hertfordſhire; and Groſvenor-ſtreet, London.

8.   CECIL, EARL of EXETER.

THE Right Hon. Brownlow Cecil, Earl of
Exeter, and Baron of Burleigh, lord lieutenant and cuſtos rotulorum of the county of Rutland,
born Sept. 21, 1725, ſucceeded his father the late
Earl Brownlow, who died November 3, 1754.   His
lordſhip married July 24, 1749, Letitia, ſole daughter and heir of Horatio Townſhend, Eſq; one of the
commiſſioners of exciſe ; who died in April 1756,
leaving no iſſue.   The late Earl married, in 1722,
Hannah Sophia Chambers, daughter of Thomas
Chambers, of Derby, Eſq; by whom he had iſſue,

1. The preſent Earl.

2. Lady Margaret Sophia, who died in 1737.

3. The Hon. Thomas Chambers, born June 25,
1728.

4. Lady Elizabeth, born June 22, 1729; and,

5. Lady Anne, born in 1734.

This noble Earl is deſcended from Robert Sitlift,
Seeſil, or Cecil, who flouriſhed in the reign of King
William Rufus ; but the greateſt of his anceſtors was
William Cecil, Lord Burleigh, lord high-treaſurer of
England, and prime miniſter to Queen Elizabeth.
The preſent Earl is deſcended from Thomas Lord
Burleigh, the eldeſt ſon of that great ſtateſman Wil-
liam Lord Burleigh.

Arms.] Barry of ten, argent and azure, over all ſix
eſcutcheons, 3, 2, and 1, ſable, each charged with a
lion rampant of the field.

Creſt.] On a chapeau, gules, turned up, ermine, a
garb, or ; ſupported by two lions, that on the dexter
ſide, argent ; the ſiniſter, azure.

Supporters.] Two lions, ermine.

Motto.] *Cor unum, via una.*

Chief Seats.] At Burleigh, near Stamford, in the county of Northampton; and Grofvenor-ftreet, London.

---

9. COMPTON, EARL OF NORTHAMPTON.

THE Right Hon. CHARLES COMPTON, Earl of NORTHAMPTON, and Baron Compton of Compton, recorder of the town of Northampton, fucceeded his uncle George, Dec. 6, 1758; and, Sept. 13, 1759, married the lady Anne Somerfet, daughter of Charles late Duke of Beaufort, by whom he has iffue a daughter, born June 26, 1760.

George Earl of Northampton, father of the two laft Earls, married, in 1686, Jane, youngeft daughter of Sir Stephen Fox, Knt. and by this lady (who died July 10, 1721) had iffue four fons and fix daughters, viz.

1. James, who fucceeded him.

2. George, who fucceeded his brother James, Oct. 3, 1754.

3. Stephen, third fon, died young.

4. Charles, the fourth fon, who died Nov. 20, 1755, married, Auguft 14, 1727, to Mary, only daughter of Sir Berkeley Lucy, Bart. by whom he had iffue two fons and four daughters, viz. Charles, the prefent Earl of Northampton; Spencer-Mary, married, firft, to Richard Haddock, and, 2dly, to —— Scott, both in the fea-fervice; Jane, married, Feb. 2, 1753, to George-Bridges Rodney, Efq; and died Jan. 28, 1757, Catharine, married, Jan. 26, 1756, to John Earl of Egmont; and Elizabeth, unmarried.

5. Lady Elizabeth, eldeft daughter, died Jan. 3, 1742-3.

6. Lady Mary, married, in April 1709, to William Gore, of Tring in Hertfordſhire, Eſq; and died in Auguſt 1737.

7. Lady Jane, who is alſo dead.

8. Lady Anne, married, Oct. 16, 1729, to Sir John Ruſhout of Northwick, and has iſſue, a ſon, and two daughters.

9. Lady Penelope; and,

10. Lady Margaret, who are both unmarried.

His Lordſhip, on July 2, 1726, married, to his ſecond lady, Elizabeth, daughter of Sir James Ruſhout, of Northwick, in the county of Worceſter, Bart. and relict of Sir George Thorold, Bart. by whom he had no iſſue; and dying, April 15, 1727, was ſucceeded by his eldeſt ſon James, the late Earl.

This noble family are deſcended from the Comptons of Compton, in Warwickſhire, who were lords of that place before the conqueſt.

Arms.] Sable, a lion paſſant-guardant, or, between three helmets, argent.

Creſt.] On a wreath a mount, vert, and thereon a beacon, or, enflamed on the top, proper; about the ſame a label, inſcribed, *Niſi Dominus.*

Supporters.] Two dragons, with wings expanded, ermine, collared with ducal collars, and chains of gold.

Motto.] *Je ne cherche que ung.*

Chief Seats.] At Caſtle-Aſhby, in Northamptonſhire; at Compton-Vinyates, in the county of Warwick; and Mount-ſtreet, London.

10. FIELDING, EARL OF DENBIGH.

THE Right Hon. Basil Fielding, Earl of Denbigh and Desmond, Viſcount Fielding and Callan, Baron Fielding of Newenham-Padox and St. Liz, and Baron Fielding of Lecaghe, and one of his

Majefty's moft honourable privy-council, was born
Jan. 3, 1719, fucceeded his father William, the late
Earl, who died Aug. 1, 1755; and married April 12,
1757, Maria, daughter to Sir John Bruce-Cotton, of
Conington, in Huntingdonfhire, Bart. by whom he
had a fon and heir, born June 15, 1760.

William, the late Earl, born Oct. 26, 1697, fuc-
ceeded Earl Bafil, his Father, March 28, 1716-17.
His lordfhip married Ifabella, daughter to Peter de
Young, of Utrecht, in Holland, and fifter to the
Marchionefs of Blandford, by whom he had iffue, an
only fon, Bafil, the prefent Earl.

Bafil, father of the late Earl, married Hefter, daughter to Sir Bafil Firebrace, Bart. and by her had iffue,
three fons, and fix daughters:

1. William, the late Earl.

2. Bafil, who died in his infancy.

3. Charles, who married, in Sept. 1737, Mary,
daughter of Sir Thomas Palmer, of Wingham, in
Kent, Bart. and relict of Sir Brook Bridges, of the
fame county, and died in Feb. 1745, leaving three
fons, and two daughters.

4. Lady Mary, the eldeft daughter, married, on
April 15, 1729, to William Cockburne, M. D. and
died in 1732.

5. Lady Bridget, married to Colonel James Ot-
way, of Kent.

6. Lady Elizabeth, who died in April 1752.

7. Lady Hefter, who died Feb. 20. 1720-1.

8. Lady Diana.

9. Lady Frances, married to Daniel, Earl of
Winchelfea and Nottingham, and died in September 1734.

This noble Earl is defcended from the Earls of
Hapfburg, in Germany. Geoffrey, Earl of Hapfburg, being oppreffed by Rodolph, Emperor of Germany, came over into England, and one of his fons
ferved King Henry III. in his wars, whofe anceftors

laying claim to the territories of Lauffenburg and Rhin-Filding, in Germany, he took the name of Filding. One of the braveft of the prefent Earl's anceftors, was Earl William, of whom Lord Clarendon obferves, " That he ferved King Charles I. from the beginning of the civil war, with unwearied pains, and exact fubmiffion to difcipline and order, as a volunteer in Prince Rupert's troop, and engaged with fingular courage in all enterprizes; but was mortally wounded in an engagement with the enemy, April 3, 1643."

Arms.] Argent, on a fefs, azure, three lozenges, or.

Creft.] On a wreath, an eagle with two heads difplayed, fable, armed and membered, or, and charged on the breaft with the above paternal coat.

Supporters.] Two bucks, proper, attired and unguled, or.

Motto.] *Crefcit fub pondere virtus.*

Chief Seats.] At Newenham-Padox, in Warwickfhire; at Martinfthorp, in the county of Rutland; and Hanover-Square, London.

11. FANE, EARL of WESTMORELAND.

THE Right Hon. JOHN FANE, Earl of WESTMORELAND, Baron le Defpenfer and Burgherfh, and Baron of Catherlough, in Ireland, chancellor of the univerfity of Oxford, and lieutenant-general of his Majefty's forces, fucceeded his brother Thomas, the late Earl, in his honours and eftate, in 1736. His lordfhip married Mary, only daughter and heir of Lord Henry Cavendifh, by whom he has no iffue.

Vere, Earl of Weftmoreland, father of the two laft and the prefent Earls, married Rachel, only daughter and heir of John Bence, Efq; by whom he left iffue, three fons, and three daughters.

1. Vere, his eldest son, who succeeded him, and died unmarried in 1699; and was succeeded by

2. Thomas, his brother, late Earl of Westmoreland, who married Catherine, daughter and heir of Charles Stringer, of Charleton, Esq; but died without issue, March 4, 1736, and was succeeded by

3. John, the present earl.

4. Lady Mary, married to Sir Francis Dashwood, Bart. by whom she had issue, Sir Francis Dashwood, and a daughter married to Sir Robert Ofton, of Beekly, in Kent, which lady is since dead.

5. Lady Catherine, married to William Paul, of Braywick, in Berkshire, Esq;

6. Lady Susan, who died, unmarried, March 11, 1734-5.

This noble Earl is descended from the Fanes, an ancient family, which resided at Badsall in Kent; from which descended Francis Fane, son and heir of Sir Thomas Fane, Knight, by Mary, his wife, sole daughter and heir to Henry Nevil, Lord Abergavenny, afterwards created Baroness Despenser. The said Francis was a Knight of the Bath; and, in the reign of King James I. created Baron Burghersh, and Earl of Westmoreland in 1624.

Arms.] Azure, three right-hand gauntlets, with their backs forward, or.

Crest.] Out of a ducal coronet, or; a bull's head, argent; pyed, sable; armed, or; and charged on the neck with a rose, gules, barbed and seeded, proper.

Supporters.] On the dexter side, a gryphon, party per fess, argent and or; his beak, fore-legs, and chain of the second, his collar, sable. On the sinister, a bull, argent; pyed, sable; armed, collared, chained, and hoofed, or; on the collar a rose, proper.

Motto.] *Ne vile Fano.*

Chief Seats.] At Apthorp, in Northamptonshire; Mereworth, Kent; Hanover-Square, London.

12. MORDAUNT, EARL of PETERBOROUGH.

THE Right Hon. Charles Mordaunt, Earl of Peterborough and Monmouth, Vifcount Avalon, Baron Mordaunt of Turvey, and Baron Mordaunt of Ryegate, fucceeded his grandfather Charles, the late Earl, in 1735; and married Mary, daughter of John Cox, Efq; of London, by which lady, who died in November 1755, he hath iffue two daughters:

1. Lady Frances, born in April 1736; and,
2. Lady Mary.

His Lordfhip married, 2dly, by whom he has a fon and heir, born May 16, 1758.

John Lord Mordaunt, father of the prefent Earl, married Frances, daughter to Charles Paulet, Duke of Bolton; and dying April 6, 1710, left iffue,

1. The prefent Earl.
2. John, lieutenant-colonel in the army, member in parliament for Chrift-Church, who, in Oct. 1735, married Mary, fifter to Scroop Lord Vifcount Howe. She died September 12, 1749.

The late Earl, Charles, grandfather to the prefent Earl, married Carey, daughter of Sir Alexander Frazer, of an antient family in Scotland, by whom he had iffue,

1. John Lord Mordaunt, father of the prefent Earl.
2. Henry, who died unmarried, Feb. 24, 1709-10.
3. Henrietta, married to Alexander Duke of Gordon, in Scotland.

The anceftors of this family received the honour of Baron, the 24th of Henry VIII. and Earl the 3d of Charles I. and are defcended from John Mordaunt of Turvey, in the county of Bedford, Efq; who was one of the King's commanders in the battle of Stoke,

near

near Newark upon Trent, againſt John Earl of Lincoln, the 2d of Henry VII. He was alſo chancellor of the dutchy of Lancaſter; and the 24th of Henry VIII. ſummoned to parliament, having married Elizabeth, daughter and coheir to Henry de Vere, Lord of Drayton and Adington.

Arms.] Argent, a chevron between three eſtoils, ſable.

Creſt.] In an Earl's coronet, or; the buſt of a Mooriſh prince, habited in a cloth of gold, all proper; and wreathed about the temples, argent.

Supporters.] Two eagles, ſilver; armed and membered, ſable.

Motto.] *Nec placida contenta quieta eſt.*

Chief Seats.] At Parſon's-Green, in the county of Middleſex; Dantzy, in Wiltſhire; Audley-ſtreet, London.

---

13. GREY, EARL of STAMFORD.

THE Right Hon HARRY GREY, Earl of STAM-FORD, Baron Grey of Groby, Bonville, and Harrington, ſucceeded Harry, the late Earl, his father, in Nov. 1739, having, in May 1736, married the Lady Mary Booth, only daughter and heir of George Earl of Warrington, by whom he hath had iſſue, three ſons, and two daughters:

1. George-Harry, Lord Grey, born Oct. 1. 1737.
2. Lady Mary Grey, born April 17, 1739.
3. Booth Grey, born Auguſt 15, 1740.
4. Lady Anne Grey, born Jan. 23, 1741-2, who died in June 1743; and,
5. John, born May 22, 1743.

Harry, late Earl of Stamford, and father of the preſent Earl, married Dorothy, daughter to Sir Nathan Wright, of Caldecote-Hall, in the county of

Warwick,

Warwick, Knt. lord-keeper of the Great Seal in the reigns of King William and Queen Anne ; and by her, who died Aug. 12, 1738, had iffue, two fons, and five daughters :

1. Harry, the prefent Earl.

2. John, who, in May 1748, married Lucy, fecond daughter of Sir Jofeph Danvers, of Swithland, in the county of Leicefter, Bart.

3. Lady Dorothy, now living.

4. Lady Catherine, married to Mynheer John Trip, poftmafter-general of Amfterdam, who died in June 1738. She married, 2dly, to Wanden Bemden, burgo-mafter of Amfterdam.

5. Lady Diana, married in Sept. 1736, to George Middleton, Efq;

6. Lady Anne, married in October 1745, to Sir Richard Acton, of Aldenham, in the county of Salop, Bart.

7. Lady Jane, married, in 1738, to George Drummond, Efq; fecretary to the Order of the Thiftle; but died in June 1752.

Thomas, Earl of Stamford, grandfon to Henry Grey, who was created Earl of Stamford, the 3d of Charles I. in the reign of King William, was made chancellor of the dutchy of Lancafter, lord-lieutenant and cuftos-rotulorum of the county of Leicefter, and of the privy-council to Queen Anne; but dying, on Jan. 31. 1719-20, without furviving iffue, his titles, and part of his eftate, defcended to the faid Harry Grey, the late Earl, fon of John Grey, third fon of Henry the firft Earl of Stamford.

This noble family are defcended from Henry de Grey, to whom King Richard I. gave the manor of Turro in Effex. Henry Lord Grey, Marquis of Dorfet, and afterwards Duke of Suffolk, was another of the anceftors of this noble Earl, who was conftituted High Conftable of England at the coronation of King Edward VI. and married the Lady Frances, daughter

of

of Charles Brandon, Duke of Suffolk, by Mary the youngeſt ſiſter of King Henry VIII. firſt married to Lewis XII. King of France; by whom he had the Lady Jane Grey, who was proclaimed Queen of England, on the death of King Edward; but the party of Queen Mary prevailing, ſhe loſt her head, as did her father the Duke of Suffolk, and her huſband Guildford Dudley, fourth ſon of the Duke of Northumberland.

Arms.] Barry of ſix, argent and azure, in chief three torteauxes, a label of three points, ermine.

Creſt.] On a wreath, an unicorn erect, ermine; armed, creſted, and hoofed, or; having a full ſun behind it, proper.

Supporters.] Two unicorn, ermine; armed, creſted, and hoofed, or.

Motto.] *A ma puiſſance.*

Chief Seats.] Enville-Hall, in Staffordſhire; Bragdate-Hall, in the county of Leiceſter; Dunham-Maſſy, in Cheſhire; Sackville-ſtreet, London.

---

14. FINCH, EARL of WINCHELSEA.

THE Right Hon. DANIEL FINCH, Earl of WINCHELSEA and NOTTINGHAM, Viſcount Maidſtone, Baron Fitz-Herbert of Eaſtwell, Baron Finch of Daventry, Lord of the Royal Manor of Wye, in Kent, and Baronet, one of the Lords of his Majeſty's moſt honourable Privy-council, a Knight of the moſt noble Order of the Garter, and one of the elder brethren of the Trinity-houſe, ſucceeded his father, Daniel, the late Earl, Jan. 21. 1729-30. His Lordſhip married, in 1729, the Lady Frances Fielding, daughter of Baſil, the late Earl of Denbigh, by whom he had iſſue one daughter, Lady Charlotte. And her Ladyſhip dying, Sept. 1734, he married, to his ſecond

2   Lady,

Lady, in Jan. 1737-8, Mary, daughter and coheir of Sir Thomas Palmer, of Wingham, in Kent, Bart. by whom he hath issue, four daughters, living:

1. Lady Heneage, born in December 1741.

2. Lady Essex, born Jan. 1. 1745-6.

3. Lady Hatton, born Feb. 23, 1746-7.

4. Lady Augusta, born in February 1750-1; and four others that died young.

Daniel Finch, Earl of Winchelsea and Nottingham, father of the present Earl, married Lady Essex Rich, second daughter to Robert Rich, Earl of Warwick; by whom he had issue, one daughter, named Mary, who married to William Saville, Marquis of Hallifax; and, after his decease, on Jan. 1. 1707-8, she married to John Kerr, late Duke of Roxburgh, and died on Sept. 19, 1718, and had issue. [See *Kerr* Earl.] His Lordship married, to his second wife, Anne, eldest daughter of Christopher, late Lord Viscount Hatton, by whom he had issue, five sons, and eight daughters.:

1. Daniel, the present Earl.

2. William, who married the Lady Anne Douglas, sister to Charles, the present Duke of Dover; which Lady Anne dying in the year 1741, without issue, he married his second wife, the Lady Charlotte, daughter to the Earl of Pomfret, in August 1746.

3. John.

4. Henry, who is not yet married.

5. Edward, married to Miss Elizabeth Palmer.

6. Lady Essex, married, on July 20, 1703, to Sir Roger Mostyn, in the county of Flint, Bart. and died May 23, 1721.

7. Lady Charlotte, married, February 4, 1725-6, to his Grace, Charles Symour, late Duke of Somerset.

8. Lady Anne, who died young.

9. Lady Elizabeth, who, in Sept. 1738, was married to the Hon. William Murray, now Lord Mansfield.

10. Lady Mary, married, on Sept. 22, 1716, to

Thomas Watfon-Wentworth, late Marquis of Rock-ingham.

11. Lady Henrietta, married to his Grace William Fitzroy, Duke of Cleveland, leaving no iffue.

12. Lady Ifabella, now living.

13. Lady Frances; and,

14. Lady Margaret: both died unmarried.

This family are defcended from Herbert Fitz Her-bert, Earl of Pembroke, and chamberlain to King Henry I. They took the name of Finch, in the reign of King Edward I.

One of the anceftors of the prefent Earl, was the Right Hon. Heneage Finch, Earl of Nottingham, who was conftituted lord high-chancellor of England in 1675; and lord high-fteward on the trials of Phi-lip Earl of Pembroke, and William Vifcount Stafford, in 1680.

This Earl was the fon of Heneage Finch, recorder of London, and fpeaker of the houfe of Commons, in 1625. He was created a Baron in 1673, and Earl of Nottingham in 1681. King William would have conftituted the Earl lord high-chancellor of Eng-land on his acceffion; but his lordfhip declined that office, and accepted the poft of principal fecretary of ftate, which he refigned in March 1693-4, not find-ing himfelf acceptable to the court, and was not em-ployed afterwards during that reign. The day after the coronation of Queen Anne, he was appointed fe-cretary of ftate again; and, while he was in this ftation, the houfe of commons twice refolved, That he highly merited the truft her Majefty repofed in him. At the acceffion of King George I. he was one of the lords juftices appointed to adminifter the government until his Majefty's arrival; and in Sept. 1714, he was made lord prefident of the council. The title of Vifcoun-tefs of Maidftone was conferred on Elizabeth, daugh-ter of Sir Thomas Heneage, captain of the guards to Queen Elizabeth, treafurer of her chamber, vice-chamberlain of her houſhold, and chancellor of the duchy of Lancaſter, wife of Sir Moyle Finch, by K. James I. in the 21ſt year of his reign, anno 1623, to her and the heirs male of her body; who dying in 1633, left iſſue (beſides ſeveral other children by her huſband Sir Moyle Finch) Sir Thomas Finch, who ſucceeded to the earldom of Winchelſea ; and who dying in 1634, was ſucceeded by his eldeſt ſon, Heneage Earl of Winchelſea, who having been very inſtrumental in the reſtoration of King Charles II. was conſtituted governor of Dover-caſtle; and, in 12 Car. II. (being deſcended from the family of Herbert) was created Baron Fitz-Herbert of Eaſtwel in Kent, and was ſoon after ſent ambaſſador to Turkey ; from which embaſſy he returned in 1669, and died in 1689. He had twenty-ſeven children by four wives, of whom William Lord Maidſtone was one, who married Elizabeth, daughter of Thomas Windham, of Norfolk, Eſq; and the Lord Maidſtone being killed in the ſeafight with the Dutch in 1672, left his lady with child of a ſon, of which ſhe was delivered, in Sept. 1672, who was baptized by the name of Charles, ſucceeded his grandfather the ſaid Heneage Earl of Winchelſea. Earl Charles died Aug. 14, 1712; and leaving no male iſſue, the honour deſcended to Heneage Finch, his uncle, ſecond ſon of the ſaid Heneage Earl of Winchelſea, and brother of the ſaid Lord Maidſtone, deceaſed ; and Earl Heneage Finch dying without male iſſue in 1726, was ſucceeded by his youngeſt brother John Finch ; which John dying without iſſue in 1729, the title of Earl of Winchelſea devolved on Daniel, late Earl of Nottingham, ſon and heir of Sir Heneage Finch, fourth ſon of Sir Moyle Finch and Elizabeth his wife, who was created Counteſs of Winchelſea 21 Jac. I. anno 1623.

Arms.] Quarterly, firſt and fourth, argent, a chevron between three gryphons paſſant, ſegreant, ſable, for Finch ; ſecond and third, gules, three lions rampant, or, for Fitz-Herbert.   *Creſt.*]

Creſt.] On a wreath, a gryphon paſſant, ſegreant, ſable.

Supporters.] On the dexter ſide a lion, or, collared ducally, gules. On the left a gryphon, ſable, alike collared, argent.

Motto.] *Nil conſcire ſibi.*

Chief Seats.] At Burley, in Rutlandſhire; at Round-ſtone, in Buckinghamſhire; at Eaſtwell, in Kent; and Sackville-ſtreet, London.

15. STANHOPE, EARL of CHESTERFIELD.

THE Right Hon. PHILIP DORMER STANHOPE, Earl of CHESTERFIELD, Baron Stanhope of Shelford, knight of the moſt noble order of the garter, and one of the lords of his Majeſty's moſt honourable privy council, born Sept. 22, 1695, ſucceeded his father Philip, the late Earl, Jan. 27, 1725-6. His lordſhip married, Sept. 5, 1722, the Lady Meloſina, Counteſs of Walſingham, by whom he has no iſſue.

Philip Stanhope, Earl of Cheſterfield, father of the preſent Earl, married Lady Elizabeth Savile, one of the daughters and coheirs of George Marquis of Halifax, and left iſſue by her four ſons and two daughters, viz.

1. Philip, the preſent Earl.

2. William, knight of the Bath, married, firſt, Margaret, daughter of John Rudge, Eſq; by whom he hath iſſue one daughter Elizabeth, married to Sir Wilbore Ellis, formerly one of the lords of the admiralty. He married, ſecondly, Miſs Crawley, daughter of John Crawley, Eſq; late alderman of London; and, thirdly, Miſs Delaval, ſiſter to Francis Blake Delaval, Eſq; Oct. 6, 1759.

3. John, who died without iſſue.

4. Charles, born Sept. 6, 1708, who died Feb. 20, 1736, without iſſue.

E 2

5. Lady

5. Lady Gertrude, married to the late Sir Charles Hotham, Bart.

6. Lady Elizabeth, married to Samuel Hill of Shenston, in the county of Stafford, Esq; who died without issue Nov. 14, 1727.

This family received their surname from the town of Stanhope, in the bishoprick of Durham, where they resided before they removed into Nottinghamshire. Sir Richard Stanhope had a large estate in the North in the reign of Henry III.   Sir Richard de Stanhope, his son, was Lord of Estwyche in Northumberland, and mayor of Newcastle; and King Edward III. in consideration of his services against the Scots, granted him a third part of the village and fishery of Paxton, in Scotland.

The honour of Baron was conferred on this noble family in the fourteenth year of King James I. and that of Earl in the fourth of Charles I.

Arms.] Quarterly, ermine and gules.

Crest.] On a wreath a tower, argent, with a demi-lion rampant, issuing from the battlements, or, crowned ducally, gules, and holding between his paws a grenade firing, proper.

Supporters.] On the dexter side a wolf, or, crowned with a ducal coronet. On the sinister a talbot, ermine.

Motto.] *A Deo & Rege.*

Chief Seats.] At Bretby in Derbyshire ; at Shelford in Nottinghamshire; at Blackheath in Kent ; and South-Audley-street, London.

---

16. TUFTON, EARL of THANET.

THE Right Hon. SACKVILE TUFTON, Earl of THANET, Baron Tufton, Lord Westmoreland and Vezey, lord of the honour of Skipton in Craven, and baronet, and hereditary-sheriff of the counties of Westmoreland and Cumberland; was born in August 1733, and succeeded his father, who died Dec. 4, 1754.

ceeded his uncle, Earl Thomas, in 1729. His lordship, in 1722, married Lady Mary Sackvile, youngeft
daughter and coheir of William Marquis of Halifax ;
by whom he had iffue,

1. Lord John, who died young.
2. Sackvile, the prefent Earl.
3. Lady Mary, who died July 25, 1758. And,
4. Lady Charlotte.

This noble family is defcended from Elfege de
Toketon, alias Tufton, lord of the manors of Sile-
ham in the county of Kent, and of Tufton in the
county of Suffex, who flourifhed in the reign of King
John, and from whom defcended John Tufton, Efq;
whofe refidence was at Hothfield in Kent. He was
fheriff of that county in the reign of Queen Elizabeth.
His fon John was created a baronet 9 Jac. I. and mar-
ried Chriftian, daughter of Sir Humphrey Brown,
Knt. one of the judges of the court of Common-
Pleas, by whom he had iffue Nicholas, created Baron
Tufton, of Tufton in Suffex, 2 Car. I. and Earl of
Thanet, in Kent, 4 Car. I.

Arms.] Sable, an eagle difplayed, ermine, within a
bordure, argent.

Creft.] On a wreath, a fea-lion, fejant.

Supporters.] Two eagles, their wings expanded,
ermine.

Motto.] *Fiel pero defdichado.*

Chief Seats.] At Hothfield in Kent ; at Newbottle
in Northamptonfhire ; and Grofvenor-ftreet, London.

---

17. MONTAGU, EARL of SANDWICH.

THE Right Hon. John Montagu, Earl of .
SANDWICH, Vifcount Hinchingbroke, Baron
Montagu of St. Neots in Huntingdonfhire, joint
vice-treafurer of Ireland, one of the elder brethren
of the Trinity-Houfe, governor of the Charter-

Houfe, recorder of the corporations of Huntingdon and Godmanchefter, lieutenant-general in the army, one of his Majefty's privy council, and F. R. S. fucceeded Edward, the late Earl, his grandfather, Oct. 20, 1729. His lordfhip married the Hon. Dorothy, daughter of Charles Lord Vifcount Fane, of the kingdom of Ireland, March 7, 1741-2 ; by whom he has iffue,

1. John Vifcount Hinchingbroke, born Jan. 26, 1743-4.

2. Edward Montagu, born June 30, 1745, died Nov. 3, 1752.

3. William-Auguftus, born in 1752.

4. Lady Mary, born Feb. 23, 1747-8.

His lordfhip was plenipotentiary at the treaty of Aix-la-Chapelle, concluded Oct. 7, 1748.

The Hon. Edward Montagu, father of the prefent Earl, married Elizabeth, only daughter of Alexander Popham, of Littlecote in Wiltfhire, Efq; and dying Oct. 3, 1722, in his father's life-time, left iffue,

1. The Lady Mary, who died young.

2. The Lady Elizabeth, married, in Sept. 1737, to Kelland Courtney, Efq;

3. John, the prefent Earl. And,

4. The Hon. William Montagu, who married Mifs Naylor, daughter of ———— Naylor, Efq; in 1748.

This noble family being a branch of the late Duke of Montagu's, derive their pedigree from Drogo de Monteacuto, who came into England with William the Conqueror.

Sir Sidney Montagu, great grandfather of the late Earl, was conftituted mafter of the court of Requefts in the reign of King Charles I. and was elected knight of the fhire for the county of Huntingdon, in 1640; but was expelled the houfe for refufing to take an oath the houfe had framed for their members, " That they would live and die with their general the Earl of Effex."

Sir Edward Montagu, his son, was born July 27, 1625, and had a commiffion from the parliament, in 1643, to raife a regiment of a thoufand men, in the county of Cambridge, which he raifed accordingly, and was in moft of the confiderable actions in that war, particularly at Nafeby in 1645, behaving with that gallantry, that he was advanced to the command of brigadier-general the fame year, when he was but twenty years of age. He was afterwards appointed with Defborough to execute the office of high-admiral, and was joined with Blake in the command of the fleet, after whofe death he had the fole command, and the addrefs, as well as the honour, of bringing the whole fleet to fubmit to King Charles II. and thereupon fet fail with them to the coaft of Holland, in order to convoy his Majefty King Charles II. to England, whereby he contributed no lefs than general Monk to the reftoration of that prince : and his Majefty, at his arrival in England, conftituted him one of the knights of the moft noble order of the garter; and, on July 13, (the fame year) 1660, in the 35th year of his age, created him Baron Montagu of St. Neots in Huntingdonfhire, Vifcount Montagu, and Earl of Sandwich : he was alfo made mafter of the King's wardrobe, admiral of the narrow feas, and lieutenant-admiral to his royal highnefs the Duke of York, lord high-admiral of England. He was afterwards appointed his Majefty's proxy at the efpoufals of the princefs Donna Catherina, the daughter of Don Pedro, King of Portugal, and had the honour of convoying that princefs to England in 1662. He had a great fhare in the victory obtained over the Dutch at fea, June 3, 1665, where eighteen of the enemy's capital fhips were taken, and fourteen more · deftroyed, and admiral Opdam blown up. He afterwards took eight Dutch men of war, two Eaft-India men, and twenty fail of other merchantmen.

He

He was appointed ambaffador extraordinary to the court of Spain, in 1666, to mediate a peace between the courts of Spain and Portugal, which he effected. He was vice admiral under the Duke of York in the fea-fight off Southwold-Bay, May 28, 1672, where he contributed greatly to the victory obtained that day; but died fighting bravely in the fervice of his country. Bifhop Parker, in the hiftory of his own times, relating this engagement, fays, " The Earl " of Sandwich having fhattered feven of the enemy's " fhips, and beat off three firefhips, at length over- " powered, fell a facrifice to his country. A gentle- " man adorned with all the virtues of Alcibiades, " and untainted by any of his vices; capable of any " bufinefs; full of wifdom; a great commander at " fea and land; learned, eloquent, affable, liberal, " and magnificent."

Arms.] Argent, three lozenges conjoined in fefs, gules; a border, fable.

Creft.] On a wreath a gryphon's head couped, or; its beak and wings fable.

Supporters.] On the dexter fide a triton, holding over his right fhoulder a trident, all proper, his ducal crown, or. On the finifter a parrot, with wings dif-clofed, vert.

Motto.] *Poft tot naufragia portum.*

Chief Seats.] At Hinchinbroke in the county of Huntingdon; and Pall-Mall, London.

---

18.   CAPEL, EARL of ESSEX.

THE Right Hon. John-William-Anne-Holles Capel, Earl of Essex, Vifcount Malden, and Baron Capel of Hadham, a lord of the bedchamber to the King; born Oct. 7, 1732, fucceeded his father William, the late Earl, Jan. 8, 1742-3; and married, Aug. 1, 1754, Mifs Charlotte, daughter of Sir Charles Hanbury

Hanbury Williams, knight of the Bath; by whom he has a daughter named Elizabeth, born Aug. 10, 1755, a son born Nov. 13, 1757, and a daughter, born July 14, 1759; and the Countess, their mother, died July 19, 1759.

William Earl of Effex, father of the prefent Earl, married, Nov. 27, 1718, to the Lady Jane Hyde, daughter of Henry Earl of Clarendon and Rochefter, and by her (who died Jan. 3, 1723-4) had iffue four daughters; whereof Lady Charlotte, born Oct. 2, 1721, married, March 30, 1752, Thomas, now Lord Hyde : the reft died unmarried.

On Feb. 2, 1725-6, his lordfhip married his fecond wife, the Lady Elizabeth Ruffel, youngeft daughter of Wriothefley, father of the late and prefent Dukes of Bedford, by whom he had three daughters and two fons, viz.

1. George Vifcount Malden, born in Jan. 1727, died young.

2. Lady Diana, born Feb. 22, 1728.

3. Lady Anne, born May 13, 1730.

4. Lady Amelia, born Sept. 9, 1731.

5. John-William-Anne, the prefent Earl.

This noble family is defcended from Sir Richard Capel, lord juftice of Ireland in the reign of King Henry VII. in 1503, whofe anceftors were lords of the manor of Capel in the county of Suffolk for many ages. But the greateft hero of this family was Arthur Earl of Effex, who was beheaded for his loyalty to King Charles I. of whom Lord Clarendon declares, " He was a man that, whoever after him " fhould deferve beft of the Englifh nation, could " never think himfelf undervalued, when he fhould " hear that his courage, virtue, and fidelity were laid. " in the balance with, and compared to, that of the " the Lord Capel."

Arms.] Gules, a lion rampant, between three crofs croflets fitchy, or.

E 5   *Creft.*]

Creſt.] On a wreath, a demi-lion rampant, couped, or, holding in his paws a croſs croſlet, fitchy,
gules.

Supporters.] Two lions, or, ducally crowned, gules.
Motto] *Fide et fortitudine.*
Chief Seats.] At Caſhioberry in Hertfordſhire;
and Groſvenor-ſquare, London.

---

19. MONTAGU, EARL of CARDIGAN.

THE Right Hon. GEORGE MONTAGU, Earl of
CARDIGAN, Baron Brudenel of Stanton-Wi-
vil, conſtable and lieutenant of Windſor-Caſtle,
knight of the moſt noble order of the garter, and
baronet, preſident of St. Luke's hoſpital, and F. R. S.
born in 1712, married the Lady Mary Montagu,
youngeſt daughter, and now one of the coheirs of
John Duke of Montagu, July 7, 1730; and ſince
the deceaſe of his Grace, has taken the name and
arms of Montagu.

His lordſhip has iſſue a ſon named John Lord Brudenell, born March 18, 1734-5; and three daughters, viz. The Ladies Elizabeth, Mary, and Henrietta.

George Brudenell, late Earl of Cardigan, ſucceeded
his grandfather in 1703, and dying in July 1732,
left iſſue by his wife the Lady Elizabeth Bruce, eldeſt
daughter of Thomas late Earl of Aileſbury, four
ſons, and two daughters, viz.

1. George, the preſent Earl of Cardigan.

2. The Hon. James Brudenell, member of parliament for Shaftſbury, whoſe daughter was married,
Sept. 2, 1758, to Sir Samuel Fludier, Knt. alderman of London, and member of parliament for Chip-
penham.

3. Robert,

3. Robert, colonel of his Majesty's forces, married to Miss Bishop, daughter to Sir Cecil Bishop, Bart. in Feb. 1759.

4. Thomas, now Lord Bruce. *See Lord Bruce.*

5. The Lady Frances, married to Oliver Tilson, Esq; And.

6. Lady Mary, married to Richard Powis, Esq; after whose death she married, June 2ς, 1754, to Thomas Bouldby, Esq;

This noble Earl is descended from William de Brudenhill, who flourished in the reigns of King Henry III. and King Edward I. the seat of the family being then at Doddington, in Oxfordshire, part of his estate lying at Adderbury and Bloxham, in that county, and another part of it in Northamptonshire.

Sir Thomas Brudenell, another of the ancestors of this noble Earl, in consideration of his loyalty and eminent services to King Charles I. was, by King Charles II. in the thirteenth year of his reign, created Earl of Cardigan, three days before his Majesty's coronation.

Arms.] Of Montagu and Monthermer quarterly two coats, the first and fourth argent, three lozenges conjoined in fess gules, within a border sable; second and third sable, a lion rampant argent, and in a canton argent, the cross of England, for Churchill.

Crest.] On a wreath a gryphon's head couped, or, with wings indorsed and beaked, sable.

Supporters.] On the dexter side a gryphon, or, beaked, winged, and four legs sable. On the sinister a wyvern, gules, collared, or, wings expanded, gules, charged on the breast in a canton azure, St. Andrew's cross, argent.

Motto.] *Spectamur agendo.*

Chief Seats.] At Dean in Northamptonshire; at Blackheath in Kent; at Windsor-Castle as constable; and Dover-street, London.

E 6   20. AN-

20. ANNESLEY, EARL of ANGLESEA.

THE Right Honourable Richard Annesley, Earl of Anglesea, Viscount Valencia, Baron Annesley of Newport-Pagnel, Baron Mount-Norris, Baron of Altham, and Baronet, succeeded his brother Arthur in 1737.

Richard Annesley, Lord Altham, father of the present Earl, married Dorothy, daughter to Mr. Davy of the county of Devon; and departing this life Nov. 25, 1701, left issue two sons and one daughter.

1. Arthur Lord Altham, who married —— a natural daughter of John Sheffield, late Duke of Buckingham, who died without issue.

2. Richard, the present Earl.

3. Elizabeth, who married Maurice Lord Haversham; and, after his decease, she was married, Anno 1746-7, to —— Fitzwilliam White, Esq;

This noble Earl is descended from Richard Annesley, of Annesley, in the county of Nottingham, who flourished in the reign of William the Conqueror, in 1079.

[*For a more particular account of the family of this noble Lord, the reader is requested to consult the third volume of this work, which contains an account of the families of the* Irish *nobility.*]

Arms.] Quarterly, first pally of six, argent and sable; over all a bend, gules.

Crest.] On a wreath, a Moor's head and bust, sidefaced and couped, proper; wreathed about the temples, argent and sable.

Supporters.] On the dexter side, a Roman knight; on the sinister, a Moorish prince, both habited and furnished, proper.

Motto.] *Virtutis Amore.*

Chief Seats.] At Belchington in Oxfordſhire; Farn-borough-place, in the county of Southampton; and Clemoling-park, in the county of Wexford in Ireland.

---

21. HOWARD, EARL of CARLISLE.

THE Right Honourable FREDERICK HOWARD, Earl of CARLISLE, Viſcount Howard of Mor-peth, and Baron Dacres of Gilleſland, born May 28, 1748, ſucceeded his father Henry Sept. 4, 1758.

Henry, the late Earl, married the Lady Frances Spencer, only daughter of Charles Earl of Sunder-land, who died July 27, 1742, and by whom he had iſſue two ſons and two daughters, viz.

1. Charles, Lord Morpeth, who died in Auguſt, 1741.

2. Robert, then Lord Morpeth, died October 20, 1743.

3. Lady Arabella, who married, in 1741, to Jo-nathan Cope, Eſq; and died in the year 1746, leaving iſſue a ſon named Charles, and a daughter named Arabella.

4. Diana, who married, Feb. 9, 1748-9, to Tho-mas Duncombe, Eſq;

His Lordſhip married to his ſecond Lady, June 8, 1743, Iſabella Byron, ſiſter to the preſent Lord Byron, by whom he had iſſue one ſon and four daughters:

1. Frederick, the preſent Earl.

2. Lady Anne, born in 1744.

3. Lady Fanny, born in 1745.

4. Lady Betty, born in 1746. And,

5. Lady Juliana.

Charles, Earl of Carliſle, father of the late Earl, married the Lady Elizabeth Capel, only ſur-viving daughter of Arthur Earl of Eſſex; and his Lordſhip dying on the 1ſt of May, 1738, left iſſue two ſons and three daughters, viz.

1. Henry, the late Earl.

2. Sir Charles Howard, lieutenant-general of his Majefty's forces, colonel of the third regiment of dragoon-guards, governor of Carlifle, member of parliament for the faid city, and knight of the Bath.

3. Lady Elizabeth, married firft to Nicholas Lord Lechmere, who dying without iffue by her, June 18, 1727, her Ladyfhip, October 25, 1728, was married fecondly to Sir Thomas Robinfon, of Rockby-park, in Yorkfhire, Bart.

4. Lady Anne, married to Richard Ingram, Lord Vifcount Irwin, of Scotland. And,

5. Lady Mary.

The faid Earl Charles was lord lieutenant and cuftos rotulorum of the counties of Weftmoreland and Cumberland, deputy e rl-marfhal of England, firft commiffioner of the trea try, governor of the town and caftle of Carlifle, vice-admiral of the adjacent coaft, and one of the privy council to King William III. He was alfo of the privy-council in the reign of Queen Anne, and one of the commiffioners to treat of an union with Scotlnd, in the year 1706; and, on the demife of Queen Anne, was appointed by the late King George I. one of the regents, fworn of the privy-council, conftituted firft commiffioner of the treafury, and conftable of the Tower; and in the year 1723, he was made governor of Windfor-caftle, and lord warden of the foreft of Windfor.

This noble Earl derives his pedigree from William Lord Howard, fecond fon of Thomas the fecond Duke of Norfolk, by Margaret his fecond wife, daughter of Thomas Lord Audley.

Arms.] Gules, on a bend, between fix crofs croflets fitche, argent, an efcutcheon, or, charged with a demi-lion rampant, pierced through the mouth with an arrow within a double treffure counterflory, gules.

Creft.] On a chapeau, gules, turned up, ermine,

a lion guardant, his tail extended, or, gorged with a ducal coronet, argent, a mullet for difference.

Supporters.] On the dexter fide a lion, argent, differenced by a mullet. On the finifter a bull, gules, armed, unguled, ducally gorged, and chained, or.

Motto.] *Volo, non valeo.*

Chief Seats.] At Caftle-Howard, in Yorkfhire; Naworth-caftle, in Cumberland; Morpeth-caftle, in Northumberland; and Soho-fquare, London.

---

22. SCOT, DUKE of BUCCLEUCH, EARL of DONCASTER.

THE Moft Noble HENRY SCOT, Duke of Buc-CLEUCH, Earl of Dalkeith, Baron Scot of Buccleuch and Efkdale, and a Peer of England by the title of Baron Scot, of Tindale in Northumberland, and Earl of Doncafter in Yorkfhire, was born Sept. 2, 1746, being great grandfon of James Duke of Monmouth and Buccleuch, and Earl of Doncafter, who was the eldeft fon of King Charles II. by Mrs. Lucy Walters, daughter of Richard Walters, Efq; and was born at Rotterdam, in Holland, April 9, 1649, and went by the name of James Crofts until his Majefty's reftoration. In the year 1662, the King fent for him over into England, and an apartment was affigned him in Whitehall. The next year the King created him Baron of Tindale, Earl of Doncafter, and Duke of Monmouth, and made him knight of the moft noble order of the garter. The fame year, 1663, he married the Lady Anne, fole daughter and heir of Francis Earl of Buccleuch, one of the greateft fortunes in Great Britain. Upon this marriage he took the name of Scot, and they were created Duke and Duchefs of Buccleuch in Scotland. He was appointed mafter of the horfe to his Majefty in 1665,

· death of his Grace the Duke of Albemarle in 1669, he was conftituted general of his Majefty's forces, lord lieutenant of the eaft-riding of Yorkfhire, governor of the town and citadel of Hull, and chief juftice in eyre of all his Majefty's forefts and chafes fouth of Trent; and in 1672 he was conftituted lord high chamberlain of Scotland.

The fame year 1672, he commanded the fix thoufand Englifh and Scots which joined the French army on the frontiers of Holland, and was conftituted lieutenant-general of the forces of Lewis XIV. being prefent at the taking of Rhineburgh, Doefburgh, and Zutphen, and at the reduction of Utrecht, where the French king kept his court for fome time. In the year 1673, he was at the fiege of Maeftricht, and commanded at the attack of the counterfcarp. The town being taken, the Duke with the Britifh forces withdrew, it not being thought for the intereft of England to affift the French in making an entire conqueft of the United Provinces.

The Duke was elected chancellor of the univerfity of Cambridge in 1674; and as he had formerly commanded the forces fent to the affiftance of the French againft the Dutch, he made a campaign under the Prince of Orange, in the year 1678, againft the French, and was at the attack of the abbey of St. Dennis.

The Field Conventiclers in Scotland breaking out into rebellion in the year 1679, and having affembled a very formidable force, the Duke of Monmouth was fent down to fupprefs them; and giving the rebels battle at Bothwell-bridge on the 22d of June, totally defeated them, taking a great number of prifoners, among whom were feveral of the murderers of the archbifhop of St. Andrew's; and returning to court in triumph, appeared at that time very high in the King's favour. Nor was he lefs in the favour of the people, on his appearing at the head of what was called the Proteftant Party, and fhewing an uncom-

mon zeal againſt thoſe who were accuſed of the Popiſh Plot; but the King falling ſick, and the Duke of
York being ſent for over from the Netherlands, and
finding the Duke of Monmouth had rendered himſelf
exceeding popular, was apprehenſive of his having
an eye upon the crown: he procured him therefore
to be diſmiſſed from all his places, and ſent abroad;
but the King recovering from his illneſs, thought it
convenient alſo that the Duke of York ſhould return
to Flanders before the meeting of the parliament.
The Duke of York thereupon reſided at Bruſſels, and
the Duke of Monmouth at Utrecht; but the Duke of
Monmouth on a ſudden returned from Holland, without the King's leave, and arriving at London on the
27th of November, about midnight, the watch gave
notice of it in the ſeveral wards. The people thereupon immediately illuminated their houſes, rung the
bells, and made bonfires, as if it had been for ſome
notable victory; but the Duke of Monmouth coming
over without the King's leave, did not think fit to
attend the court: and ſoon after his friends the Lords
Shaftſbury, Ruſſel, and ſeveral other perſons of diſ-
tinction, preſented the Duke of York as a recuſant
at the bar of the court of King's-Bench, which made
the Duke of York their profeſſed enemy. The King
calling the next parliament to meet at Oxford, the
Duke of Monmouth, the Earl of Eſſex, and ſeveral
other Lords, petitioned his Majeſty that the parliament might not ſit at Oxford, where they ſuggeſted
the houſes could not act with freedom; but that he
would be pleaſed to order them to ſit at Weſtminſter,
the uſual place, where they might conſult and act
with ſafety. This petition was ſigned,

Monmouth,	Stamford,	Paget,
Kent,	Eſſex,	Gray,
Huntingdon,	Shaftſbury,	Herbert,
Bedford,	Mordaunt,	Howard,
Saliſbury,	Evers,	Delamere.

The King frowned on the petitioners, and gave them no anſwer; and on the 21ſt of March, 1680-81, the parliament met at Oxford, and a bill was brought into the houſe for excluding the Duke of York from the crown, and ſecuring the nation againſt a popiſh ſucceſſor, read the firſt time on the 28th of March, 1681, and ordered a ſecond reading. Whereupon the King came to the houſe, and made a ſpeech, wherein he obſerved, That their beginnings were ſuch, that he could expeᶜt no good ſucceſs from their debates, and therefore diſſolved them; and a plot, denominated the Ryehouſe-plot, being diſcovered at this time, the Earls of Shaftſbury and Eſſex, Lord Ruſſel, Col. Sydney, and ſeveral more, were taken into cuſtody as conſpirators, and ſoon after the Duke of Monmouth; but the Duke was admitted to bail, and the King, being ſatisfied he was not concerned in that part of the plot relating to the Ryehouſe, granted his Grace a pardon, who thereupon went over to Holland, where he remained till the death of King Charles II. which happened on Feb. 6, 1684-5.

The Duke of Monmouth being ſtrongly poſſeſſed with an opinion that his mother was married to King Charles II. and that conſequently he had an undoubted right to the Britiſh crown, adviſed with the Earl of Argyle, and the reſt of his friends in Holland, on the feaſeableneſs of making a deſcent in England, and aſſerting his right to that throne. They were pretty unanimous as to the probability of ſucceſs, the Duke being ſo exceeding popular, and the nation generally jealous of the King's deſign to introduce popery; only one party were of opinion, that things were not yet ripe; that it were better to wait till the King had made ſome advances towards the alteration of religion, and the people's fears of popery heightened. Others inſiſted, that they were more likely to ſucceed if they made the attempt before the King was well ſettled on his throne, and while the

Duke's

Duke's intereſt was ſo conſiderable in England; but the Earl of Argyle being for an immediate deſcent, and embarking in order to make a diverſion in the Duke's favour in Scotland, it was carried for an immediate deſcent upon England: whereupon the Duke hired a frigate of thirty-two guns, and three ſmall tenders, one of which was detained by the Dutch, on the Engliſh miniſter (Skelton) applying to the States to prevent theſe ſhips ſailing. However, the Duke proceeded in his voyage with the frigate and two tenders, and, after a tedious ſtormy paſſage, arrived at Lime in Dorſetſhire the 11th of June, 1685, his whole force not amounting to two hundred men, including officers; but having brought over arms for five thouſand more, and great numbers of the country-people joining him, his forces ſoon became very formidable, the militia conſtantly flying before him.

From Lime the Duke marched croſs the country to Taunton-Dean in Somerſetſhire, where he cauſed himſelf to be proclaimed King, and ſet a price upon the King's head, as the King had upon the Duke's, and cauſed him to be attainted of high treaſon in the parliament, which was then ſitting. Whereupon the Duke, in his declaration, called the parliament a ſeditious aſſembly; and advancing afterwards to Bridgwater, he continued his march towards Bath and Briſtol: but receiving advice that a body of regular troops was in full march for the Weſt, he thought proper to retire to Bridgwater again, where he had lain but a little while before the King's forces arrived within three or four miles of that town, commanded by the Earl of Feverſham and Lord Churchill, afterwards Marlborough, who encamped on Sedgmore; of which the Duke receiving advice, and being at the ſame time informed that the officers fell to drinking every evening, and continued at it till morning, and that their outguards were very negligent in their duty, he formed a deſign to ſurpriſe the camp of the

royaliſts

royalifts in the night-time; but his guides, either through ignorance or treachery, led the Duke's forces a great way round about, infomuch that it was broad daylight when they arrived at the camp of the royalifts, whom they found ready to receive them. However the Duke's foot fought very bravely, and bid fair for victory, till the Lord Gray, who commanded the horfe, abandoned the infantry, and left the field; or rather, he found his cavalry, which confifted only of country-fellows, whofe horfes would not ftand fire, were foon put into confufion, when they were charged by regular troops; whereupon a total rout fucceeding, the Duke endeavoured to make his efcape; but was taken the next day, and being brought up to town, was fuffered to fee the King, and beg his life; but was however executed on Tower-hill on Wednefday July 15, 1685. But furely never was the death of any prince more lamented by the people, who would not be perfuaded he was dead, but remained in expectation of feeing him appear in arms again, for fome years.

[For a particular account of the intermediate anceftors and the family of this noble Duke, the reader is requefted to confult the fecond volume of this work, under the title of Duke of Buccleuch.]

Arms.] Quarterly, firft and fourth, the arms of King Charles II. with a battooned gobonated, pearl and faphire; fecond and third, the arms of Scot, viz. topaz, a bend, faphire, charged with an eftoil between two crefcents, topaz.

Creft.] A ftag paffant, proper.

Supporters.] On each fide, a woman richly attired in an antique habit, their under robe emerald, the middle one faphire, the uppermoft ruby, and on their heads a plume of three feathers, pearl.

Motto.] *Amo.*

Chief Seats.] At Hall-place, in Berkfhire; at Dalkeith, near Edinburgh, in Scotland; and in Grofve-

23. COOPER, EARL of SHAFTESBURY.

THE Right Honourable ANTHONY ASHLEY COOPER, Earl of SHAFTESBURY, Baron Aſhley of Winborne St. Giles, Baron Cooper of Pawlet, Baronet, lord lieutenant and cuſtos rotulorum of the county of Dorſet, and of the town of Poole, recorder of Shafteſbury, and F. R. S. ſucceeded Anthony, the late Earl, his father, in February 1712-13. His Lordſhip married, on the 12th of March, 1724-5, the Lady Suſan Noel, ſiſter to Baptiſt Earl of Gainſborough ; by which Lady, who died in June 1758, he had no iſſue. His Lordſhip married, ſecondly, Mary ſecond daughter to Jacob the preſent Viſcount Folkſtone.

Anthony late Earl of Shaftesbury, father of the preſent Earl, was born Feb. 26, 1670. He married, in 1709, Jane, daughter of Thomas Ewer, of Buſhyhall in Hertfordſhire, Eſq; by whom he had iſſue, Anthony, the preſent Earl, his only ſon. This Lady died in November 1751.

This noble Earl is deſcended from Richard Cooper, who flouriſhed in the reign of King Henry VIII. and purchaſed the manor of Paulet, in the county of Somerſet, of which the family are ſtill proprietors. But his anceſtor, who makes the greateſt figure in hiſtory is, ſir Anthony Aſhley Cooper, who was afterwards created Earl of Shaftesbury, and conſtituted lord high chancellor of England. He is generally admired for his great parts and learning. He was a ſtudent of Exeter-college in Oxford, from whence he removed to Gray's-inn, one of the Inns of Court, where he made a conſiderable proficiency in the ſtudy of the law. He was elected member of parliament for Tukesbury in Glouceſterſhire, in the parliament that

then about twenty-five years of age. In the beginning of the civil war, 'tis said he raised a regiment for the service of King Charles I. being then sheriff of the county of Dorset, and made governor of Weymouth in that county; but colonel William Ashburnham being made governor of the county of Dorset, whereby Weymouth became dependent on him, Sir Anthony, imagining that his loyalty was suspected, came up to London, and offered his service to that part of the parliament which sat there, who gave him a regiment of horse, and the command of all their forces in Dorsetshire. But notwithstanding he appeared a hearty champion in the cause of the parliament, he seems to have opposed Cromwell's usurpation with great spirit; whereupon Sir Anthony, and above a hundred more of the same stamp, being kept out of the house of commons by force, published a remonstrance, setting forth that the Protector had assumed absolute and arbitrary power, and that every man ought to assist in opposing it. That the small number of members he suffered to remain in the house could not pretend to be the representatives of the people; they were not entrusted to consent to any thing in behalf of the nation, if the rest were excluded from sitting and debating matters in the house; which had such an influence on the next convention the Protector called, that they began to question his authority; whereupon he dissolved them, and ever after discountenanced and oppressed the Presbyterian and Republican party. Whereupon Sir Anthony and his friends began to turn their eyes upon the King, believing his restoration would prove a less evil than the tyrannical government they were under; and as the King's circumstances were very low at this time, and he appeared forsaken by all the princes of Europe, they did not doubt but they should get the Presbyterian sect established, and the prerogatives of the crown considera-

ftoration. After the death of Cromwell, the Rump parliament appointed him one of their council of ftate, and a commiffioner for managing the affairs of their army, which did not divert him from his defign of reftoring the King, 'tis faid; and, in the year 1659, he was accufed before the Rump, of keeping a cor-refpondence with his Majefty, and raifing men to join Sir George Booth for that end; for which he was imprifoned, with a great many other men of fi-gure. He was, however, acquitted of the charge, and afterwards intrufted by the Rump with the com-mand of of a regiment of horfe, being one of the firft which declared for general Monk and a free parlia-ment; and, when the convention had declared for the King, he was one of the twelve members fent by that houfe to the King, with fix peers, to invite his Ma-jefty to return and take the government of the king-dom upon him: whereupon the King, with this com-mittee of parliament, embarked for England, and ar-rived at Dover, May 25, 1660, and coming to Can-terbury the next day, general Monk, and Sir Antho-ny Afhley Cooper, was fworn of the privy council; and Sir Anthony was afterwards appointed one of the commiffioners for the trial of the regicides; and, three days before the coronation, he was created Ba-ron Afhley of Winbourne St. Giles's; foon after he was conftituted chancellor and under-treafurer of the Exchequer; and, in May 1667, he was conftituted one of the commiffioners of the treafury. In 1672 he was created Lord Cooper of Pawlet, in the county of Somerfet, and conftituted lord high-chancellor of England.

vifed his Majefty alfo to iffue his declaration for the
indulgence of the Diffenters, which the parliament refolved was a difpenfing with the penal laws; and yet,
when the matter came to be debated in the houfe of
lords, none cenfured it more feverely. On the other
hand, it is faid, he promoted the teft for rendering
Papifts incapable of enjoying any office or place of
truft, which obliged the Duke of York to lay down
his poft of high-admiral, and all the other places he
held ; which the court refenting, the feals were taken
from Lord Shaftesbury, and he became as ftrenuous
an oppofer of the court, as ever he had been an ad-
vocate for its meafures.

He was, however, conftituted prefident of the
council in April 1679 ; but continuing his oppofition
to the Duke of York, and endeavouring to get him
excluded from the crown, he was laid afide again in
March following, and became exceeding popular
among the Presbyterian and Republican party ; and
no man profecuted thofe who were charged with the
Popifh plot with greater violence : but his enemies
rendering him fufpected of being in a plot of another
nature, he thought fit to retire to Holland, where he
died Jan. 22, 1682-3.

He had married three wives; 1. Margaret, daughter of Thomas Lord Coventry, by whom he had no
children. 2. The Lady Frances, daughter of David
Earl of Exeter, by whom he had his fon Anthony,
afterwards Earl of Shaftesbury. 3. He married
Margaret, daughter of William Lord Spencer, by
whom he had no iffue.

Arms.] Argent, three bulls paffant, fable, armed
and unguled, or.

Creft.] On a chapeau, gules, turned up, ermine,
a bull paffant, fable, gorged with a mural coronet,
and armed, or.

Supporters.] On the dexter fide a bull fable, his ducal collar, or. On the finifter, a talbot, azure, gorged as the dexter.   *Motto.*]

Motto.] *Love, serve.*

Chief Seats.] At Winborne St. Giles, in the county of Dorset ; at Rockburn-house, in the county of
Southampton ; and in Margaret-street, Grosvenor-
square, London.

---

24. L E E, E A R L of L I T C H F I E L D.

THE Right Hon. GEORGE HENRY LEE, Earl
of LITCHFIELD, Viscount Quarendon, Baron
of Spelsbury, and Baronet, and custos-brevium in the
court of Common-Pleas, succeeded George-Henry,
the late Earl, his father, Feb. 15, 1742-3, and married Diana, only daughter of Sir Thomas Frankland,
Bart. by whom he has no children.

George-Henry Lee, late Earl of Litchfield, father
of the present Earl, born March 12, 1689, married,
July 14, 1716, Frances, daughter of Sir John Hales,
of Woodchurch, in the county of Kent, Bart. by
whom he had issue, three sons and five daughters:

1. George-Henry, the present Earl.

2. Edward-Henry, who married, Sept. 29, 1743,
to Miss Derander, since dead.

3. Charles-Henry, who died July 7, 1740.

4. Lady Charlotte, married, in Jan. 1744-5, to the
Lord Viscount Dillon.

5. Lady Mary, married, July 31, 1742, Cosmas
Nevil, of Holt in Leicestershire, Esq;

6. Lady Frances, married to Lord Cornbury, son
to the last Earl of Clarendon.

7. Lady Harriot, married to Lord Bellew, died
in April 1752.

8. Lady Anne, married Hugh Lord Clifford, Dec.
17, 1749.

Fitzroy-Henry Lee (the admiral) brother of the
late Earl, died April 19, 1750; and Robert Lee, an
other

other brother, married Miss Kitty Stonehouse, daughter of Sir John Stonehouse, Bart. of Berkshire.

This noble Earl is descended from Sir Walter Lee, of Wyburnbury, in the county of Chester, the family taking their name from the lordship of Lee, in the said parish, where they resided in the reign of King Edward III.   Sir Henry, another of the ancestors of this noble Earl, was of the privy-council to King Henry VII. and King Henry VIII.   He also served King Edward VI. Queen Mary, and Queen Elizabeth, being very eminent for his abilities, both as a statefman and a soldier.

Arms.] Argent, a fess between three crescents, sable.

Crest.] In a marquis's coronet, or, a demi stone column, argent ; and on its capital a bird's leg, erazed at the thigh, perched, preyed on by a faulcon, all proper.

Supporters.] Two lions ermine, each gorged with a plain collar, argent, having thereon three crescents, sable.

Motto.] *Fide & Constantia.*

Chief Seats] At Ditchley in Oxfordshire ; and in Bruton-street, London.

25. BERKELEY, EARL OF BERKELEY.

THE Right Honourable FREDERICK AUGUSTUS BERKELEY, Earl of BERKELEY, Viscount Dursley, Baron Berkeley of Berkeley-castle, Mowbray, Segrave, and Breaus of Gower, born May 24, 1745, succeeded his father Augustus, the late Earl, Jan. 9, 1755.

The late Earl married, May 7, 1744, Elizabeth, daughter of Henry Drax, Esq; of Charborough in Dorsetshire, one of the ladies of the bedchamber to her royal highness the princess of Wales ; and by her, who was married, 2dly, to Robert Nugent, Efq; one of the lords of the treafury, and by whom fhe had a daughter, born Dec. 10, 1758, he had iffue,

'Frederick-Auguftus, the prefent Earl.

James, born July 25, 1747, who died the year after.

The ladies Louifa, Elizabeth, and Frances, all three born July 28, 1748, but died foon after.

Lady Georgina-Augufta, born Sept. 28, 1749.

Lady Elizabeth, born in December 1750.

George-Cranfield, born Aug. 10, 1753.

This noble family are defcended from Robert Fitz-Harding, who obtained a grant of Berkeley-caftle in Glouceftershire (which the family ftill inherit, and from whence they obtained the furname of Berkeley) from Henry Duke of Normandy, afterwards King of England, the faid Robert Fitz-Harding, being defcended from the royal line of the Kings of Denmark.

Arms.] Gules, a chevron between ten croffes pattee, fix above, and four below, argent.

Creft.] On a wreath a mitre, gules, garnifhed, or, charged with the paternal coat.

Supporters.] Two lions, argent, the finifter having a ducal crown, and plain collar and chain, or.

Motto.] *Dieu avec nous.*

Chief Seats.] At Berkeley-caftle in Glouceftershire; and at Craneford in Middlefex.

---

26. BERTIE, EARL of ABINGDON.

THE Right Hon. WILLOUGHBY BERTIE, Earl of ABINGDON, and Baron Norris of Rycote, fucceeded his father Willoughby, the late Earl, June 10, 1760.

Willoughby, the late Earl, fon of James, fecond fon of James the firft Earl of Abingdon, born Nov. 28, 1692, fucceeded Montagu his uncle, and married, in Aug. 1727, Anna Maria, daughter of Sir John Collins, Bart. by whom he had issue three sons and seven daughters, viz.

1. James Lord Norris, who was burnt in his bed at Rycote.

2. Willoughby, second son, now Lord Norris, born Jan. 16, 1740.

3. Peregrine, third son, born March 13, 1741.

4. Lady Elizabeth.	8. Lady Eleonora.
5. Lady Jane.	9. Lady Mary, born Nov.
6. Lady Bridget.	12, 1746. And,
7. Lady Anne.	

10. Lady Sophia, born Nov. 6, 1748.

Sir James Bertie, Knt. father of the present Earl, born March 13, 1673, married, in Jan. 1691-2, Elizabeth, daughter and heiress of George Lord Willoughby of Parham, by whom he had issue,

1. Willoughby, the present Earl.

2. Edward, who died Sept. 21, 1733.

3. The Rev. William Bertie.

4. John.

5. Lady Bridget, who married to Robert Coytmor, of Carnarvonshire, Esq; by whom she had issue a son and two daughters.

The first of the family of Bertie that bore the title of Earl of Abingdon, was James Bertie, Lord Norris of Rycote, being created Earl of Abingdon in 1682, 34 Car. II. who married Eleonora, eldest daughter of Sir Henry Lee, of Ditchley in Oxfordshire, by whom he had issue six sons and three daughters, viz.

1. Montagu, the late Earl.	4. Robert.
2. James.	5. Peregrine.
3. Henry.	6. Charles.

7. Lady Bridget, married to Richard Lord Viscount Bulkeley, of the kingdom of Ireland.

8. Lady Anne, married to Sir William Courtney, of Powderam-castle, in Devonshire. And,

9. Lady Mary, who died unmarried. The said Earl James, their father, died in 1699.   *Arms.*]

Arms.] Argent, three battering-rams barways, proper, armed and garnifhed, azure ; an annulet for difference.

Creft.] On a wreath, the head and buft of a king couped, proper, crowned ducally, and charged on the cheft with a fret, or.

Supporters.] On the dexter fide a pilgrim, or friar, vefted in ruffet, with his ftaff and pater-nofter in his hand, or.   On the finifter, a favage wreathed about the temples and middle with ivy, proper ; on each of their chefts a fret, or.

Motto.] *Virtus ariete fortior.*

Chief Seats]. At Witham, in Berkfhire ; Rycote, in Oxfordfhire; Lincoln's Inn Fields, London.

27. NOEL, EARL of GAINS-BOROUGH.

THE Right Hon. THOMAS NOEL., Earl of GAINSBOROUGH, Vifcount Campden of Campden, Baron Noel of Ridlington, Baron Hicks of Ilmington, Baron Noel of Titchfield, and baronet, fucceeded his brother Baptift, the late Earl, in May 1759.

Baptift, the late Earl, born June 8, 1740, fucceeded his father Baptift, March 21, 1750-1, and died upon his travels at Geneva.

Baptift, father of the late and prefent Earls, had iffue by Elizabeth Chapman, his wife, who married, 2dly, in Nov. 1756, Thomas Noel, Efq;

1. Lady Elizabeth, born in 1731.

2. Lady Jane, born in 1733, married to Gerrard Anne Edwards, Efq;

3. Lady Juliana, born in 1734-5.

4. Lady Penelope, born in 1735-6, and died young.

5. Lady Anne, born in 1737.

6. Bap-

6. Baptift, the late Earl.

7. Lady Lucy.

8. Thomas, the prefent Earl.

9. Charles, who died young.

10. Mary.

11. Sufanna.

12. Sophia.

Baptift Noel, Earl of Gainfborough, and grand-father of the prefent Earl, fucceeded his coufin Baptift-Wriothefley, Earl of Gainfborough, in 1690. He married the Lady Dorothy, fecond daughter of John Duke of Rutland, who died April 17, 1714, in the 29th year of her age, leaving iffue, three fons and three daughters, viz.

1. Baptift, father of the late Earl.

2. John, who died Dec. 26, 1718.

3. James.

4. Lady Catharine.

5. Lady Sufannah, married to Anthony-Afhley Cooper, Earl of Shaftesbury.

6. Lady Mary, who died young, in 1718.

This noble Earl is defcended from —— Noel, who came into England with William the Conqueror; and in confideration of his fervices, obtained a grant of feveral manors and lands of very great value.

Arms.] Or, fretty of ten pieces, gules, a canton, ermine.

Creft.] On a wreath, a buck at gaze, argent; attired, or.

Supporters.] Two bulls, argent; armed and unguled, proper.

Motto.] *Tout bien ou rien.*

Chief Seats.] At Extonbrook in the county of Rutland; and Cavendifh-fquare, London.

28. D'ARCY,

48. D'ARCY, EARL of HOLDERNESS.

THE Right Hon. ROBERT D'ARCY, Earl of HOLDERNESS, Baron D'Arcy, Menel, and Conyers, one of his Majesty's principal secretaries of state, and of the privy-council, and lord lieutenant of the North-riding of the county of York, keeper of the liberty and forest of Richmond, constable of Middle-ham-castle in Yorkshire, and governor of the Charter house, succeeded his father Robert in Jan. 1721-2; and, in Nov. 1743, married Mary, daughter of the Sieur Doublet, one of the nobles of Holland, by whom he had issue,

1. George, born in Sept. 1745, who died at two years of age.

2. Thomas, born May 7, 1750, and died in July following.

3. Lady Amelia, born Oct. 12, 1754.

Robert, late Earl of Holderness, father of the present Earl, married the Lady Frederica, eldest daughter and coheir to Meinhardt Sconbergh, Duke Sconbergh in England, and died Jan. 20, 1721-2, leaving issue, besides the present Earl, a daughter, named Louisa Carolina, married to William Earl of Ancram, who had issue by her one son and a daughter.

This noble Earl is descended from Norman D'Arcy, who came over with the Conqueror; and it appears in Doomsday-Book, where the general survey of England made by the Conqueror is recorded, that Norman D'Arcy held of him thirty-three lordships in Lincolnshire, by the immediate grant of the Conqueror.

Arms.] Quarterly, first, azure, semee of cross croslets, and three cinquefoils, argent, for D'Arcy. Second, azure, three bars gemel, and a chief, or. Third, azure, a maunch, or, for Conyers. Fourth, gules, a saltire, argent, thereon a mullet, for Nevile.

Crest:]

Crest.] On a wreath, a spear broken in three pieces, or, headed, argent, and banded together at their middle by a ribbon, gules.

Supporters.] On the dexter side a tyger, argent ; on the sinister a bull, sable, armed, or.

Motto.] *Un Dieu, un Roy.*

Chief Seats.] At Hornby-castle in Yorkshire ; at Aston, Hurdwick, and Patrick-Brampton in the same county ; and Arlington-street, London.

29. WINDSOR-HICKMAN, EARL of PLYMOUTH.

THE Right Hon. OTHER-LEWIS WINDSOR HICKMAN, Earl of PLYMOUTH, and Baron Windsor of Bradenham in Buckinghamshire, lord lieutenant and custos rotulorum of the county of Glamorgan, comptroller of Cheshire and Flintshire, and constable of Flint-castle, born May 12, 1731, succeeded his father Other, the late Earl, in his honours and estate, Nov. 27, 1732, and married, Aug. 11, 1750, Catharine, eldest daughter of Thomas Lord Archer, by whom he has issue,

1. Other Lord Windsor, born May 30, 1751,.
2. Thomas, born May 19, 1752.
3. Andrew, who died the day he was born.
4. Lady ——, born Dec. 3, 1755.
5. Lady ——, born May 3, 1757,
6. A son born Sept. 23, 1758 ; and,
7. Another son, born Jan. 4, 1760.

Other Hickman Windsor, late Earl of Plymouth, father of the present Earl, born June 30, 1707, was married, May 7, 1730, to Elizabeth, only daughter to Thomas Lewis, of Soberton, Esq; and by her (who died Nov. 9, 1733) had issue only one son, viz. the present Earl.

This

This noble Earl is descended from Robert Fitz-Hickman, lord of the manor of Bloxham in Oxford-shire, 56 Hen. III. in 1272; and he is maternally descended from the noble family of the Windsors, who were barons of the realm at the time of the conquest. Thomas Windsor, great-grandfather of the present Earl, having raised a troop at his own charges, and served King Charles I. with great courage and fidelity during the continuance of the civil wars, and suffered very much during Cromwell's usurpation, was immediately after the restoration, viz. in the twelfth year of King Charles II. restored to the stile and title of Lord Windsor; and in the thirty-fourth of King Charles II. created Earl of Plymouth.

Arms.] Gules, a saltire, argent, between twelve cross croslets, or,

Crest.] On a wreath, a buck's head erazed, proper, attired, or.

Supporters.] Two unicorns, argent, armed, crested, tufted, and hoofed, or,

Motto.] *Je me fie en Dieu.*

Chief Seats.] At Hewel Grange, in the county of Worcester and Warwick; at Peel-Hall in Cheshire; and Hanover-square, London.

---

30. STAFFORD-HOWARD, EARL of STAFFORD.

THE, Right Hon. JOHN PAUL STAFFORD-HOWARD, Earl of STAFFORD, Baron Stafford of Stafford-castle, in the county of Stafford, succeeded his nephew William Matthias Stafford on his decease, which happened Feb. 28, 1750-1.

The present Earl married, in June 1738, Elizabeth, daughter of A. Ewen of the county of Somerset, Esq; and Elizabeth his wife, eldest daughter of John St. Albin of Alfoxton in the same county, Esq;

F 5

William,

William, the second Earl of Stafford, father of the late Earl, succeeded his uncle Henry, and died in Jan. 1733. He married Anne, daughter of George Holman of Warkworth, Esq; by whom he had issue, 1. William Matthias, the late Earl. 2. Lady Mary, who married the Count de Chabot in France. 3. Lady Anastasia; and, 4. Lady Anne, both nuns at Paris.

The late Lord married, in July 1743, Henrietta, daughter of Richard Cantillon, Esq; by whom he had no issue.

This noble Earl is descended from Robert de Toeni, who attended William Duke of Normandy in his invasion of England; and, at the time of the general survey, was possessed of more than a hundred lordships in England, and of the castle of Stafford in Warwickshire, from whence the family took the name of Stafford.

Arms.] Gules, in the middle, a bend between six cross croslets, argent, a shield, or, therein a demilion rampant, pierced through the mouth with an arrow, as in the Duke of Norfolk's.

Crest.] Out of a ducal coronet, per pale, sable and gules, a swan issuing, proper.

Supporters.] On the dexter side, a lion, argent; charged on the shoulder with a crescent, sable. On the sinister, a swan, with wings expanded, proper; gorged with a ducal coronet, party-per-pale, gules and sable.

Motto.] *Abstulit qui dedit.*

Chief Seats.] At Sheffnal-manor, in the county of Salop; in Germain street, London.

31. LUMLEY-SAUNDERSON, EARL of SCARBOROUGH.

THE Right Hon. RICHARD LUMLEY SAUNDER-
SON, Earl of SCARBOROUGH, Vifcount and Baron Lumley, of Lumley-caftle; and Vifcount Lumley
of Waterford in the kingdom of Ireland; fucceeded
his father Thomas, the late Earl, March 15, 1752,
and married, Dec. 12, 1752, Barbara, fifter to Sir
George Saville of Rufford in Nottinghamfhire, Bart.
by whom he has iffue,

1. George Auguftus, born Oct. 24, 1753.
2. Lady Frances Barbara Ludlow Lumley, born
Feb. 25, 1756.
3. A fon, born April 3, 1757.
4. A fon, born June 22, 1760.

Thomas, the late Earl of Scarborough, married
the Lady Frances, daughter of George Hamilton,
Earl of Orkney, by whom he has had iffue two fons
and three daughters, viz.

1. Richard, the prefent Earl.
2. George, who died Dec. 11, 1739.
3. Lady Frances, married, in June 1753, to Peter
Ludlow of Ardfallah, in the county of Meath in Ireland, Efq; now Lord Ludlow.
4. Lady Anne. And,
5. Lady Harriot, who died Nov. 6, 1747.

Richard Lord Vifcount Lumley, grandfather of the
prefent Earl, was, on the 10th of April, 1689, advanced to the dignity of Vifcount Lumley of Lumley-
caftle; and on the 15th of April, 1690, (1 William
and Mary) created Earl of Scarborough. He married
Frances, only daughter and heir of Sir Henry Jones,
of Afton in Oxfordfhire; and, departing this life on
the 17th of Dec. 1721, had iffue feven fons and four
daughters, viz.

1. Henry, who died July 14, 1710.

F 6　　　　　　　　2.

2. Richard, who fucceeded his father, died unmarried in February, 1739-40.

3. William, who was killed in an engagement at fea, April 9, 1709.

4. Thomas, the late Earl.

5. Charles Lumley, Efq; who died Aug. 11, 1727.

6. John, who died in October, 1739. And,

7. James.

8. Lady Mary, married to George Montagu, late Earl of Hallifax, and had iffue. See Earl of *Hallifax.*

9. Lady Barbara, married to the Hon. Charles Leigh, of Leighton in Bedfordfhire, Efq;

10. Lady Anne; married to Frederick Frankland, Efq; and died without iffue in Feb. 1739-40. And,

11. Lady Henrietta. The Lady Frances, their mother, died in March, 1737.

This noble Earl is defcended from Liulph, a nobleman of great fame, in the reign of Edward the Confeffor, and took the name of Lumley, from Lumley-caftle, in the bifhopric of Durham, where the family refided many years.

Arms.] Argent, a fefs, gules, between three parrots, proper, collared as the fecond, being the arms of the ancient Barons Thweng, from one of the heirs whereof his Lordfhip is lineally defcended; but the ancient arms of Lumley are, gules, fix martlets, argent.

Creft.] On a wreath, in her neft, proper, a pelican feeding her young, argent, vulned, proper.

Supporters.] Two parrots, with wings expanded, proper, i. e. vert, beaked and membered, gules.

Motto.] *Murus æneus confcientia fana.*

Chief Seats.] At Sandbeck, in Yorkfhire; at Stanftead, in Suffex; at Glentworth, in Lincolnfhire; and in Grofvenor-ftreet, London.

32. NEWPORT, EARL of BRADFORD.

THE Right Hon. Thomas Newport, Earl of Bradford, Vifcount Newport, and Baron of High-Ercal, fucceeded his brother Richard in honour and eftate, who died unmarried. He is a lunatic, and unmarried.

Richard, the late Earl, fucceeded his brother Henry, who died Dec. 23, 1734.

Richard, father of the prefent and the two preceding Earls, married Mary, daughter of Sir Thomas Wilbraham of Woodhey in the county of Chefter, Bart. and by her, who died in 1738, had four fons, Henry, Richard, Thomas, and William, of which the three firft fucceeded him, and William died before his father; and four daughters, Lady Mary, who died unmarried; Lady Elizabeth, married in Sept. 1718, to James Cocks of the city of Worcefter, Efq; Lady Anne, on the 8th of April, 1719, to Sir Orlando Bridgman of Blodwell in the county of Salop, Bart. and the Lady Diana to Algernoon Coote, the fixth Earl of Montrath in Ireland. His Lordfhip died June 4, 1723, and was fucceeded by his eldeft fon Henry.

The anceftors of this family were very inftrumental in bringing Wales under the dominion of the crown of England, particularly Sir William Newport, who defeated 8000 Welfh in Glamorganfhire, in the fixth year of King Henry IV. This family alfo contributed to the Revolution in 1688, and fetting King William and Queen Mary on the throne.

Creations.] Baron Newport of High-Ercal in Shropfhire, by letters-patent dated Oct. 14, 1642, 18 Car. I. Vifcount Newport of Bradford in Shropfhire, 11th March, 1674, 27 Car. II. and Earl of Bradford in the fame county May 11, 1694, 6 Will. and Mary.

Arms.]

Arms.] Argent or chevron gules between three leopards faces, fable.

Creft.] On a wreath an-unicorn's head erafed, gules, armed and gorged with a ducal coronet, or.

Supporters.] Two leopards guardant, proper.

Motto.] *Ne fupra modum fapere.*

Chief Seats.] At High-Ercal in Shropfhire, at Eaton in the fame county, and at Wefton in Staffordfhire.

---

33. DE ZULEISTEIN, EARL of ROCHFORD.

THE Right Hon. WILLIAM HENRY NASSAU DE ZULEISTEIN, Earl of ROCHFORD, Vifcount Tunbridge, Baron of Enfield, groom of the ftole to his Majefty, one of his Majefty's privy council, lord lieutenant and cuftos rotulorum of the county of Effex, and vice-admiral of the coafts in the fame county; was born Sept. 17, 1717, fucceeded his father Frederick the late Earl in June 1738; and married Lucy, daughter of Edward Young, Efq; of Durnford, near Sarum, in Wiltfhire, by whom he has no iffue.

Frederick, late Earl of Rochford, father of the prefent Earl, married Elizabeth, daughter of Richard Savage, Earl Rivers; and dying in June, 1738, left iffue, befides the prefent Earl, Richard Savage Naffau, born June 1, 1723, who was married, Dec. 24, 1751, to the Dutchefs Dowager of Hamilton, by whom he has a fon, William Henry, born July 28, 1754; another fon, born Sept. 5, 1756; and a daughter, born Nov. 3, 1754.

This noble Earl is defcended from Frederick Naffau de Zuleiftein, natural fon of Frederick Naffau Prince of Orange, grandfather of King William III. which Frederick de Zuleiftein was general of foot in

the

the Dutch fervice, and was killed at the battle of Woerden, in.defence of his country, in 1672.

His fon William Henry was fent by the Prince of Orange to King James II. to congratulate him on the birth of the Prince of Wales; but chiefly to learn how the Englifh ftood affected towards him, and he carried back with him to Holland fuch invitations from many of the nobility and gentry, as encouraged the Prince and the States to make a defcent in England foon after, whereby the Revolution was effected.

He ferved under King William in the wars of Ireland, and the Netherlands; and in confideration of his merit, and near alliance to his Majefty, was created Earl of Rochford, &c.

Arms.] Quarterly, firft, azure femee of billets, and a lion rampant, gules, crowned with a ducal coronet, azure; argent, a fefs, gules; four gules, two lions paffant, guardant in pale, or; over all in an efcutcheon, gules; three gules, argent, and fometimes a lion rampant, fable.

Creft.] In a ducal coronet, or, a pair of buck's horns, gules.

Supporters.] Two lions erminois, ducally crowned, azure.

Motto.] *Spes durat Avorum.*

Chief Seats.] At Eafton, in Suffolk; at Loughtonhall and Ofyth, in the county of Effex; and at Zuleftein, in Holland.

---

34. KEPPEL, EARL of ALBEMARLE.

THE Right Hon. George Keppel, Earl of Albemarle, Vifcount Bury, Baron Afhford of Afhford in Kent, and lieutenant-general, was born April 8, 1724; and his father dying the 22d of Dec. 1754, he fucceeded to his honours and eftates.

His

His father, William Anne Keppel, late Earl of Albemarle, one of the lords of his Majefty's bedchamber, colonel of the fecond regiment of foot guards, a lieutenant-general, governor of Virginia, ambaffador to France, and knight of the moft noble order of the garter, was born June 5, 1702, fucceeded his father Arnold Jooft in 1718; and on the 21ft of Feb. 1722-3, was married to the Lady Anne Lenox, fifter to his Grace the late Duke of Richmond, and by her had iffue eight fons and feven daughters, viz.

1. George, the prefent Earl.

2. Commodore Auguftus Keppel, captain of the Torbay man of war.

3. James, died young.

4. William, captain in the firft regiment of footguards, and gentleman of the horfe to his Majefty.

5. Frederick, chaplain in ordinary to his Majefty, and one of the prebends of Windfor; married to Mifs Walpole, daughter of Sir Edward Walpole, a knight of the Bath, Sept. 13, 1758, by whom he had a daughter, born June 18, 1759.

6. Lady Sophia; and,

7. Lady Mary, both dead.

8. Lady Anne, died in Jan. 1754,

9. Lady Naffau,

10. Thomas, and,

11. Edward, all three dead.

12. Lady Caroline.

13. Lady Elizabeth.

14. Henry.

15. Lady Amelia, died young.

Arnold Jooft Van Keppel, Earl of Albemarle, grandfather of the prefent Earl, defcended from an ancient noble family of the province of Gelderland, being a younger fon of Bernard Van Pallant, Lord of Keppel, by Agnes Charlotte Elizabeth, the daughter of Jacob Van Wafferaer, Lord Opdam: The faid Arnold came over into England with the Prince of Orange in 1688,

5

to whom he was very dear. He was a member of the nobles of Holland, deputy-forester of that province, and general of the Dutch horse in the service of the States General.

He married in Holland, in 1701, Isabella, second daughter of S. Gravemoor, general of the forces of the States General, by whom he had issue the late Earl, his only son; and the Lady Sophia, his only daughter, married to John Thomas, Esq; He died at the Hague, in the forty-eighth year of his age, Anno 1718.

Arms.] Gules, three escallop-shells, argent.

Crest.] In a ducal coronet, or, a demi-swan close, proper.

Supporters.] Two lions, ducally crowned, or.

Motto.] *Ne cede malis.*

Chief Seats.] At Durhams, near Barnet, in the county of Middlesex; and at Voorst and Loo in Holland; Bolton-street, London.

---

35. COVENTRY, EARL OF COVENTRY.

THE Right Hon. GEORGE WILLIAM COVENTRY, Earl of COVENTRY, Viscount Deerhurst, lord lieutenant and custos rotulorum of the county and city of Worcester, and a lord of the bedchamber to his Majesty, succeeded his father the late Earl William, who died March 18, 1751.

His Lordship married, March 5, 1752, Maria, eldest daughter of John Gunning, Esq; by his wife Bridget, daughter of John Viscount Mayo, in Ireland, by whom he has,

1. Lady Elizabeth Anne, born in 1753, died Aug. 22, 1756.

2. Lady Maria Alicia, born in Dec. 1754.

3.

3. Lady Anne Margaret.

4. Lady ——, born March 18, 1757; and,

5. A fon and heir, born April 28, 1758.

The late Earl, father of the prefent, married Elizabeth, daughter to Mr. John Allen of the city of Weftminfter, by whom he had iffue three fons.

1. Thomas Henry, Vifcount Deerhurft, who died in the year 1744.

2. George William, the prefent Earl.

3. John Bulkeley.

Walter Coventry, Efq; father of the late Earl, married Anne, daughter of Simon Holcomb, of Devon, Efq; by whom he had iffue four fons:

1. Walter, who died on the 5th of April, 1677.

2. William, the late Earl.

3. Thomas, who married Mary, daughter and heir of —— Green, of Henley in Buckinghamfhire, Efq;

4. Henry, married to Anne, daughter to Mr. Coles of the city of Oxford.

This noble Earl is defcended from John Coventry, a native of the city of Coventry, and afterwards mercer and lord mayor of London in the reign of Henry V. from whom defcended Thomas Coventry, one of the juftices of the court of Common-pleas in the reign of Queen Elizabeth, whofe fon Thomas was recorder of London, and afterwards lord-keeper of the great feal in the reign of King Charles I. of whom Earl Clarendon gives the following character, ‘ That he difcharged all the offices he went through ‘ with great abilities, and fingular reputation of inte- ‘ grity: That he enjoyed his place of lord-keeper ‘ with univerfal reputation; juftice was never better ‘ adminiftered for the fpace of fixteen years, even to ‘ his death, being then near fixty years of age.’

His youngeft daughter Dorothy, who married Sir John Packington, is faid to have written *The whole Duty of Man.*

Arms.]

Arms.] Sable, a fefs, ermine, between three crefcents, or.

Creft.] On a wreath a garb, or, and thereon a
dunghill-cock perched, gules, comb, wattles, and
leg, or.

Supporters.] Two eagles, wings expanded, argent;
membered and beaked, or.

Motto.] *Candidè & Conftanter.*

Chief Seats.] At Crome d'Abitot, in Worcefterfhire;
Grofvenor-fquare, London.

36. VILLIERS, EARL of JERSEY.

THE Right Hon. WILLIAM VILLIERS, Earl of
JERSEY, Vifcount Villiers of Dartford, and
Baron of Hoo, one of the lords of his majefty's privy
council, fucceeded his father William, the late Earl,
July 13, 1721; and married, June 23, 1733, the
Lady Anne Egerton, daughter to Scroop late Duke
of Bridgwater, and relict of Wriothefley Ruffel, late
Duke of Bedford, by whom he had iffue two fons, viz.

1. Frederick William, Lord Villiers, who died in
October, 1742. And,

2. George Bufhy, the prefent Lord Villiers, born
June 9, 1735.

William Villiers, Earl of Jerfey, father of the prefent Earl, married Judith, only daughter to Frederick
Hern, Efq; by whom he had iffue two fons and one
daughter:

1. The prefent Earl.

2. Thomas Villiers, his fecond fon, now Lord
Hyde. See Lord HYDE.

3. Lady Barbara, married, in 1725, to Sir William
Blacket, of the county of Northumberland, Bart. but
he dying on the 27th of Auguft, 1728, fhe was married, on the 13th of March, 1728-9, to Bufhy Manfel,
Efq; late Lord Manfel, and has iffue one only daughter, viz. Lady Barbara.   The

The Countefs, their mother, died in July, 1735.

This noble Earl is defcended from the family of Villiers in Normandy, fome of whom came over to England with the Conqueror; feveral manors and land in England being foon after granted to Pagan de Villiers, one of this Earl's anceftors.

Arms.] Argent, on a crofs of St. George, gules, five efcallop-fhclls, or; a crefcent for difference.

Creft.] On a wreath a lion rampant, argent, and ducally crowned, or.

Supporters.] Two lions, argent, crowned with ducal coronets, or; each having a plain collar, gules, charged with three efcallop-fhells of the fecond.

Motto.] *Fidei Coticula Crux.*

Chief Seats.] At Middleton-ftony, in Oxfordfhire; Grofvenor-fquare, London.

---

37. POULET, EARL POULET.

THE Right Hon. JOHN POULET, Earl POULET, Vifcount and Baron Poulet of Hinton St. George, lord lieutenant and cuftos rotulorum of the county of Somerfet, fucceeded his father the late Earl John, May 28, 1743, and is yet unmarried.

John Lord Poulet, father of the prefent Earl, was created Vifcount of Hinton St. George, and Earl Poulet, Dec. 29, 1706. His Lordfhip married Bridget, daughter and coheir to Peregrine Bertie, Efq; brother to Robert Earl of Lindfey, by whom he had four fons and four daughters, viz.

1. John, the prefent Earl.

2. Peregrine, who died in October, 1752.

3. Vere, who married, in 1754, Mary, daughter of Richard Butt, of Arlington in the county of Gloucefter, Efq; by whom he had a fon and heir, born in April, 1756.

4. Anne.

5. Lady Bridget, married, May 21, 1724, to Po-lexfen Baftard, of Kettley in Devonfhire, Efq; and has iffue, William, Edmond, and Baldwin Polexfen.

6. Lady Cathàrine, married, June 26, 1725, to John Parker, Efq; of Barrington in Devonfhire, and has iffue, Henrietta, Catharine, Bridget, John, and Montague; and died Aug. 16, 1758.

7. Lady Sufanna; and,

8. Lady Rebecca, both unmarried.

This noble Earl is defcended from a younger branch of the Duke of Bolton's family.

Arms.] Sable, three fwords in pile, their points in bafe, argent; pomels and hilts, or.

Creft.] On a wreath, an arm embowed, and bran-difhing a broad fword, all proper.

Supporters.] On the dexter fide, a favage man; on the finifter, a woman, both proper, wreathed about their temples and loins with ivy, vert.

Motto.] *Gardez la Foy.*

Chief Seats.] At Hinton St. George, in Somerfet-fhire; at Buckland, in Dorfetfhire; in York-build-ings, London.

38. GODOLPHIN, EARL of GODOLPHIN.

THE Right Hon. Francis Godolphin, Earl of Godolphin, Vifcount Rialton, Baron Go-dolphin, and Baron Helfton, governor of the Scilly Iflands, and one of the Lords of his Majefty's moft honourable privy-council, was born on the 3d of Sep-tember, 1678, and fucceeded the late Earl his father on his death, Sept. 15, 1712. He married the Lady Henrietta, eldeft daughter of John Duke of Marl-borough, who became Dutchefs of Marlborough on her father's deceafe. The Earl had iffue by her three fons and three daughters:

I,

1. William, Marquis of Blandford, who died without iſſue.

2. Henry, who died young.

3. Lady Margaret, who died young.

4. Lady Henrietta, married to his Grace Thomas Pelham Holles, Duke of Newcaſtle.

5. Lady Mary, married to his Grace Thomas Duke of Leeds.

Sidney Earl of Godolphin, third ſon of Sir Francis Godolphin, and father of the preſent Earl, married Margaret, fourth daughter of Thomas Blagne, Eſq; by whom he had iſſue only the preſent Earl, of whom his mother died in child-bed in September, 1678.

At the Revolution, 1688, his Lordſhip and many other noble Peers voted for a regency during the life of King James, propoſing to have made the Princeſs of Orange, his eldeſt daughter, regent; but it being carried to proclaim the Prince and Princeſs of Orange King and Queen, and to veſt the executive power ſolely in the Prince, he ſubmitted to it, and was conſtituted one of the commiſſioners of the treaſury again, and in 1690 firſt commiſſioner.

In the beginning of the reign of Queen Anne, in the year 1702, he was ſworn into the office of lord-treaſurer of England: in 1704, he was elected one of the knights of the moſt noble order of the garter; and in 1706, was appointed one of the commiſſioners to treat of an union with Scotland; and on concluding the treaty of union, was conſtituted lord high treaſurer of Great Britain.

This noble Earl is deſcended from the family of Godolphin, which reſided on the manor of Godolphin in the county of Cornwal, about the time of the Conqueſt, and from whence they took their ſurname.

Arms.] Gules, an eagle, with two heads diſplayed between three fleurs-de-lis, argent.

Creſt.] On a wreath, a dolphin naiant, embowed proper.

Sup-

Supporters.] Two eagles reguardant, with their wings difplayed, argent.

Motto.] *Francha Leale Toge.*

Chief Seats.] At Godolphin in Cornwall, Tilfheade in Wiltfhire, and Hogmagog near New-market, Suffolk; St. James's, Stable yard, London.

---

39. CHOLMONDELEY, EARL of CHOLMONDELEY.

THE Right Hon. GEORGE CHOLMONDELEY, Earl of CHOLMONDELEY, Vifcount Malpas and Kells, and Vifcount Cholmondeley of Nantwitch, Baron of Newburgh, and Baronet, a knight of the Bath, lieutenant-general of his Majefty's forces, one of his Majefty's moft honourable privy council; lord lieutenant, cuftos rotulorum, and vice-admiral of Chefhire; governor of the caftle of Chefter; lord lieutenant of Anglefey, Caernarvon, Flint, Merioneth, and Montgomery; and fteward of the royal manor of Shene in Surry. On the 14th of Sept. 1723, he married Mary, only daughter of Sir Robert Walpole, late Earl of Orford, by whom he had iffue three fons, viz.

1. George, Vifcount Malpas, born October 17, 1724, married, Jan. 19, 1746-7, to Hefter, daughter and heir of Sir Francis Edwards, Bart. by whom he has iffue.

2. Robert, born Nov. 2, 1727, now in holy orders, and auditor-general of his Majefty's revenues in America, married to Mifs Mary Woffington, by whom he has iffue.

3. Frederick, who died an infant.

And his Lady dying in the year 1732, his Lordfhip ftill remains a widower.

He fucceeded his father, the late Earl, in his honours and eftate, May 7, 1733.

George,

George, the father of the prefent Earl, married Elizabeth, daughter of Heer Van Baron Rutenburgh, by whom he had iffue two fons and three daughters, viz.

1. George, the prefent Earl.

2. James, lieutenant-general of his Majefty's forces, who married the Lady Penelope, daughter and heir of James Earl of Barrymore, by whom he has no iffue.

3. Lady Henrietta, unmarried.

4. Lady Elizabeth, married, Jan. 23, 1730-1, to Edward Warren, of Poyton in Chefhire, Efq;

5. Lady Mary, unmarried.

This noble Earl is defcended from the antient family of Egerton, Barons of Malpas in Chefhire, in the time of the Conqueft ; from whom alfo the Duke of Bridgewater is defcended.

Arms.] Gules, two helmets in chief, proper, garnifhed, or; in bafe, a garb of the third.

Creft.] On a wreath, a demi-gryphon rampant, fable ; beaked, winged, and membered, or, holding a helmet, proper.

Supporters.] On the dexter fide, a gryphon, fable ; its beak, wings, and fore-legs, or. On the finifter, a wolf of the fecond, gorged with a collar perflew, vaire.

Motto.] *Caffis tutiffima virtus.*

Chief Seats.] At Cholmondeley, in the county of Chefter ; in Mount-ftreet, London.

---

40. HARLEY, Earl of OXFORD.

THE Right Hon. Edward Harley, Earl of Oxford and Mortimer, and Baron Harley of Wigmore, was born Sept. 2, 1726, fucceeded his father Edward the 11th of April, 1755 ; and married, July 11, 1751, Sufannah, daughter of William Archer, of Wexford in Berkfhire, Efq; but as yet has no iffue.

Edward,

Edward, the late Earl, married, in March 1725, Martha, eldeft daughter of John Morgan, of Trede-gar in Monmouthfhire, Efq; by whom he had iffue,

1. The prefent Earl.

2. Robert, born Sept. 10, 1727, died Jan. 12, 1760.

3. John, born Sept. 29, 1728.

4. Thomas, born Aug. 24, 1730, married, March 15, 1752, to Mifs Bangham, daughter of Edward Bangham, Efq;

5. William, born May 3, 1733.

6. Martha, born Nov. 23, 1736. And,

7. Sarah, who died in April, 1737.

This noble Earl is faid to be defcended from the Harleys in France. Others are of opinion, that the Harleys of France are defcended from a family of that name in Shropfhire, which refided in England long before the Conqueft, and that the prefent Earl alfo is defcended from the Shropfhire family.

Arms.] Or, a bend cottifed, fable.

Creft.] On a wreath, a caftle, argent, tripple towered, with a demi-lion rampant, gules, iffuing out of the battlements of the middle tower.

Supporters.] Two angels, proper, the habit and wings difplayed, or.

Motto.] *Virtute & Fide.*

Chief Seats.] At Eyewood and Brampton-brian-caftle in the county of Hereford; in Henrietta ftreet, Cavendifh-fquare, London.

---

41. SHIRLEY, EARL FERRERS.

THE Right Hon. WASHINGTON SHIRLEY, Earl FERRERS, Vifcount Tamworth, and Baronet, a captain in the royal navy, fucceeded his brother Lawrence May 5, 1760, and is yet unmarried.

Lawrence, the late Earl, was fon of Lawrence Shirley, brother to the former Earl Henry, and fuc-

G   ceeded

ceeded his said uncle Henry in Aug. 1745; and on Sept. 16, 1752, married Mary, youngeft daughter of Sir William Meredith, of Henbury in Chefhire, Bart. from which Lady he was feparated by act of parliament: but having committed the horrid crime of murder, by fhooting Mr. Johnfon, his own fteward, through the body with a piftol, in January 1760, the February following he was brought prifoner to London; and in April was tried by his Peers in Weftminfter-hall, and found guilty of wilful murder; for which crime he had fentence paffed upon him by Lord Henley, lord high fteward on that trial, to be hanged, and his body anatemifed, as the law directs in cafes of murder: which fentence, after a fortnight's refpite, was put in execution, and he was hanged at Tyburn May 5, 1760.

Sir Robert Shirley, Bart. was created Vifcount Tamworth, and Earl Ferrers, in 1711. He married Elizabeth, daughter and heir of Lawrence Wafhington, Efq; by whom he had ten fons and feven daughters; but three of the fons only furvived him, viz.

1. Wafhington; and,

2. Henry, who were fucceffively Earls Ferrers.

3. Lawrence, father of the prefent Earl.

Wafhington, late Earl Ferrers, married Mary, daughter of Sir Richard Levings, Bart. and by her had iffue three daughters, his coheirs, viz.

1. Lady Elizabeth, married to Jofeph Gafcoigne Nightingale, of Enfield, Efq; by whom fhe had a fon, Wafhington, who died unmarried Jan. 23, 1754; and a daughter, Elizabeth, fole heir to her brother, married the fame year to Wilmot Vaughan, Efq; by whom fhe had a fon, born May 9, 1755; but fhe died two days after.

2. The Lady Selina, married to Theophilus, Earl of Huntingdon; and,

3. Lady Mary, married to Thomas Needham, Lord Vifcount Kilmurry of Ireland.

This

This family is maternally defcended, by the Ferrers's, from a confiderable Norman Baron, who was poffeffed of a great eftate in Warwickfhire, Lincolnfhire, Northamptonfhire, and Derbyfhire, by the favour of the Norman Conqueror, as appears by Domefday-book.

Arms.] Paly of fix, ôr and azure; a canton, ermine.

Creft.] On a wreath, the buft of a Saracen fidefaced and couped, proper; wreathed about the temples, or and azure.

Supporters.] On the dexter fide, a talbot, ermine, his ears, or, and his ducal collar, gules; on the finifter, a rein-deer, of the laft attired, argent, gorged with a ducal coronet of the third billet, or.

Motto.] *Honor virtutis præmium*; *& malgre l'envie.*

Chief Seats.] At Stanton-Harold, in Leicefterfhire; Aftwell, in Northamptonfhire; and Chartley-caftle in Staffordfhire; Great Marlborough-ftreet, London.

---

42. WENTWORTH, EARL OF STRAFFORD.

THE Right Hon. WILLIAM WENTWORTH, Earl of STRAFFORD, Vifcount Wentworth, of Wentworth-Woodhoufe, Baron of Stainborough, Roby, Newmarfh, and Overfley, and Baronet, and F. R. S. fucceeded his father Thomas, the late Earl, in Nov. 1739; and married, April 28, 1741, the Lady Anne Campbell, fecond daughter to the late Duke of Argyle, by whom he has no iffue.

Thomas, father of the prefent Earl, was created Earl of Strafford Sept. 4, 1711. He married the fame year Anne, the fole daughter and heir of Sir Henry Johnfon, by whom he had iffue one fon and three daughters, viz.

1. William, the prefent Earl.

2.

2. Lady Anne, married to William Conolly, of Ireland, Efq;

3. Lady Lucy, married, in 1747-8, to Col. George Howard.

4. Lady Henrietta, married, in 1744, to Henry Vernon, Efq; and has iffue.

The late Earl was bred a foldier, and was advanced gradually to the poft of lieutenant-general. He ferved in the army with great applaufe, during the war againft France; and particularly in the battles of Steinkirk and Landen : he ferved alfo in the army of the allies in the reign of Queen Anne; but was however fent ambaffador to the court of Ruffia, and afterwards to the States-General, and was one of the plenipotentiaries at the treaty of Utrecht, figned April 11, 1713. He was alfo conftituted the firft lord commiffioner of the admiralty, and confequently one of the lords juftices for the adminiftration of the government on the death of Queen Anne, until the arrival of his Majefty King George.

This family took their name from the manor of Wentworth in Yorkfhire, of which they were poffeffed in the reign of William the Conqueror.

Arms.] Sable, a chevron between three leopards heads, or.

Creft.] On a wreath a gryphon paffant, argent.

Supporters.] On the dexter fide a gryphon, argent; on the finifter, a lion, or.

Motto.] *En Dieu eft tout.*

Chief Seats.] At Wentworth-caftle in Yorkfhire; at Boughton in the county of Northampton; at Twickenham in Middlefex; and St. James's-fquare, London.

43. LEGGE,

43. LEGGE, EARL of DARTMOUTH.

THE Right Hon. WILLIAM LEGGE, Earl and Baron of DARTMOUTH, Vifcount Lewifham, and recorder of Litchfield, fucceeded William, the late Earl, his grandfather, Dec. 15, 1750, and married, Jan. 11, 1755, Frances-Catharine, fole daughter and heir of the late Sir Charles Gunter-Nicholl, knight of the Bath, by whom he has iffue,

George, Lord Vifcount Lewifham, born Oct. 4, 1755; another fon born Feb. 4, 1757; and a daughter born May 18, 1759.

George, Lord Vifcount Lewifham, eldeft fon of William the late Earl, and father of the prefent Earl, married Elizabeth, the daughter and heir of Sir Arthur Kaye, Bart. and dying in his father's life time, Aug. 29, 1732, left iffue,

1. The prefent Earl.
2. Anne. And,
3. Elizabeth.

And his lady furviving him, married Francis, Lord North and Guilford.

William Legge, Baron Dartmouth, grandfather of the prefent Earl, was born in 1672, and created Vifcount Lewifham and Earl of Dartmouth in 1713. He married in 1700, the Lady Anne Finch, daughter of the Right Hon. Heneage Finch, Earl of Aylesford, by whom he had iffue fix fons and two daughters, viz.

1. George, father of the prefent Earl, who died Aug. 29, 1732.
2. Heneage, born in 1703-4, now one of the barons of his Majefty's Exchequer, married, in 1739, to Mifs Catharine Fogg, niece to Sir John Barnard, by whom he had iffue, and died Aug. 28, 1759.
3. William, who died in his infancy.

G 3   4. Henry,

4. Henry, born in March 1708, chancellor and under-treasurer of the Exchequer, and one of the lords commissioners of the Treasury, who married Mary, sole daughter and heir of Edward Lord Stawell, now Baroness Stawell, and has issue a son, born Feb. 22, 1757.

5. Edward, who died in 1747.

6. Robert, who died in his minority.

7. Lady Barbara, married to Sir Walter Bagot of Blithfield, in Staffordshire, Bart.   And,

8. Lady Anne, married to Sir Lister Holt, Bart.

The Right Hon. George Legge, Baron Dartmouth, father of the late Earl William, was admiral of the fleet sent to demolish Tangier, in the reign of King Charles II. in 1683; and, in the reign of King James II. was constituted master of the horse, general of the ordnance, and constable of the Tower of London; and made admiral of the fleet, designed to intercept the Dutch, who were bringing over the Prince of Orange in 1688; but he was not able to perform that service, being detained in the Thames mouth by contrary winds; or, as some insinuate, he did not attempt it, because he knew his officers were not hearty in the service, and the Prince landed at Torbay in Devonshire, without interruption, on Nov. 5.   But however that was, he was deprived of all his employments at the revolution; and being committed to the Tower in the year 1691, died there the 25th of Oct. the same year.

This noble Earl is descended from Signior de Lega, an Italian nobleman, who flourished in Italy in the year 1297.   What time the family came into England is uncertain; but it appears they were settled at Legge's-Place, near Tunbridge, in Kent, for many generations; and Thomas, one of their ancestors, was twice lord-mayor of London, viz. in 1346, and 1353.

Arms.] Azure, a buck's head caboched, argent.

Crest.]

Creſt.] In a ducal coronet, or, a plume of three oſtrich feathers, party-par-pale, argent and gules.

Supporters.] On the dexter ſide a lion, argent, ſemee of fleurs-de-lis, ſable, and crowned as the creſt. On the ſiniſter a buck, argent, ſemee of mullets, gules.

Motto.] *Gaudet tentamine virtus.*

Chief Seats.] At Sandwell-Hall in Staffordſhire; at Black-Heath in Kent; and Charles-ſtreet, St. James's-ſquare, London.

44. PAGET, EARL of UXBRIDGE.

THE Right Hon. HENRY PAGET, Earl of Uxbridge, Baron Paget of Beaudefert, and of Burton, only ſon of Thomas Cateſby, Lord Paget, ſucceeded Henry Paget, Earl of Uxbridge, his grandfather, in Aug. 1743.

Thomas-Cateſby, Lord Paget, father of the preſent Earl, married, May 3, 1718, the Lady Elizabeth, ſiſter to the Hon. Scroop Egerton, afterwards created Duke of Bridgwater; and his lordſhip dying in Jan. 1741-2, left iſſue living, Henry, his only ſon, now Earl of Uxbridge.

Henry, grandfather of the preſent Earl, was created a peer of Great Britain, by the title of Lord Burton, Baron of Burton, in the county of Stafford, Dec. 31, 1711, 10 Anne; and Earl of Uxbridge in the county of Middleſex, Oct. 19, 1714, 1 Geo. I. His lordſhip married Mary, daughter and coheir to Thomas Catesby, of Whiſton in the county of Northampton, Eſq; by whom he had iſſue Thomas-Catesby, his only ſon; and his lady dying Nov. 1, 1734, he married, ſecondly, in 1739, Elizabeth, daughter of Sir Walter Bagot, of Blithfield, Bart.

This

This noble Earl is defcended from Sir William, af-. terwards Lord Paget, who was fecretary of ftate in the reign of King Henry VIII. and fent ambaffador both to the Emperor and the French king, and concerned in many important negotiations, being one of the ableft minifters of that reign.

That King made him one of his executors, and appointed him to be of the council to his fon and fucceffor King Edward VI. in which reign he was alfo fecretary of ftate, and was fent ambaffador to the Emperor Charles V. to negotiate an alliance againft France. In the reign of Queen Mary he was conftituted lord privy-feal.

Henry, Earl of Uxbridge, great-grandfather of the prefent Earl, being fent ambaffador to Turkey, had the honour of negotiating and concluding the peace of Carlowitz, between the Emperor of Germany and the Grand Signior, in the year 1698.

Arms.] Sable, on a crofs ingrailed, between four eagles difplayed, argent; five lions paffant of the firft.

Creft.] On a wreath, a demi-tyger rampant, fable, gorged with a ducal coronet, and tufted and mained, argent.

Supporters.] Two tygers, as in the creft.

Motto.] *Per il fuo contrario.*

Chief Seats.] At Drayton in Middlefex; at Beaudefert in Staffordfhire; and Conduit-ftreet, London.

45. BENNET, EARL of TANKERVILLE.

THE Right Hon. CHARLES BENNET, Earl of TANKERVILLE, Baron Offulfton, fucceeded his father Charles, the late Earl, March 14, 1753.

The late Earl married Camilla, daughter of Edward Colvile of Whitehoufe, in the bifhopric of Durham, Efq; by whom he has iffue two fons and one daughter, viz.   I.

1. Charles, the prefent Earl, who married Alicia, third daughter of Sir John Aftley, Bart. in 1742, and has iffue, Charles Bennet, Lord Offulfton, born Nov. 15, 1743; John-Grey, who died in the fecond year of his age; Lady Camilla-Elizabeth; Lady Frances-Alicia, and a fon, born April 3, 1757.

2. George, born in 1727.

3. Lady Camilla, married, Jan. 14, 1754, to Gilbert-Fane Fleming, Efq;

Charles, Lord Offulfton, grandfather of the prefent Earl, was created Earl of Tankerville, 1 Geo. I. and in July 1695, he married the Lady Mary, only daughter of Ford Lord Grey of Wark; which lady died May 31, 1710, by whom he had iffue four fons and three daughters, viz.

1. Charles, the late Earl.

2. John.

3. Henry, who died unmarried.

4. Grey, alfo died unmarried, Nov. 19, 1724.

5. Lady Bridget, eldeft daughter, married to John Wallop, Lord Vif. Limington, and died Oct. 12, 1738.

6. Lady Annabella, fecond daughter, married to William Paulet, Efq; and

7. Lady Mary, married, Aug. 6, 1720, to William Wilmer, of Sywell in Northamptonfhire, Efq; and died May 24, 1729.

This noble Earl is defcended from the family of the Bennets in Berkfhire, who flourifhed in the reign of King Edward III.

Arms.] Gules, a bezant between three demi lions rampant, argent, with a mullet for difference.

Creft.] On a wreath a demi-lion rampant, argent, holding in his paws a bezant; and fometimes out of a mural coronet, or, a lion's head, argent, charged with a bezant on his neck.

Supporters.] Two lions, argent, each charged on its fhoulder with a bezant, and crowned ducally, or.

Motto.] *De bon vouloir fervir le roy.*

Chief

Chief Seats.] At Chillingham-caftle in Northum-berland; and St. James's-fquare, London.

---

46. FINCH, EARL of AILESFORD.

THE Right Hon. HENEAGE FINCH, Earl of AILESFORD, and Baron of Guernfey, fucceeded his father Heneage, the late Earl, June 26, 1757. He married, Oct. 6, 1750, Lady Charlotte Seymour, youngeft daughter of Charles, Duke of Somerfet, by whom he has iffue fix fons and one daughter.

1. Heneage, born July 15, 1751.
2. Charles, born June 4, 1752, N. S.
3. William, born May 27, 1753.
4. Charlotte, born May 28, 1754.
5. John, born May 22, 1755.
6. A fifth fon, born April 26, 1756. And,
7. A fixth fon, horn March 11, 1760.

Heneage, the late Earl, fucceeded his father Heneage, Earl of Ailesford, July 22, 1719. He married Mary, daughter and heir of Sir Clement Fifher of Packington in Warwickfhire, Bart. by whom he had iffue one fon and four daughters.

1. Heneage, the prefent Earl.
2. Lady Anne.
3. Lady Mary, married to William late Lord Vifcount Andover.
4. Lady Elizabeth. And,
5. Lady Frances, who married in April 1741, to Sir William Carew, of Powderham-caftle.

This noble Lord is defcended from the fame anceftors with the Earl of Winchelfea.

Arms.] Argent, a chevron between three gryphons paffant, fable; a crefcent for difference.

Creft.] On a wreath, a gryphon paffant, fable.

Supporters.] On the dexter fide a gryphon, fable, gorged with a ducal collar, or. On the finifter, a lion of the fecond, ducally gorged, azure.   *Mot-*

Motto.] *Aperto vivere voto.*

Chief Seats.] At Ailesford in Kent; at Albury in Surry; at Packington in Warwickſhire; and Cavendiſh-ſquare, London.

---

47. HERVEY, EARL of BRISTOL.

THE Right Hon. GEORGE-WILLIAM HERVEY, Earl of BRISTOL, Lord Hervey of Ickworth, his Majeſty's ambaſſador at the court of Madrid, ſucceeded his grandfather John, late Earl of Briſtol, in Jan. 1750-1,

John Lord Hervey, eldeſt ſon of John late Earl of Briſtol, by Elizabeth his wife, daughter of Sir Thomas Felton, Bart. and father of the preſent Earl, born Oct. 15, 1696, was created Lord Hervey of Ickworth, in the county of Suffolk, June 12, 1733, and married, Oct. 24, 1720, Mary, daughter of brigadiergeneral Nicholas Lee Pell, and had iſſue by her four ſons and four daughters, viz.

1. George-William, the preſent Earl, born Aug. 31, 1721.
2. John-Auguſtus, born May 19, 1724, a captain in the navy, and member of parliament for Bury.
3. Frederick, born in Auguſt 1730.
4. William, born May 13, 1732.
5. Lady Le Pell, married, Feb. 26, 1742-3, to Conſtantine Phipps, Eſq;
6. Lady Mary, married to George Fitzgerald, Eſq;
7. Lady Amelia-Carolina Naſſau; and,
8. Lady Caroline.

His Majeſty was pleaſed to grant, by his warrant dated June 6, 1753, to the daughters of the Lord Hervey, the ſame place and precedency in all aſſemblies, as daughters of Earls of Great Britain.

John late Earl of Briſtol, and grandfather of the preſent Earl, born Aug. 27, 1665, was created Baron

Hervey

Hervey in the second year of Queen Anne, and Earl of Briftol, 1 Geo. I. 1714. He married to his firft wife, Ifabella, daughter and fole heirefs of Sir Robert Carr, of Sleeford, in Lincolnfhire, Bart. by whom he had iffue one fon and two daughters, viz.

1. Carr, born Sept. 17, 1691, who died Nov. 14, 1723.

2. Ifabella, his eldeft daughter, died in November 1711, unmarried. And,

3. Elizabeth, fecond daughter (of whom her mother died in child-bed, March 7, 1692-3) died an infant.

In the year 1695, his lordfhip married his fecond wife, Elizabeth, daughter and fole heirefs of Sir Thomas Felton, of Playford, in the county of Suffolk, Bart. by whom he had iffue eleven fons and five daughters, viz.

1. John, late Lord Hervey, above-mentioned.

2. Thomas, born Jan. 20, 1698; married Mifs Anne Cavaflin of Ireland.

3. William, born Dec. 25, 1699, and married in 1729, Elizabeth, daughter of Thomas Ridge, of Portfmouth, Efq;

4. Henry, born Jan. 5, 1700, married, in 1730, to Catharine, fifter to Sir Thomas Afton, Bart. and died in Nov. 1748.

5. Charles, born April 5, 1703, is prebend of Ely. He married Mifs Martha Howard, daughter of Col. Howard.

6, 7, and 8, died foon after they were born.

9. James-Porter, born June 24, 1706, fince dead.

10. Felton, born Feb. 12, 1711-12, groom of the bedchamber to the Duke, married Dorothy, daughter of Solomon Afhley, Efq;

11. James, born March 5, 1712-13, fince dead.

12. Lady Elizabeth, married to the Right Hon. Buffy Manfel, late Lord Manfel, and died Dec. 3, 1727.

3

13 Lady.

13. Lady Anne.

14. Lady Barbara, died unmarried, July 24, 1727.

15. Lady Louisa-Carolina, married Sept. 23, 1731, Sir Robert Smith, of Westminster, Bart.

16. Lady Henrietta, died in August 1732.

This noble family derive their pedigree from Robert Fitz-Hervey, a younger son of Hervey, Duke of Orleans, who came over from France with William the Conqueror.

Arms.] Gules, on a bend, argent, three trefoils sliped, proper.

Cress.] On a wreath, a leopard, passant, (holding in his dexter paw a trefoil sliped, proper) bezantee and gorged with a ducal coronet, and chained, or.

Supporters.] Two leopards, proper, bezantee, and with collars and chains, or.

Motto.] *Je noublieray jamais.*

Chief Seats.] At Ickworth in Suffolk; at Asgarbye in Lincolnshire; and St. James's-square, London.

---

48. CARTERET, EARL GRANVILLE.

THE Right Hon. JOHN CARTERET, Earl GRANVILLE, Viscount Carteret, Baron Carteret of Hawnes, and Baronet, knight of the most noble order of the garter, lord-president of his Majesty's most honourable privy-council, a governor of the Charter-house, one of the society for propagating the gospel in foreign parts, and hereditary sheriff of the island of Jersey, born April 22, 1691, succeeded his father George Lord Carteret, in the barony of Carteret, in Sept. 1695, and succeeded to the earldom of Granville on the death of his mother the Lady Grace, Countess of Granville, in Oct. 1744.

He married, Oct. 24, 1710, Frances, only daughter of Sir Robert Worsley, Bart. by whom he had issue three sons and five daughters, viz.

I.

1. Robert, born Sept. 21, 1721.

2. Lady Grace, married to Lionel Talmafh, Earl of Dyfert in Scotland, in July 1729, and died July 23, 1755.

3. Lady Louifa, married, in 1733, to Thomas Lord Vifcount Weymouth. [*See* Weymouth *Vifcount.*]

4. Lady Georgina-Carolina, married to the late Hon. John Spencer, brother to the Duke of Marlborough ; and fince, to the Right Hon. William Earl Cowper.

5. Lady Frances, married, in 1743, to John Marquis of Tweeddale. Another daughter and two fons died in their minority.

His Lordfhip married to his fecond wife Lady Sophia, eldeft daughter of Thomas Fermer, Earl of Pomfret, in 1744, and has iffue a daughter, named Sophia, born in Aug. 1745, of whom her mother died in child-bed.

His Lordfhip was appointed ambaffador-extraordinary and plenipotentiary to the Queen of Sweden, Jan. 25, 1718-19, and arrived at Stockholm June 30, 1719, where he offered the King of Great Britain's mediation to the Queen, in order to make peace between Sweden and Denmark, and between Sweden and the Czar of Mufcovy, which fhe accepted; and a treaty between Sweden, Pruffia, and Hanover, was proclaimed at Stockholm March 9, 1719-20. He had the honour of concluding the peace alfo between Denmark and Sweden, in 1720.

His Lordfhip returning to England, was, on the death of James Craggs, Efq; fecretary of ftate, on the 5th of March, 1720-1, advanced to that poft.

The Duke of Newcaftle fucceeding Lord Carteret in his office of fecretary of ftate, April 3, 1724, his Lordfhip was conftituted lord lieutenant of Ireland.

His Lordfhip continuing lord lieutenant of Ireland until the death of his late Majefty in 1727, he was continued in that poft by his prefent Majefty, and remained

mained lord lieutenant until June 19, 1730, when he was succeeded by his Grace the Duke of Dorset.

Lord Carteret had no public employment from the year 1730 to 1741, when he was again declared principal secretary of state.

His Lordship being one of the eight noble lords who were proprietors of Carolina, and his Majesty having purchased the shares of seven of them, Lord Carteret's eighth part was set out by commissioners, who allotted him that part of North Carolina which lies contiguous to Virginia, which was confirmed to him by his Majesty.

Lord Carteret resigning the seals on the 24th of Nov. 1744, William Earl of Harrington, was constituted principal secretary of state in his stead.

The family of Carteret is of Norman extraction, and had their surname from their signiory or lordship of Carteret, in Normandy. In the Annals of Normandy, and the History of the Holy Wars, there is honourable mention made of the lords of the house of Carteret.

George Lord Carteret, father of the present Earl, married the Lady Grace Granville, youngest daughter of John Earl of Bath, who died in Sept. 1695, leaving one daughter and three sons, viz.

1. Lady Jemima, who died unmarried in 1733.

2. George, the eldest, died an infant.

3. John, now Earl Granville.

4. Philip, died in the 19th year of his age, in 1710.

The Lady Grace, their mother, in consideration of the great services of her father John Granville, Earl of Bath, who was entrusted by King Charles II. to bring about the restoration, was, by the late King George, in the first year of his reign, created Viscountess Carteret, and Countess Granville, with limitation of those honours to John her son, the present Earl, with remainder of the title of Viscount Carteret,

teret, to Edward Carteret, his-uncle, and the heirs of his body.

This family derive their pedigree from the Granvilles of Normandy. Three brothers of this name attended William the Conqueror in his descent upon. England, and contributed to the victory he obtained over King Harold, at Hastings in Suffex, in the year 1066, and had several manors and lands in England conferred on them by that prince, in consideration of their eminent services.

Arms.] Quarterly, first and fourth, gules, four fusils in fess, argent, for Carteret; second and third, gules, three clarions or claricords, or, for Granville.

Crest.] Above a wreath, upon a mount, a squirrel sejant, all proper.

Supporters.] Two winged deer, gules; attired, or.

Motto.] *Loyall devoir.*

Chief Seats.] At Hawnes, in the county of Bedford ; and Arlington-street, London.

---

49. MONTAGU DUNK, EARL of HALIFAX.

THE Right Hon. George Montagu Dunk, Earl of Halifax, Viscount Sunbury, and Baron Halifax, first lord commissioner of trade and plantations, lieutenant-general of his Majesty's forces, lord lieutenant and custos rotulorum of the county of Northampton, and one of his Majesty's most honourable privy-council, was born Oct. 5, 1716, succeeded George, his father, the late Earl, May 9, 1739; and married, July 2, 1741, Miss Anne Dunk, daughter of —— Dunk, Esq; of Hawkhurst, in the county of Kent, which lady dying in 1753, left three daughters, viz.

1. Lady Anne, born in April 1742.
2. Lady Frances, born in May 1743. And,

3. Lady

3. Lady Elizabeth, born in Nov. 1745.

George, late Earl of Halifax, father of the prefent Earl, married Richarda-Pofthuma, daughter of Richard Saltenftall of Chippen-warden in the county of Northampton, Efq; by whom he had a daughter named Lucy, married to Francis Earl of North and Guildford. [See North and Guildford Earl.] He married to his fecond wife the Lady Mary Lumley, eldeft daughter of Richard Earl of Scarborough, by whom he had iffue one fon and fix daughters, viz.

1. George, the prefent Earl.

2. Lady Frances, married, in Jan. 1738-9, to Sir Roger Burgoyne, Bart. of Sutton, in the county of Bedford, and has iffue.

3. Lady Anne, married, in Sept. 1740, to Sir Danvers Ofborn, of Chickfands in the county of Bedford, Bart. and dying in July 1743, left iffue.

4. Lady Mary, married, in Dec. 1743, to Henry Archer, Efq; brother to the prefent Lord Archer.

5. Lady Barbara;

6. Lady Elizabeth, married, in 1747, to James Johnfton, Efq; and has iffue, one fon, James, and a daughter, Charlotte.

7. Lady Charlotte, married, in 1748-9, to Jofeph Irkyll, of Dallington in the county of Northampton, Efq; and has iffue.

The original of this family will be found in that of the Duke of Manchefter's, of which this of Halifax is a branch.

Charles Montagu, firft Earl of Halifax, of this family, and grand uncle of the prefent Earl, was conftituted one of the lords commiffioners of the treafury in 1691; and in 1694, was appointed chancellor and under-treafurer of the Exchequer; and the coin being exceedingly debafed and diminifhed, he formed the defign of calling in the money, and recoining it in the year 1695, and effected it within the fpace of two years. To facilitate which, and fupply

the

the want of money, when the old money was called in, he projected the issuing of exchequer-bills : whereupon the commons came to a resolution in the year 1697, " That the Hon. Charles Montagu, Esq; chan-" cellor of the Exchequer, for his good services to " the government, did deserve his Majesty's favour." He was constituted first lord commissioner of the Treasury in the year 1698, and resigning that post in the year 1700, obtained a grant of the office of auditor of the receipt of the Exchequer, and the same year was created Baron Halifax, with remainder to George Montagu, Esq; late Earl of Halifax, eldest son of Edward Montagu, Esq; his eldest brother, and the heirs of his body ; and dying without issue by his lady, the daughter of Sir Christopher Yelverton, was succeeded in his honour by the said George, late Lord Halifax.

The descent of this noble family is from the Earls of Manchester, ancestors to the Duke of that name.

Arms.] Argent, three fusils conjoined in fess, gules, a border, sable.

Crest.] On a wreath, a gryphon's head couped, or, with a beak and wings, sable, and a portcullis on its neck of the second.

Supporters.] Two gryphons, argent, gutty de sang, their wings expanded, gules, and each charged on the neck with a portcullis, sable.

Motto.] *Otium cum dignitate,*

Chief Seats.] At Horton in Northamptonshire ; at Bushy-park in Middlesex ; and Grosvenor-square, London.

50. YELVERTON, EARL of SUSSEX.

THE Right Hon. HENRY YELVERTON, Earl of SUSSEX, Viscount Longueville, Baron Grey of Ruthyn, and Baronet, succeeded his brother George-

Au-

Auguftus, the late Earl, who died unmarried, Jan. 8, 1758; and Jan. 17, 1757, married Mifs Hall, by whom he has a daughter born June 19, 1759.

Talbot Earl of Suffex, father of the late and prefent Earls, was created Earl of Suffex, Aug. 3, 4 Geo. I. He married Lucy, daughter to Henry Pelham, of Lewes in Suffex, Efq; and dying in Oct. 1731, left iffue by her two fons, George the late Earl, and Henry, the prefent Earl.

This noble Earl is defcended from the Yelvertons of Norfolk, who flourifhed in the reign of Edward II. whofe feat was at Rackheath, near Norwich.

Sir Chriftopher Yelverton, another of the anceftors of this noble Earl, was chofen fpeaker of the houfe of commons in the 39th of Queen Elizabeth, and in the 44th year of her reign, was made one of the judges of the King's Bench, as he was alfo in the reign of King James I. and his fon Sir Henry Yelverton was a judge of the Common-Pleas in the reign of King Charles I. whofe reports are in great efteem at this day.

Arms.] Argent, three lions rampant, and a chief, gules.

Creft.] On a wreath, a lion paffant reguardant, gules.

Supporters.] On the dexter fide, a wyverne, or, on the finifter, a lion reguardant, gules.

Motto.] *Foy en tout.*

Chief Seat.] At Eafton-Manduit in the county of Northampton.

51. COWPER, EARL COWPER.

THE Right Hon. WILLIAM COWPER, Earl COWPER, Vifcount Fordwich, Baron Cowper of Wingham, and Baronet, lord lieutenant and cuftos rotulorum of the county of Hertford, and fellow

of

of the Royal Society, born in 1709, succeeded William, his father, the late Earl, Oct. 10, 1723; and married, June 27, 1737, Lady Henrietta, youngest daughter and coheir of Henry, Earl of Grantham, and had issue one son, George, Viscount Fordwich, born in Aug. 1738, and a daughter named Caroline, born June 20, 1733; and married in July, 1753, to Henry Seymour, Esq; He married to his second wife, Lady Georgina-Caroline, daughter of the Right Hon. John Earl of Granville, and widow of the Hon. John Spencer, brother to the late Duke of Marlborough, and mother to the Hon. John Spencer, Esq;

William, late Earl Cowper, father of the present Earl, was bred to the study of the law; and soon after he was called to the bar, was appointed one of the King's council in the reign of King William, and of Queen Anne's council in the next reign; and that Queen constituted him lord keeper of the great seal of England in the year 1705; and in 1707, after the treaty of Union, lord chancellor of Great Britain, which post he held until the year 1710: and on the accession of the late King George, was constituted lord high chancellor again. It is observed to his honour, that he refused to accept new years gifts from the counsellors at law, which had been long given to his predecessors; and what is still more to his honour, he foresaw and opposed the destructive measures pursued in the year 1720, by the South-sea directors, and some of the ministry. He was created a Peer by the stile and title of Lord Cowper, Baron Cowper of Wingham in the county of Kent, 5 Anne, 1706, Viscount Fordwich and Earl Cowper, 4 George I. 1717.

His Lordship married Judith, daughter and heiress of Sir Robert Booth, of London, Knight, by whom he had only one son, that died an infant; and after her decease he married the daughter of John Clavering, Esq; by whom he had issue two sons and two daughters, viz.

I.

1. William, the prefent Earl.

2. Spencer Cowper, who married Dorothy, daughter of Charles, Vifcount Townfhend, in May 1743.

3. Lady Sarah, who died Dec. 7, 1758.

4. Lady Anne, married, in 1731, to James-Edward Colleton, Efq;

This noble Earl is defcended from Simon Cowper, fheriff of London, in the fourth year of King Edward II. 1310. Sir William Cowper, another of his anceftors, who refided at the caftle of Hertford, was eminent for his hofpitality and charity, making it his bufinefs, in the decline of life, to vifit and relieve his poor neighbours at their houfes, and died much lamented, Anno 1664, in the 83d year of his age.

Arms.] Argent, three martlets and a chief engrailed, gules; on the latter, as many annulets, or.

Crest.] On a wreath, a lion's gamb erected and erafed, or, holding a branch, vert; fructed, gules.

Supporters.] Two bay horfes, with tails docked, proper.

Motto.] *Tuum eft.*

Chief Seats.] At Colne-green, in Hertfordfhire; at Ratling-court, in the county of Kent; and Grofvenor-fquare, London.

---

52. STANHOPE, EARL STANHOPE.

THE Right Hon. PHILIP STANHOPE, Earl STANHOPE, Vifcount Stanhope of Mahon, and Baron of Elvafton, fucceeded his father James, the late Earl, Feb. 5, 1720-1. He married, in 1745, Lady Grizel, daughter of Thomas, Lord Haddington, by whom he has iffue, Philip Lord Vifcount Stanhope, and the Hon. Charles Stanhope.

James Stanhope, father of the prefent Earl, was created Vifcount Stanhope of Mahon, and Baron Stanhope

hope of Elvafton, July 21, 1717; and on April 7, 1718, created Earl Stanhope. He married, Feb. 24, 1712-13, Lucy, daughter of Thomas Pitt, of Stratford, in Wiltfhire, Efq; and his Lordfhip, dying Feb. 5, 1720, had iffue by her (who died Feb. 24, 1722-3) three fons and one daughter:

1. Philip, now Earl Stanhope; and,

2. Lucy, a daughter, twins, born Aug. 15, 1714..

3. George, born Dec. 28, 1717, died unmarried.

4. James, who died in the tenth year of his age, April 21, 1730. And,

' 5. Lady Jane.

He was appointed commander in chief of the Britifh forces in Spain in the reign of Queen Anne, in 1708; and the fame year fubdued the ifland of Minorca. He commanded the Englifh forces alfo at the battles of Almanara and Saragoffa in the year 1710, to which victories he greatly contributed, and facilitated the march of King Charles III. to Madrid, of which he took poffeffion foon after. He was conftituted firft commiffioner of the treafury, and chancellor of the Exchequer, in 1717; and in the year 1718, principal fecretary of ftate.

Alexander Stanhope, Efq; the late Earl's father, was the only fon of Philip the firft Earl of Chefterfield, by his fecond wife, Anne, daughter of Sir John Packington, Bart.

Arms and *Creft.*] The fame as the Earl of Chefterfield; a crefcent for difference.

Supporters.] On the dexter fide, a talbot, ermine. On the finifter, a wolf, or, ducally crowned, azure; each charged on the fhoulder with a crefcent, azure.

Motto.] *A Deo & Rege.*

. *Chief Seats.*] At Chevening, in the county of Kent; Hanover-fquare, London.

53. SHERARD, EARL of HARBOROUGH.

THE Right Hon. BENNET SHERARD, Earl of HARBOROUGH, Baron Sherard of Harborough in England, and Baron of Leitrim in Ireland, fuc-. ceeded Philip, the late Earl, his father, July 20, 1750. His Lordſhip married, in June, 1738, Lady Elizabeth, daughter of Ralph, Earl of Verney, by whom he has iſſue four ſons, Charles, Harry, James, and William; and three daughters, Elizabeth, Charlotte, and Mary. This Lady dying, his Lordſhip, July 2, 1757, married Miſs Noel, daughter to the Hon. Juſtice Noel, by whom he has a daughter, born March 12, 1759.

Philip, late Earl of Harborough, and father of the preſent Earl, ſucceeded Earl Bennet, his couſin, Oct. 16, 1732. He married Annè, ſole daughter and heir of Nicholas Pedley, Eſq; and by her, who died Feb. 16, 1749-50, had iſſue ſix ſons and eight daughters, of which are living,

1. The preſent Earl.
2. The Hon. Philip Sherard.
3. Lady Dorothy, who married James Torkington, Eſq; and has iſſue ſeveral ſons and daughters.
4. Lady Lucy. And,
5. Lady Suſanna.

This noble Earl is lineally deſcended from Schirard, who was poſſeſſed of manors and lands·to a great value in the counties of Cheſhire and Lancaſhire in the reign of William the Conqueror. Geoffrey, another of this Earl's anceſtors, was three times ſheriff of Rutlandſhire, in the reigns of King Edward IV. and King Richard III.

Arms.] Argent, a chevron, gules, between three torteauxes.

Creſt.] In a ducal coronet, or, a peacock's tail erect, proper.

Supporters.] Two rams, argent, armed and un-guled, or.

Motto.] *Hostis honori invidia.*

Chief Seats.] At Stapleford, in Leicestershire; Whisfendine, in Rutlandshire; Chelsea.

---

54. P A R K E R, E A R L of MACCLESFIELD.

THE Right Hon. GEORGE PARKER, Earl MAC-CLESFIELD, Viscount Parker, and Baron of Macclesfield, one of the tellers of his Majesty's Exchequer, vice-president of the Foundling-hospital, high steward of Henley upon Thames, and president of the Royal Society, succeeded Thomas, the late Earl, his father, April 28, 1732; and on the 18th of Sept. 1722, married Mary, eldest daughter and co-heir of Ralph Lane, Esq; a Turkey merchant, by which Lady, who died June 4, 1753, he has issue two sons:

1. Thomas, Lord Viscount Parker, born Oct. 12, 1723, married Dec. 12, 1749, to Miss Mary Heathcote, eldest daughter to Sir William Heathcote, of Hursley, Bart. by whom he has issue.

2. George Lane, born Sept. 6, 1724, who is yet unmarried.

His Lordship married, a second time, in Novemb. 1757, Miss Nesbit.

Thomas Parker, late Earl of Macclesfield, father of the present Earl, was, March 19, 1715, created Lord Parker, and Baron of Macclesfield; and Nov. 5, 1721, advanced to the dignities of Viscount Parker of Ewelme, in Oxfordshire, and Earl of Macclesfield. His Lordship married Janet, daughter and coheir of —— Carrier, of Wickworth, in the county of Derby, Esq; by whom he left issue,

1. The present Earl; and,

2. The Lady Elizabeth, married, April 7, 1720, to William Heathcote, of Hursley, in the county of Southampton, Esq; (since created Bart.) by whom she had issue, Thomas, Samuel, Gilbert, Henry, Mary Viscountess Parker, Elizabeth, and Jennetta.

The late Earl was constituted lord chief justice of the King's-bench in the year 1710; and in the year 1718, he was constituted lord chancellor of England, in which high office he remained six years.

This noble Earl is descended from Thomas Parker, who flourished in the reign of King Edward III. and then possessed the manor of Lees, near Norton, in the county of Derby, which still retains the name of Norton-lees.

Arms.] Gules, a chevron between three leopards faces, or.

Crest.] A leopard's head erased and guardant, or; ducally gorged, gules.

Supporters.] Two leopards reguardant, proper, each gorged with a ducal coronet, gules.

Motto.] *Sapere aude.*

Chief Seats.] At Sherburn-castle, in Oxfordshire; St. James's-square, London.

---

55. FERMOR, EARL of POMFRET.

THE Right Hon. GEORGE FERMOR, Earl of POMFRET, and Lord Lempster, succeeded his late father, Thomas, July 8, 1753.

The said late Earl, July 14, 1720, married Henrietta Louisa, daughter and heiress of John Lord Jeffreys, Baron of Wem, by the Lady Charlotte Herbert, daughter and heir of Philip, Earl of Pembroke and Montgomery, and by her had issue four sons and six daughters.

1. George, the present Earl.
2. William, who died in 1744.

3. John; and,

4. Thomas, both dead.

5. Lady Sophia, married, in 1744, to John, Earl Granville; and died in 1745.

6. Lady Charlotte, married to the Right Hon. William Finch, Efq; brother to the Earl of Winchelfea.

7. Lady Henrietta, married to John Conyers, of Copthall in Effex, Efq;

8. Lady Juliana, married in Aug. 1751, to Thomas Penn, one of the proprietors of Penfilvania.

9. Lady Louifa.

10. Lady Anne, married July 15, 1754, to Thomas Dawfon, Efq;

This noble family, who were formerly called Ricards, were antiently feated at Somerton, upon the river Cherwell in the county of Oxford, where they had large poffeffions, as far back as the time of King Henry VII.

Arms.] Quarterly, firft and fourth, argent, a fefs, fable, between three lions heads erafed, gules. The fecond and third, azure, a faltire, argent, between four eagles difplayed, or.

Creft.] Out of a ducal coronet, or, a cock's head iffuing, gules; crefted and wattled, or.

Supporters.] Two lions, proper.

Motto.] *Hora e fempre.*

Chief Seats.] At Eafton-Nefton, in the county of Northampton; Prince's-ftreet, Grofvenor-fquare, London.

56. GRAHAM, EARL GRAHAM.

THE Right Hon. WILLIAM GRAHAM, Earl and Baron GRAHAM of Belford in Scotland, and Earl of Belford in the county of Northumberland in England, Duke of Montrofe in Scotland, and chancellor of the college of Glafgow, fucceeded his father

James

James, late Earl of Belford, &c. in 1741. His Lordſhip married, in Oct. 1742, the Lady Lucy Manners, daughter of John, late Duke of Rutland, by whom he has iſſue.

His Grace William Graham, late Earl of Belford, and Duke of Montroſe, ſecond ſon of James Duke of Montroſe, married the Lady Chriſtian Carnegie, daughter of David Earl of Northeſk, by whom he had iſſue,

1. James, Marquis of Graham, who died in his infancy.

2. David, Marquis of Graham, and firſt Earl of Belford.

3. William, the preſent Earl of Belford.

4. Lord George, who died unmarried.

5. Lady Margaret, who died unmarried.

This noble Earl is deſcended from the valiant Greme, or Graham, who forced his way through that barrier formed by the Britons to defend their country, erected between Dunbritton and Edinburgh friths, and from him called Graham's Dyke.

[*The Reader will meet with a more particular account of this noble family under the title of Duke of* Montroſe, *among the Peers of* Scotland, *in the ſecond Volume of this Work.*

Arms.] Quarterly, firſt and fourth, or, on a chief, ſable, three eſcallop-ſhells, or. Second and third, argent, three roſes, gules, barbed and ſeeded, proper.

Creſt.] On a wreath, an eagle, wings hovering, or, preying on a ſtork on its back, proper.

Supporters.] Two ſtorks cloſe, argent; beaked and membered, gules.

Motto.] *Ne oublie.*

Chief Seats.] At Glaſgow, in the county of Lanerk; at Kincairn, in the county of Perth; at Myndock-caſtle, in the county of Lennox; and in Upper Groſvenor-ſtreet, London.

57. KER, EARL OF WAKEFIELD.

THE Right Hon. JOHN KER, Duke of Roxburgh in Scotland, and Earl and Baron KER
of WAKEFIELD in Yorkſhire, Engliſh honours, ſucceeded his father, Robert, late Duke of Roxburgh,
who died Aug. 20, 1755.

His Grace is deſcended from the noble family of
Drummond, formerly called Drymen, which flouriſhed
in the reign of Alexander II. King of Scotland, and
were anceſtors of all the Britiſh Kings of the Stuart
race.

> [*For an account of this noble family the reader may
> conſult the ſecond Volume of this Work, under the
> title of* Duke of Roxburgh, *among the Peers of*
> Scotland.]

Arms.] Quarterly, firſt and fourth, vert, on a chevron, between three unicorns heads erazed, argent;
as many mullets, ſable. Second and third, gules,
three muſcles, or.

Creſt.] On a wreath, an unicorn's head erazed,
argent; armed, or.

Supporters.] Two ſavages, each holding a club over
his ſhoulder, and wreathed about his temples and
loins with ivy, all proper.

Motto.] Pro Chriſto & Patria dulce Periculum.

Chief Seats.] At Bray, in the county of Bucks;
Hanover-ſquare, London.

58. WALDEGRAVE, EARL WALDEGRAVE.

THE Right Hon. JAMES WALDEGRAVE, Earl
WALDEGRAVE, Viſcount Chewton, Baron
Waldegrave of Chewton, and Baronet, a teller of the
Exchequer, lord warden and ſteward of the Stanne-
ries

ries and Dutchy of Cornwall, one of his Majefty's moft honourable privy council, and knight of the moft noble order of the garter, fucceeded James the late Earl, his father, in his honours and eftate, April 11, 1741; and married, in Dec. 1754, Mifs —— Drax, daughter of Henry Drax, Efq; member of parliament for Wareham, and fifter to the countefs of Berkeley; which Lady dying, he married, May 15, 1759, Maria, fecond daughter to Sir Edward Walpole, knight of the Bath, by whom he has a daughter, born March 24, 1760.

James, Earl Waldegrave, father of the prefent Earl, was created Vifcount Chewton, and Earl Waldegrave, Sept. 13, 1729. He married, in the year 1714, Mary, fecond daughter to Sir John Webb, of Hatherop, in Gloucefterfhire, Bart. by whom he had two fons and a daughter, viz.

1. James, the prefent Earl, born March 4, 1714-15.

2. Major-general John Waldegrave, a knight of the Bath, and groom of his Majefty's bedchamber; who, in 1751, married the Lady Elizabeth, daughter of John, Earl Gower, by whom he has iffue. His Lady was, in May 1758, delivered of two daughters.

3. Lady Henrietta, born Jan. 2, 1716-17, who married, July 7, 1734, to the Hon. Edward Herbert, only brother to the late Marquis of Powis, who died in November following, leaving her with child; and fhe was delivered in June, 1735, of a daughter, named Barbara.

This Earl was appointed ambaffador extraordinary and plenipotentiary to the Emperor of Germany in 1727; and ambaffador and plenipotentiary to the King of France in 1730.

Henry, grandfather of the prefent Earl, was created Lord Waldegrave on the 20th of January, 1685. His Lordfhip married Henrietta, natural daughter of King James II. by Mrs. Arabella Churchill, fifter to John, late Duke of Marlborough, and by her had iffue two fons and one daughter, viz.

1. James, late Earl Waldegrave.
2. Henry, who died unmarried. And,
3. Arabella, a nun.

This noble Earl is defcended from John de Walde-grave, who was fheriff of London in the year 1205, in the feventh year of King John.

Arms.] Party per pale, argent and gules.

Creft.] In a ducal coronet, or, a plume of five oftrich feathers, party per pale, argent and gules.

Supporters.] Two talbots, fable, eared, or, and each gorged with a mural coronet, argent, mafoned, fable.

Motto.] *Cælum non animum.*

Chief Seats.] Naveftoke in Effex; Albemarle-ftreet, London.

59. ASHBURNHAM, EARL of ASHBURNHAM.

THE Right Hon. JOHN ASHBURNHAM, Earl of ASHBURNHAM, Vifcount St. Afaph, and Baron of Afhburnham, one of the lords of his Majefty's bedchamber, ranger and keeper of Hyde-park, and St. James's-park, born Oct. 30, 1724, fucceeded his father John, the late Earl, March 10, 1736-7; and June 28, 1756, was married to Mifs Crawley, daugh-ter to John Crawley, Efq; late alderman of London, by whom he had a fon, Vifcount St. Afaph, born Feb. 2, 1758, who died the 13th of the fame month; and a daughter, born Nov. 8, 1759.

John, Baron of Afhburnham, father of the prefent Earl, was created Vifcount St. Afaph, and Earl of Afhburnham, May 14, 1730. His Lordfhip married to his firft wife, Oct. 21, 1710, the Lady Mary Butler, daughter to James, late Duke of Ormond, who dying without iffue, Jan. 2, 1712, in the 23d year of her age, he married, fecondly, July 24, 1714, Henrietta,

coun-

countcfs of Anglefea, who died June 26, 1718, in the thirty-firft year of her age, leaving an only daughter, the Lady Anne Afhburnham, who died unmarried Aug. 8, 1732. He married to his third wife the Lady Jemima Grey, fecond daughter to Henry, Duke of Kent; which Lady died July 27, 1731, leaving iffue John, the prefent Earl; and his Lordfhip died in the 49th year of his age.

This noble Earl is defcended from Piers, Lord Efhbernham, high fheriff of the counties of Surry, Suffex, and Kent, and conftable of Dover-caftle, in the reign of King Harold: he defended that caftle againft William the Conqueror to the laft extremity.

Arms.] Gules, a fefs between fix mullets, argent.

Creft.] Out of a ducal coronet, or, an afh-tree, proper.

Supporters.] Two greyhounds, fable, collared and chained, or.

Motto.] *Le Roy & l'Eftat.*

Chief Seats.] At Afhburnham in Suffex, and Teddington in Middlefex; Whitehall, Weftminfter.

---

60. HOWARD, EARL of EFFINGHAM.

THE Right Hon. THOMAS HOWARD, Earl of EFFINGHAM, Lord Howard, deputy earl-marfhal of England, colonel of the 34th regiment of foot, major-general, and one of the chief fearchers of the cuftoms in the port of London, fucceeded Francis, the late Earl, his father, in Feb. 1742-3, and married, Feb. 14, 1744-5, Elizabeth, daughter of Peter Beckford, Efq; grandfon of Sir Thomas Beckford, Knt. by whom he hath iffue,

1. Thomas Lord Howard, born Jan. 13, 1746-7.
2. Richard, born Feb. 29, 1747-8.
3. Lady Elizabeth.

4.

4. Lady Anne.

5. Lady Maria.

Francis Howard, late Earl of Effingham, father of the prefent Earl, was created Earl of Effingham, Dec. 8, 1731. His Lordfhip married Diana, daughter of major-general O Farrel, by whom he had iffue Thomas, the prefent Earl. After the death of which Lady he married Anne, fifter to Robert Briftow, Efq; by whom he had iffue a fon, named George, who died in his infancy.

This noble Earl is defcended from the Lord William Howard, fon of Thomas, the fecond Duke of Norfolk, who commanded the royal navy which defeated the Spanifh Armada in 1588. He alfo commanded the Englifh fleet in 1596, in that memorable expedition when Cadiz was taken, and all the Spanifh men of war and galleons in the harbour were deftroyed.

Arms and *Creft*.] The fame as the Duke of Norfolk's, a mullet for difference.

Supporters.] Two lions, argent; on the fhoulder of each a mullet for difference.

Motto.] *Virtus mille fcuta.*

Chief Seats.] At Great Bookham, in the county of Surry; and in Upper Grofvenor-ftreet, London.

---

61. WALPOLE, EARL of ORFORD.

THE Right Hon. GEORGE WALPOLE, Earl of ORFORD, Vifcount Walpole, Baron Walpole, and Baron of Haughton, one of the lords of his Majefty's bedchamber, lord lieutenant and cuftos rotulorum of the city and county of Norwich, and fteward of the corporation of Yarmouth, fucceeded his father Robert, April 1, 1751.

Robert, the late Earl, married Margaret, fole daughter and heir of Samuel Rolls, of Haynton in

Devonfhire,

Devonſhire, Eſq; by whom he had iſſue George, the preſent Earl, born April 2, 1730.

Sir Robert Walpole, father of the ſaid late Earl of Orford, was born in 1674, and choſen to repreſent the borough of King's-Lynn in parliament, in 1700, and ſerved for that corporation in every parliament almoſt, until he was created an Earl. He was conſtituted firſt lord commiſſioner of the Treaſury, and chancellor of the Exchequer, in Oct. 1715, which poſt he held during all the reign of King George I. and in the reign of King George II. until he was advanced to the peerage (except between the years 1717 and 1721) and he was, while a commiſſioner, elected knight of the garter in 1726, and created Earl of Orford, Feb. 9, 1741-2.

He married to his firſt wife Catharine, daughter of John Shorter, Eſq; by whom he had iſſue three ſons and one daughter.

1. Robert, the late Earl.

2. Sir Edward, clerk of the Pells in the Exchequer.

3. Horatio, uſher of the Exchequer. And,

4. Lady Mary, married, in 1723, to George Earl of Cholmondeley.

Their mother, Sir Robert's firſt wife, dying in 1737, he married, the ſame year, Mary Skerret, daughter and heir of Thomas Skerret, Eſq; who died in June 1738, by whom he had no iſſue after marriage.

This family took their name from Walpole in Norfolk, where they reſided before the conqueſt.

Arms.] Or, on a feſs between two chevrons, ſable, three croſs croſlets of the firſt.

Creſt.] On a wreath, the buſt of a man, ſide-faced, couped, proper, ducally crowned, with a long cap on, gules, thereon a catharine wheel, or; which creſt belonged to the family of Robſart, and was, in memory of the ſervices of Sir John Robſart, knight of the garter, againſt the Saracens.

H 5

Supporters.] On the dexter fide an antelope, and on the finifter fide a buck, both argent, attired, proper, gorged with collars, checky, or, and azure, each having a chain thereto affixed, and their hoofs or.

Motto.] *Fari quæ fentiat.*

Chief Seats.] At Houghton-Hall in the county of Norfolk; at Piddleton in the county of Dorfet; at Haynton in Devonfhire; and Green-ftreet, Grofvenor-fquare, London.

---

62. STANHOPE, EARL of HARRINGTON.

THE Right Hon. WILLIAM STANHOPE, Earl of HARRINGTON, Vifcount Peterfham, Baron of Harrington, lieutenant-general, colonel of the 2d troop of horfe-grenadier-guards, and comptroller of the cuftoms in the port of Dublin, fucceeded his father William, the late Earl, Dec. 8, 1756.

William, the late Earl, married Anne, daughter and heir of colonel Edward Griffith, by whom he had iffue two fons, William and Thomas, twins, born Dec. 18, 1719, of which their mother died in child-bed.

William, the prefent Earl, married, in Aug. 1746, to the Lady Caroline Fitz-Roy, eldeft daughter of his Grace Charles, late Duke of Grafton, by whom he hath iffue,

1. Lady Carolina, born March 11, 1746-7.
2. Lady Ifabella, born April 4, 1748.
3. Lady Emilia, born May 24, 1749.
4. Lady Henrietta, born Oct. 26, 1750.
5. Charles, Vifcount Peterfham, born March 20, 1753.
6. William-Fitzroy, born June 26, 1754.
7. Henry, born in 1755.
8. Lady ———, born March 31, 1760.

William

William the late Earl, was appointed ambaffador to Spain in 1729, and concluded the treaty of Seville there, Nov. 9, the fame year. He was, June 12, 1730, made one of his Majefty's principal fecretaries of ftate, and refigning the feals in 1741, was declared prefident of the council. He was conftituted fecretary of ftate again in 1744, upon the refignation of Earl Granville; and was, Nov. 4, 1746, conftituted lord lieutenant of Ireland; in which poft he was fucceeded by his Grace the Duke of Dorfet. As to the antiquity of this family, *fee the Earl of* Chefterfield.

Arms.] Quarterly, ermine and gules, a crefcent on a crefcent for difference.

Creft.] On a wreath, a tower, argent, with a demi-lion rampant, iffuing from the battlements, or, holding between his paws a grenade firing, proper.

Supporters.] On the dexter fide a talbot, argent, gutte de poix; on the finifter a wolf, erminois; each fupporter gorged with a garland or chaplet of oak, vert, fruéted, or.

Motto.] *A deo & rege.*

Chief Seats.] At Peterfham in Surry; at Linby in the county of Nottingham; and St. James's, Stable-yard, London.

---

63. PULTENEY, EARL of BATH.

THE Right Hon. WILLIAM PULTENEY, Earl of BATH, Vifcount Pulteney, Baron of Heydon, one of the lords of his Majefty's moft honourable privy council, and F. R. S. was appointed fecretary of war in Sept. 1714, and in May 1723, conftituted cofferer of his Majefty's houfhold, and fworn of the privy-council in Feb. 1741-2; alfo in July 1742, was created Baron of Heyden, Vifcount Pulteney, and Earl of Bath. His Lordfhip, Dec. 27,

1714,

1714, married Anna-Maria, daughter of John Gumeley, of Thiftleworth, in the county of Middlefex, Efq; by which Lady, who died Sept. 13, 1758, he has iffue one only fon, William Lord Vifcount Pulteney, promoted to the rank of lieutenant-general of his Majefty's forces, Aug. 25, 1759.

William Pulteney, Efq; father of the prefent Earl, married Mary, daughter of ——— Floyd, Efq; by whom he had iffue four fons, viz.

1. William, now Earl of Bath.

2. Henry Pulteney, Efq; lieutenant-general and colonel of the 13th regiment of foot.

3. Corbet, who was killed at the fiege of Lifle in 1708, unmarried.

4. Thomas, who alfo died unmarried.

Their father, the faid William Pulteney, Efq; married to his fecond wife Arabella, daughter of George Earl of Berkley, by whom he had three daughters, of which two died in their minority, and Elizabeth, the third daughter, died in France in 1748.

This noble Earl is defcended from Sir John Pulteney, who was four times lord-mayor of London, in the reign of King Edward III.

Arms.] Argent, a fefs dancettee, gules, in chief three leopards heads, fable.

Creft.] On a wreath, a leopard's head erafed, fable, gorged with a ducal coronet, or.

Supporters.] On each fide a leopard, argent, gutte de poix; collared dancette, gules.

Motto.] *Quo virtus.*

Chief Seat.] In Piccadilly, London.

64. WALLOP, EARL of PORTSMOUTH.

THE Right Hon. JOHN WALLOP, Earl of PORTSMOUTH, Vifcount Lymington, and Baron Wallop of Farley-Wallop, governor of the ifle of of Wight, conſtable of Cariſbroke-caſtle, ſteward, ſurveyor, receiver, and bailiff of all manors, lands, &c. in the iſland, and vice-admiral of the ſaid iſland, married, in 1716, Lady Bridget, eldeſt daughter of Charles Bennet, Earl of Tankerville, by which lady, who died Oct. 12, 1738, he had iſſue,

1. John Viſcount Lymington, born Aug. 3, 1718, married, July 12, 1740, Catharine, daughter and heir of John Conduit of Cranbery, in Hampſhire, by Catharine his wife, coheir of the celebrated Sir Iſaac Newton, and dying in 1749, left iſſue by his lady, who died April 15, 1750, three ſons, John, now Viſcount Lymington, Henry, Barton, and Bennet, alſo a daughter, Catharine.

2. Bridget, who died in June 1736.

3. Borlace, died in April 1741.

4. Mary, died young.

5. Charles.

6. Anne, who died March 3, 1759.

The four following, Bluet, Elizabeth, Henry, and Bennet, died young.

His Lordſhip married, 2dly, Elizabeth, eldeſt daughter to James Lord Griffin, and relict of Henry Grey of Billingbear, in the county of Berks, Eſq;

This noble Earl is deſcended from the Wallops of Hampſhire, a Saxon family, which were poſſeſſed of lands of a conſiderable value in that county, at the time of the conqueſt.

Arms.] Argent, a bend wavy, ſable.

Creſt.] On a wreath, a mermaid, holding in her dexter hand a mirror, in the other a comb, all proper.

Supporters.] Two chamois, or wild goats, ſable.

Motto.] *En ſuivant la veriete.*

Chief Seats.] At Huſbands, in Hants; and Billing-bear in the county of Berks; and New Burlington-ſtreet, London.

65. GRE-

65. GREVILE, EARL BROOKE.

THE Right Hon. Francis Grevile, Earl Brooke and Warwick, and Lord Brooke, Baron Brooke of Beauchamp-court in Warwickſhire, lord lieutenant and cuſtos rotulorum of the county of Warwick, knight of the moſt antient and noble order of St. Andrew, born in 1719, ſucceeded his father William as Lord Brooke, in July 1727; and July 7, 1746, was created Earl Brooke of Warwick-caſtle in the county of Warwick ; and, on the death of the late Earl of Warwick, was created Earl of Warwick, Nov. 27, 1759. His Lordſhip married, May 16, 1742, the Hon. Elizabeth Hamilton, eldeſt daughter to the Lord Archibald Hamilton, by whom he had iſſue,

1. George Lord Grevile, born September 16, 1746.

2. Charles-Francis, born May 12, 1749.

3. Louiſa-Auguſta, born April 14, 1743.

4. Frances-Elizabeth, born May 11, 1744.

5. Charlotte-Mary, born July 6, 1745.

6. Iſabella, born March 1, 1748, who died the ſame day.

7. Charles-Francis, born May 12, 1749. And,

8. Robert Fulke, born Feb. 3, 1750-1.

William Lord Brooke, father of the preſent Earl, married Mary, ſecond daughter and coheir of the Hon. Henry Thynne, Eſq; and by her (who died March 29, 1720) had iſſue three ſons, viz.

1. William, who died in his infancy.

2. Fulke-Grevile, who alſo died young. And,

3. Francis, now Earl Brooke.

The ſaid William Lord Brooke, their father, died July 28, 1727, in the thirty-third year of his age.

The

The anceftors of this noble family are of Norman extraction, and came over to England with William the Conqueror, who conferred manors and lands on them in England, of a confiderable value; and at length they obtained the government of the caftle of Warwick, the prefent feat of the family.

Arms.] Sable, on a crofs, within a border ingrailed, or, five pellets.

Creft.] In a ducal coronet, or, a fwan, with wings expanded, argent; beaked, fable.

Supporters.] Two fwans, argent; beaked and membered, fable; and ducally gorged, or.

Motto.] *Vix ea noftra voco.*

Chief Seats.] At Warwick-caftle in Warwickfhire; at Richmond in the county of Surry; and Grofvenor-fquare, London.

---

66. GOWER, EARL GOWER.

THE Right Hon. GRANVILLE-LEVESON GOWER, Earl GOWER, Vifcount Trentham, and Lord Gower, Baron of Sittenham, and Baronet, mafter of the horfe, lord lieutenant and cuftos rotulorum of the county of Stafford, governor of the Charter-houfe, and one his Majefty's moft honourable privy-council.

He married, in 1744, Elizabeth, daughter of Nicholas Fazakerley, Efq; who died of the fmall-pox, May 19, 1745, by whom he had a fon named John, who died the fame day. He married to his fecond wife, March 31, 1748, the Lady Louifa Egerton, daughter of George Duke of Bridgwater, by whom he hath iffue,

1. Lady Louifa, born Oct. 22, 1749.
2. Lady Carolina, born Nov. 2, 1753.
3. A fon born dead, Aug. 16, 1755.
4. George Vifcount Trentham, born in Feb. 1758.

2   Sir

Sir John Levefon Gower, Bart. grandfather of the prefent Earl, was created a peer of Great Britain, by the title of Lord Gower, and Baron of Stittenham, in the county of York, March 16, 1702-3, 2 Ann. He married the Lady Catharine, eldeft daughter to John Duke of Rutland, and by her had iffue four fons and two daughters.

1. Catharine, who died April 20, 1712, in the 17th year of her age.

2. Jane, married to John Proby, of Elton-Hall, Efq; who died in childbed June 10, 1726.

3. John, the late Earl Gower, who married, in 1712, the Lady Evelyn Pierpoint, youngeft daughter to —— Evelyn, late Duke of Kingfton ; and by her had iffue four fons and fix daughters. This Lady dying in 1727, his Lordfhip, in 1733, married Penelope, daughter of Sir John Stonehoufe, Bart. and relict of Sir Henry Atkins, Bart. by whom he had only one daughter. This Lady dying in 1735, he married the Lady Mary, daughter and coh.ir of Anthony Earl of Thanet, by whom he had iffue one daughter and three fons.

4. William, who, on May 26, 1730, was married to Anne, fifter to Sir Richard Grofvenor, of Eaton-Hall, Bart. which Lady died Dec. 13, the year following.

5. Thomas, who died Aug. 12, 1727, in the 29th year of his age.   And,

6. Baptift.

This ancient family are lineally defcended from Sir Allan Gower, fheriff of the county of York, and Lord of Sittenham in that county, at the time of the Norman conqueft ; which eftate of Sittenham is in poffeffion of the prefent Earl.

John Gower, fon of Sir Thomas Gower, cotem-porary with Chaucer, or rather his mafter, one of his lordfhip's anceftors, is efteemed one of the beft poets of that age, and a great improver of the Eng.ifh language.

language. He died in a very advanced age in the year 1402.

Arms.] Quarterly, firſt and fourth, barry of eight, argent and gules; over all, a croſs-flory, ſable, for Gower. Second and third, azure, three laurel-leaves erect, or, for Leveſon.

Creſt.] On a wreath, a wolf paſſant, argent; collared and chained, or.

Supporters.] Two wolves, argent, each having a collar and main, or.

Motto.] *Frangas, non flectes.*

Chief Seats.] At Trentham in the county of Stafford; at Sittenham in Yorkſhire; at Bill-Hill, near Ockingham in Berkſhire; and Upper Brook-ſtreet, London.

67. HOBART, EARL OF BUCKINGHAMSHIRE.

THE Right Hon. JOHN HOBART, Earl of BUCKINGHAMSHIRE, Lord Hobart, Baron Hobart of Blickling, and Baronet, comptroller of his Majeſty's houſhold, one of the lords of his Majeſty's bedchamber and privy-council, ſucceeded the late Earl John, his father, Sept. 22, 1756.

John, the late Earl, born in 1692, was created Lord Hobart, and Baron Hobart of Blickling in the county of Norfolk, May 28, 1728; alſo on Aug. 20, 1746, was created Earl of Buckinghamſhire. His Lordſhip married, to his firſt wife, Judith, daughter to Robert Brittiffe, of Baconſthorp, in Norfolk, Eſq; by whom he had iſſue three ſons, viz.

1. Henry, who died an infant.

2. John, the preſent Earl.

3. Robert, who died young in 1733.

Alſo five daughters, of whom Dorothy only is living, married to Capt. Hotham, of the foot-guards,

aid

aid-de-camp to Lord Ligonier, and eldeft fon of Beaumont Hotham, Efq; one of the commiffioners of the cuftoms.

His Lady dying in 1726, he married in 1728, Elizabeth, fifter to Robert Briftow, Efq; by whom he had two fons, viz.

1. George, member of parliament for St. Ives, and married, in May 1757, to Albina, daughter of Lord Vere Bertie, by whom he has a fon born March 3, 1758, and another born May 5, 1760.

2. Henry.

Sir Henry Hobart, Bart. lord chief juftice of the common-pleas, was one of the anceftors of this noble Earl, whofe reports are ftill in much efteem among the learned of the law.

Arms.] Sable, a ftar of eight rays, or, between two flanches, ermine.

Creft.] On a wreath, a bull paffant, party per-pale, fable and gules, all bezanty, and a ring in his nofe, or.

Supporters.] On the dexter fide a ftag; on the finifter, a talbot; both proper, reguardant, each having a radiant collar and line, or.

Motto.] *Auctor pretiofa facit.*

Chief Seats.] At Blickling in the county of Norfolk; and at Hill ftreet, London.

68. FITZ-WILLIAM, EARL FITZ-WILLIAM.

THE Right Hon. WILLIAM FITZ-WILLIAM, Earl FITZ-WILLIAM, Vifcount Milton, Lord Fitz-William, and Baron of Milton in England; alfo Earl Fitz-William, Vifcount Milton, and Baron Fitz-William of Liffer, or Lifford in Ireland, was born May 30, 1748, and fucceeded his father William, the late Earl, who died Aug. 10, 1756.

The

The late Earl, on June 22, 1744, married the Lady Anne Wentworth, eldeſt daughter of Thomas Marquis of Rockingham, by which Lady, who died May 4, 1759, beſides the preſent Earl, he has left iſſue ſix daughters, viz.

1. Lady Anne, born March 25, 1744.
2. Lady Charlotte, born July 14, 1746.
3. Lady Frances, born Oct. 22, 1750.
4. Lady Amelia-Maria, born Dec. 12, 1751.
5. Lady Henrietta, born March 20, 1753.   And,
6. Lady Dorothy, born May 22, 1754.

This noble Earl is deſcended from Sir William Fitz-William, marſhal of the army of William the Conqueror, at the battle of Haſtings in Suſſex, by which victory that prince made his way to the throne of England.

Sir William Fitz-William, another of the anceſtors of this noble Earl, was three times conſtituted lord lieutenant of Ireland, in the reign of Queen Elizabeth, and was five times one of the lords juſtices of that kingdom, and general and commander in chief of the army there ; and having ſerved her Majeſty in that kingdom near thirty years, ſhe permitted him to return to England, where he died in a very advanced age, in the year 1599.

Arms.] Lozenges, argent, and gules.

Creſt.] In a ducal coronet, or, a triple plume of feathers, argent.

Supporters.] Two ſavage men, proper; wreathed about their heads and waiſts, vert; and in their exterior hands a tree eradicated, the top broken off, alſo proper.

Motto.] *Appetitus, rationi, pareat.*

Chief Seats.] At Milton in the county of Northampton ; and St. James's-ſqnare, London.

69, HER-

69. H E R B E R T,   E A R L OF
P O W I S.

THE Right Hon. HENRY-ARTHUR HERBERT, Earl of Powis, Vifcount Ludlow, Lord Herbert of Cherbury, Baron Powis of Powis-caftle, and Baron Herbert of Cherbury and of Ludlow, lord lieutenant and cuftos rotulorum of the county of Salop, and lieutenant-general of his Majefty's forces, was created Lord Herbert of Cherbury, Dec. 21, 1743; and, on the death of William Herbert, Marquis of Powis, who died March 8, 1747-8, and left his Lordfhip his whole eftate, he was farther advanced to the dignity of Baron Powis, of Powis-caftle, Vifcount Ludlow, and Earl of Powis, May 27, 21 Geo. II. and was alfo created Lord Herbert, Baron Herbert of Cherbury, and of Ludlow, Oct. 7, 1749 ; and in default of iffue male, to defcend to Richard Herbert, Efq; his brother, and his heirs male ; and in default of fuch iffue, to Francis Herbert, of Ludlow in the county of Salop, Efq; and the heirs male of his body.

His Lordfhip married, March 30, 1751, Barbara, only daughter and heir of the Hon. Edward Herbert, Efq; only brother of William Marquis of Powis ; and of his wife the Lady Henrietta, only daughter of James Earl of Waldegrave, by whom he hath iffue two daughters and a fon, viz.

1. Lady Georgina, born Jan. 10, 1752.

2. Lady Augufta, born Sept. 18, 1753.

3. George Edward Arthur Henry, Lord Vifcount Ludlow, born July 7, 1755.

4. Lady ——, born Oct. 9, 1757.

Sir Francis Herbert, Bart. father of the prefent Earl, married Dorothy, daughter of John Oldbury, of London, Merchant, and dying Feb. 27, 1718-19, left iffue five fons and three daughters, viz.

1. Henry

1. Henry Arthur, the prefent Earl.

2. Richard, who died May 16, 1754.

3. Francis, who died unmarried in 1730.

4. Herbert; and,

5. John, who both died in the year 1719.

6. Urania, married to Coulfton Fellows, of Eggef-ford in Devonfhire, Efq; then knight of the fhire for the county of Huntington.

7. Dorothy, married to John Harris, of Pickwell in Devonfhire, Efq;

8. Florentia, who died in the year 1720.

This noble Earl is defcended from —— Herbert, a natural fon of King Henry I. of which family there have been as many brave and worthy men as any family in the Britifh peerage has produced.

Arms.] Party-per-pale, azure and gules, three lions rampant, argent; armed and langued, or.

Creft.] On a wreath, a wyvern, with wings expanded, vert, holding in his mouth a finifter hand, couped at the wrift, gules.

Supporters.] On the dexter fide, a lion, argent, femee of rofes, armed and langued, gules. And on the finifter fide, a lion, azure; femee of flower-de-lis, or.

Motto.] *Fortitudine & Prudentia.*

Chief Seats.] At Powis-caftle, in Montgomery-fhire; at Oakley-park, in Shropfhire; in Berkeley-fquare, London.

70. PERCY-SMITHSON, EARL of NORTHUMBERLAND.

THE Right Hon. HUGH PERCY-SMITHSON, Earl of NORTHUMBERLAND, Lord and Baron of Warkworth, and Baronet, knight of the moft noble order of the garter, one of the lords of his Majefty's bedchamber, lord lieutenant and cuftos ro-tulorum

tulorum of the county of Northumberland, and F. R. S. grandfon and heir of Sir Hugh Smithfon, of Stonwick in Yorkfhire, Bart. on the death of Algernon Seymour, late Duke of Somerfet, was created Earl of Northumberland, and Baron of Warkworth in the fame county, on the 7th of February, 1749-50. His Lordfhip married, July 18, 1740, the Lady Elizabeth Seymour, only daughter of Algernon Seymour, late Duke of Somerfet, and Earl of Northumberland and Egremont, by whom he hath iffue two fons and one daughter. *See Baronefs* PERCY.

1. Hugh, Lord Warkworth, born Aug. 14, 1742.

2. Algernon, born Jan. 21, 1749-50. And,

3. The Lady Elizabeth Anne Frances, born April 6, 1744.

This noble Earl is defcended from the family of the Smithfons, of Newfham in Yorkfhire, which appears to have been poffeffed of lands in that county in the reign of King Richard II.

Arms.] Quarterly, firft and fourth, azure, five fufils in fefs, or; the arms of Percy, fecond and third, or, a lion rampant, azure; the arms of the Dukes of Brabant.

Creft.] On a chapeau, gules; a lion paffant, azure.

Supporters.] On the dexter fide, a lion, azure; on the finifter an unicorn, argent, collared gabonè, or, and azure.

Motto.] *Efperance en Dieu.*

Chief Seats.] At Sion-houfe, near Brentford; and Tottenham, both in the county of Middlefex; Warkworth, Alnwick, and Prudhoe caftles, in the county of Northumberland; Stanwick and Ayrmin in Yorkfhire; and at Northumberland-houfe, London.

71. WYNDHAM, EARL OF EGREMONT.

THE Right Hon. CHARLES WYNDHAM, Earl of Egremont, Lord and Baron of Cockermouth, and Baronet, lord lieutenant and custos rotulorum of the county of Cumberland, succeeded his father Sir William Wyndham, Baronet, in 1740; and on the death of Algernon, Duke of Somerset, his uncle, without issue male, was created Earl of Egremont, and Baron of Cockermouth, in the county of Cumberland, to him and his heirs male; and in default of such issue, to descend to his brother Percy Wyndham-Obrien, now Earl of Thomond in Ireland. His Lordship, March 12, 1750-1, married Alicia Maria, daughter of George, Lord Carpenter, by whom he has,

1. George, Lord Cockermouth, born Dec. 7, 1751.
2. Lady Elizabeth Alicia Maria, born Nov. 30, 1752.
3. Lady Frances, born July 10, 1755.
4. Lady ———, born Sept. 5, 1756.
5. A son, born Oct. 8, 1759.

Sir William Wyndham, Baronet, father of the present Earl, only son of Sir Edward Wyndham, Bart. was master of the buck-hounds, secretary at war, chancellor of the Exchequer, and also of the privy-council to her late Majesty Queen Anne. He married to his first wife, July 21, 1708, the Lady Catherine Seymour, second daughter of his Grace Charles, Duke of Somerset, by whom he had two sons and two daughters, viz.

1. Charles, now Earl of Egremont.
2. Percy Obrien, now Earl of Thomond in Ireland. *See Earl of* Thomond *in the* Irish *Peerage.*
3. Catherine, who died unmarried in April, 1734. And,
4. Elizabeth, married, in 1749, to the Honourable
George

George Grenville, Efq; one of the lords of the treafury.

His firft Lady dying, he married the Lady Maria-
Catherine, widow of the Marquis of Blandford, and
daughter of M. Peter d'Jong, of Utrecht in the Netherlands, by whom he had no iffue.

This noble Earl is defcended from Ailwardus, a
Saxon of diftinction, who refiding at Wymondham,
now Wyndham, in the county of Norfolk, took the
furname of Wyndham from thence.

Arms.] Azure, a chevron between three lions
heads, erafed, or.

Creft.] A lion's head, erafed, within a fetter-lock,
or.

Supporters.] On the dexter fide, a lion rampant,
azure, winged invertedly, or; on the finifter fide, a
gryphon, argent, guttè de fang.

Motto.] *Au bon Droit.*

Chief Seats.] At Orchard-Wyndham, and Witham,
in Somerfetfhire; Petworth, in the county of Suffex;
and Wrefil-caftle in Yorkfhire; Privy-garden, London.

72. GRENVILLE-TEMPLE, EARL TEMPLE.

THE Right Hon. RICHARD GRENVILLE-TEM-
PLE, Earl TEMPLE, Vifcount and Baron Cobham, lord privy-feal, and lord lieutenant of the
county of Buckingham, a knight of the garter, was
born Sept. 26, 1711. He married, May 9, 1737,
Anna, one of the daughters and coheirs of Thomas
Chambers, in the county of Middlefex, Efq; and had
one only daughter by her, who died July 14, 1742.

The title of Vifcountefs Cobham being limited to
Mrs. Grenville, and her heirs male, after the death
of her brother the late Lord Vifcount Cobham without iffue, fhe became Vifcountefs Cobham on her
brother

brother Lord Cobham's death, which happened Sept,
13, 1749, and in October following she was created
Countess Temple; and dying Oct. 7, 1752, the Earldom descended on the Hon. Richard Grenville Temple, the present Earl, commonly called Lord Vifcount Cobham, at that time member of parliament
for Buckingham. In Dec. 1756, his Lordship was
appointed first commissioner of the admiralty, which
office he resigned in April 1757, when he was appointed lord privy seal.

Besides this noble Lord, Mrs. Grenville had issue,

2. The Hon. George Grenville, treasurer of the
navy, and one of his Majesty's most honourable privy
council.   He married Elizabeth, daughter of Sir William Wyndham, Bart. by whom he has several children.

3. Henry, who died in May, 1716.

4. James, one of the lords commissioners of the
treasury, who married the daughter of James Smyth,
of Harding in Hertfordshire, Esq; who died Dec.
14, 1757.

5. Henry, late governor of Barbadoes. He married,
Oct. 11, 1757, Margaret, daughter of —— Banks,
Esq; and has one daughter, born August 2, 1758.

6. Thomas, who was killed on board his Majesty's ship the Defiance, which he commanded, in
an engagement with a French squadron, which was
taken and destroyed May 3, 1747.

7. Lady Hester, married to the Right Hon. William Pitt, Esq; one of his Majesty's principal secretaries of state, and has issue a son, born Oct. 10, 1756;
another son, born May 28, 1759; and a daughter,
born April 22, 1758.

Hester, the late Countess Temple, mother of the
present Earl, was daughter of Sir Richard Temple, a
knight of the Bath, who married Mary, daughter of
—— Knap, of Weston in the county of Oxford, Esq;

I   and

and had four fons and fix daughters, of which two died young.

Chriftian, the third daughter, was married to Sir Thomas Lyttleton, of Frankley in the county of Worcefter, Bart. Maria, firft to Dr. Weft, prebendary of Winchefter; and, 2dly, to Sir John Langham, of Cottefbroke in the county of Northampton, Bart. Hefter, the fecond daughter, late Countefs Temple, married to Richard Grenville, of Wotton in Bucks, Efq; and Penelope to Mofes Berenger, of the city of London, Efq;

Of the fons, which were Richard, Purbeck, Henry, and Arthur, the three laft died unmarried; and Richard was created Vifcount Cobham on the 19th of October, 1714. He married Anne, daughter to Edmund Halfey, Efq; member of parliament for Southwark; by which Lady, who died March 29, 1760, he had no iffue; and his Lordfhip dying, was fucceeded, purfuant to the limitation, by his eldeft furviving fifter Hefter, the late Countefs Temple.

This branch of the family of Grenville, or Granville, has been feated at Wotton under Barnwood in Buckinghamfhire, ever fince the reign of King Henry I. being more than 600 years.

Arms.] Quarterly, in the firft and fourth, vert, on a crofs, argent, five torteaux, gules, for Grenville. In the fecond and third, for Temple, quarterly, or, an eagle difplayed, fable and argent; two bars, fable, each charged with three martlets, or.

Creft.] In a ducal coronet, a martlet clofe, or.

Supporters.] On the dexter, a lion party-per-fefs embattled, or, and gules; on the finifter, a horfe, argent, powdered, with eaglets, fable.

Motto.] *Templa quam dilecta.*

Chief Seats.] At Stow and Wotton, both in Bucks; Pall-Mall, London.

73. HARCOURT, EARL of HARCOURT.

THE Right Honourable SIMON HARCOURT Earl of HARCOURT, Lord Vifcount Newnham, and Baron Harcourt, one of the Lords of his Majefty's privy council, Lieutenant General, and F. R. S. fucceeded Simon, late Lord Vifcount Harcourt, his grand-father, July 29, 1727, as Lord Vifcount Harcourt; was created Earl Harcourt, of Stanton Harcourt, and Vifcount Newnham, in Oct. 1749. His Lordfhip married Rebecca, daughter and heir of Charles Le Bafs, Efq; by whom he has iffue, two fons and two daughters, viz.

1. George-Simon Vifcount Newnham, born Aug. 1, 1736.

2. William, born March 20, 1742-3.

3, Lady Elizabeth, born Jan. 18, 1738-9. And,

4. Lady Anne, born in June, 1741, who is fince dead.

Simon Harcourt, the father of the prefent Earl, married Mifs Elizabeth Evelyn, daughter of John Evelyn, Efq; and dying in 1721, he left iffue, two daughters and one fon, viz.

1. Elizabeth.

2. Martha, who married George Venables Vernon, of Sudbury, in Derbyfhire, Efq;

3. Simon, the prefent Earl.

Simon, Lord Vifcount Harcourt, Grandfather of the prefent earl, was Attorney-General, in 1707, in the reign of Queen Anne, and 1710 was conftituted Lord Keeper of the Great Seal of England, and was advanced to the poft of Lord High Chancellor of Great Britain, April 17, 1712. In the reign of King George I. he was one of the Lords of his Majefty's privy-council, and in the years 1723, 1725, and 1727, was one of the Lords Juftices, during his Majefty's abfence in his German dominions.

l 2   This

This noble Earl is defcended from the Harcourts of Normandy, who took their name from a place called Harcourt, in that province, where the family ufually refided.   Gervaife, Count de Harcourt, with his two fons, Jeffery and Arnold, came over with the conqueror, when he invaded England, in 1066.

Arms.] Gules, two bars, or.

Creft.] In a ducal coronet, or, a peacock clofe, proper.

Supporters.] Two lions, or, each gorged with two bars gemels, gules.

Motto.] *Le bon temps viendra.*

Chief Seats.] At Stanton-Harcourt, Cokethrop, and Newnham, all in the county of Oxford;   Cavendifh-fquare, London.

74. SEYMOUR-CONWAY, EARL of HERTFORD.

THE Right Honourable FRANCIS SEYMOUR-CONWAY, Earl of HERTFORD, Vifcount Beauchamp, Lord Conway, Baron of Ragley, and Baron of Killultagh in Ireland, knight of the moft noble order of the garter, one of his Majefty's privy council, a lord of his Majefty's bedchamber, and lord lieu-tenant and cuftos rotulorum of the county of War-wick, fucceeded his father Francis as Lord Conway, Feb. 4, 1731-2, and was created Vifcount Beauchamp, and Earl of Hertford, Aug. 3, 1750.   His lordfhip married in May 1741, Lady Ifabella Fitz-Roy, fecond daughter of his Grace, Charles, late Duke of Grafton, by whom he has iffue,

1. Francis, Lord Vifcount Beauchamp, born Feb. 12, 1742-3.

2. Lady Anne, born Aug. 1, 1744.

3. Henry, born Dec. 15, 1746.

4. Lady-Sarah-Frances, born Sept. 27, 1747.

5. Robert,

5. Robert, born Dec. 20, 1748.

And the ladies, 6. Gertrude, 7. Frances, 8. Elizabeth, and 9. another daughter born Jan. 4, 1756.

Francis, late Lord Conway, father of the prefent earl, was created Baron Conway of Ragley, in the county of Warwick, and Baron Conway of Killultagh, in the county of Antrim in Ireland, March 17, 1702-3. His Lordfhip married the Lady Mary Hyde, third daughter of Lawrence, Earl of Rochefter, and by her, who died on the 23d of January, 1708-9, had iffue, four daughters, viz. Letitia, Mary, Henrietta, and Catherine, of which the eldeft only is living. He married, 2dly, Jane, daughter of——Bowden, Efq; by whom he had iffue, a daughter, named Jane, of whom fhe died in child-bed, Feb. 13, 1715-16. He married, 3dly, Charlotte, daughter of Sir John Shorter, by whom he left iffue, two fons and one daughter, viz.

1. Francis, now Earl of Hertford.

2. Henry, Lieut. General of his majefty's forces, married the Countefs Dowager of Ailesbury, and daughter of General Campbell, by whom he has a daughter, Anne.

3. Anne, married, in 1755, to John Harris, Efq; of Hayne, in Devonfhire.

This noble lord is a branch of the family of the ancient dukes of Somerfet, nearly related to the crown.

Arms.] Quarterly, firft and fourth, Sable, on a bend, cottized, argent; a rofe between two annulets, gules, for Conway, 2 and 3 quarters are quarterly, viz. 1 and 4, or; on a pile, gules between fix fleurs-de-lis, azure; three lions paffant, guardant, or, being a coat of augmentation, 2d and 3d, gules; two wings conjoined in lure, or, for Seymour.

Creft.] On a wreath, the buft of a Moor, fide-faced, couped, proper; and wreathed about the temples, argent and azure.

I 3 *Sup-*

Supporters.] Two Moors, each wreathed as the creft, holding in their exterior hands a fhield, azure, garnifhed, or; the dexter charged with the fun in its glory, the other with a crefcent, argent.

Motto.] *Fide & amore.*

Chief Seats.] At Sandywell in the county of Gloucef-ter; Taplow in Bucks; Ragley in Warwickfhire; Lif-burne in Ireland; Grofvenor-ftreet, London.

75. NORTH, EARL OF GUILFORD.

THE Right Honourable FRANCIS NORTH, Earl of GUILFORD, Lord North and Guilford, one of the lords of his Majefty's bed-chamber, was born April 13, 1704, and fucceeded his father in 1729, as Lord Guilford. Oct. 31, 1734, he fucceeded to the title of Lord North, by the death of William Lord North and Grey; and on the 8th of March 1752, was created Earl of Guilford.

His lordfhip married the 16th June, 1728, the Lady Lucy, daughter of George, late Earl of Halifax, by whom he has iffue, 1. one fon, named Frederick, Lord North, born the 13th of April, 1732; who on the 20th of May, 1756, was married to Mifs Speke, of Dillington in Somerfet, a great heirefs, by whom he had a fon, George Auguftus, born in 1757, and a daughter born Feb. 16, 1760; and 2. a daughter named Lucy, who died an infant; and his lady dying May 7, 1734, he married again in Jan. 1735-6, Elizabeth, relict of George, Lord Vifcount Lewifham, eldeft fon of William, Earl of Dartmouth, by whom he had iffue,

3. Lady Louifa.

4. Francis, deceafed.

5. Brownlow. And,

6. Charlotte, who died in 1748.

And

And his fecond lady dying, his lordfhip married Mary, relict of Lewis Watfon, Earl of Rockingham, in June, 1751.

Francis, the late Lord Guilford, father of the prefent lord, married firft, Elizabeth, third daughter to Fulk Greville Lord Brooke, but by her had no iffue. 2dly, Alice, daughter and one of the coheirs of Sir John Brownlow of Belton, by whom he had iffue three fons. 1. Francis, now Earl of Guilford, 2. Brownlow, 3. Peregrine, who both died infants; and a daughter Alice, who died unmarried.

This noble lord is lineally defcended from Sir Edward North, who was advanced to the dignity of a baron under the title of Lord North, in the firft year of the reign of Queen Mary.

Creations.] Baron North of Kirtling in the county of Cambridgefhire, by writ of fummons to parliament, the 17th of Feb. 1553, 1 Mary; and Baron Guilford, by letters patent, the 27th of September, 1683, 35 Car. II. and Earl of Guilford, 1752.

Arms.] A lion paffant, or, between three fleurs-de-lis, argent.

Creft.] On a wreath a dragon's head erafed, fable, ducally gorged and chained, or.

Supporters.] Two dragons ducally gorged and chained, or, winged, fable.

Motto.] *Animo & fide.*

Chief Seats.] At Kirtlage in Cambridgefhire; at Durdans in Surry; at Wroxton-abbey in Oxford-fhire; and Grofvenor-fquare, London.

76. CORNWALLIS, EARL CORNWALLIS.

THE Right Honourable CHARLES CORNWAL-LIS, Earl CORNWALLIS, Vifcount Brome, Lord Cornwallis of Eye, conftable of the tower of

London, Lord Lieutenant of the Tower hamlets, and one of the Lords of his Majesty's most honourable privy council, was born the 29th of March, 1700, and succeeded his father Charles as Lord Cornwallis, the 19th of January, 1721-2.

He married in 1722, Elizabeth, daughter of Charles, the late Lord Viscount Townshend, by whom he has issue, four sons: Charles, born Dec. 31, 1738; Harry, born Sept. 10, 1740; James, born Feb. 25, 1742; and William, born Feb, 20, 1743; and three daughters, the Lady Elizabeth, who married in 1753, to Bowen Southwell, Esq; Charlotte, who married in 1756, to the Rev. Dr. Madan of Chiswick, and Mary.

Charles, the late and third Lord Cornwallis, married in June, 1699, Charlotte, daughter and sole heir to Richard Butler, Earl of Arran, by whom he had nine sons and three daughters. 1. Charles, Earl Cornwallis. 2. James, born Sept. 16, 1701, died May 28, 1727. 3. Stephen, born Dec. 23, 1703 died in May 1743. 4. John, born Dec. 23, 1706. 5. Richard, born Sept. 17, 1708, died in Feb. 1740-1. 6. Edward, born Feb. 22, 1712-13, a major-general in the army, and member of parliament for the city of West-minster, married March 17, 1753, to Miss Maria Townshend, daughter to the late Lord Townshend. 7. Frederick, a twin with Edward, Lord Bishop of Litchfield and Coventry. 8. William, born March 12, 1713-14, deceased. 9. Henry, born May 22, 1715, deceased. 10. Charlotte. 11. Elizabeth, both died infants. 12. Mary, died unmarried.

Of this noble family which has been long of great repute in Norfolk and Suffolk, was John Cornwallis, Esq; who in 1377, the 1st of Richard II. was sheriff of London.

Creations.] Baron Cornwallis of Eye in Suffolk, by Letters patent, the 20th of April, 1661, 13 Car. II. Viscount Broome in the county of Suffolk, and Earl Cornwallis, the 30th of June, 1753, 27 Geo. II.

Arms.

Arms.] Quarterly, firſt and fourth, ſable, gutty, d'eau, on the feſs, argent, three Corniſh choughs, proper.

Creſt.] On a wreath, a mount, vert, and thereon a ſtag lodged, argent, attired, or, having about his neck a garland of laurel, proper.

Supporters.] Two ſtags attired and gorged, argent.

Motto.] *Virtus, vincit invidiam.*

Chief Seats.] At Broome in Suffolk; at Culford-hall in the ſame county; Hill-ſtreet, London.

77. YORKE, EARL of HARDWICKE.

THE Right Hon. Philip Yorke, Earl of Hard-wicke, Viſcount Royſton, Lord Hardwicke, Baron Hardwicke, lord high ſteward of the univerſity of Cambridge, and one of his Majeſty's moſt honourable privy council.

He was, on the 23d of March, 1720, appointed ſolicitor-general to the late King George; and on the 31ſt of January, 1723, attorney-general.

In Oct. 1733, he was conſtituted lord chief juſtice of the King's Bench; and on the 21ſt of Feb. 1736-7, lord-high-chancellor, which office he reſigned in 1756.

In July 1749, he was choſen high ſteward of the univerſity of Cambridge.

His Lordſhip married Margaret, one of the daughters of Charles Cocks, of the city of Worceſter, Eſq; by whom he hath five ſons and two daughters now living.

1. Philip, Lord Viſcount Royſton.

2. Charles, of Lincoln's-Inn; who, with his brother John, had the office of clerk of the crown in the court of Chancery conferred on them, June 27, 20 Geo. II. He was choſen in the laſt parliament, member for Rygate, as alſo in the preſent parliament; and in

I 5

May, 1755, married Miss Catherine Freeman, daughter of William Freeman, of Hertfordshire, Esq; by which lady, who died July 10, 1759, he has a daughter, born the fifteenth of February 1756.

3. Joseph was captain of a company in the first regiment of foot guards, with the rank of lieutenant-colonel, and aid-de-camp to his Royal Highness the Duke, at the battle of Fontenoy, in 1745. In 1749, when the Earl of Albemarle went ambassador extraordinary to the French court, he went over secretary to the embassy: and being aid-de-camp to his majesty, he was, in Sept. 1751, appointed minister plenipotentiary to the states-general. He was chosen a member in the last parliament for East-Grinstead in Sussex, as also in the present parliament, which met May 31, 1754; and was constituted colonel of a regiment of foot, March 29, 1755, and major general.

4. John, who with his brother Charles, is clerk of the crown, was in November, 1753, elected member of parliament for Higham Ferrers in Northamptonshire, in the room of John Hill, Esq; and serves for the same place in the present parliament.

5. The Rev. and Hon. James York, was ordained at Cambridge, in April 1754; and soon after on a vacancy, made a prebend of Bristol, and rector of great Horsley in Essex.

His lordship's two daughters were, Lady Elizabeth, married to George, Lord Anson, and died June 1, 1760; and Lady Margaret, married in 1749, to John Heathcote, Esq; son and heir of Sir John Heathcote, Bart.

His eldest son Philip, now Lord Viscount Royston, on the 14th of Dec. 1738, was appointed one of the tellers of the exchequer; and on the 22d of May, 1740, was married to the lady Jemima Campbell, only daughter of John, now Earl of Breadalbin, by the Lady Amabel Grey, eldest daughter and coheir of Henry de Grey, late Duke of Kent, by whom he has two daughters, Amabel, born the 2d of Jan, 1750-1,

I.   and

and Mary Jemima, born Feb. 9, 1756; and her Ladyship, by defcent from his Grace the faid Duke of Kent, is Marchionefs Grey. His Lordship in Sept. 1757, was appointed Lord Lieutenant of the county of Cambridge.

Arms.] Argent, a faltire, azure, with a bezant in the center.

Creft.] On a wreath of colours, a lion's head erafed, proper; collared, gules; charged with a bezant.

Supporters.] On the dexter fide, a lion guardant, or; collared, gules; charged with a bezant. On the finifter fide, a ftag, proper; attired and unguled, or; and collared in like manner.

Motto.] *Nec cupias, nec metuas.*

Chief Seats.] At Hardwicke, in the county of Gloucefter; Wimple, in Cambridgefhire; Great Ormond-ftreet, London.

78. VANE, EARL of DARLINGTON.

THE Right Hon. HENRY VANE, Earl of DAR-LINGTON, Vifcount and Baron Barnard of Bar-nard-Caftle, in the bifhoprick of Durham, colonel of a company in the fecond regiment of foot-guards, lord lieutenant, and vice admiral of the county of Durham, and mayor of Durham, fucceeded his father, Henry, the late Earl, who died March 6, 1758.

His Lordship, March 10, 1757, married Mifs Low-ther, fifter of Sir William Lowther, bart. by whom he had a daughter born May 3, 1759.

Henry, the late Earl, in 1725, married the Lady Grace Fitz-roy, fecond daughter of Charles, Duke of Cleveland, by whom he had three fons and three daughters, viz.

1. Henry, the prefent earl.

2. Frederick, born the 26th of June, 1732.

I 6
3. The

3. Raby, born Jan. 2, 1736.

4. Lady Anne, married in March 1746, to the Hon. Charles Hope Weir, of Cragie-Hall, in Scotland, Efq; Brother to the Earl of Hopetoun.

5. Lady Mary, married in Oct. 1752, to Ralph Carr, of Cocken, in the county of Durham, Efq; and,

6. Lady Henrietta, born Dec. 26, 1738.

Of the family of Vane, which were antiently feated in Wales, and from thence tranfplanted to Hilden and Badfel in Kent, was Sir Henry Vane, knight, who in 1356 was fo made by the Black Prince, at the battle of Poictiers, and from him this noble family and that of the earl of Weftmoreland are defcended.

Creations.] Baron Barnard, July 8, 1699, 10 Wm. III. Vifcount Barnard, and Earl Darlington, April 3, 1754, 27 Geo. II.

Arms.] Azure, three finifter gauntlets, or.

Creft.] A dexter hand in armour, couped at the wrift, proper, holding a fword argent, hilt and pomel, or.

Supporters.] On the dexter fide a griphon, argent; on the finifter an antelope, or, each gorged in a plain collar, azure. The dexter fide charged with three left hand gauntlets, otherwife three martlets, or.

Motto.] *Nec temere nec timide.*

Chief Seats.] At Raby Caftle, in the bifhopric of Durham; St. James's Square, London.

---

79   BELASYSE, EARL FAUCONBERG.

THE Right Hon. Thomas Belasyse, Earl Fauconberg, Vifcount Fauconberg, and Baron Fauconberg, one of the Lords of his Majefty's bed-chamber, born April 27, 1699, fucceeded the late Vifcount Thomas, his father, in 1718; and was advanced to the dignity of an Earl in 1756, 29 Geo. II.

On

On the 5th of Auguft, 1726, he married Catharine, daughter and heir of John Betham, of Rowington, in Warwickfhire, Efq; by which lady, who died May 30, 1760, he has had iffue three fons and four daughters, viz.

1. Thomas, who died an infant.

2. A fecond Thomas, born June 29, 1740, who died in the 12th year of his age.

3. Henry, Vifcount Fauconberg, born in 1742.

4. Lady Catharine.

5. Lady Barbara, married to the Hon. George Barnwell, Efq;

6. Lady Mary. And,

7. Lady Anne.

Thomas, Vifcount Fauconberg, father of the prefent Earl, married Bridget, daughter of Sir John Gage, of Firle, in Suffex, Bart. by whom he had iffue,

1. The prefent Earl.

2. Henry. And,

3. John, who died in their infancy.

4. Rowland, the third fon, unmarried.

5. Mary, the eldeft daughter, was married April 4, 1721, to John Pitt, Efq; third fon of Thomas Pitt, Efq; governor of Fort St. George, in the Eaft-Indies, who is fince dead.

Anne, fecond daughter, and,

3. Penelope, both dead.

This noble lord is defcended from Belafis, a Norman knight, who came over with William the Conqueror, and was general of the forces fent to reduce the city and ifle of Ely to the obedience of that prince.

Arms.] Quarterly, firft and fourth, a chevron ; gules between three fleur-de-lis, azure : fecond and third, argent, a pale ingrailed between two pallets plain, fable.

Creft.] On a wreath, a lion couchant guardant azure.

Supporters.] On the dexter fide, a buck holding in

his

5

his mouth a branch of oak fructed, all proper; on the finister an unicorn, azure, armed, crefted, and unguled, or.

Motto.] *Bonne & belle affex.*

Chief Seats.] At Newborough-hall, and Allerton-caftle in Yorkfhire; at Sutton in Chefhire; at St. Thomas's near Stafford; and Great George ftreet, London.

---

80. FOX, EARL OF ILCHESTER.

THE Right Hon. STEPHEN FOX, Earl of ILCHESTER, Lord Ilchefter and Stavordale, Baron Strangeways of Woodford-Strangeways, Baron of Redlynch, and joint comptroller of accounts of the army, was created Lord Ilchefter in Somerfetfhire, and Baron Strangeways, of Woodford-Strangeways in Dorfetfhire, May 11, 1741, 14 Geo. II. and Lord Ilchefter and Stavordale in Somerfetfhire, and Baron of Redlynch in the fame county, with remainder to the Right Hon. Henry Fox, Efq; his brother, the 3d of January, 1746-7, 20 Geo. II. and he was created Earl Ilchefter in June, 1756. His Lordfhip married in March, 1736, Elizabeth Horner, only daughter and heir of Thomas Strangeways Horner, of Wells, in the county of Somerfet, Efq; by whom he hath iffue, two fons and fix daughters, viz.

1. Henry Thomas, Lord Ilchefter, born July 29, 1747.

2. Stephen-Strangeways-Digby, born Dec. 3, 1751.

3. The Lady Sufannah Sarah-Louifa, born Feb. 1, 1742-3.

4. The Lady Charlotte-Elizabeth, born March 11, 1743-4, and died March 16, 1755.

5. The

5. The Lady Juliana-Judith, born July 10, 1744-5, who died April 24, 1749.

6. The Lady Lucy, born Dec. 15, 1748.

7. The Lady Chriftian-Henrietta-Caroline, born Jan. 3. 1749-50. And,

8. Lady Frances Muriel, born Aug. 1755.

Sir Stephen Fox, father of the prefent Earl, married Mifs Elizabeth Whittle, only daughter of Mr. William Whittle, of Lancafhire, by whom he had iffue.

1. Stephen, who died in France.

2. Charles, Efq; who married Elizabeth-Carr Trollop, only daughter and heir of Sir William Trollop, of Lincoln, Bart. and died without iffue, in 1713.

3. Stephen, who died in 1675.

4. William, who died in 1680.

5. James, who died in 1677.

6. John, who died in 1667.

7. Elizabeth, married Dec. 27, 1673, to John Lord Cornwallis, by whom he had iffue, Charles, late Lord Cornwallis.

8. Margaret, the fecond daughter, died unmarried, in 1687.

9. Jane, the youngeft daughter, married, in 1685, to George, Earl of Northampton, and died in 1721. [*See* Northampton, *Earl.*]

The faid Sir Stephen Fox, in 1703, married Chriftian, daughter of the Rev. Mr. Charles Hope, of Nafely, in Lincolnfhire, by whom he had iffue, two fons and two daughters, viz.

1. Stephen, now Earl of Ilchefter.

2. The Right Hon. Henry Fox, Efq; pay-mafter general of his Majefty's forces, and one of his Majefty's moft Hon. privy council. He married in May, 1744, the Lady Georgina-Carolina, Lenox, eldeft daughter of his Grace Charles, late Duke of Richmono, by whom he had iffue, four fons, Stephen, born Feb. 20, 1744. Henry-Charles, who died in 1746;

Charles.

Charles-James, born Jan. 14; 1748-9; and Henry Edward Fox, born March 4, 1755.

3. Charlotte, only surviving daughter of the said Sir Stephen Fox, married to the Hon. Edward Digby, Efq; and is mother to the prefent Lord Digby.

Arms.] Ermine on a chevron, azure, three foxes heads erazed, or; and in a canton, azure, a fleur-de-lis, or.

Creft.] On a chapeau, azure, turned up, ermine, a fox, fejant, or.

Supporters.] On the dexter fide, a fox, ermine; frettee, or; collared dovetail, azure; three fleurs-de-lis of the fecond. On the finifter fide, a fox, proper; collared in like manner.

Motto.] *Faire fans dire.*

Chief Seats.] At Redlynch, near Bruton in Somerfetfhire; in Burlington-ftreet, London.

A SHORT

A
SHORT VIEW
OF THE
PEERAGE
OF
ENGLAND.

1. DEVEREUX, VISCOUNT HEREFORD.

THE Right Hon. EDWARD DEVEREUX, Viscount HEREFORD, and Baronet, Premier Viscount of England, fucceeded Price, the late Vifcount, in Aug. 1748. He married Catharine, daughter of Richard Myton, of Garth, in the county of Montgomery, Efq; who died Feb. 2, 1748-9, leaving iffue by him,

1. Bridget, born May 9, 1739.

2. Arthur, born March 20, 1740, and died July 15, the fame year.

3. Edward, born Feb. 10, 1740-1.

4. Arthur, born Feb. 10, 1741-2, and died Sept. 1743.

5. Catharine, born Feb. 7, 1742-3.

6. George, born April 25, 1744.

Price, the late and tenth Vifcount Hereford, born July 9, 1694, married Jan. 3, 1720, Elizabeth, only daughter of Leicefter Martin, Efq; which lady dying without iffue, he married July 30, 1740, Eleonora, daughter of—Price, of Rhwlas, in Merionethfhire, Efq;.

Arthur Devereux, Efq; father of the prefent Vifcount, married Mifs Glynn, daughter of Evan Glynn, Efq; by whom he had iffue, two fons, Arthur and Vaughan,

Vaughan, who died in their minority; and their mother dying alfo, he married Mifs Elizabeth Glynn, daughter of Richard Glynn, Efq; by whom he had iffue, Edward, the prefent Lord Vifcount Hereford, who fucceeded Price, late lord, who died without iffue; and having proved his difcent from the late Walter, Vifcount Hereford, who died in 1588, he took his feat in the houfe of peers, April 3, 1750.

Of this family was Robert Devereux, Earl of Effex, general of the parliament army againft king Charles I.

This noble lord is defcended from Evreux, of Normandy, from which town the family took their name. His anceftors, attending William the Conqueror in his defcent on England, were rewarded for their fervices with manors and lands taken from the Englifh of a very great value.

Arms.] Argent, a fefs, gules, in chief three tor-teauxes.

Creft.] In a ducal coronet, or, a talbot's head, argent; eared gules.

Supporters.] On the dexter fide, a talbot argent; eared, gules; with a ducal coronet of the fecond. On the finifter, a rein deer of the laft, attired, gorged with a ducal coronet, and chained, or.

Motto.] *Bafis virtutum conftantia.*

Chief Seat.] At Nanteribba, in Montgomeryfhire.

2. BROWN, VISCOUNT MONTAGU.

THE Right Hon. Anthony Brown, Vifcount Montagu, fucceeded his father Henry, the late vifcount, June 25, 1717; and in 1740, married Barbara, third daughter of Sir John Webb, of Hathorp, in the county of Gloucefter, Bart. by whom he had iffue, feveral children, whereof one fon, Anthony and one daughter, Mary, are living.

Henry,

Henry, Lord Vifcount Montagu, father of the pre-fent Vifcount, married Barbara, daughter of James Walfingham, of Chefterford in Effex, Efq; and left iffue, one fon and fix daughters.

1. Anthony, the prefent vifcount.
2. Mary. And,
3. Elizabeth, both dead.
4. Barbara, married to Ralph Salvin, Efq;
5. Catharine, married to George Colingwood, Efq;
6. Anne, married to Anthony Kemp, Efq;
7. Henrietta, married to——Harcourt, Efq;

This noble lord is defcended from Sir Anthony Brown, who was made knight of the bath, at the co-ronation of King Richard II.

Arms.] Sable, three lions paffant in bend, between two double cotifes, argent.

Creft.] On a wreath, an eagle difplayed, vert.

Supporters.] Two wolves, argent; with each a plain collar and chain, or.

Motto.] *Suivez raifon.*

Chief Seats.] At Cowdry in Suffex.

3. FIENES, VISCOUNT SAY AND SELE.

THE Right Hon. RICHARD FIENES, Vifcount and Baron Say and Sele, fucceeded Laurence, late Vifcount Say and Sele his coufin, in Dec. 1742. He married Jan. 28, 1754, Ifabella, daughter of Sir John Tirrel, and relict of John Pigot of Dodderfhill, in the county of Bucks, Efq;

Richard Fienes, a clergyman, father to the pre-fent Lord Vifcount Say and Sele, married Penelope, daughter of George Chamberlain, of Wardingdon, in Oxfordfhire, Efq; by whom he had iffue,

1. Richard his fon, now vifcount Say and Sele.

2. Sufannah, married to —— Gordon, of Green-wich, Efq;   3. Pene-

3. Penelope, who married Richard Wykham, of Strateley, in the county of Oxford, Esq;

4. Elizabeth, married to the Rev. Mr. Henry Quartley, rector of Wicken in Northampton.

5. Celicia.

The said Laurence, late Viscount Say and Sele, second son of John Fienes, third son of William Viscount Say and Sele, succeeded to that title on the death of Nathaniel, Viscount Say and Sele, Feb. 24, 1709-10; and dying unmarried, was succeeded by the present viscount.

This noble lord is descended from John, Baron Fienes, hereditary constable of Dover-castle, and Lord Warden of the cinque-ports in the twelfth century.

Arms.] Azure, three lions rampant, or.

Crest.] On a wreath, a wolf sejant, argent; his radiant collar and chain, or.

Supporters.] Two wolves, argent; gorged and chained, or.

Motto.] *Fortem posce animum.*

Chief Seats.] At Dodderhill in Bucks; Golden-Square, London.

4. TOWNSHEND, VISCOUNT TOWNSHEND.

THE Right Hon. CHARLES TOWNSHEND, Viscount TOWNSHEND of Raynham, and Baron Townshend, of Lynn-Regis, an Baronet, succeeded his father Charles, the late viscount, in June 1738. His lordship married Audrey, daughter and sole heir of Edward Harrison, of Hertfordshire, Esq; governor of Fort St. George in India, and by her hath issue four sons and one daughter:

1. George, Brigadier General of his Majesty's Forces born Feb. 28, 1723-4, was in May 1758 appointed colonel of the 28th regiment of Foot, and in 1751, married the lady Charlotte Compton, only daugh-

daughter and heir to James, Earl of Northampton, and baronefs Ferrers of Chartley, by whom he has issue, one son, George, born May 7, 1753; and a daughter, Charlotte, born Oct. 15, 1754.

2. Charles, who on the 15th of Auguft, 1755, married Lady Caroline, eldeft daughter and coheir of his Grace, John Duke of Greenwich, widow of Francis, Earl of Dalkeith, fon and heir of Francis, Duke of Buccleugh.

3. Edward, who died unmarried.

4. Roger, an officer in the army.

5. Audrey, unmarried.

Charles, Lord vifcount Townfhend, father of the prefent vifcount, married Elizabeth, daughter and fole heir to Thomas, Lord Pelham, who died May 11, 1711, leaving iffue, four fons and one daughter:

1. Charles, the prefent vifcount.

2. Thomas, who on May 2, 1730, was married to Albina, daughter of Col. John Selwyn.

3. William, who on May 29, 1725, was married to Henrietta, only daughter of the Lord William Paulet, by whom he had iffue one fon and four daughters.

4. Roger; and,

5. Elizabeth, married to Charles, Lord Cornwallis.

His Lordfhip in July, 1713, married Dorothy, Daughter of Robert Walpole, in the county of Norfolk, Efq; by whom he had iffue four fons and two daughters, viz.

1. George, Vice-Admiral of the white.

2. Auguftus, who died in 1745.

3. Horatio, commiffioner of the victualling-office.

4. Edward, prebend of Weftminfter, married, in May 1747, a daughter of Brigadier Gen. Price.

5. Dorothy, married in 1743, to Spencer Cowper, brother to the prefent Earl Cowper, and Dean of Durham.

6. Mary, married to the Hon Col. Edw. Cornwallis.

The late Lord Vifcount Townfhend was apointed principal fecretary of ftate in the reign of King

George I. in 1720, and continued fo to the end of his Majefty's reign ; when upon refigning the feals, they were returned to him again by his prefent Majefty, King George II. who continued him principal fecretary of ftate, to the year 1730.

This family are of Norman extraction, and came into England about the time of the conqueft.

Arms.] Azure, a chevron, ermine between three efcalop fhells, argent.

Creft.] On a wreath, a buck, fable, attired proper.

Supporters.] On the dexter fide, a buck, fable; on the finifter, a greyhound, argent.

Motto.] *Hæc generi incrementa fides.*

Chief Seats.]At Raynham-hall and Stiffcay-hall, in the county of Norfolk ; Grofvenor-ftreet, London.

5. THYNNE, VISCOUNT WEYMOUTH.

THE Right Hon. Thomas Thynne, Vifcount Weymouth, and Baron Thynne, of Warminfter, and Bart. high fteward of Tamworth, born Sept. 13, 1734, fucceeded Thomas the late vifcount his father, in his honour and eftate, Jan. 12, 1750-1 ; and married May 22, 1759, the Lady Elizabeth Bentinck, eldeft daughter of the prefent Duke of Portland, by whom he has a daughter, born March 26, 1760.

Thomas Thynne, late vifcount Weymouth, father of the prefent Vifcount, fucceeded to the title and eftate of his grandfather's elder brother Thomas, Lord Vifcount Weymouth, in 1714; he married on the 6th of Dec. 1726, the Lady Elizabeth Sackville, daughter of his Grace Lionel Duke of Dorfet, which lady died June 29, 1729. His lordfhip married July 3, 1733, Louifa, daughter of the Right Hon. John Earl Granville, by whom he ! iffue three fons, viz.

1. Thomas, the prefent Vifcount.

2. James;

2. James; and

3. Henry-Frederick, of whom her ladyſhip died in child-bed, Dec. 25, 1736.

Of this family was Thomas Thynne, Eſq; who was ſhot in his coach on the 12th of February, 1682, by ſome aſſaſſins employed by Count Coningſmark, a German nobleman, to murder him, looking upon this gentleman as a ſuccefsful rival; of which there is an account on his monument in the ſouth iſle of Weſtminſter-abbey; whereon is his effigies cumbent, and in the front his figure in a coach, with three aſſaſſins ſurrounding it, and one of them firing at him with a blunderbuſs. The three aſſaſſins were foreigners in the count's ſervice, and were all of them convicted and executed; while the count, who ſet them to work was ſpared, and permitted to return to Germany.

This noble family are deſcended from the Bottevilles of Poictou in France, who came over into England in the reign of King John, and ſettled at Longleate in Wiltſhire, where they aſſumed the name of Thynne.

Arms.] Barry of ten, or and ſable.

Creſt. On a wreath, a rein-deer, or.

Supporters.] On the dexter ſide, a rein deer, or, gorged, with a plain collar, ſable; on the ſiniſter, a lion, gules.

Motto.] *J'ay bonne cauſe.*

Chief Seats.] At Drayton Baſſit, in Warwickſhire; Botsfield in Longleate, Wiltſhire; Cravenſtreet, London.

6. HATTON, VISCOUNT HATTON.

THE Right Hon. WILLIAM HATTON, Viſcount HATTON, of Cretton, and Baron Hatton of Kerby, born in 1690, ſucceeded his father the late Viſcount, in 1706, and is yet unmarried.

Chri-

Chriftopher, Lord Hatton, father of the prefent vifcount, was created vifcount Hatton, Jan 17, 1682. He married firft the lady Cecilia Tufton, third daughter of John Earl of Thanet, by whom he had iffue,

1. Anne, married to Daniel Finch, late Earl of Winchelfea and Nottingham: (*See Earl of* Winchelfea)

2. Margaret, and,

3. Elizabeth, who died young.

And the lady, their mother, dying, he married in 1676, his fecond wife Frances, only daughter to Sir Henry Yelverton, by whom he had iffue, but all died young; and fhe dying, May 15, 1684, his lordfhip married to his third wife, Elizabeth, daughter and coheir of Sir William Haflewood, of Maidwell in Northamptonfhire, and by her had three fons and three daughters.

1. William, the prefent vifcount.

2. Charles.

3. John.

4. Elizabeth.

5. Penelope; and,

6. Anne, who are all unmarried.

This noble lord is defcended from Sir Chriftopher Hatton, who was captain of the guard to Queen Elizabeth; afterwards vice-chamberlain, and of her majefty's privy-council, and in 1587, was conftituted lord high chancellor of England, and the next year was elected knight of the garter.

He was defcended from Ivon, Vifcount of Coutantin in Normandy, whofe pofterity came over into England foon after the conqueft, and fettled in the county of Chefter, and afterwards in Northamptonfhire.

Arms.] Azure, a chevron between three garbs, or.

Creft.] On a wreath, a hind at gaze, or.

Supporters.] Two horfes, argent; bridled, fable.

Motto.] *Virtus Tutiffima Caffis.*

Chief Seat.] At Kirby in Northamptonfhire.

7. St.

7. ST. JOHN, VISCOUNT BOLINGBROKE.

THE Right Hon. FREDERICK ST. JOHN, Lord Vifcount BOLINGBROKE, and St. John, Baron St. John of Lydiard-Tregoze, and Baron St. John of Batterfea, fucceeded to the Honours and Eftates of his Uncle the late Lord Vifcount Bolingbroke, who died in the Year 1754.

The prefent Vifcount was, the fame year, admitted into the Houfe of Lords, and in September 1757, was married to Lady Diana Spencer, daughter to his Grace the late Duke of Marlborough.

Henry, the late Lord Vifcount Bolingbroke, was foon after the acceffion of Queen Anne, made fecre-tary of War, and in 1708, fecretary of ftate. On the 24th of October, 1713, he was conftituted lord lieu-tenant, and cuftos rotulorum of the county of Effex; but in 1714, his honours and eftate were forfeited by an act of attainder.

He was afterwards reftored in blood, and his pater-nal eftate fecured to his heirs.

His firft wife was Frances, daughter and coheir of Sir Henry Winchcomb. His fecond wife was Maria-Clara de Champs de Marefilly, marchionefs de Vil-lette, born of a noble family in France.

His lordfhip having no iffue by either of them, his honours defcended to his nephew Frederick, the pre-fent lord vifcount Bolingbroke.

This noble lord is defcended from the lords of Ba-fing in Hampfhire, who were barons at the time of the Conqueft.

Arms.] Argent, on a chief, gules, two mullets, pierced, or,

Creft.] On a wreath, a mount proper, and there-from a falcon rifing, with bells, or, and ducally gorg-ed, gules.

K   *Supporters.*]

Supporters.] Two eagles with wings expanded, or, crowned ducally, gules, and upon each breaft a pair of horfes hemes, tied at the top and bottom, proper, within which is party-per pale, argent and gules.

Motto.] *Nec quærere nec fpernere Honcrem.*

Chief Seats.] At Batterfea ; in Surrey ; at Lydiard in Wilts; and Charles-ftreet, Berkeley-fquare, London.

---

8. BOSCAWEN, VISCOUNT FALMOUI H.

THE Right Hon. Hugh Boscawen, Vifcount Falmouth, Baron Bofcawen-Rofe, one of his Majefty's privy council, lieutenant-general of his Majefty's forces, and captain of the yeomen of the guards, fucceeded Hugh, the late vifcount his father, Oct. 25, 1734. He married married Maria Ruffel, widow of —— Ruffel, by whom he has no iffue.

Hugh, Vifcount Falmouth, father of the prefent Vifcount, was by Queen Anne, created Lord Vifcount Falmouth, &c. and was groom of the bed-chamber to his Royal Highnefs the Prince of Denmark. On the acceffion of his late Majefty, he was made comptroller of his Majefty's houfhold ; and on the 13th of June 1720, 6 George I. was created Baron of Bofcawen-Rofe and Vifcount Falmouth. He married Charlotte, eldeft daughter and coheir of Charles Godfrey, Efq; by whom he had iffue eight fons and ten daughters, viz.

1. Hugh, the prefent Vifcount.

2. Edward, admiral of the blue, one of the lords of the admiralty, and one of his majefty's privy-council, married to Mifs Glanville of St.Clere in Kent, in December 1742, by whom he has iffue fons and daughters. In conjunction with General Amherft, he took the ifland of Cape-Breton from the French in July 1758, and took and deftroyed five French men of war in Auguft 1759.

3. George, a major-general in the army, married the Hon. Mifs Trevor.

4. John, colonel of a regiment of foot, married Mifs Surman, who died Jan. 18, 1749.

5. William-Frederick, who died unmarried.

6. Nicholas, D. D. dean of St. Buriens in Cornwal, married a daughter of—Woodward, relict of—Hatton.

7. Lady Charlotte, married to Henry Moor, Earl of Drogheda, who died in April 1735.

8. Lady Anne, married to Sir Cecil Bifhop, Bart. and is fince dead.

9. Lady Mary, married in Aug. 1732, to John Evelyn, Efq; alfo dead.

10. Lady Lucy, married to Charles Frederick, Efq; and,

11. Lady Kitty, who died unmarried.

The reft died young and unmarried.

This noble Lord is defcended from Richard Bof- cawen, of the town of Bofcawen, in the county of Cornwall, who flourifhed in the reign of K. Edward VI.

Arms.] Ermine, a rofe, gules, barbed and feeded, proper.

Creft.] On a wreath, a boar paffant, gules, armed, briftled and unguled, or.

Supporters.] Two fea-lions, Goutes des Larmes, argent.

Motto.] *In Cælo Quies.*

To which Arms are added a fefs between two rofes, being the Lady's arms.

Chief Seats.] At Tregothan, in the county of Corn- wall; St. James's-fquare, London.

9. BYNG, VISCOUNT TORRINGTON.

THE Rt. Hon. GEORGE BYNG, Vifcount Tor- RINGTON, Baron Byng and Baronet, born in 1739, fucceeded George, the late Vifcount his father, April 6, 1750.

George

George, the late Vifcount, and father of the prefent Vifcount, fucceeded Pattee, his brother, in Jan.
1746-7; he was colonel of a regiment of foot, and in
Oct. 1747, was conftituted major-general of his Majefty's forces: he married, 1736, Elizabeth, daughter
of —— Daniel, Efq; fon of Sir Peter Daniel, Knt.
who died April 7, 1756, by which lady, who died
March 17, 1759, he had iffue two fons, viz.

1. George, the prefent vifcount; and

2. John.

George, grandfather of the prefent Vifcount, was
created a Baronet Nov. 15, 1715, and Baron and
Vifcount Sept. 9, 1721; he married in 1691, Margaret, daughter of James Mafter, of Eaft-Langden in
the county of Kent, Efq; and by her, who died April
1, 1756, he had eleven fons and four daughters, of
which thofe who furvived him were,

1. Pattee, who fucceeded him.

2. George, the late vifcount.

3. Robert, commiffioner of his Majefty's navy, and
governor of Barbadoes, married Elizabeth, daughter
of Jonathan Forward, Efq; and died in Oct. 1740,
leaving iffue three fons.

4. John, admiral of the blue, who, agreeable to the
fentence of a court-martial, was fhot on board his
majefty's fhip the Monarque, in Portfmouth harbour,
March 14, 1757.

5. Edward, married in 1730, Mary, daughter and
heir of John Bramfton, of Screens in Effex, Efq;
He died 1756. And,

6. Sarah, his only furviving daughter, married John Osborn, Efq; fon of Sir John Osborn, of
Chickfand, in the county of Bedford, Bart. by whom
fhe had a fon Sir D'Anvers Osborn, Bart. married in
1740, to the Lady Mary Montagu, daughter of
George late Earl of Halifax.

This noble Lord is defcended from the Byngs of
Wrotham, in the county of Kent, who flourifhed
there in the reign of king Henry VII.

Arms.] Quarterly, fable and argent; in the firft a lion rampant of the fecond.

Creft.] On a wreath, fable and argent, an antelope paffant, ermine ; horned, tusked, flafhed, maned and hoofed, or ; langued, gules.

Supporters.] On the dexter fide, an antelope, ermine ; horned, maned, and hoofed, or ; ftanding on a fhip gun, proper. And on the finifter fide, a feahorfe, proper ; finned, or ; on a like gun.

Motto.] *Tuebor.*

Chief Seats.] At Southill, in Bedfordfhire ; Privygarden, Whitehall, London.

10. FITZGERALD, VISCOUNT LEINSTER.

THE Right Hon. JAMES FITZ GERALD, Vifcount LEINSTER in England, Earl of Kildare, and Baron of Offaley, Premier Earl and Baron of the kingdom of Ireland, fucceeded his father Robert in his Eftate, and in the Earldom of Kildare and Barony of Offaley, in February, 1743-4. His Lordfhip was created a Peer of Great Britain Feb. 28, 1746-7, by the title of Vifcount Leinfter of Taplow, in the county of Buckingham. He married, Feb. 7, 1746-7, the Lady Emilia, daughter of his Grace Charles, late Duke of Richmond, by whom he hath iffue, George, born Jan. 15, 1747-8, and Robert, Caroline Mabel, and Emilia.

Robert, the late Earl of Kildare, father of the prefent Earl, fucceeded John the eighteenth Earl of Kildare, his father in 1707. He married in March, 1708-9, the Lady Mary O'Brien, eldeft daughter of William, Earl of Inchiquin, and had iffue, four fons and eight daughters, viz.

1. William, Lord Offaley, born in Jan. 1714-15, died an infant. .

2. George

2. George, who died young.
3. James, now Vifcount Leinfter, &c.
4. Charles, who died in 1733.
5. Lady Mary, eldeft daughter.
6. Lady Elizabeth.
7. Lady Henrietta.
8. Lady Catherine.
9. Lady Anne, and,
10. Lady Frances; which fix daughters all died young.

11. Lady Margaret, born in July, 1722, and married, in 1748, to the Lord Vifcount Hilfborough.

12. Lady Charlotte, who died in October 1743.

·· This noble Lord is defcended from Walter Fitz-Other, who poffefled feveral lordfhips in the counties of Hampfhire and Buckinghamfhire, in the reign of Edward the Confeffor; and was warden of all the forefts in Berkfhire, and Caftellan of Windfor in the reign of William the Conqueror. Maurice Fitz-Gerald, another of this Lord's anceftors, contributed very much to the conqueft of Ireland in the reign of King Henry II. and was rewarded with a great eftate in lands in the province of Leinfter, and particularly the Barony of Offaley, and the caftle of Wicklow, and died, covered with honours, in the year 1177, 24 Hen. II.

' The late Lord's father preferved the city of Dublin from being plundered and burnt, after king James's defeat at the battle of the Boyne, in 1690.

· [*For a more particular and fatisfactory account of this noble family, the reader is directed to confult the third Volume of this work, containing an Account of the Peerage of Ireland.*]

Arms.] Pearl, a faltire, ruby.

Creft.] On a wreath, a monkey at gaze, proper; environed about the middle, and chained, topaz.

Supporters.] Two monkeys environed and chained, as the creft.

Motto.]

Motto.] *Crom aboo.*

Chief Seats.] At Maynooth, Cartown, and Dullard-
ftown, all in the county of Kildare, in Ireland.

---

11. BOUVERIE, VISCOUNT FOLKESTON.

THE Right Hon. Jacob Bouverie, Vifcount
Folkeston, Lord Longford, and Baron of
Longford, and Baronet, and prefident of the fociety
for encouraging arts, manufactures, and commerce,
fucceeded his brother, Sir Edward de Bouverie, in
his honour and eftate, in Nov. 1736; and on the 29th
of June 1747, was created Lord Longford, Baron of
Longford in the county of Wilts, and Vifcount Fol-
kelton of Folkefton, in the county of Kent. He
married Mary, daughter and fole heir of Bartholomew Clarke, of Roehampton, in the county of Surry, Efq; by whom he has living two fons and four
daughters, viz.

1. William, married in Jan. 1747, to Harriot, only
daughter and heir of Sir Mark Stewart-Pleydel, of
Colefhill in Berkfhire, Bart. which Lady dying in May
1750, left one fon Jacob, born in March 1750. He
married 2dly, Sept. 5, 1751, Rebecca, daughter of John
Alleyn of Barbadoes, Efq; by whom he has iffue William Henry, born in Oct. 1752, and Bartholomew,
born Oct. 29, 1753.

2. Edward.

3. Anne.

4. Mary, married March 16, 1759, to Anthony,
the prefent Earl of Shaftfbury.

5. Charlotte, and,

6. Harriot.

His Lady dying in Nov. 1739, he married in April
1741, the Hon. Elizabeth Marfham, eldeft daughter
of Robert late Lord Romney, by whom he has had
two fons,

1. Jacob,

1. Jacob, who is fince dead. And,

2. Philip, born in October 1746, now living.

William, eldeft fon of Sir Edward de Bouverie, Knt. father of the prefent Vifcount Folkefton, was created a Baronet in 1713. He married Mary, daughter of James Edwards of London, Efq; by whom he had iffue, a fon Edward, who died young : his fecond wife was Anne, daughter and fole heir of David Urry, of London, Efq; by whom he had feveral children, of whom three fons and two daughters only lived to maturity, viz.

1. Edward, who fucceeded him in 1717, and married Mary, daughter and coheir of John Smith, Efq; was fucceeded by,

2. Jacob, his brother, the prefent Vifcount.

3. Chriftopher, who died unmarried.

4. Jane, married to John Allen-Pufey, of Pufey in Berkfhire, Efq; who died in 1742, without iffue.

5. Anne, who is unmarried.

This noble Lord is defcended from the Defboveries, of the caftle Defboveries, near the city of Lifle, in Flanders, who came into England on account of the perfecution for religion in that country, and fettled at Canterbury.

Arms.] Party-per-fefs, or and argent, an eagle difplayed, with two heads, fable.

Creft.] On a wreath, a demi-eagle difplayed, fable; beaked and ducally gorged, or ; on his breaft a crofs corflet, argent.

Supporters.] On each fide, an eagle reguardant, fable ; gorged with a ducal coronet, charged on the breaft with a crofs corflet, argent.

Motto.] *Patria cara, Carior Libertas.*

Chief Seats.] At Longford, near Salisbury, in Wiltfhire ; in Clifford-ftreet, London.

A SHORT

A
SHORT VIEW
OF THE
PEERAGE
OF
ENGLAND.

1. NEVILLE, LORD ABERGAVENNY.

THE Right Hon. GEORGE NEVILLE, Lord ABER-GAVENNY, Premier Baron of England, Lord Lieutenant, and cuſtos rotulorum of the county of Suſſex, ſucceeded his father William late Lord Abergavenny, Sept. 21, 1744.

His Lordſhip married, Feb. 5, 1753, Henrietta, daughter of Thomas Pelham, late of Stanmere in the county of Suſſex, Eſq, who in Feb. 1755, was brought to bed of a ſon and heir, named Henry.

William, the late and 14th Lord Abergavenny, father of the preſent Lord, married, in May 1725, Catherine daughter of Lieutenant general Tatton, and widow of the late Edward, Lord Abergavenny, and by her, who died on the 4th of December 1728, had iſſue, a ſon George, the preſent Lord; and daughter Catherine. His Lordſhip married again May 20, 1732, the Lady Rebecca, daughter of Thomas, Earl of Pembroke, and by her who died Oct. 20, 1758, had iſſue three daughters and one ſon, viz.

1. Harriot, born Nov. 17, 1734.

2. Mary, born June 13, 1736, and died Aug. 2, 1758.

3. The

3. Sophia, born March 14, 1738, and died Jan. 3, 1759.

4. William, born in October 1741.

This noble Lord is defcended from John of Gaunt, fourth fon of king Edward III.

Arms.] Gules on a faltire, argent, a rofe of the firft, barbed and feeded, proper.

Creft.] In a ducal coronet, or, a bull's head, argent; pied, fable ; armed of the firft, and charged on the neck with a rofe, gules.

Supporters.] Two bulls, argent, pied, fable, armed unguled, collared, and chained, or.

Motto.] *Ne vile velis.*

Chief Seats.] At the caftle of Abergavenny, in Monmouthfhire ; at Eridge, and Kidbrook-Hall, in Suffex; and Charles-ftreet, Berkley-fquare, London.

2. T O U C·H E T, L O R D A U D·L E Y.

THE Right Hon. John Touchet, Earl of Castlehaven, in Ireland, Baron Audley of H leigh, and Baron of Orier in England, fucceeded his father James, who died in October 1740.

James Touchet, late Earl of Caftlehaven, and Baron Audley, fucceeded his father James, in 1700, married Elizabeth, daughter of Henry Lord Arundel, and had iffue, a fon, born April 15, 1723, named John, the prefent Lord Audley.

This noble Lord is defcended from the ancient family of the Touchets of Normandy, which attended William the Conqueror in his expedition to England in the year 1066.

Arms.] Ermine, a chevron, gules.

Creft.] In a ducal coronet, or, a fwan rifing, argent ; ducally gorged of the firft.

Sup-

Supporters.] Two wyverns, with wings expanded fable.

Motto.] *Je le tiens.*

Chief Seats.] At Hileigh-Castle in Staffordshire; and Castle-Haven, in Ireland.

---

3. BARRET-LENNARD, LORD DACRE.

THE Rt. Hon. THOMAS BARRET-LENNARD, Lord DACRE, born in 1716, succedeed his mother Anne, Baroness Dacre, who became heir to that title and estate on the death of her elder sister Barbara, in 1740. She married first Richard Barret-Lennard, Esq; who died soon after, by whom she had a son, viz. Thomas Barrett-Lennard, now Lord Dacre, who married Anne, daughter of Sir John Pratt, Knt. and had issue a daughter, named Anna Barbara, who died 1749.

The said Anne, Baroness Dacre, afterwards married Henry father of the present Lord Teynham, and had issue. *See Lord* Teynham. She was married lastly, to the Hon. Rob. Moor, Esq; a younger son of Henry Earl of Drogheda of the kingdom of Ireland, by whom she had one son named Henry.

Thomas Lennard Lord Dacre, father of the late Baroness, was created Earl of Suffex, Oct. 5, 26 Charles II. He married Lady Anne Fitzroy, natural daughter of king Charles II. by Barbara Dutchefs of Cleveland, by whom he had issue one son and two daughters.

1. Charles; and
2. Henry, who died in their infancy.
3. Barbara; and,
4. Anne.

Who on their father's death in 1715, became heirs to the Barony of Dacre, which was held in abeyance between them, till the Lady Barbara, who married Charles Skelton, Esq; a general officer in the service of the king of France, dying without issue in the year 1740, the Lady Anne, her sister, then became sole heir to her father; and was succeeded by her son the present Lord Dacre.

This noble family were long resident at Chevening in Kent; they were barons originally by tenure and writ of summons the 25th of Edward I. 1297; also by writ of summons 36 Henry VI. 1460, again declared 2 James I. 1604.

Arms.] Quarterly, first and fourth, or, on a fesse gules, three fleurs-de-lis of the first for Lennard; second and third, party-per-pale, barry of four, counter-changed, argent and gules, for Barret.

Crest.] An Arabian dog's head, argent, langued, gules, eyes, or, issuing out of a ducal coronet, or; and sometimes a hydra, proper, on a wreath, argent and gules, being the Barret-crest.

Supporters.] On the dexter side, an alant argent, langued gules, with a spiked collar, chain, and clog, or; on the sinister side, a bull, gules, horned, or, collared with a ducal coronet and chain, or,

Motto.] *Pour bien desirer.*

Chief Seats.] Bell-house, in Essex, Bruton-street, London.

---

4. WEST, LORD DELAWARR.

THE Right Hon. JOHN WEST, Lord DELAWARR, one of his Majesty's most honourable privy-council, knight of the Bath, lieutenant-general, and colonel of the first troop of horse-guards, governor of the island of Guernsey, master forester of the Bailiwic of Fritham in the New Forest, and F. R. S. was born April 4, 1693, and succeded his father John, the late Lord, May 26, 1723.

He married in 1721, the Lady Charlotte Maccarty daughter to Donagh Earl of Clancarty in Ireland, a n by her had issue two sons and two daughters, viz.

1. John,

1. John, born in 1729, married Aug, 1756, to Miſs Whynyard, daughter of the late general, by whom he had a ſon born in April 1757, and a ſon born July 31, 1758.

2. George, born in 1733, was in Nov. 1759, appointed captain-lieutenant in the foot-guards, with the rank of lieutenant-colonel.

3. Henrietta-Cecilia, born in 1730.

4. Diana, born in 1731; and married to Colonel Clavering, Nov. 9, 1756.

His Lady dying in 1734-5, his Lordſhip married in 1744, his ſecond Lady, Anne reliǎ of Lord Abergavenny, which Lady died in June 1748, leaving no iſſue.

John, father of the preſent Lord, married Margaret, ſole daughter and heir of John Freeman, merchant, and died on the 26th of May 1723, leaving iſſue by her, John, the preſent Lord, and a daughter Elizabeth, who in Auguſt 1724, was married to Thomas Diggs, of Chilham Caſtle in Kent, Eſq; and had iſſue two ſons, Weſt and Dudley.

This noble family is deſcended from the Weſts, a great family in the weſt of England; but in the reign of Edward II. they appear to have been ſeized of manors and lands in the county of Warwick.

Thomas Lord Delawarr, one of his Lordſhip's anceſtors, was captain-general of Virginia in 1609; and going over thither, contributed more to the planting and ſupporting the firſt Engliſh colonies there, than any of the adventurers in the reign of K. James I.

Arms.] Argent, a feſs dancette, ſable.

Creſt.] In a ducal coronet, or, a gryphon's head, azure; ears and beak of the firſt.

Supporters.] On the dexter ſide, a wolf coward, argent; his plain collar, or. On the ſiniſter, a cockatrice of the ſecond, his wings diſplayed, gules and or.

Motto.] *Jour de ma vie.*

Chief Seats.] At Whorwell, in Hampſhire; Bolderwood, Hants; Sheffeld-place, Suſſex; Hanover-Square, London.   5. STOUR-

5. STOURTON, LORD STOURTON.

THE Right Hon. WILLIAM STOURTON, Lord Stourton, Baron Stourton, fucceeded his brother Charles, who died without iffue the 11th of March 1753. He married Winifred, daughter of Philip Howard, of Buckenham in Norfolk, Efq; brother to the prefent duke of Norfolk, by whom he hath iffue.

Charles-Philip, born Aug. 22, 1752; and two daughters, viz.

1. Catherine, born Aug. 6, 1750. And
2. Charlotte-Mary, born Sept. 16, 1751.

Thomas, the 13th Lord Stourton, father of the laft and prefent Lords, married Catherine, daughter of Richard Frampton, of Bitfton in the county of Dorfet, Efq; and by her had two fons the late and prefent Lords, and three daughters Mary, Catherine, and Jane.

This noble Lord is defcended from Sir Ralph Stourton, of Stourton in Wiltfhire, who oppofed William the Conqueror in the weft of England, until he granted Sir Ralph and his followers the terms they infifted on.

Arms.] Sable, a bend, or between fix fountains, proper.

Creft.] On a wreath, a demi-grey-friar, habited in ruffet; girt, or; holding a fcourge of three lafhes with knots, gules.

Supporters.] Two fea-dogs, proper; fcaled on their backs, and finned, or.

Motto.] *Loyal je ferai durant ma vie.*

Chief Seat.] At Stourton-Caftle, in Staffordfhire.

6. VERNEY, BARON WILLOUGHBY of BROKE.

THE Right Hon. JOHN-PEYTO VERNEY, Baron Willoughby of Broke, born in 1738, fucceeded his uncle Richard, the late Lord, who died the 11th of Auguft, 1752.

The late Lord Richard, married Margaret, daughter of Mr. Nehemiah Walker, of the county of Monmouth, by whom he hath had issue one son, who died an infant

This noble Lord is descended from William de Vernai, who flourished in the reign of king Henry I. *Anno.* 1419.

Arms.] Gules, three crosses recercele, verded, or, a chief vaire, ermine and erminois.

Crest.] On a wreath, the bust of a man couped and affronte, proper, crowned ducally, or.

Supporters.] Two antelopes, argent, spotted gules, armed, crested and unguled, or.

Motto.] *Vertue vaunceth.*

Chief Seats.]At Compton Murdack and Chesterton, in Warwickshire.

---

7. N O E L, L O R D WENTWORTH.

THE Right Hon. EDWARD NOEL, Lord WENTworth, of Nettlested, and Baronet, succeeded Martha, Baroness of Wentworth in 1745, and married Judith, daughter of William Lamb of Farndish, in the county of Northampton, Esq; by whom he has issue one son named Thomas, born November 18, 1745; and a daughter Judith,

Sir Clobery Noel, Bart. father of the present Lord, married Elizabeth, daughter of Thomas Rowney of Oxford, Esq; by whom he had issue, six sons and one daughter, viz.

1. Edward, the present Lord.

2. The Rev. Clobery Noel.

3. Thomas, captain of one of his Majesty's ships of war, was mortally wounded in the action off Port-mahon with the French in May 1756, and soon died after at Gibraltar.

4. The

4. The Rev, John Noel.

5. The Rev. Rowney Noel.

6. William-James Noel, who died young. And;

7. Mary.

This noble Lord is defcended from the fame anceftor with the Earl of Strafford.

Arms.] Quarterly, firft and fourth, frette, gules, a
canton ermine, for Noel; fecond, a chevron between
three leopards faces, or, for Wentworth; three gules,
on a chief, indented, fable; three martlets, argent,
for Lovelace.

Creft.] On a wreath, a buck at gaze, argent,
armed, or.

Supporters.] Two gryphons, argent.

Motto.] *Penfes a Been.*

Chief Seats.] At Kirkby Mallory, in Leicefterfhire;
Saville-Row, London.

---

8. WILLOUGHBY, LORD WILLOUGHBY OF PARHAM.

THE Right Hon.. Hugh Willoughby, Lord
Willoughby of Parham, in Suffolk, prefident
of the fociety of Antiquaries, and F. R. S. fucceeded his father Charles, the late Lord, June 12, 1715.

Charles, the late Lord Willoughby of Parham, father of the prefent Lord, married Hefter, youngeft
daughter of Henry Davenport in Lancafhire, Efq; by
whom he had iffue, the prefent Lord, and a daughter
named Hellen.

This noble family is defcended from Sir John de
Willoughby, a Norman knight, who attending William the Conqueror into England, had the Lordfhip
of Willoughby in Lancafhire conferred on him.

Sir John Willoughby, another of the anceftors of this
noble Lord, attended king Edward III. in his wars in
France, and was in the battle of Poitiers, where

John,

John the French king, was taken prifoner in 1356.

Arms.] Or, frette, azure.

Creft.] On a wreath, the head and buft of a fara-
cen couped, and affronte, proper, crowned ducally.

Supporters.] On the dexter fide, an oftrich, argent,
beaked and membered, or, and in its beak an horfe-
fhoe, or; on the finifter, a favage wreathed about
the temples and loins with wild ivy, proper.

Motto.]

Chief Seats.] At Shaw-place and Worfley in the
county of Lancafter; Craven-ftreet, London.

---

9. CAREY, LORD HUNSDON.

THE Right Hon. WILLIAM-FERDINAND CAREY,
Baron of Hunfdon, fucceeded Robert, Lord
Hunfdon, in 1702; but refiding in Holland, did not
take his feat in the houfe of Peers till March 1707-8.
His Lordfhip in Jan. 1717-18, married Grace, daughter to Sir Edward Waldo, knight; but by her had
no iffue.

His Lordfhip, who is the eighth Lord Hunfdon, is
the fon of William Carey, and grandfon of Ferdinand
Carey, who was a colonel in the fervice of the States-
General, and died in the bed of honour at the fiege
of Maeftricht.

This noble Lord is defcended from Adam de Kerrey
or Carey, Lord of Caftle-Kerrey in Somerfetfhire, who
flourifhed in the reign of king Edward I.

Henry Carey, Efq; another of his lordfhip's anceftors, was nearly allied to Queen Elizabeth, and much
confided in by her, who advanced him to the title of
Baron Hunfdon, in the firft year of her reign, and
fettled four thoufand pounds *per Ann.* upon him,
having fpent great part of his own eftate in her fervice before fhe came to the crown.

She made him governor of Berwick in the tenth
year

year of her reign; during which command, he made several incurfions into Scotland, and fubdued the rebels commanded by Lord Dacres, who had formed a defign of fetting the Queen of Scots at liberty; whereupon the Queen made him general of the marches of Scotland, and lord chamberlain of her houfhold; and in the year of the Spanifh invafion, 1588, he commanded an army of 34000 foot and 2000 horfe, appointed for the fafety of the Queen's perfon.

Arms.] Argent, on a bend, fable, three rofes of the field, barbed and feeded, proper.

Creft.] On a wreath, a fwan with wings expanded, argent, beaked and membered, fable.

Supporters.] On the dexter fide a ram, argent, fpotted gules and azure, armed, ducally gorged and chained, or; on the finifter, a male gryphon of the firft, his beak, fore legs, plain collar chained, and rays, or.

Motto.] *Comme je trouve.*

---

10. ST. JOHN. LORD ST. JOHN of BLETSOE.

THE Right Hon. John St. John, Lord St. John of Bletfoe, and Baronet, fucceeded his father John, the late Lord June 24, 1757; and Dec. 13, 1755, married Mifs Simond, daughter of Peter Simond, Efq; merchant of London, by whom he had a daughter born Sept. 10, 1759.

John, the late Lord, married March 6, 1724-5, Elizabeth, daughter of Sir Ambrofe Crawley, of Greenwich, in the county of Kent, knight, and by her has had iffue, fix fons and fix daughters, viz.

1. John, the prefent Lord, born Nov. 15, 1725.

2. Andrew, the fecond fon, born Dec. 23, 1726, who died in January following.

3. Mary, the eldeft daughter, born Nov. 21, 1728.; married Oct. 16, 1754, to Henry Drax, Efq;

4. Ambrofe,

4. Ambrose, born May 23, 1730, who died Dec. 13, 1740.

5. St. Andrew, born Jan. 17, 1731-2.

6. Elizabeth, born Dec. 12, 1733.

7. Jane, born July 19, 1735.

8. Barbara, born Sept. 19, 1737.

9. Anne, born Jan. 31, 1738 9.

10. Henry, born June 1, 1740.

11. Lettice, born Dec. 7. 1741; and,

12. Ambrose, born October 17, 1743.

St. Andrew, the seventh Lord, grandfather of the present baron, had eight sons and seven daughters.

1. Mary, married to the Rev. William Foster.

2. Elizabeth, married to John Livesay, of Berks, Esq;

3. Jane.

4. Barbara.

5. Jane.

6. Anne, all died in their infancy.

7. Elizabeth, married to John Lucy of Hennick in the county of Bedford, Esq;

8. Oliver, the eldest, died unmarried.

9. St. Andrew, who had a posthumous son, named St. Andrew, and on whom devolved the title of Lord St. John of Bletsoe, as successor to Paulet, Earl of Bolingbroke; but he died in May, 1714, about two years of age, and the title devolved on,

10. William his uncle; which William dying in Oct. 1720, unmarried, was succeded by

11. Rowland, and he dying in July, 1722, unmarried, the honour came to,

12. John, father of the present Lord, his next brother.

13. Paulet.

14. Beauchamp.

15. Henry, who died unmarried.

This is the eldest branch of the ancient family of St. John, of Stanton St. John, in the county of Oxford.

Arms.]

Arms.] Argent on a chief, gules, two mullets pierced, or.

Creft.] On a mount, vert, a falcon rifing, belled, or, and ducally gorged, gules.

Supporters.] Two monkies, proper.

Motto.] *Data fata fecutus.*

Chief Scats.] At Melchburn in Bedfordſhire ; Woodford in the county of Northampton ; and Thriftſtreet, Soho.

11. PETRE, LORD PETRE.

THE Right Hon. ROBERT EDWARD PETRE, Baron Petre of Writtle, fucceeded Robert-James, the late lord his father, in honour and eſtate, in July 1742.

Robert-James, Lord Petre, father of the prefent lord, was born June 3, 1713; and married May 2, 1732, the daughter of James, late Earl of Derwentwater, by which lady, who died March 31, 1760, he had iſſue, Robert-Edward, his Son, now Lord Petre, and three daughters.

Robert, Loid Petre, grandfather of the prefent lord, married, March 1, 1711-12, Catherine, daughter of Bartholomew Walmeſley, in Lancaſhire, Eſq; and died March 22, 1712-13, leaving his lady then with child, who was brought to bed of a fon, named Robert, the late Lord Petre, which lady in April 1733, was married again to the Right Hon. Charles Lord Struton.

This noble lord is defcended from Sir William Petre, who was of the privy-council, and principal fecretary of ſtate in the reigns of king Henry VIII. king Edward VI. Queen Mary, and Queen Elizabeth ; and he negotiated the marriage between Queen Mary and Philip II. of Spain ; and was feven times fent ambaſſador to foreign princes.

Arms.] Gules, a bend, or, between two efcallop ſhells, argent.

Creft.

Creſt.] On a wreath, two lions heads erafed and indorſed, the firſt, or, the other, azure, each gorged with a plain collar counter-changed.

Supporters.] According to Lilly, on the right fide a lion reguardant, azure, collared, or; on the left fide a lion reguardant, or, collared, azure.

Motto.] *Sans Dieu rien.*

Chief Seats.] At Thorndon, Ingarſton, and Writtle-park, all in the county of Eſſex; at Dunkelagh, in the county of Lancaſter; and Brook-ſtreet, London.

---

12. ARUNDEL, LORD ARUNDEL OF WARDOUR.

THE Right Hon. HENRY ARUNDEL, Lord ARUNDEL of Wardour, and Count of the ſacred Roman empire, born March 31, 1740, ſucceeded his father Henry, the late lord, who died Sept. 21, 1756.

Henry, the late lord, born Oct. 4, 1717, married Mary, daughter of Richard Beeling Arundel, Eſq; by whom he had iſſue, Henry, the preſent lord, and Thomas, who married May 19, 1760, Miſs Mary Porter.

Henry, Lord Arundel of Wardour, grand-father of the preſent lord, was born Feb. 16, 1693, and ſucceeded to the honour on the death of his father, June 29, 1726. His lordſhip married Eleanor Elizabeth, daughter of the baron Everard, of Leige, by whom he had iſſué, beſides the late lord, two ſons, Thomas and James-Everard.

He married, after the death of his firſt lady, Anne, Daughter of William Herbert, late Marquis of Powis, by whom he had no iſſue. She died on the 8th of March, 1747-8.

This noble lord is deſcended from Roger de Arun-del, who came over to England with William the Conqueror, Anno 1066, who rewarded his ſervice

with

with twenty-eight manors in Somerfetſhire, taken from the Engliſh.

. Thomas, another of this Lord's anceſtors, was made a count of the empire, by the emperor Rodolph, in conſideration of his ſervices againſt the Turks.

Arms.] Sable, ſix ſwallows, three, two, and one, argent.

Creſt.] On a wreath, a wolf paſſant, argent.

Supporters.] On the dexter ſide, a lion guardant, erminois, viz. yellow powdered with black, ducally crowned, or. On the ſiniſter, an owl, argent; with wings diſcloſed, or; crowned as the dexter.

Motto.] Deo Data.

Chief Seat.] At Wardour-Caſtle, in Wiltſhire.

---

13. BLIGH, LORD CLIFTON.

THE Right Hon. JOHN BLIGH, Lord CLIFTON, Baron Clifton of Leighton Bromfwold, in Enggland, Earl and Viſcount Darnley, and Baron Clifton of Rathmore in Ireland, ſucceeded his brother Edward, the late lord, in 1747, and is yet unmarried.

John Bligh, Lord Clifton, father of the preſent lord, was created Baron Clifton of Rathmore, in the county of Meath, the 1ſt of Auguſt, 1722; and, on the 5th of February following, Viſcount Darnley of Athboy in the ſame county; alſo on the 1ſt of June, 1725, Earl of Darnley in Ireland, and died Sept 12, 1728, aged 41, having married Theodoſia Hyde, then only daughter and heir of Edward, Earl of Clarendon, who died July 30, 1722, leaving iſſue, two ſons and three daughters, viz.

1. Edward the late lord, who died in Auguſt 1747, unmarried,

2. John, the preſent lord.

3. Lady Mary, married to William Tighe, Eſq;

4. Anne, who married to Edward Ward, Eſq;

5. Theo-

5. Theodofia, married to William Crofbie, Efq;

The great grand-father of this noble lord, who lived in London, going over to Ireland, in the time of Oliver Cromwell, as an agent to the adventurers there, acquired a good eftate, and laid the foundation for the grandeur of this family.

Arms.] Azure, a gryphon fegreant, or; armed and langued, gules; between three crefcents, argent.

Creft.] On a wreath, a gryphon's head erafed, or..

Supporters. Two Gryphons, with wings expanded, or; each having a Ducal Collar and chain, azure.

Motto.] *Finem refpice.*

Chief Seats.] At Rathmore, in the county of Meath, in Ireland; Cobham-hall, in Kent; and Berkley-fquare, London.

---

14. D O R M E R, L O R D D O R M E R.

THE Right Hon. CHARLES DORMER, LORD DORMER of Wenge, and Baronet, fucceeded Charles, the late Lord Dormer, his father, July 2, 1728, and is yet unmarried.

Charles, Lord Dormer, father of the prefent lord, fucceeded to the title on the death of Rowland, Lord Dormer. He married to his firft wife, Catherine, daughter of —— Fettyplace, in the county of Oxford, Efq; by whom he had iffue, two fons, viz.

1. Charles the prefent lord. And,

2. John Dormer, Efq; who married Mary Bifhop, daughter of Sir Cecil Bifhop, of Parham, in the county of Suffex, Bart. by whom he had iffue, eight children, whereof Charles, eldeft fon, married to Lady Mary Talbot, fifter to the right Hon. George Talbot, Earl of Shrewfbury; and Elizabeth, married Nov. 21, 1753, to the faid Earl.

The

The said Charles, late Lord Dormer, married secondly, Elizabeth, daughter of Richard Bidulph, of the county of Stafford, Efq; by whom he had issue, fourteen children, of which four sons and four daughters are living, viz.

1. William, unmarried.

2. Robert,

3. Jofeph, and,

4. Francis, who are all three unmarried.

5. Anne, and,

6. Elizabeth, both unmarried.

7. Frances, third surviving daughter, married in 1726, to William Plowden, Efq; by whom she had fifteen children, of which twelve are living.

8. Mary, the youngest surviving daughter, is yet unmarried.

This noble lord is descended from the Dormers of Weft-Wiccomb, in Buckinghamshire; of which family was Sir Michael Dormer, lord mayor of London, in 1541, 21 Henry VIII.

Arms.] Azure, ten billets, four, three, two, and one, or; on a chief of the second, a demi-lion rampant, naissant, sable.

Creft.] On a wreath, a right-hand glove, proper; surmounted by a falcon, argent.

Supporters.] Two falcons, argent; armed, membered, and belled, or.

Motto.]

Chief Seats.] At Peterly, in the county of Bucks; Edfworth, in the county of Hants.

---

15. ROPER, LORD TEYNHAM.

THE Right Hon. HENRY ROPER, Lord TEYNHAM, succeeded his brother Philip in his honour and estate, June 1, 1727. He married in July, 1733, ——— daughter of Edmund Powel, of Sandford, in Oxfordshire, Efq; by whom he has had issue,

1. An-

1. Anthony, born March 12, 1741, who died July 20, the fame year.

2. Mary Catherine, born Dec. 24, 1742.

3. Winifred, born Dec. 5, 1743.

4. Chriftopher, who died Sept. 15, 1747. And,

5. Thomas, born Feb. 3, 1744-5.

Henry, Lord Teynham, father of the late, and prefent lord, married Catherine, daughter of Philip Smith, Lord Vifcount Strangford in Ireland, by which lady, who died April 16, 1711, he had two fons.

1. Philip, who fucceeded him; but died in June, 1727, in the 19th year of his age.

2. Henry, the prefent lord. And,

3. Elizabeth, married to John Webb, Efq; and died Nov. 14, 1736.   His Lordfhip married to his fecond lady, Mary, fifter to Sir William Gage, of Furle in Suffex, Bart. but by her had no iffue.   He married, thirdly, Lady Anne, late Baronefs Dacre, fecond daughter of Thomas Lennard, Earl of Suffex, and widow of Richard Lennard, of Woodhoufe, Efq; by whom he had iffue, two fons and one daughter, viz.

1. Charles, who died in 1755, having married Mifs Trevor, by whom he left feveral children.

2. Henry, a clergyman. He married the daughter of William Chetwin, Efq;

3. Anne.

This noble lord is defcended from the Ropers of Canterbury, who flourifhed in the reign of King Edward III.

Arms.] Party-per-fefs, azure and or, a pale, and three roe-buck's heads erazed, counterchanged.

Creft.] On a wreath, a lion rampant, fable ; holding a ducal coronet between his paws, or.

Supporters.] On the dexter fide, a buck, or. On the finifter, a tyger reguardant, argent.

Motto.] *Spes mea in Deo.*

Chief Seats.] At Linfted-Lodge, in the county of Kent; and Brook-ftreet, London.

L

MAY-

16 MAYNARD, LORD MAYNARD.

THE Right Hon. CHARLES MAYNARD, Lord MAYNARD of Eftaynes Parva, and Baron Maynard, Baron Maynard of Wickloe, in Ireland, and baronet, fucceeded his brother Grey, late Lord Maynard, in April 1745, and is yet unmarried.

Banafter, Lord Maynard, father of the prefent lord, marrried the lady Elizabeth Grey, daughter to Henry, late Earl of Kent, and by her, who died on the 23d of September, 1714, had iffue, eight fons and three daughters, viz.

1. William, who died before his father, in the 50th year of his age, in 1716-17, unmarried.

2. Banafter, fecond fon, died young.

3. Henry, third fon, fucceeded his father, in March, 1718-19, and died unmarried, Dec. 9, 1742.

4. Banafter.

5. Anthony, and,

6. Robert, who all died young.

7. Grey, who fucceeded his brother Henry, in Dec. 1742; died in April, 1745, unmarried.

8. Charles, the prefent lord.

9. Amabella, the eldeft daughter, married Sir William Lowther, of Swillington in the county of York, Bart.

10. Dorothy, who married Robert Hefilridge, Efq;

11. Elizabeth.

This noble lord is defcended from——Maynard, who came over with William the Conqueror, and whofe name is inferted in the roll among thofe who were in the conqueror's army at the battle of Haftings.

Arms.] Argent, a chevron, azure, between three finifter hands erect, couped at the wrift, gules.

Creft.] On a wreath, a ftag trippant, or.

Supporters.] On the dexter fide, a ftag, proper. On the finifter, a talbot, argent; pyed, fable; and gorged with a plain collar, gules.   *Motto.*]

Motto.] *Manus jufta nardus.*

Chief Seats.] At Eafton-Parva, in the county of Effex; Grofvenor-fquare, London.

---

17. MURRAY, LORD STRANGE.

THE Moft noble JAMES MURRAY, Lord STRANGE, of Knockyn in England, Duke of Athol in Scotland, and lord of the Ifle of Man. His grace took his place as Lord Strange, in the houfe of Peers, in March, 1736-7.

The Barony of Strange devolved on his grace James Murray, on the death of James Stanley, Earl of Derby, as great-grandfon and heir of James, Lord Strange, fon and heir of John Duke of Athol, fon and heir of John Marquis of Athol, by the Lady Amelia Sophia, daughter of James, Lord Strange.

[*An account of the family of this noble lord may be feen in the fecond volume, among the peers of Scotland, under the title of Duke of Athol.*]

Arms.] Quarterly, 1ft and 4th, azure; three mullets, argent; within a double treffure, flowered and counter-flowered, or; 2d and 3d, quarterly, viz. 1ft and 4th, paly of 6, fable and or; 2d and 3d, or; a fefs cheque, azure and argent.

Creft.] A demi-favage, holding in his dexter hand a key, or; and in his finifter a dagger, proper.

Motto.] *Furth fortune, and fill the fetters.*

Supporters.] On the dexter, a lion rampant, argent; collared, azure; charged with three mullets, argent; on the finifter, a favage, proper, wreathed about the loins with laurel.

Chief Seats.] Blair-Caftle, and Dunkeld in Perth-fhire; Grofvenor-fquare, London.

18. LEIGH,

18. LEIGH, LORD LEIGH.

THE Right Hon. EDWARD LEIGH, Lord LEIGH, of Stoneley, and Baronet, born the 1st of March, 1742, succeeded Thomas, late Lord Leigh, his father, Nov. 30, 1749.

Thomas, late Lord Leigh, father of the present lord, succeeded Edward, Lord Leigh, his father, in 1737-8. His lordship married Maria-Rebecca, daugh- . ter of   by whom he had issue, three sons and one daughter, viz.

1. Thomas, who died young.
2. Thomas, who died in 1741.
3. Edward, the present Lord Leigh.
4. Mary.

The said Maria-Rebecca, his wife, dying Dec. 9, 1746, he married to his second lady, in Dec. 1747, Catherine, daughter of Rowland Berkeley, of Cotheridge, in the county of Worcester, Esq; by whom he left issue, one daughter, Anne, born Oct. 28, 1748.

This family took their name from the town of High-Leigh in Cheshire, where they resided before the Norman conquest.

Arms.] Gules, a cross ingrailed, argent, a lozenge in the dexter chief of the second.

Crest.] On a wreath, an unicorn's head erased, argent; armed and mained, or.

Supporters.] Two unicorns, argent; armed and mained, or.

Chief Seats.] At Stoneley-abby, in Warwickshire; and at Fleathamstead, in the same county.

---

19. BYRON, LORD BYRON.

THE Right Hon. WILLIAM BYRON, Lord BYRON, of Rochdale, born Nov. 5, 1722, succeeded William, late Lord Byron, his father, Aug. 8,

3   1736,

1736, married March 28, 1747, Elizabeth, only daughter and sole heiress of Charles Shaw, Esq; of the county of Norfolk, by whom he had issue, two sons, William, born June 7, 1748, who died the May following, and William, his second son, born Oct. 27, 1749, and two daughters, the eldest of which died June 1, 1760.

William, Lord Byron, father of the present lord, born Jan. 4, 1669, married the Lady Mary, sister to Scroop, late Duke of Bridgewater, which lady died April 11, 1703, and his lordship married again Dec. 19, 1706, the Lady Frances-Wilhelmina, third daughter of William Bentinck, Earl of Portland, by whom he had issue, three sons and one daughter.

1. George, born Oct. 1, 1707, and died July 6, 1720.

2. William, born July 6, 1709, and died a few days after.

3. William-Henry, born Oct. 23, 1710, died soon after. And,

4. Frances, born Aug. 10, 1711, and died Sept. 21, 1724.

Which Frances-Wilhelmina, Lady Byron, dying March 31, 1712, his lordship in 1720 married Frances, second daughter of William, late Lord Berkley, of Stratton, by whom he had issue, one daughter and five sons.

1. Isabella, born Nov. 10, 1721, married in 1742, to the Earl of Carlisle.

2. William, the present Lord Byron.

3. John, born Nov. 8, 1723, married to Miss Trevanion.

4. Richard, born Oct. 28, 1734, student of Christ's church, in Oxford.

5. Charles, born April 6, 1726, who died May 16, 1731.

6. George, born April 22, 1730.

Which William, Lord Byron, their father died Aug. 8, 1736, and his lady is since married to Sir Thomas Hay, Bart.

From

From Doomſday-book it appears, that this family were poſſeſſed of numerous manors and lands in the reign of the conqueror; and that Sir John Byron, one of his lordſhip's anceſtors, attended King Edward III. in his wars in France.

Sir John Byron, another of this lord's anceſtors, was a great ſoldier, and performed many ſignal actions in the civil wars, in defence of king Charles I. to whom he continued faithful to the laſt.

Arms.] Argent, three bendlets enhanſed, gules.

Creſt.] On a wreath, a mermaid, with her comb and mirrour, all proper.

Supporters.] Two horſes cheſnut.

Motto.] *Crede Biron.*

Chief Seats.] At Linby, Newſtead Abbey, and Bull-well park, in Nottinghamſhire; Great Marlborough-ſtreet, London.

---

20 W A R D, L O R D W A R D.

THE Right Hon. JOHN WARD, Lord WARD, Baron of Birmingham, and recorder of the city of Worceſter, born in March, 1704, ſucceeded William, the late Lord Dudley and Ward, in the barony of Birmingham, in May, 1740, and on Dec. 26, 1723, he married Anna Maria, daughter of Charles Bour-chier, Eſq; by whom he has one ſon named John, born in 1724; and ſhe dying Dec. 12, 1725, his Lordſhip married, in Jan. 1744-5, Miſs Mary Carver, daughter of John Carver, Eſq; by whom he has iſſue William, born Jan. 21, 1750.

William Ward, Eſq; father of the preſent lord, married Mary, daughter of John Grey, of Enfield-hall in Staffordſhire, Eſq; third ſon of Henry the firſt Earl of Stamford, by whom he left iſſue two ſons and two daughters:

1. John, the preſent Lord Ward.

2. The

2. The Rev. Mr. William Ward, rector of King's Swinford and Himley, deceased.

3. Frances, married to George Rook, of St. Laurence, in Kent, Esq; who is since dead. And,

4. Anne, unmarried.

The anceſtors of this noble lord were antiently of the county of Norfolk, of which was Simon Ward, who had large poſſeſſions in the reign of Edward I. and was in France and Scotland in the reigns of king Edward II. III.

Arms.] Chequey, or and azure, a bend ermine.

Creſt.] In a ducal coronet, or, a lion's head azure.

Supporters.] Two angels haired and winged, or, their under robes ſanguine, and their uppermoſt azure.

Motto.] *Comme je fus.*

Chief Seats.] At Dudley-caſtle, Himley-hall, and Sedgeley-park, in Staffordſhire; Upper Brook-ſtreet, London.

---

21. LANGDALE, LORD LANGDLE.

THE Right Hon. MARMADUKE LANGDALE, Lord LANGDALE, ſucceeded his father, the late lord, Dec. 12, 1718, married Elizabeth, youngeſt daughter of William Lord Widdrington, and by her has iſſue one ſon and two daughters:

1. Marmaduke, his heir apparent, married to Conſtantia, daughter of the late Sir John Smyth of Acton Burnel, in Shropſhire, Bart, by whom he has iſſue two daughters, Conſtantia and Elizabeth.

2. Dorothy, married to Sir Walter Vavaſour, of Haſſewood, in Yorkſhire, Bart. And,

3. Elizabeth, unmarried.

Marmaduke, late Lord Langdale, father of the preſent lord, married Frances, daughter of Richard Draycotte, of Painefly in Yorkſhire, Eſq; by whom

L 4   he he had issue one son, the present Lord Langdale, and two daughters, viz. Elizabeth, married to Peter Middleton of Stockley in Yorkshire, Esq; and Frances, married to Nicholas Blundel, of Crosby in Lancaster, Esq;

This noble lord is descended from the Langdales of Yorkshire, who resided at the town of Langdale (from whence they took their name) in the reign of King John; but his ancestor, who makes the greatest figure in history, is Sir Marmaduke Langdale, who raised forces in the north of England, in defence of King Charles I. was victorious in numberless battles and sieges; and when his majesty, by the united forces of England and Scotland, was at length overpowered, he attended King Charles II. in his exile, and returned to England with his majesty at the restoration.

Arms.] Sable, a chevron between three estoils, argent.

Crest.] On a wreath, a star, argent.

Supporters.] Two bulls, sable, armed, crested, and ungulled, argent.

Motto.] Post tenebras lucem.

Chief Seats.] At Holme in Spaldingmore, and Dalton, both in Yorkshire; Golden-Square, London.

22. BERKLEY, LORD BERKLEY of STRATTON.

THE Right Hon. JOHN BERKLEY, Lord BERKLEY of Stratton, one of the Lords of his Majesty's privy council, and Captain of his Majesty's band of gentlemen pensioners, March 24, 1701, succeeded the late William Lord Berkley, whose father, Sir John Berkley, was by King Charles II. created Lord Berkley, of Stratton, in 1658.

The late William Lord Berkley, married Frances, youngest daughter of Sir John Temple, of East-Sheen,

in

in Surry, Knt. by whom he had issue three sons, and four daughters, viz.

1. John, the present lord.

2. William, who died March 25, 1733.

3. Charles, who married in 1745, Frances, daughter of Col. John West, by whom he has two daughters, Frances, Jane, and Sophia; and a son, Maurice John.

4. Jane, who died in 1744.

5. Frances, married in 1720, to William late Lord Byron. *See* Byron *Lord.*

6. Barbara, married March 29, 1726, to John Trevanion, Esq; and,

7. Anne, married in May 1737, to James Cocks, Esq;

This noble lord is descended from Sir Maurice Berkley, second son of Lord Berkley, of Berkley-castle, who flourished in the reign of King Edward II. and king Edward III. and was celebrated for his valour and conduct in the wars of Scotland and France.

This family were eminent also for their services to King Charles I. and King Charles II. during the civil war, and at the restoration.

Arms.] Gules, a chevron, ermine between ten crosses pattee, argent.

Crest.] On a wreath, an unicorn passant, gules.

Supporters.] Two Savages, with clubs over their shoulders, and wreathed about their temples and loins with ivy.

Motto.] *Pauca suspexi pauciora dispexi.*

Chief Seats.] At Abby-Bruton in Somersetshire, and Berkley square, London.

---

23. ARUNDEL, LORD ARUNDEL of TRERISE.

THE Right Hon. John Arundel, Lord Arundel, of Trerise, born Nov. 21, 1701, succeeded his father John, the late lord, Sept. 24, 1706, and

married

married Elizabeth, fifter to Thomas Wentworth, late Earl of Strafford, by whom he has no iffue.

John Lord Arundel, father of the prefent lord, married Jane, daughter of Dr. William Beaw, lord bifhop of Landaff, and dying Sept. 24, 1706, was fucceeded by his only fon John, the prefent Lord Arundel.

John Lord Arundel, grandfather to the prefent lord, married Margaret, daughter and fole heir of Sir John Ackland, of Devonfhire, knight, by whom he had iffue,

1. John, the late Lord Arundel.

2. Gertrude, married to Sir John Bennet, of Hof-kihs in Hertfordfhire, Bart.

He married to his fecond wife Barbara, daughter to Sir Henry Slingfby of the county of York, Bart. by whom he had iffue one fon Richard, next heir to the prefent lord, who married in September, 1732, the Lady Frances Manners, fifter of his Grace John Duke of Rutland, by whom he had no iffue.

This family came into England with William the Conqueror; and at the time of the general furvey, in the twentieth year of that reign, were poffeffed of twenty-eight lordfhips in Somerfetfhire.

John Arundel, of Trerife, one of his lordfhip's an-ceftors, took up arms in defence of King Charles I. with four of his fons, and two of them loft their lives in his majefty's fervice.

Arms.] Quarterly, 1ft and 4th, fable; fix fwallows clofe, 3, 2, and 1, argent; 2d and 3d, fable, three chevronels of the fecond.

Creft.] On a chapeau, gules, turned up ermine a fwallow, argent.

Supporters.] Two-panthers guardant, or, fpotted of various colours, incenfed proper, i. e. with fire iffu-ing out of their mouths and ears.

Motto.] *Nulli præda.*

Chief Seat.] At Trerife in Cornwall.

25. CRA-

24. CRAVEN, LORD CRAVEN.

THE Right Hon. FULWAR CRAVEN, Lord CRA-VEN, fuccecded his brother William, late Lord Craven, in his honour and eftate, in Aug. 1739, and is yet unmarried.

William Craven, Lord Craven, father of the late and prefent Lord, was born Oct. 4, 1668, and married Elizabeth, daughter of Humberfton Skipwith, Efq; by whom he had iffue, three fons,

1. William, late Lord Craven.
2. Fulwar, the prefent Lord. And,
3. Robert, who died unmarried.

His Lorfhip died Oct. 9, 1711, and was fucceeded by William, his eldeft fon, who married Anne, daughter to Frederick Tilney, of Rotherwick, by whom he had iffue, one daughter, who died Nov. 21, 1725.

This noble Lord is defcended from John Craven, of Appletreewick, in the county of York, who flourifhed in the reigns of Henry VII. and Henry VIII.

Arms.] Argent, a fefs between fix crofs croflets, fitchy, gules.

Creft.] On a chapeau, gules, turned up, ermine, a gryphon of the fecond beaked, or.

Supporters.] Two gryphons, ermine.

Motto.] *Virtus in actione confiftit.*

Chief Seats.] At Comb-Abbey, in Warwickfhire; Hampfted-Marfhal, in the county of Berks; George-ftreet, London.

---

25. CLIFFORD, LORD CLIFFORD.

THE Right Hon. HUGH CLIFFORD, Lord CLIF-FORD, of Chudleigh, born Sept. 29, 1726, fucceeded Hugh his father, late Lord Clifford, March 26, 1732; and married Lady Anne Lee, daughter of

George-

George-Henry Lee, late Earl of Litchfield, Dec. 17. 1749, by whom he has issue.

Hugh, Lord Clifford, father of the present Lord, born in 1700, married Elizabeth, daughter of Edward Blount, in the county of Devon, sister to the Dutchess of Norfolk, by whom he had issue, four sons and two daughters, viz.

1. Hugh, the present Lord.
2. Edward.
3. Henry, who died an infant.
4. Thomas, born after his father's decease, August 22, 1732.
5. Elizabeth, who died an infant. And,
6. Mary.

This noble Lord is descended from Walter de Clifford, of Clifford-castle in the county of Hereford, who came over into England with the Conqueror; of which family was fair Rosamond, mistress to King Henry II.

Sir Thomas Clifford, who was created Baron Clifford of Chudleigh, in the 24th of King Charles II. was constitured lord high treasurer of England the same year.

Arms.] Cheque, or and azure; a fess, gules, a crescent for difference.

Crest.] Out of a ducal coronet, or, a wyvern rising, gules.

Supporters.] On the dexter side a wyvern with wings expanded, azure; on the sinister, a monkey, proper, invironed about the loins, and chained, or.

Motto.] *Semper paratus.*

Chief Seats.] At Ugbrook, near Chudleigh in Devonshire; at Cannington, near Bridgwater, in the county of Somerset; Jermyn-street, London.

26. BOYLE,

26. BOYLE, BARON BOYLE.

THE Right Hon. John Boyle, Baron Boyle of Marlton, and Earl of Corke and Orrery in Ireland, born Jan. 2, 1706-7, succeeded Charles, his father, late Earl of Orrery, in 1731. His lordship married, May 9, 1728, the Lady Harriot Hamilton, daughter to George, Earl of Orkney, by which Lady, who died in 1739, he had issue two sons and one daughter, viz.

1. Charles, Lord Boyle, born Jan. 27, 1728-9, who in 1753, married Susannah, daughter of Henry Hoar, of Stourhead in Wiltshire, Esq; by whom he had issue one son, born in 1754, but died the year following; also a daughter, Henrietta, now living. His Lordship died Sept. 16, 1759.

2. Hamilton Boyle, born Feb. 3, 1729-30.

3. Lady Elizabeth, who married Thomas Worsley, Esq; son of Sir James Worsley, Bart. of Pitewell, in Hampshire.

He married to his second wife Mrs. Margaret Hamilton, daughter of John Hamilton, Esq; of Caledon in the county of Tyrone in Ireland, in June 1738, by whom he has issue living,

1. Edmund, born Nov. 21, 1742. And,

2. Lady Lucy.

Charles, Earl of Orrery, father of the present Earl, was created Baron Boyle, of Marston, in the county of Somerset, Sept. 10, 1711. He married Elizabeth Cecil, daughter to John, Earl of Exeter, grandfather of the present Earl; which Lady died a few years after her marriage, leaving issue by him, an only son, John, the present Earl of Orrery.

The machine called the Orrery, invented by the late Earl Charles, will perpetuate his memory to the latest posterity.

A

[*A more particular account of this noble family, the Reader will meet with under the title of Earl of Corke and Orrery in the third Volume of this work, among the Peers of Ireland.*]

Arms.] Party-per-bend crenelle, argent and gules, cresent for difference.

Crest.] On a wreath, a lion's head erazed, party-per-pale crenelle, argent and gules.

Supporters.] Two lions party-per-pale; the dexter gules and argent; the sinister of the second and first.

Motto.] *Honor virtutis præmium.*

Chief Seats.] At Marston, in the county of Somerset; at Caledon, in the county of Tyrone in Ireland; Great George-street, London.

---

27. HAY, LORD HAY.

THE Right Hon. THOMAS HAY, Lord HAY of Pedwardin, Viscount Dupplin, and Earl of Kinnoul in Scotland, one of his Majesty's privy-council, chancellor of the dutchy of Lancaster, and his Majesty's ambassador extraordinary and plenipotentiary to the court of Portugal, succeeded his father George-Henry, the late Earl, July 29, 1758, and married May 12, 1741, to Miss Arnley, of Wiltshire, who died in June 1753, leaving no issue.

The Earls of Kinnoul, who have resided for many generations in Perthshire, in North-Britain, were ancestors of this noble Lord.

[*A particular account of this noble family, the Reader will meet with, in the second Volume of this work, under the title of Earl of Kinnoul, among the Peers of Scotland.*]

Arms.] Quarterly, first and fourth, azure, an unicorn saliant, argent; armed, crested, and unguled, or; within a bordure, or; charged with eight thistles, proper; and as many demi-roses, gules; leaved, barbed,

barbed, and feeded, proper ; conjoined upon one ftem, fecond and third argent ; three efcutcheons, gules.

Creft.] On a wreath, an husbandman couped at the knees, habited in dark grey, with ruffet breeches, a red waiftcoat, and a Highland bonnet, azure ; holding over his right-fhoulder a double ox-yoke, proper.

Supporters.] Two husbandmen, habited as the creft, their ftockings ruffet, and fhoes brown ; the dexter bearing over his fhoulder the culture of a plough ; and the finifter, the plough-paddle, all proper.

Motto.] *Renovate animos.*

Chief Seats.] At Brodefworth, in Yorkfhire ; at Dup-lin-Houfe, in Scotland ; and Whitehall, London.

---

28. WILLOUGHBY, LORD MIDDLETON.

THE Right Hon. FRANCIS WILLOUGHBY, Lord MIDDLETON, of Middleton, and Baronet, fuc-ceeded his father Francis, the late Lord, Aug. 4, 1758. Francis, the late Lord fucceeded his father Thomas, April 2, 1729, and married on the 25th of July 1723, Mary, fecond daughter of Thomas Edwards, of the Middle-Temple, Efq; by whom he has had iffue,

1. Francis, the prefent Lord.

2. Thomas. And,

3. A daughter that died young.

Thomas, Lord Middleton, grandfather of the pre-fent Lord, was created Lord Middleton, Jan. 1, 1711. His Lordfhip married Elizabeth, daughter and coheir of Richard Rothwell, of Stapleford, Bart. by whom he had iffue, four fons, viz.

1. Francis, the late Lord.

2. Thomas Willoughby, Efq; who married Eliza-beth, fole daughter and heir of Thomas Southby, in Yorkfhire, Efq; who died in 1742, leaving iffue, fe-veral children.

3. Rothwell, who is yet unmarried.

4. Henry, who died unmarried.

This noble Lord is defcended from Sir Thomas Willoughby, lord chief juftice of the Common-pleas in the reign of King Henry VIII.

Arms.] Quarterly, firft and fourth, or; fretty, azure, for Willoughby of Parham and Eresby. Second and third, or, on two bars, gules, three water bougets, argent, for Willoughby of Middleton and Wollaton.

Creft.] On a wreath, the buft of a man, couped and affrontee, proper; crowned ducally, or.

Supporters.] On the dexter fide, a pilgrim, or grey-friar, in his habit, proper; with his beads, crofs, &c. and a ftaff in his right-hand, or. On the finifter, a favage with a club in his exterior hand, wreathed about the temples and middle with ivy, all proper; each fupporter holding a banner, gules; fringed, or; enfigned with an owl, argent; crowned, ducally collared, and chained, or; the owl being the creft of Willoughby of Middleton and Wollaton.

Motto.] *Verite fans peur.*

Chief Seats.] At Wollaton-Hall, in Nottingham-fhire; and at Middleton, in the county of Warwick.

---

29. TREVOR, LORD TREVOR.

THE Right Hon. JOHN TREVOR, Lord TREVOR of Bromham, and F.R.S. fucceeded his brother Thomas, late Lord Trevor, the 22d of March 1753, and married May 31, 1731, Elizabeth, daughter of that celebrated author, Sir Richard Steele, Knt. by whom he has now living an only daughter, Diana.

The late Lord married in 1730, Elizabeth, only daughter and heir of Timothy Burrel of Cuckfield, Efq; and by her, who died in Aug. 1734, has one daughter, Elizabeth, married to his Grace Charles, late Duke of Marlborough. *See Duke of* Marlborough.

Thomas

Thomas Trevor, Lord Trevor, father of the late and prefent Lords, was created Lord Trevor of Bromham, Jan. 1, 1711. He married to his firft wife Elizabeth, daughter and coheir of John Searle, of Finchley, in Middlefex, Efq; by whom he had two fons and three daughters, viz.

1. Thomas, late Lord Trevor.

2. John, the prefent Lord.

3. Anne.

4. Letitia, married to Peter Cock, of Camberwell, Efq; and,

5. Elizabeth.

His Lordfhip married, fecondly, Anne, daughter of Robert Weldon, Efq; by whom he had three fons,

1. Robert, who has taken the firname and arms of Hampden.

2. Richard Trevor, D. D. lord bifhop of Durham.

3. Edward, who died young.

He was made follicitor-general in the year 1692, and attorney-general in 1695; and in the reign of Queen Anne, was conftituted lord chief-juftice of the Common-pleas; in 1725, lord privy-feal ;- and in 1730, was made prefident of his Majefty's moft honourable privy-council.

This noble Lord is defcended from Rourd Wieduck, one of the moft antient families of Wales, faid to have flourifhed in the reign of King Arthur; but the firft who had the name of Trevor, was Tudor Trevor, Earl of Hereford.

Arms.] Party-per-bend, finifter, ermine and erminois, a lion rampant, or.

Creft.] On a chapeau, gules; turned up, ermine; a wyvern rifing, fable.

Supporters.] Two wyverns reguardant, fable.

Chief Seats.] At Bromham, in Bedfordfhire; Mount-Pleafant, near Barnet, in Middlefex; Peckham, in Surry; and Bond-ftreet, London.

30. MASHAM, LORD MASHAM.

THE Right Hon. SAMUEL MASHAM, Lord Masham and Baronet, remembrancer of his Majefty's court of Exchequer, and auditor-general to the Prince of Wales, fucceeded his father Samuel, the late Lord, Oct. 16, 1758, and in Oct. 1736, married Harriot, daughter of Sawley Winnington in the county of Worcefter, Efq; by whom he has no iffue.

Samuel, father of the prefent Lord, was created Lord Mafham of Oates, in the county of Effex, Jan. 1, 1711. He married Abigail, daughter to Francis Hill, a Turkey merchant ; by which Lady, who died Sept. 6, 1734, he had iffue, two daughters and three fons. viz.

1. George, who died unmarried.
2. Samuel, the prefent Lord.
3. Francis, who died unmarried.
4. Anne, who married April 11, 1726, to Henry Hoar, Efq; which Lady died March 4, 1727.
5. Elizabeth, youngeft daughter, died on Oct. 25, 1724, in the fourteenth year of her age.

Sir Francis Mafham, Bart. father of the prefent Lord, married Mary, daughter of Sir William Scot, Bart. of Rouen in Normandy, by whom he had iffue, eight fons and one daughter. He married to his fecond wife Damaris, daughter of Ralph Cudworth, D. D. and had iffue, one fon, Francis-Cudworth Mafham, who died May 17, 1731; and the faid Sir Francis, their father, died in March 1702-3, in the 77th year of his age.

This noble Lord is defcended from Sir John Mafham, who flourifhed in the reign of King Henry VI. and was buried at Thorneham, in the county of Suffolk, in 1455.

Arms.] Or, a fefs hemette, gules, between two lions paffant, fable.

Creft.]

Creſt.] On a wreath, a gryphon's head couped, or, between two wings erect, gules.

Supporters.] On the dexter ſide, a lion, ſable ; on the ſiniſter, a leopard guardant, proper, each having an eaſtern crown, or.

Motto.] *Mihi juſſa capeſſere.*

Chief Seats.] At Oates-hall, in the county of Eſſex ; and Burlington-ſtreet, London.

31. FOLEY, LORD FOLEY.

THE Right Hon. Thomas Foley, Lord Foley, of Kidderminſter, ſucceeded his father Thomas, the late Lord Foley, in his honour and eſtate, Jan. 22, 1732-3, and is yet unmarried.

Thomas Foley, Lord Foley, father of the preſent Lord, was by Queen Anne, created a peer of this realm, by the title of Lord Foley, Baron Foley of Kidderminſter, January 1, 1711. His Lordſhip married Mary, daughter and ſole heireſs of Thomas Strode, Eſq; by whom he had iſſue, four ſons and two daughters, of which Thomas, the preſent Lord, and Elizabeth, only are living.

He is deſcended from an ancient family in the county of Worceſter.

Arms.] Argent, a feſs, ingrailed between three cinquefoils, within a plain border, ſable.

Creſt.] On a wreath, a lion rampant, argent; holding between his paws an eſcutcheon of the arms of Foley.

Supporters.] Two lions, argent ; femee of cinque-foils, ſable.

Motto.] *Ut proſim.*

Chief Seats.] At Whitley-Court, in the county of Worceſter ; Hanover-ſquare, London.

32. BATHURST, LORD BATHURST.

THE Right Hon. ALLEN BATHURST, Baron Bathurst of Battlesden, treasurer to the Prince of Wales, was created Lord Bathurst, Jan. 1, 1711. His Lordship married Catherine, daughter and heir of Sir Peter Apsley, by whom he hath issue, four sons and five daughters, viz.

1. Benjamin, born Aug. 12, 1711, and married Nov. 26, 1732, Elizabeth, daughter of Charles, late Earl of Ailesbury; but by her has no issue.

2. Henry, a judge in the court of Common-pleas, who married Mrs. Philips.

3. John, deceased.

4. Allen, fellow of New-College, Oxford.

5. Frances, married Aug. 5, 1731, to William Woodhouse, Esq; who died in March 1735. She married, secondly, to James Whitshed, of the kingdom of Ireland, Esq; by whom she has no issue.

6. Catherine, married in 1737, to Henry Courtney, Esq;

7. Jane, the third daughter, married in April 1744, James Buller, member of parliament for the county of Cornwall.

8. Leonora, married in 1752, to colonel Urmston.

9. Anne, married in 1752, to the Rev. Mr. Benson.

Sir Benjamin Bathurst, father of the present Lord, married Frances, daughter of Sir Allen Apsley, Knt. by whom he had issue, three sons and one daughter, viz.

1. Allen, the eldest son, the present Lord.

2. Peter, the second son, married to Miss How, daughter and heir of Charles How, of Gritworth, in the county of Northampton, Esq; and she dying, he married to his second wife the Lady Selina Shirley, eldest daughter of Robert, Earl Ferrers, by his second wife.

3. Ben-

3. Benjamin Bathurſt, Eſq; the youngeſt ſon, married the daughter and coheir of — Poole, of Kemble, in Wiltſhire, who died in child-bed, 1737-8, having had twenty-one children, whereof ſeven ſurvived her. He married, 1742, to his ſecond wife, Miſs Broderick, only daughter of Dr. Broderick.

4. Anne, married to Henry Pye, of Farrington, in Berkſhire, Eſq;

This noble Lord is deſcended from the Bathurſts, of Bathurſt-Caſtle, near Battle-Abbey in the county of Suſſex.

Arms.] Sable, two bars, ermine ; in chief three croſſes, pattee, or.

Creſt.] On a wreath, a dexter arm in mail, embowed, and holding a club with ſpikes, all proper.

Supporters.] Two ſtags argent ; each gorged with a collar gemel, ermine.

Motto.] *Tien ta foy.*

Chief Seats.] At Ruskins in the county of Bucks ; at Cirenceſter, in Glouceſterſhire ; and St. James's-ſquare, London.

33. ONSLOW, LORD ONSLOW.

THE Right Hon. Richard Onslow, Lord Onslow, and Bart. lord lieutenant and cuſtos rotulorum of the county of Surry, and knight of the moſt honourable order of the Bath, born in the year 1713, ſucceeded Thomas, his father, the late lord, in June 1740. He married the year following, Mary Ellwell, daughter of the late Sir Edward Ellwell, by whom he has no iſſue.

Thomas, Lord Onſlow, father of the preſent lord, married Elizabeth, ſole daughter and heir of Mr. Knight, of the iſland of Jamaica, and by her, who died April 19, 1731, had iſſue, an only ſon, Richard, the preſent lord.

Sir

Sir Richard Onflow, eldeft fon of Sir Arthur Onflow, and grandfather to the prefent lord, was one of the knights of the fhire for the county of Surry in the reign of King James II; and in the reign of King William, was one of the lords of the admiralty, and fpeaker of the houfe of commons; and fworn of the privy-council to Queen Anne, in 1710. On the acceffion of his late majefty, he was conftituted one of the lords of the treafury, and chancellor and under-treafurer of the exchequer; and having been a ftrenuous afferter of the proteftant intereft, was created lord Onflow, Baron of Onflow, in the county of Salop, June 25, 1716, with limitation, for want of iffue male, to his uncle, Denzil Onflow, of Pyrford, Efq; and the heirs male of his body. He married Elizabeth, daughter of Sir Henry Tulfe, by whom he had iffue, two fons and two daughters, viz.

1. Thomas, late Lord Onflow.

2. Richard, who died young.

3. Elizabeth, who married to Thomas Middleton, of Standfted-Montfitchet, in the county of Effex; and after his death, fhe married fecondly to Samuel Baldwin, Efq; and,

4. Mary, who married to Sir John Williams, of Stoke, in the county of Suffolk, Knt.

This noble lord is defcended from the Onflows of Shropfhire, who flourifhed in the reign of King Henry III. They took their name from their manor of Onflow, or Ondeflow, in that county.

Arms.] Argent, a fefs, gules, between fix Cornifh choughs, proper.

Creft.] On a wreath, a faulcon, proper; legged and belled, or; feeding on a partridge, proper.

Supporters.] Two faulcons, with wings difclofed, proper; legged and belled, or.

Motto.] *Semper fidelis.*

Chief Seats.] At Weft Clandon, in Surry; Marlborough-ftreet, London.

54. MAR.

34 MARSHAM, LORD ROMNEY.

THE Right Hon. ROBERT MARSHAM, Lord ROMNEY, fucceeded his father, the late Lord Romney, Nov. 28, 1724; and married Mifs Pym of the ifland of St. Kitts, by whom he had iffue, four fons and four daughters, viz.

1. Robert, born in May 1743.
2. Charles, born in Jan. 1745-6.
3. John, fince dead.
4. Prifcilla, born in Jan. 1750-1.
5. Elizabeth. 6. Frances, born April 1755. 7. A fon, bcrn Oct. 22, 1757, and 8. A daughter, March 1, 1759.

Robert Marfham, Lord Romney, father of the prefent lord, was created Lord Romney June 25, 1716, 2 Geo. I. His Lordfhip married Elizabeth, daughter and coheir of Sir Cloudefley Shovel, by whom he had iffue Robert, now Lord Romney, and two daughters, Elizabeth, who married in May, 1741, the Right Hon. Jacob Bouverie, Lord Vifcount Folkefton; (*See* Folkefton, *Vifcount,*) and Harriot, who is yet unmarried. His lady furviving, fhe married John, late Lord Carmichael, and Earl of Hyndford, in Scotland.

This noble lord is defcended from the Marfhams of the town of Marfham, in the county of Norfolk, from which town they took their name.

Arms] Argent, a lion paffant in bend, gules, between two bendlets, azure.

Creft.] On a wreath, a lion's head erafed, gules.

Supporters.] Two lions, azure; femee of crofs croflets and ducally gorged, or.

Motto.] *Non fibi fed Patriæ.*

Chief Seats.] At the Mote, near Maidftone in Kent, and at Cuxton, in the fame county; Clifford-ftreet, London.

35. CADOGAN, LORD CADOGAN.

THE Right Hon. Charles Cadogan, Lord Cadogan, Baron of Oakley, colonel of the second troop of horse-guards, governor of Gravefend and Tilbury fort, and lieutenant-general, fucceeded his brother William, the late Lord, July 5, 1726. He married Elizabeth, daughter of Sir Hans Sloan, Bart. by whom he hath iffue, one fon, Charles-Sloan Cadogan, born Oct. 29, 1728, who married in 1747, Frances Bromley, daughter of the late Lord Montfort, by whom he has iffue, a fon, named Charles-Henry; and three other fons, viz. William, Edward, and George.

Henry Cadogan, Efq; father of the late and prefent lord, married Bridget, daughter to Sir Hardrefs Waller, Knt. by whom he had two fons, viz.

William, the eldeft fon, late Earl of Cadogan, who diftinguifhed himfelf in a great many battles againft the French; efpecially at the battle of Tanniers near Mons, in 1709, and was on the 21ft of June, 1716, created a peer of Great Britain, by the title of Lord Cadogan, baron of Reading; and on the 8th of May, 1718, 4 George I. was created Baron of Oakley, Vifcount Carverfham, and Earl of Cadogan, with remainder of the barony of Oakley, to Charles his brother. His lordfhip married Margaretta Cecilia Munter, daughter of William Munter, counfellor of the court of Holland, by whom he had iffue, two daughters, viz.

1. Sarah, married to Charles, late Duke of Richmond; and,

2. Margaret, married to Count Bentinck.

And dying on the 17th of July, 1726, the title of Baron of Oakley, devolved on Charles, his only brother, now Lord Cadogan.

Earl Cadogan, was made colonel of a regiment of Horfe, and brigadier-general in 1704; and at the

bat-

battles of Schellenrberg and Hochſtet, the ſame year, behaved with great bravery.

In 1706, he was appointed plenipotentiary to the Spaniſh Netherlands, and advanccd to the degree of a major-general; and in 1709, was conſtituted lieutenant-general: he was dangerouſly wounded in the neck at the ſiege of Mons. On the acceſſion of the late King George I. he was made maſter of the robes, and colonel of the ſecond regiment of horſe-guards; and in 1716, was made governor of the iſle of Wight, and plenipotentiary to the States of Holland. On the Duke of Marlborough's death, in 1722, he was appointed maſter general of the ordnance, and colonel of the firſt regiment of foot-guards. No officer was ſo much relied on by the late Duke of Marlborough, as Lord Cadogan. He had the care of marking out almoſt every camp during the war in the Netherlands and Germany, in the reign of Queen Anne, which he executed with ſo much ſkill, that it is obſerved, the duke was never ſurpriſed or attacked in his camp during all that war.

This noble lord is deſcended from Kehdlin, Prince of Powis in Wales, from whom deſcended William Cadwygan, or Cadogan, of Llanbeder, in the county of Pembroke, another of the anceſtors of Lord Cadogan.

Arms.] Quarterly, 1ſt and 4th, gules; a lion rampant reguardant, or; 2d and 3d, argent; three boars heads couped, ſable.

Creſt.] Out of a ducal coronet, or; a gryphon's head, vert.

Supporters.] On the dexter ſide, a lion reguardant, or; on the ſiniſter, a gryphon reguardant, vert; each gorged with a double treſſure, flowered and counter-flowered, gules.

Motto.] *Qui invidet minor eſt.*

Chief Seats.] At Caverſham in Oxfordſhire; Bruton-ſtreet, London.

36. DUCIE-MORTON, LORD DUCIE.

THE Right Hon. Matthew Ducie Morton, Lord Ducie, and Baron of Morton, in Staffordshire, succeeded his father, the late Lord Ducie, May 2, 1735.

Matthew Ducie Morton, father of the present lord, was created Lord Ducie and Baron Morton, June 13, 1720. His lordship married Arabella, daughter and coheir of Thomas Prestwich, of Holm, Bart. by whom he had issue, three sons and four daughters:

1. Matthew, the present lord.

2. Rowland Lewis, who is dead.

5. Charles who married Miss Anne Wyat, daughter of ——— Wyat, of Windsor, in Berkshire, Esq; and had issue by her a son, named Benjamin, that died.

4. Elizabeth, his eldest daughter, married first to Richard Syms, of Black-heath, Esq; and secondly, to Francis Reynolds, only son and heir of Thomas Reynolds, Esq;

5. Mary,

6. Arabella; and,

7. Penelope, all three dead.

This noble lord is descended from the Ducies in Normandy. After they came into England, king Edward I. conferred on them the lordship of Morton, in Staffordshire, and several other lordships and manors, which the family enjoyed for many ages.

Sir Robert Ducie, one of his lordship's ancestors, was lord mayor of London in the reign of king Charles I. and though he lent his Majesty 80,000 l. which was lost by the king's being driven from London, he died however worth 400,000 l.

Arms.] Argent, a chevron, gules, between three square buckles, sable.

Crest.]

Creſt.] Out of a wreath, a moor-cock riſing, proper, comb and wattles, gules.

Supporters.] Two unicorns, argent, armed maïned,
tufted, and hoofed, or; each gorged with a ducal coronet, party-per-pale, or and gules.

Motto.] *Perſeverando.*

Chief Seats.] At Spring-park and Tortworth, in
the county of Glouceſter; Brook-ſtreet, London.

---

37. KING, LORD KING.

THE Right Hon. WILLIAM KING, Lord KING,
Baron of Ockham, ſucceeded his brother Peter,
on the 22d of March, 1754.

Peter, the firſt Lord King, was choſen recorder of
the city of London, July 27, 1708, and on the 12th
of September following, had the honour of knight-
hood conferred on him. He was cohſtituted Lord
chief juſtice of the common-pleas, in the 1ſt year of
King George I. in Michaelmas term, 1714, and on
the 5th of April following, was ſworn of his majeſty's
moſt hon. privy council. On May 19, 1725, 11 Geo.
I. he was created a peer of this kingdom, by the title
of Lord King, baron of Ockham, in the county of
Surry, and in June, the ſame year, declared Lord
high chancellor of England, which he reſigned in
Nov. 1733. His lordſhip married Anne, daughter
of Richard Seys, of Boverton, Eſq; and departing this
life, July 22, 1734, left iſſue by her four ſons and two
daughters:

1. John, his eldeſt ſon, who ſucceeded him in honour and eſtate, married in May, 1729, Elizabeth,
daughter of Robert Fry, of Devonſhire, Eſq; but
dying Feb. 10, 1739-40, without iſſue, was ſucceeded by,

2. Peter, late Lord King, the ſecond ſon, who
dying unmarried in 1754, was ſucceeded by,

3. Wil-

3. William, now Lord King.

4. Thomas, the fourth son, married in 1734, a lady of an ample fortune in Holland, and has issue, two sons, Peter and Thomas, and two daughters.

5. Elizabeth, who died in 1749; and,

6. Anne.

Arms.] Sable, three spears heads erect, argent; embowed, gules; on a chief, or; as many pole-axes, azure.

Crest.] On a wreath, a dexter arm, couped below the elbow and erect, habited, azure; and thereon three spots, or; turned down, argent; the hand proper, grasping a truncheon, sable, the top broken off, and the bottom enameled of the second.

Supporters.] Two English mastiffs reguardant, proper; each having a plain collar, gules.

Motto.] *Labor ipse voluptas.*

Chief Seats.] At Ockham, in the county of Surry; St. James's-street London.

---

38   M O N S O N, L O R D M O N S O N.

THE Right Hon. JOHN MONSON, Lord Monson, and Baronet, succeeded John, his father, the late lord, in July 1748.

His lordship in June, 1752, married Theodosia, daughter of John Maddison, in the county of Lincoln, Esq; by whom he has issue, John, his son and heir, born in 1753; a daughter named Arabella, born in 1754, another son, George Henry, born in 1755; and a third son, born March 12, 1758.

Sir John Monson, Bart. father of the present lord, was created Lord Monson, May 28, 1728. His lordship married the Lady Margaret Watson, youngest daughter of Lewis, Earl of Rockingham, and had issue three sons, viz.

1. John, the present Lord Monson, born July 23, 1727.

2. Lewis, born Nov. 28, 1728, to whom Thomas, late Earl of Rockingham left his estate, on condition

of his taking the name of Watſon. On the 16th of February he was appointed one of the auditors of the imprefs and foreign accounts, firſt fruits, tenths, cuſtoms, and of the mint and coinage. He married, Oct. 12, 1752, Grace, the third daughter of the late Right Hon. Henry Pelham, Eſq; by whom he hath iſſue, two ſons, viz. Lewis Thomas, born April 18, 1754, and Henry, born April 20, 1755. On May 20, 1760, he was created Baron Sondes of Lees Court, in the county of Kent.

3. George, born April 18, 1730.

This noble lord is deſcended from John Monſon, who flouriſhed in the reign of king Edward III. from whom deſcended another John, who attended King Henry V. in his wars in France.

Sir William Monſon, another of this lord's anceſtors, applying himſelf to the ſea, was made an admiral by queen Elizabeth, and was at the taking and plundering the city of Cadiz, with the Earl of Eſſex, in 1596; he was alſo at the taking a galleon of 1600 tons, worth a million of ducats, in which were, alſo the Marquis of Sancta-Cruz, and 300 other Spaniſh gentlemen; he continued admiral in the reigns of King James I. and King Charles I. dying about the commencement of the civil war, and is ſtill celebrated for his judicious naval tracts.

Arms.] Or, two chevrons, gules.

Creſt.] On a wreath, a lion rampant, ſuſtained by a pillar, or.

Supporters.] On the dexter ſide, a lion, or; having a collar and chain azure; the collar charged with three creſcents of the firſt; on the ſiniſter, a gryphon, argent; its collar and chain as the dexter, and its fore legs, azure.

Motto.] *Preſt pour mon pais.*

Chief Seats.] At South Carlton and Northod, both in the county of Lincoln; at Broxborn, in Hertfordſhire; Piccadilly, London.

39. TALBOT, LORD TALBOT.

THE Right Hon. WILLIAM TALBOT, Lord
Talbot, Baron of Henfol, fucceeded his father
Charles, the late lord, in Feb. 1736-7. In Feb. 1733-4,
he married Mary, daughter and fole heir of Adam
Cardonnel, Efq; by whom he has one fon, William,
born Nov. 5, 1739, and a daughter, Cecil, married
to —— Rice, of Newton in Caermarthenfhire.

Charles, Lord Talbot, fon of the late Right Rev.
William Talbot, lord bifhop of Durham, and father
of the prefent lord, was created Lord Talbot, and
Baron of Henfol, Dec. 5, 1733. His lordfhip married
Cecil, daughter and heir of Charles Matthews, of
Glamorganfhire, Efq; and by her had iffue five
fons, viz.

1. Charles-Richard Talbot, who died in Sept. 1733.
2. William, now Lord Talbot.
3. John, who married May 30, 1737, Mifs Henrietta Maria, fecond daughter of Sir Matthew Decker,
of Richmond, Bart. and after her death, married a
daughter of Lord Chetwynd. He died Sept. 22, 1756.
4. Edward, who died an infant. And,
5. George, a clergyman.

The faid late Lord Charles, was made folicitor-
general, in 1726, and lord high chancellor of Great-
Britain, in 1733; which poft his lordfhip held till
his death, in Feb. 1736-7.

This noble lord is defcended from Sir Gilbert Talbot, of Grafton, knight of the garter, third fon of
John, the fecond Earl of Shrewfbury.

Arms.] Gules, a lion rampant, within a border engrailed, or; a crefcent for difference.

Creft.] On a chapeau, gules, turned up, ermine,
a lion, or; his tail extended.

Supporters.] Two talbots, argent; accolled with a
double nefure flory, collared gules.

Motto.]

Motto.] *Humani nihil alienum.*

Chief Seats.] At Caftle-Menych, and Henfol, in the county of Glamorgan; Barrington in Gloucefter-fhire; Lincoln's-Inn-Fields, London.

---

40. BROMLEY, LORD MONTFORT.

THE Right Hon. Thomas Bromley, Lord Montfort, Baron of Horfeheath, high fteward of the town of Cambridge, fucceeded his father Henry, the late lord, who died Jan 1, 1755.

John Bromley, Efq; grandfather of the prefent lord, died in 1707, leaving two fons, viz.

1. John Bromley, Efq; who died unmarried in Nov. 1718. And,

2. Henry, the late Lord Montfort, who married the fifter and fole heir of Sir Francis Wyndham, Bart. of Trent, in the county of Somerfet, by whom he had iffue Thomas, of whom fhe died in child-bed, and a daughter, Frances, married to Charles Sloan Cadogan, fon and heir of Charles Lord Cadogan.

This noble lord is maternally defcended from Sir Walter Bromleghe, of Bromleghe, in the county of Stafford, who flourifhed in the reign of king John.

Sir Thomas Bromley, another of his lordfhip's anceftors, was conftituted lord-high-chancellor of England, 21 Eliz. in which poft he died, 29 Eliz.

Arms.] Quarterly, per pale, dovetail, gules and or.

Creft.] Upon a wreath, a demi-lion rampant, fable; iffuing out of a mural crown, or; holding a ftandard, vert; charged with a gryphon paffant, argent.

Supporters.] On the dexter fide, an unicorn cream-coloured, gorged with a ducal coronet, thereto a chain reflected over his back, horned and unguled, or. On the finifter fide, an horfe, argent; pellited, collared, dovetail, azure; thereon three lozenges, or.

M 4

Motto.

Motto.] *Non inferiora fecutus.*

Chief Seats.] At Horfe-heath, in the county of Cambridge ; Queen-ftreet, May-fair, London.

41. HOW, LORD CHEDWORTH.

THE Right Hon. John-Thynne How, Lord Chedworth, and Baron of Chedworth, lord-lieutenant and cuftos rotulorum of the county of Gloucefter, and conftable of St. Brionel's caftle in the foreft of Deane, fucceeded John, the late Lord his father, in April 1742, and married Sept. 23, 1751, Martha, daughter and coheir of Sir Philip Parker Long, of Arwarton in Suffolk, Bart. but as yet hath no iffue.

John, late Lord Chedworth, father of the prefent Lord, was created Lord Chedworth, Baron of Chedworth, in the county of Gloucefter, May 12, 1741, 14 Geo. II. His Lordfhip married Dorothy, eldeft daughter of Henry Frederick Thynne, Efq; Grandfather of Thomas, the prefent Lord Vifcount Weymouth, by whom he had iffue, fix fons and two daughters.

1. John the prefent Lord Chedworth.

2. Henry-Frederick.

3. Thomas, married to Mifs White, about the year 1746.

4. Charles.

5. James, married July 5, 1755, to Mifs Howarth, daughter of Sir Humphry Howarth.

6. William.

7. Mary. And,

8. Anne.

This noble lord is defcended from the Hows of Somerfetfhire, who refided in that county for many generations, where they were poffeffed of a great eftate, and of other lands in Devonfhire and Effex.

Sir Scrope How appeared very zealous and active in bringing about the Revolution in 1688, and joined

with

with the Earl of Nottingham and other Lords and
gentlemen in fubfcribing a declaration : " That they
" owned it to be rebellion to refift a king that go-
" verned by law ; but he was always accounted a
" tyrant that made his will the law ; and to refift
" fuch a one, they juftly efteemed no rebellion, but
" a neceffary and juft defence."

Arms.] Or, a fefs between three wolves heads
couped, fable ; a crefcent for difference.

Creft.] On a wreath, a dexter arm in armour, erazed below the elbow, lying fefs-ways, and holding
in the hand a fcymetar erected, all proper ; hilted
and pomelled, or ; pierced through a boar's head,
couped, fable.

Supporters.] On the dexter fide, a lion, argent ; pellited, armed, and langued, gules. And on the finifter
fide, an angel, proper ; the face profile, with brown-
ifh hair, habited crimfon, the under garment, azure ;
the wings, argent ; pinioned of the fourth.

Motto.] *Juftus & propofiti tenax.*

Chief Seats.] At Stawell in Glouceftershire ; Wifh-
ford, in Wiltshire ; and Curzon-ftreet, London.

42. EDGCUMBE, LORD EDGCUMBE.

THE Right Hon. RICHARD EDGCUMBE, Lord
EDGCUMBE, Baron of Mount Edgcumbe, lord
lieutenant and cuftos rotulorum of the county of
Cornwal, fucceeded his father the late Lord Nov.23,
1758.

Richard, the late Lord, born in 1680, was created
Baron Edgcumbe of Mount Edgcumbe, in the county
of Devon, April 20, 1742, 15. Geo. II. His Lordfhip married Matilda, daughter of Sir Henry Furnefe,
of Walderfhair in the county of Kent, Bart. by whom
he had iffue two fons.

M 5.   1. Ri-

1. Richard, the prefent Lord.

2. George, a captain in the navy, and commodore of a fquadron in the Eaft-Indies.

Sir Richard Edgcumbe, Knt. father of the late Lord, born in 1639, married the lady Anne Montagu, fecond furviving daughter of Edward, late Earl of Sandwich, by whom he had iffue, two fons and fix daughters, viz.

1. John, who died an infant in 1674.   And,

2. Richard, the late Lord.

3. Anne.

4. Mary.

5. Elizabeth.

6. Catherine.

7. Anne.   And,

8. Margaret, who are all fince dead.

This Sir Richard, died in 1688, his Lady furviving him forty-one years.

The anceftors of this noble Lord received their name from their manor of Edgcumbe in Devonfhire. One of this Lord's anceftors was Sir Richard Edgcumbe, who came over to England with the Earl of Richmond, having a great fhare in the victory he obtained over King Richard III. at Bofworth, by which the Earl made his way to the throne of England.

Arms.] Gules, on a bend, ermine; cottifed, or; three boars heads couped, argent.

Creft.] On a wreath, or and gules, a boar paffant, argent; a chaplet about the neck of oak leaves, fructed, proper.

Supporters.] On each fide, a greyhound, argent; gutte-de-poix, collared, dovetail, gules.

Motto.] *Au playfire fort de Dieu.*

Chief Seats.] At Mount-Edgcumbe, near Plymouth, in Devonfhire; in Upper Grofvenor-ftreet, London.

43. S A N-

43. SANDYS, LORD SANDYS.

THE Right Hon. SAMUEL SANDYS, Lord SANDYS, Baron of Omberſley, and one of his Majeſty's moſt honourable privy council, lord warden and chief juſtice in Eyre of all his Majeſty's foreſts, parks, chaces, and warrens beyond Trent, was created Lord Sandys, and Baron of Omberſley in the county of Worceſter, Dec. 20, 1743, 17 Geo. II. He married in 1724, Letithea, the eldeſt daughter and heir of Sir Thomas Tipping, of Wheatfield, in the county of Oxford, Bart. by whom he has had iſſue, ſeven ſons and three daughters.

1. Edwin, member of parliament for Droitwich, in Worceſterſhire.

2 Cheek, who died in 1737.

3. Thomas, who died in 1728.

4. Martin, lieut. col. of the ſecond regiment of foot-guards, married June 17, 1760 to Miſs Trumbull, with an immenſe fortune.

5. Letithea.

6. William, who died Oct. 31, 1749.

7. Anne.

8. John.

9. Catherine, who died in 1736.

10. Henry, who died in 1737.

Edwin Sandys, Eſq; father of the preſent Lord, eldeſt ſon of Samuel Sandys, Eſq; married Alice, daughter of Sir James Ruſhout, of Northwick, Bart. by whom he had two ſons and one daughter.

1. Samuel, the preſent Lord.

2. Edwin, who died young. And,

3. Alice, who died unmarried.

This noble Lord is deſcended from the ancient family of Sandys of Furneſe in Lancaſhire, from which deſcended the Right Rev. Edwin Sandys, biſhop of

Wor-

Worcefter, and afterwards archbifhop of York, in the reign of Queen Elizabeth, one of the anceftors of the prefent Lord.

Arms.] Or, a fefs dancette between three crofs croflets fitchee, gules.

Creft.] A gryphon fegreant per fefs, or and gules.

Supporters.] On each fide, a gryphon per fefs, or and gules, collared dancette of the laft.

Motto.] *Probum non pænitet.*

Chief Seats.] At Omberfley, near Worcefter; in Upper Grofvenor-ftreet, London.

44. BRUCE-BRUDENEL, LORD BRUCE.

THE Right Hon. THOMAS BRUCE-BRUDENEL, Lord BRUCE of Tottenham, youngeft fon of George, late Earl of Cardigan, fucceeded to the title of Lord Bruce, on the death of Charles, Earl of Ailesbury, Feb. 10, 1746-7, when the title of Earl of Ailesbury became extinct. *See* Cardigan *Earl.*

The faid Charles, late Earl of Ailesbury, was created Lord Bruce of Tottenham in Wiltfhire, 19 Geo.II. 1746, with limitation of that honour to his nephew, the prefent Lord Bruce. His Lordfhip married Lady Anne Saville, eldeft daughter and coheir to William, Marquis of Halifax, by whom he had two fons and two daughters.

1. George, born in 1707, who died young.

2. Robert, who married in 1728-9, Frances, daughter of Sir William Blacket, of Newcaftle upon Tyne, Bart. and died without iffue.

3. Lady Mary, his eldeft daughter, married in Dec. 1728, to Henry Bridges, Marquis of Carnarvon, now duke of Chandos, and died in Auguft 1738.

4. Lady Elizabeth, married in 1732, to the Hon. Benjamin Bathurft, Efq; fon and heir to Allen, Lord Bathurft.

The faid Earl Charles, married to his fecond wife, the Lady Juliana Boyle, fecond daughter of Charles, late Earl of Burlington, who died without iffue by him, in 1738.

He married again in June, 1739, Caroline, only daughter of John Campbel, Efq; and dying Feb. 10. 1746-7, left iffue by her, a daughter, named Mary, married in 1757, to the Duke of Richmond.

Arms.] Argent, a chevron, gules, between three fteel caps, azure, differenced by a martlet, fable ; being the diftinction of a fourth fon.

Creft.] On a wreath, a fea horfe naiant, argent, mane and tail, or.

Supporters.] (Granted March 24, 1746-7.) On either fide a favage wreathed about the temples, and girt about the loins with ivy, all proper; holding in their exterior hands a banner ftreaming over their heads, or, charged with a faltier, and chief, gules, on a canton argent, a lion rampant, azure, the ftaff and point proper.

Motto.] *Think and Thank.*

Chief Seat.] Tottenham-Foreft in Wiltfhire.

---

45. FORTESCUE, LORD FORTESCUE.

THE Right Hon. MATTHEW FORTESCUE, Lord FORTESCUE, of Caftle-hill, married June 8, 1752, Anne, fecond daughter of John Campbell, of Calder in Scotland, and of Stackpole-court in the county of Pembroke, Efq; by whom he hath iffue,

1. Hugh, born March 12, 1753.
1. Matthew, born April 12, 1754. And,
3. John, born March 6, 1755.

Hugh Fortefcue of Filleigh, Efq; married Bridget, fole daughter and heir of Hugh Bofcawen of Tregothan,

than, in Cornwal, Efq; by Margaret, his wife, fourth-
daughter, and at laft, coheir of Theophilus, Earl of
Lincoln and Baron Clinton, by whom he had two
fons, Hugh and Theophilus; and by a fecond wife
Lucy, fecond daughter to Matthew, Lord Aylmer,
he had Matthew, now Lord Fortefcue : and the fifters
of Margaret, daughter of the Earl of Lincoln having
no iffue, the Barony of Clinton devolved on Hugh
fon and heir of the forementioned Hugh and Bridget,
who was afterwards July 5, 1746, created Earl Clinton and Baron Fortefcue of Caftle-hill, Devon ; and
in default of iffue male, the faid title of Baron Fortefcue to defcend to Matthew, his youngeft brother,
and the heirs male of his body. Theophilus, his
Lordfhip's brother, died unmarried, and his Lordfhip dying unmarried May 2, 1751, the Barony of
Fortefcue defcended to the prefent Lord.

This noble Lord is defcended from the Fortefcues
of Winfton in Devonfhire, who flourifhed in the reign
of King Edward I. from whom defcended John Fortefcue, who was lord chief juftice of Ireland, in the
reign of King Edward VI.

Arms.] Azure, a bend engrailed, argent, cottized,
or.

Creft.] On a wreath, a plain fhield, argent.

Supporters.] Two grey-hounds, argent, each having
a ducal collar, or, with a double treffure, gules.

Motto.] *Forte fcutum falus ducum.*

Chief Seats.] At Filleigh, in the county of Devon,
of late called Caftle-Hill; Ebrington in Gloucefterfhire ; and Grofvenor-fquare, London.

46. ANSON, LORD ANSON.

THE Right Hon. GEORGE ANSON, Lord ANSON,
Baron of Soberton, vice admiral of England,
firft lord of the Admiralty, and one of the lords of
his Majefty's privy-council, was created Lord Anfon,
Baron

Baron Soberton of the county of Southampton, June 10, 1747, 21 Geo. II. His Lordſhip married April 25, 1748, Elizabeth, eldeſt daughter of the Right Hon. Philip, Lord Hardwick, now Earl of Hardwick, and formerly lord chancellor of Great-Britain, by which Lady, who died June 1, 1760, he had no iſſue.

William Anſon, Eſq; father of the preſent Lord, married Iſabel, daughter and coheir of Charles Carrier, of Wirkworth, in the county of Derby, Eſq; and ſiſter to the Counteſs of Macclesfield, mother of the preſent Earl of Macclesfield.

The ſaid William Anſon, the Admiral's father, died in Auguſt 1720, leaving iſſue, two ſons and four daughters, viz.

1. Thomas Anſon, of Shugborough, Eſq; member of parliament for Litchfield.

2. George, Lord Anſon.

3. Jenetta, married to ———— Adams, Eſq; and has iſſue.

4. Iſabella.

5. Anna. And,

6. Joanna.

This noble Lord is deſcended from the Anſons of Staffordſhire, a family which reſided at Dunſtan in that county for ſeveral generations; until William Anſon, Eſq; purchaſed the manor of Shugborough in that county, in the reign of King James, and made it his chief ſeat.

Arms.] Argent, three bends ingrailed, gules; and a creſcent.

Creſt.] Out of a ducal coronet, the top of a ſpear, argent.

Supporters.] On the dexter ſide, a ſea horſe, argent; on the ſiniſter, a ſea lion, of a dun-mouſe colour, each gorged with four gemels, or.

Motto.] *Nil deſperandum.*

Chief Seats.] Moor-Park in Hertfordſhire; and Soberton, in the county of Southampton.

47. DUNCOMBE, LORD FEVERSHAM.

THE Right Hon. Anthony Duncombe, Lord Feversham, and Baron of Downton, was created Lord Feverſham, in the county of Kent, and Baron of Downton in Wiltſhire, June 23, 1747. His Lordſhip married the Hon. Margaret, daughter of George Verney, late Lord Willoughby of Brook, and ſiſter to the preſent Lord, who dying in Oct. 1755, left iſſue, a daughter, who died an infant, and three ſons.

1. Charles, and
2. Anthony, who died young. And,
3. George, who alſo died in Auguſt, 1741.

His Lordſhip married for his ſecond Lady, Nov. 2, 1756, Frances, daughter of Peter Bathurſt, of Clarendon Park in Wiltſhire, Eſq; by whom he had a daughter born Nov. 12, 1757, and her Ladyſhip died the 21ſt of the ſame month. His Lordſhip married 3dly, Anne, daughter of Sir Thomas Hales of Howlett in Kent, Bart. Aug. 8, 1758, by whom he has a daughter, born June 9, 1759.

Anthony Duncombe, Eſq; youngeſt brother of Sir Charles Duncombe, father of the preſent Lord Feverſham, married Jane, eldeſt daughter and coheir of the Hon. Frederick Cornwallis, Eſq; ſecond ſon of Frederick Lord Cornwallis, treaſurer of the houſhold to King Charles II. by whom he had three ſons and ſeven daughters, whereof Anne, the eldeſt, who married to John Sawyer of Haywood in Berkſhire, Eſq; and Anthony, now Lord Feverſham, only are living.

This noble Lord is deſcended from the Duncombes of Barley-End in Buckinghamſhire. Sir Charles Duncombe, uncle of the preſent Lord, was lord-mayor of London, in 1709.

Arms.]

Arms.] Per chevron ingrailed, gules and argent ; three talbots heads erafed counterchanged.

Creft.] A horfe's thigh bent at the joint, fable ; the fhoe, argent, iffuing out of a ducal coronet, or.

Supporters.] On each fide, a dark grey horfe, gutte d'or, ducally collared, or.

Motto.] *Deo, Regi, Patriæ.*

Chief Seats.] At Barford, near Downton in Wilt-fhire ; in Grofvenor-ftreet, London.

---

48. LIDDELL, LORD RAVENSWORTH.

THE Right Hon. HENRY LIDDELL, Lord RA-VENSWORTH, and Baronet, was created Lord Ravenfworth, in the county of Durham, June 29, 1747, 21 George II. His Lordfhip married in April 1735, Anne, only daughter of Sir Peter Delme, Knt. alderman and lord-mayor of London, by whom he hath iffue, one daughter, named Anne, married Jan. 29, 1756, to Lord Eufton, now Duke of Grafton.

Sir Thomas Liddell, father of the prefent Lord, eldeft fon of Sir Henry Liddell, Bart. married Jane, eldeft daughter of James Clavering, of Greencroft, in the county of Durham, Efq; and dying in 1715, in his father's life-time, left iffue, now living, Henry, Lord Ravenfworth ; two other fons and a daughter, all died young. Thomas, his youngeft fon, married Margaret, fifter to George Bowes, Efq; and has iffue, one fon living, named George.

This noble Lord is defcended from the ancient Lords of Liddell Caftle, in the county of Durham, where they have been proprietors of great coal-works time out of mind.

Arms.] Argent, frettee, gules ; on a chief of the fecond, three leopard's faces, or.

Creft.] On a wreath, a lion rampant, fable ; crowned, or.

Supporters.] On each fide a leopard, or, fpotted, purple, gorged with a mural crown of the fecond.

Motto.] *Unus & Idem.*

Chief Seats.] At Ravenfworth-caftle, and Newton, both in the county of Durham ; Eflington, in Northumberland ; in St. James's-fquare, London.

49. ARCHER, LORD ARCHER.

THE Right Hon. Thomas Archer, Lord Archer, Baron of Umberflade, recorder of Coventry, and cuftos rotulorum of the county of Flint, was created Lord Archer, and baron of Umberflade, in the county of Warwick, July 14, 1747, 21 George II. He married Catherine, youngeft daughter of Sir Thomas Tipping, of Wheatfield in Oxfordfhire, Bart. by whom he hath iffue, one fon and two daughters. Her ladyfhip died July 20, 1754.

1. Andrew.

2. Catherine, who married in July, 1750, to the Right Hon. the Earl Plymouth, And,

3. Anne, married to Edward Tournour of Shillinglet park, in Suffex, Efq; March 15, 1756.

Sir Andrew Archer, father of the prefent lord, fon of Thomas Archer, Efq; married Elizabeth, daughter of Sir Samuel Dafhwood, lord mayor of London, in 1702, by whom he had iffue, three fons and four daughters, viz.

1. Thomas, now Lord Archer.

2. Henry, who married in 1743, the lady Mary Montagu, third daughter of George, late Earl of Halifax.

3. Daniel, deceafed.

4. Anne.

5. Elizabeth.

6. Sarah ; and,

7. Diana, who married to Thomas Chaplin, of Blankney-hall in Lincolnfhire, Efq;

This

This noble lord is defcended from John de Archer, who came over from Normandy with William the Conqueror; and this family is one of the moft antient in Warwickfhire, being fettled at Umberflade in that county, ever fince the reign of Henry II. John, another of his lordfhip's anceftors, was champion to Thomas Earl of Warwick, in the reign of king Henry III. And Thomas was Lord Prior of St. John's of Jerufalem, in the 14th of King Edward II.

Arms.] Azure, three arrows, or.

Creft.] Out of a mural crown, or; a wyvern's head, argent.

Supporters.] Two wyverns reguardant, argent, gorged with a mural crown, or.

Motto.] Sola bona quæ honefta.

Chief Seats.] At Umberflade near Stratford in Warwickfhire; at Pirgo near Rumford in Effex; Grofvenor-fquare, London.

---

50. PONSONBY, LORD PONSONBY.

THE Right Hon. WILLIAM PONSONBY, Lord PONSONBY, Baron Penfonby, of Syfonby, in England, Earl and Baron of Befborow, and Vifcount Duncannon in Ireland, and one of the lords of the treafury, fucceeded his father Brabazon, the late lord, in July 1758, and married in July, 1739, the lady Carolina Cavendifh, eldeft daughter of William, late Duke of Devonfhire, by which lady, who died Jan. 20, 1760, he hath iffue two daughters, Catherine and Charlotte, and one fon, John, born in 1749. Brabazon, the late lord, married Sarah, widow of Hugh Colvil, Efq; by whom he had iffue three fons.

1. William, the prefent lord.

2. The Hon. John Penfonby, Efq; one of the commiffioners of the revenue in Ireland, who married in

Sept.

Sept. 1743, the lady Elizabeth, second daughter to William, Duke of Devonshire.   And,

    3. Richard.

Sir William Ponsonby, father of the present lord, was created baron of Besborow, in the county of Kilkenny, in Ireland, in 1721, and Viscount Duncannon of the county of Wexford, in Feb. 1722-3.   He married Mary, Sister to Brabazon Moor, in the county of Louth, Esq; and by her had issue three sons and three daughters, viz.

    1. Brabazon, who succeeded him in Nov. 1724, the late Lord Ponsonby.

    2. Henry, who married the lady Frances Brabazon, youngest daughter of Chambre, earl of Meath, and was killed at the battle of Fontenoy, in May, 1745.

    3. Foliot, who died in Oct. 1746.

    4. Elizabeth, married to Col. Thomas Newcomen.

    5. Dorothy; and

    6. Letitia.

This noble family received their name from the lordship of Ponsonby, in the county of Cumberland, of which they were long proprietors; but are descended from an ancient family of Picardy in France, that came over with the Conqueror, when he made the descent upon England, in 1066.

[*For a more particular account of this noble family, we refer the reader to the third volume of this work, where he will find it treated of under the title of Earl of Besborow, among the peers of Ireland.*]

Arms.] Gules, a chevron between three combs, argent.

Crest.] In a ducal coronet, azure; three arrows envelloped with a snake, proper.

Supporters.] On each side two lions reguardant, azure.

Motto.] *Pro rege, lege, grege.*

Chief Seats.] At Besborow in the county of Kilkenny, and Sysonby in the county of Leicester.

                  51. BEAU-

51. BEAUCLERK, LORD VERE.

THE Right Hon. VERE BEAUCLERK, Lord VERE of Hanworth, third fon of his Grace, Charles, late Duke of St. Alban's, born July 14, 1699, was conftituted one of the commiffioners of the office of high-admiral of England and Ireland in 1737-8, which he refigned in July 1749. In March 1750, he was created Lord Vere of Hanworth, in Middlefex; and in April 1736, he married Mary, eldeft daughter and coheir of Sir Thomas Chambers, of Hanworth, in Middlefex, Bart. and has had iffue three fons ; of whom Auberry only is living, and a daughter named Mary. (*See Duke of St.* Alban's.)

Arms.] Quarterly in the firft and fourth, quarterly, France and England with a batoon, gules, charged with three rofes, argent; fecond and third quarterly, gules, and or, in the firft quarter a mullet, argent, for Vere.

Creft.] On a chapeau, gules ; turned up ermine ; a lion paffant, or, crowned party-per pale, argent and gules, and gorged with a collar, gules, charged with three rofes, argent.

Supporters.] The fame as the Veres, earls of Oxford. On the dexter fide a boar, azure; armed, crined and membered, or; on the finifter a harpie, or ; face and neck, proper.

Motto.] *Vero nil verius.*

Chief Seats.] Hanworth-Houfe, near Ifleworth in Middlefex; St. James's-fquare, London.

---

52. VILLIERS, LORD HYDE.

THE Right Hon. THOMAS VILLIERS, Lord Hyde of Hindon, in the county of Wilts, fecond fon to William, late Earl of Jerfey, on March 30, 1752, married the Lady Charlotte Hyde, only daugh-

ter

ter of William Earl of Effex, by his wife, the Lady
Jane, daughter and coheir of Henry Earl of Clarendon, by whom he has iffue, a fon born Dec. 26, 1752,
another born Nov. 23, 1759, and other children.
On June 1, 1756, his Lordfhip was created a Baron,
by the name and ftile of Lord Hyde of Hindon, in
the county of Wilts, to extend to the heirs-male of
his body, by the Lady Charlotte Hyde ; and in default of fuch iffue, the title of Baronefs Hyde of Hindon, as aforefaid, to devolve to the faid Lady Charlotte Hyde, and the heirs-male of her body. For the
anceftors of this noble Lord, *See Earl of* Jerfey.

Arms.] Argent, on a crofs, gules ; three efcallop
fhells, or; on an efcutcheon of pretence, azure ; a
chevron, between three lozenges, or.

Supporters.] On either fide, an eagle, wings, or ;
ducally collared and legged, or ; each charged on the
breaft with a crofs, argent.

Chief Seats.] At Hindon, Wilts ; Grove, Hertfordfhire ; Downing-ftreet, London.

---

53. WALPOLE, LORD WALPOLE.

THE Right Hon. Horatio Walpole, Lord
Walpole, of Woolterton in Norfolk, fucceed-
ed his father Horatio, the late Lord, who was created
Baron Walpole, in June 1756, and died in Feb. 1757.
(*See Earl of* Orford.)

Arms.] Or, on a feffe between two chevrons, fable,
three crofs croflets, a crefcent for difference.

Supporters.] On the dexter fide, a royal hart, proper, charged with a crofs croflet, and on the fhoulder
a crefcent, or; and on the finifter, a lion rampant,
charged with a crofs croflet, and on the fhoulder with
a crefcent, fable.

Chief Seat.] Woolterton, in Norfolk.

54. MUR-

54. MURRAY, LORD MANSFIELD.

THE Right Hon. WILLIAM MURRAY, Lord MANSFIELD, baron of Mansfield, in the county of Nottingham, lord chief juftice of the court of king's bench, one of his Majefty's moft honourable privy council, and one of the governors of the charter-houfe, was created a peer in Oct. 1756.

His lordfhip is brother to Lord Vifcount Stormont, one of the fixteen peers for Scotland; and is married to the lady Elizabeth, fifter to the prefent Earl of Winchelfea and Nottingham, by whom he has no iffue.

[*For a more particular account of this noble lord's family, the reader is defired to confult the fecond volume of this work under the title of Vifcount Stormont, among the peers of Scotland.*]

Arms.] Azure, three mullets, argent, within a double treffure, or.

Supporters.] On either fide, a lion rampant, gules, the dexter femeed with mullets; the finifter with croffes patty, argent.

Motto.] *Uni æquus virtuti.*

Chief Seats.] Cane-wood, near Hampftead in Middlefex; Lincoln's-Inn fields, London.

55. HILL, LORD HARWICH.

THE Right Hon. WILLS HILL, Earl of HILS-BOROUGH, Vifcount and Baron Kilwarling, in the kingdom of Ireland, and one of his Majefty's moft hon. privy council, was on Nov. 24, 1756, advanced to the dignity of a peer of Great Britain, by the name, ftile and title of Lord Harwich, Baron of Harwich, in the county of Effex; and to defcend to the heirs-male of his body.

3

[*For*

[For a more particular account of the family of this no-ble lord, confult the Earl of Hilsborough, in the third volume of this work, among the peers of Ireland.]

Arms.] Sable, on a feffe, argent, between three leopards, paffant, guardant, or; three efcallops, gules.

Creft.] On a wreath, a rein deer's head, couped and erect, gules, collared and horned, or.

Supporters.] Dexter fide, a leopard, proper, ducally collared and chained; finifter, by a rein deer, gules; or, collared and chained as the laft.

Motto.] *Netentes aut perfice.*

Chief Seat.] At Timwefton in the county of Bucks.

56. LYTTELTON, LORD LYTTELTON.

THE Right Hon. GEORGE LYTTELTON, Baron of FRANKLEY, in Worcefterfhire, and Baronet, one of his Majefty's moft hon. privy council, and F. R. S. Son and heir of Sir Thomas Lyttelton, born Jan. 17, 1708-9, was chofen, in feveral parliaments, one of the reprefentatives for the borough of Oak-hampton in Devon; was, in 1737, appointed prin-cipal fecretary to the Prince of Wales; and in 1744, conftituted one of the lords commiffioners of the treafury, which he refigned in 1754, on being ap-pointed cofferer to his majefty's houfhold. The fame year, he was made privy counfellor; and in Dec. 1755, having refigned the office of cofferer to his Majefty's houfhold, he was made chancellor of the Exchequer; and was created baron of Frankley, by letters patent, dated Nov. 19, 1757, 30 Geo. II.

This noble lord, married, June 15, 1742, Lucy, daughter of Hugh Fortefcue of Filleigh, in Devon, Efq; by whom he has iffue, one fon, Thomas, and a daughter named Lucy, now living.

Their mother dying, Jan. 19, 1746-7, he married
a fe-

a fecond time, viz. Aug. 10, 1749, Elizabeth Rich, daughter of Sir Robert Rich, Bart. by whom he has no iffue.

Sir Thomas Lyttelton, the father of this lord, married, May 8, 1708, Chriftian, daughter of Sir Richard Temple of Stowe, in Bucks, Bart. and maid of honour to Queen Anne, by whom he had iffue fix fons and fix daughters.

1. George, the prefent Lord Lyttelton.

2. Thomas, who died unmarried, April 16, 1729, being at that time page of honour to the Princefs Royal.

3. Charles, L. L. D. dean of Exeter, one of his Majefty's chaplains in ordinary, and rector of Alvechurch in Worcefterfhire.

4. Richard, who died in his infancy.

5. Another Richard, formerly page of honour to her late majefty queen Caroline, now lient. general of his majefty's forces, knight of the bath, mafter of the jewel office, and member of parliament for Poole, in Dorfetfhire. He married, Dec. 14, 1745, Rachel, dutchefs dowager of Bridgwater, and daughter of Wriothefly Duke of Bedford.

6. William-Henry, appointed governor of South Carolina, in Jan. 1755.

7. Chriftian, married to Thomas Pitt of Boconnock, in Cornwal, Efq; and died, June 4, 1750.

8. Anne, married to the Rev. Francis; Ayfcough, D. D. prebendary of Winchefter, and formerly preceptor to the prince of Wales and Prince Edward.

9. Mary.

10. Penelope.

11. Amelia, all deceafed,

12. Hefter, now living, unmarried.

This family appear to have been of very antient ftanding and confiderable rank, at South Lyttelton and Frankley in Worcefterfhire: for fo early as the 9th Edward II. Thomas de Luttelton (or Lyttelton)

N   was

was chofen knight of the fhire for that county. His fon Thomas, was Efquire of the body, to king Richard II. Henry IV. and Henry V. and his great grandfon Thomas, was knight of the bath, and judge of the common pleas. This Sir Thomas Lyttelton was the author of the famous Treatife on Tenures, which Lord Coke fo learnedly commented upon, and ftiles him the Englifh Juftinian, and father of the law. He flourifhed under kings Henry VI. and Edward IV. Sir Thomas, father of the prefent lord, fat in three parliaments, as knight of the fhire for the county of Worcefter; and in one for Camelford, in Corn-wal. He was many years one of the lords com-miffioners of the admiralty, and died Sept. 14, 1751, aged fixty-fix.

Arms.] Argent, a chevron between three efcallops, fable.

Creft.] On a wreath, a Moor's head in profile, couped proper, with a rowl about the head, argent and fable.

Supporters.] Two tritons or mermen, with tridents, all proper.

Motto.] *Ung dieu, ung roy.*

Chief Seats.] At Hagley-Hall in Worcefterfhire, (Frankley Houfe, the antient feat of the family being burnt in the laft civil war) and Over-Arley in Staf-fordfhire; Hill-ftreet, London.

57. HENLEY, LORD HENLEY.

THE Right Hon. ROBERT HENLEY, Baron HENLEY, Lord Keeper of the great feal of Great Britain, and one of his Majefty's moft hon. privy council, was created Baron Henley of Grange, in the county of Southampton, March 29, 1760.

Arms.] Quarterly firft and fourth azure, a lion ram-pant argent, crowned with a ducal coronet, or, with-

in

in a border, argent, charged with eight torteauxes ﹔ fecond and third, three battering rams.

Creft.] A demi lion ducally crowned.

Supporters.] On the dexter fide, a lion rampant, ducally crowned and femeed with torteauxes ; on the finifter, a ftag fem eed with torteauxes.

Motto.] *Sola et unica virtus.*

Chief Seat.] At Grange in the county of Southampton.

---

58. PETTY, LORD WYCOMBE.

THE Right Hon. JOHN PETTY, Lord WYCOMBE, Baron of CHEPING-WYCOMBE, in the county of Buckingham, and Earl of Shelburne, Vifcount Fitzmaurice, and Baron of Dunkerton, in the county of Waterford, in the kingdom of Ireland, was advanced to the dignity of a peer of Great Britain, as above, May 20, 1760.

Arms.] Ermine, on a bend, fapphire, a magnetic needle pointing at a pole ftar, topaz, together with the arms of the Earl of Kerry, quartered, with a crefcent for difference.

Creft.] On a wreath a bee-hive, befet with be , diverfely volant proper.

Supporters.] On the dexter fide a pegafus, ermine, bridled, crined, winged, unguled, topaz, charged on the fhoulder with a fleur-de-lis, fapphire ; on the finifter fide, a gryphon, topaz.

Motto.] *Ut apes geometriam.*

Chief Seat.] At Cheping-Wycombe, in the county of Bucks.

[*For an account of the family of this noble lord, the reader is defired to confult the third volume of this work under the title of Earl of Shelburne, among the peers of Ireland.*]

N 2   59. MON-

59. MONSON-WATSON, LORD SONDES.

THE Right Hon. Lewis Monson-Watson, Lord Sondes, of Lees Court, in the county of Kent, was advanced to the degree of a peer as above, May 20, 1760.

This noble lord is brother to the prefent Lord Monfon. *See Lord* Monfon.

ch *Arms.*] Quarterly, firft and fourth argent, on a chevron engrailed, azure, between three martlets, able, as many crefcents, or; fecond and third, or; two chevrons, gules.

Creft.] A griffin's head erafed argent, with a ducal coronet, or.

Supporters.] On the dexter fide, a griffin argent, gorged with a ducal coronet, or; on the finifter, a bear argent, collared, or.

Motto.] *Efto quod effe videris.*

Chief Seats.] Lees Court, near Feverfham, in the county of Kent; and at Rockingham caftle, Northamptonfhire.

A

SHORT VIEW

OF THE

PEERESSES

OF

ENGLAND.

I. CAMPBELL, MARCHIONESS GREY.

THE Moſt noble JEMIMA CAMPBELL, Marchionefs GREY, and Baronefs Lucas of Crudwel, only daughter of John, now Earl of Breadalbin, by the lady Amabel Grey, eldeſt daughter and coheir of Henry de Grey, late Duke of Kent, ſucceeded to the title of Marchionefs Grey, &c. on the death of her grandfather the ſaid Henry, late duke of Kent, in June, 1740. She married May 22, the ſame year, to the Right Hon. Philip Yorke, Lord Vifcount Royſton, eldeſt ſon of Philip, Earl Hardwicke, by whom ſhe has iſſue, two daughters, Amabel, born Jan. 22, 1751; and Mary Jemima, born Feb. 9, 1756.

Henry, late Duke of Kent, grandfather of the preſent Marchionefs, was lord chamberlain of the houſhold to Queen Anne, and ſworn of her Majeſty's privy council, and was created Vifcount Goodrich, of Goodrich-caſtle, in the county of Hereford, Earl of Harold, in the county of Bedford, and Marquis of Kent, Dec. 14, 1706; and, on April 28, 1710, was created Duke of Kent. He was alſo of the privy-council to his late Majeſty King George I. gentleman of the bedchamber, and lord ſteward of his Majeſty's houſhold.

His

His grace married Jemima, eldeft daughter of Thomas, Lord Crew, of Steane, by whom he had four fons and feven daughters, viz.

1. Anthony, born in Feb. 1695-6, ftiled Earl of Harold, afterwards called up to the houfe of peers, as Lord Lucas of Crudwel, in the county of Wilts. He married in April, 1718, Lady Mary Tufton, daughter of Thomas, Earl of Thanet, and died in July, 1723, without iffue.

2. Henry, born April 1, 1697; died in Dec. 1717.

3. Lucas, And,

4. George, died young.

5. Lady Amabel, eldeft daughter, and mother of the prefent marchionefs, married John, Earl of Breadalbin in Scotland, and died March 2, 1726-7.

6. Lady Jemima, married to John, late Earl of Afhburnham.

7. Lady Henrietta, born in Oct. 1703; who died in Jan. 1716-17.

8. Lady Anne, married Lord Charles Cavendifh, brother to his Grace, William, late Duke of Devonfhire.

9. Lady Mary, married to the Rev. Dr. Gregory, dean of Chriftchurch in Oxford.

10. Lady Jane. And,

11. Lady Carolina, both died in their infancy.

This noble family is defcended from Rollo, or Fulbert, who was chamberlain to Robert Duke of Normandy, and of his gift had the caftle and honour of Croy, in Picardy, from whence his pofterity affumed their furname, which was afterwards written de Grey, which Rollo had a daughter, Arlotta, mother of William the Conqueror, and a fon, John, ftiled Lord de Croy. From him defcended Henry, grandfather of the prefent marchionefs, who was, in a lineal fucceffion, the thirteenth Earl of Kent.

Arms.] Barry of fix pieces, argent and azure in chief, three torteauxes, the arms of Grey.

Creft.

Creft.] On a chapeau, gules, turned up, ermine, a wyvern fejant, or ; laying his dexter talon on the ftock of a tree erected, fable.

Supporters.] Two wyverns, or ; their wings dif-clofed.

Motto.] *Stat religione parentum.*

Chief Seats.] At Wreft-Houfe, in Bedfordfhire ; St. James's-fquare, London.

---

2. CONINGSBY, COUNTESS CONINGSBY.

THE Right Hon. MARGARET CONINGSBY, Coun-tefs, Vifcountefs, and Baronefs CONINGSBY of Hampton-Court, was created Baronefs and Vifcoun-tefs Coningsby in the county of Hereford, the 26th of Jan. 1716, 3 Geo. I. fucceeded her father Thomas, the late Earl, as countefs Coningsby, in April 1729; and married April 11, 1730, Sir Michael Newton, fon of Sir John Newton, of Barrs-court, in the county of Gloucefter, Bart. Knt. of the Bath, and had iffue, by him, who died April 6, 1743, one fon, John, Lord Vifc. Coningsby, born in Oct. 1732, and died an infant.

Thomas Coningsby, Efq; father of the prefent Countefs, being véry inftrumental in the Revolution, was created Baron Coningsby of Clanbraffil in Ireland the 7th of April, 4 Will. and Mary. He was alfo of the privy-council in the reign of Queen Anne ; and vice-treafurer and pay-mafter of the forces in Ireland, in the year 1704 ; and created Baron Coningsby of Coningsby, in the county of Lincoln, the 18th of June, 2 Geo. I. and Earl Coningsby, April 13, 1719. He married Barbara, daughter of Ferdinando Gorges, of Eye in the county of Hereford, Efq; by whom he had iffue, three fons and four daughters, viz.

1. Thomas, married a daughter of John Carr, of the county of Northumberland, Efq; and had two

fons,

fons, Thomas, who died unmairied, and Richard, who fucceeded his grandfather as Lord Clanbriffel, married Judith, daughter of Sir Thomas Lawley, of Spoon-hill in the county of Salop, Bart. and died Dec. 18, 1729, without iffue.

2. Humphry.

3. Ferdinando.

4. Meliora, married to Thomas, Lord Southwell, in Ireland.

5. Barbara, married to George Ayres, of Ayres-court, in Ireland, Efq;

6. Lettice, married to Edward Denny, of Tralee in the county of Kerry in Ireland, Efq;

7. Mary.

His firft wife dying, he married Lady Frances Jones, daughter of Richard, Earl of Ranelagh in Ireland, by whom he had iffue,

1. Richard, who died young.

2. Margaret, now Countefs of Coningsby. And,

3. Frances, married to the late Sir Charles Hanbury Williams, Knt. of the Bath.

This family took its name from the town of Coningsby in the county of Salop, where it antiently refided.

Arms.] The fame as her father bore, viz. gules, three conies fejant, argent.

Creft.] In a ducal coronet, or, five oftrich feathers, and on the plume thereof, a coney fejant, all argent.

Supporters.] Two lions, gules, each charged on the fhoulder with three billets, and ducally crowned, or.

Motto.] *Veftigia nulla retrorfum.*

Chief Seats.] At Hampton-court in the county of Hereford ; and Hill-ftreet, London.

3. S C H U-

3. SCHULENBERG, COUNTESS of WALSINGHAM.

THE Right Hon. Melesina de Schulenberg, Countefs of Walsingham, and Baronefs of Schulenberg and Aldborough, was created countefs of Walfingham, in the county of Norfolk, and Baronefs of Aldborough, in the county of Suffolk, the 7th of April 1722, 8 Geo. I. and is faid to be niece to the late dutchefs of Kendal. She married on the 5th of Sept. 1733, the Right Hon. Philip Dormer, Stanhope, Earl of Chefterfield, by whom fhe has no iffue.

Arms.] Two coats, quarterly, viz. firft and fourth, or, a lamb paffant in fefs, quartered, gules and argent, enfigned on the head with three ftandards of the fecond; fecond and third, argent, three eagles couped at the thigh, gules.

Supporters.] Two favages, each holding a club over his arm, and wreathed about his temples and loins with ivy, all proper.

4. WALMODEN, COUNTESS of YARMOUTH.

THE Right Hon. Amelia-Sophia Walmoden, Countefs and Baronefs of Yarmouth, was created Baronefs and Countefs of Yarmouth, in the county of Norfolk, April 4, 1740, in the 13th year of his Majefty's reign.

She is daughter of the late general Francis Wendt, commander in chief of his Majefty's Hanoverian forces, who died in 1749. She was married to the Baron de Walmoden, by whom fhe hath two fons,

1. Francis, Baron of Walmoden, married in Aug. 1752, to Frederica, third daughter of Erneft, Baron Steinborge, of the council of Regency at Hanover. And,

N 5 2. Lewis

2. Lewis Walmoden.

Arms.] Or, three merrions pale, argent and azure.

Supporters.] Granted by John Anftis, King at Arms. On the dexter fide, a lion guardant, or ; and on the finifter fide, a lion, guardant, azure, gorged, with a double treffure, flory, counter-flory, azure, as the dexter is.

5. TUFTON-COKE, BARONESS CLIFFORD.

THE Right Hon. MARGARET TUFTON-COKE, Baronefs CLIFFORD, and countefs dowager of Leicefter, born June 16, 1700, was created Baronefs Clifford, Aug. 13, 1734, as heir to the Lady Anne Clifford, late wife of Richard, late Earl of Dorfet, and fole daughter and heir of George, Earl of Cumberland, &c. She married in July 1718, Thomas Coke of Holkham, in the county of Norfolk, Efq; who was created Lord Lovel, May 28, 1728, and afterwards Vifcount Coke, and Earl of Leicefter, and had iffue by the faid Earl, Edward, Vifcount Coke, and heir apparent to the Barony of Clifford, who died in 1753, and her husband the Earl of Leicefter dying without iffue, in April 1759, his titles became extinct ; and upon the death of her Ladyfhip, without iffue, the titles of the Barony of Clifford will be extinct.

Thomas, Earl of Thanet, father of the prefent Baronefs, fon of John, Earl of Thanet, by Margaret his wife, daughter and heir of Richard, Earl of Dorfet, married Catherine, daughter and coheir of Henry Cavendifh, Duke of Newcaftle, by whom he had iffue. *See Earl of* Thanet.

6. COMPTON-TOWNSHEND, BARONESS FERRERS.

THE Right Hon. the Lady CHARLOTTE COMPTON' Baroneſs FERRERS, of Chartley, ſucceeded Elizabeth, her mother, in that honour, March 13, 1740. She married in Dec. 1751, the Hon. George Townſhend, eldeſt ſon and heir of the preſent Lord Townſhend, by whom ſhe has iſſue. *See Viſc.* Townſhend.

Elizabeth, mother of the preſent Baroneſs, ſucceeded to the title of Baroneſs Ferrers, of Chartley, on the death of Robert, Earl Ferrers, her grandfather, Dec. 25, 1717, the Hon. Robert Shirley, her father, eldeſt ſon of the ſaid Earl Ferrers, dying in the lifetime of his father, Feb. 25, 1698-9. She married in 1715-16, the Right Hon. James Compton, late Earl of Northampton, by whom ſhe had iſſue, three ſons and five daughters, who except the preſent Baroneſs, all died young. *See* Northampton *Earl.*

Arms.] Quarterly, 1 and 4, a lion paſſant guardant, or; between three helmets, argent; for Compton 2 and 3, ſable; Vaire, or and gules. The Arms of Ferrers.

---

7. SMITH, BARONESS DUDLEY.

THE Right Hon. ANNE SMITH, Baroneſs DUDLEY' ſucceeded to the Barony of Dudley, upon the death of Ferdinando Dudley Lea, her brother, the late Lord, who died in Oct. 1757, unmarried.

William Lea, father of the late Lord, married Frances, ſiſter of William Ward, late Lord Dudley, and by her, who died in 1737, had iſſue, two ſons and five daughters.

1. Ferdinando, late Lord Dudley.
2. William, who died unmarried.
3. Anne, the preſent Baroneſs, married to William Smith, of Ridgeacre in Shropſhire, Gent. and has iſſue, two ſons and three daughters.

N 6   4. Francis

.4. Frances, married to Mr. Walter Woodcock, Efq;

5. Mary, who died unmarried.

6. Catherine, married to Mr. Thomas Jordain.

7. Elizabeth, who is unmarried.

Arms.] Argent, on a pale, between two leopard's faces, fable, three crefcents, or.

Creft.] An unicorn, argent, gutte de poix, gorged, with a double treffure, fleury and counter-fleury, gules.

Supporters.] On either fide, a lion double queve, vert; armed and langued, gules; gorged with a ducal coronet, thereto a cordon affixed, paffing between the fore-legs, and reflected over the back, or.

Motto.] *In feipfo totus teres.*

Chief Seat.] At Ridgrace, in Shropfhire.

---

8. PIERCY-SMITHSON, BARONESS PIERCY.

THE Right Hon. ELIZABETH SMITHSON, Baronefs PIERCY, and Countefs of Northumberland, who by defcent, became Baronefs Piercy, on the death of Algernon, late Duke of Somerfet, her father, in Feb. 1749 50. She married in 1740, Sir Hugh Smithfon, Bart, now Earl of Northumberland, by whom fhe has iffue. *See Earl of* Northumberland.

Jofceline Piercy, the 11th Earl of Northumberland, dying May 21, 1670, without iffue male, the title of Baronefs Piercy devolved on Elizabeth, his only daughter and heir. She married in 1679, Henry Cavendifh, Earl of Ogle, fon and heir to Henry, Duke of Newcaftle, who was to have borne the name and arms of Piercy; but he dying Nov. 1, 1680, left her a virgin-widow, and very young. She was afterwards claimed in marriage by Thomas Thynne, of Long-Leat in the county of Wilts, who was on that account murdered by the contrivance of Count Coningfmark, Feb. 12, 1681. On the 30th of March

1680, fhe was married to Charles Seymour, Duke of Somerfet, both being under age, by whom fhe had iffue,

1. Algernon, who fucceeded to the Baronies of Piercy, &c.
2. Piercy Seymour.
3. Charles, who died unmarried.
4. Elizabeth.
5. Catherine.
6. Anne. And,
7. Frances, who died unmarried.

Algernon, married Frances, eldeft of the two daughters and coheirs of Henry Thynne, Efq; only fon of Thomas, Vifcount Weymouth, by whom he had one fon, George, Vifcount Beauchamp, who died Sept. 11, 1744 ; and a daughter, the Lady Elizabeth, the prefent Baronefs. *See Duke of* Somerfet.

Arms.] The fame as the Earl of Northumberland's.

9. WILSON, BARONESS BERNERS.

THE Right Hon. —— WILSON, Lady BERNERS, only daughter and heir of Thomas Knyvet, of Mutford in the county of Suffolk, Efq; fecond furviving fon of Thomas Knyvet, Efq; eldeft fon and heir of Sir Thomas Knyvet, of Afhwelthorpe, fucceeded, in Dec. 1743, Catharine, late Baronefs Berners, who was lineally defcended and became the fole heir of Sir John Bourchier, the firft Lord Berners.

In the reign of William the Couqueror, Hugh de Berners, anceftor of this noble family, was of Everfdone, in the county of Cambridge; and in 1195, Robert de Berners, another anceftor of this Lady, gave a fine of two hundred marks, for obtaining the King's favour and reftitution of his Lordfhip.

Arms] Quarterly, firft and fourth, argent, a line within a border engrailed, fable, fecond and third, quarterly, or, and vert.

10. LEGGE, BARONESS STAWEL.

THE Right Hon. MARY LEGGE, Baroneſs STAWEL, of Somerton in the county of Somerſet, was thus created May 20, 1760, with limitations to her and her heirs male by her preſent huſband the Right Hon. Henry Bilſon Legge, Eſq; uncle to the preſent Earl of Dartmouth. *See Earl of* Dartmouth.

Her Ladyſhip was only daughter and heir to Edward the laſt Lord Stawel, who died April 13, 1755, (upon whoſe death the title became exinćt) by his wife Mary, daughter and heir of Sir Hugh Stewkley, Bart. who died in July 1740. She married Sept. 3, 1750, the Right Hon. Henry Bilſon Legge, Eſq; chancellor and under treaſurer of the Exchequer, and one of the lords commiſſioners of the Treaſury, by whom ſhe has a ſon, born Feb. 27, 1757, and other children.

Her Ladyſhip is deſcended from Adam de Stawel, who flouriſhed about the time of the Norman Conqueſt.

Arms.] Ruby, a croſs lozenges, pearl.

Creſt.] On a chapeau ruby, turned up ermine, an eagle diſplayed argent, from its mouth a ſcroll, inſcribed with this motto, *En parole je vis.*

Supporters.] Two beaſts (by moſt termed mantigers) bodied, &c. in form of lions, with human viſages proper, armed with a ſort of horn like thoſe of a ſatyr or goat, and maned and tufted, or.

Motto.] *En parole je vis.*

Chief Seat.] At Aldermarſton in the county of Berks.

LORDS SPIRITUAL.

Names.	Sees.	Year.	In the room of
Dr. Thomas Secker,	Bristol, —	1734	Cecil, translated.
	Oxford, —	1737	Potter, translated.
	Canterbury, —	1758	Hutton, deceased.

Arms.] The field, or, an episcopal staff in pale, azure; and ensigned with a cross patee, argent; surmounted of a pall of the last, charged with four crosses; formed, fitched, diamond-edged, and fringed, as the second.

Dr. John Gilbert,	Landaff, —	1740	Mawson, translated.
	Salisbury, —	1748	Sherlock, translated.
	York, —	1757	Hutton, translated.

Arms.] Gules, two keys in saltier, in chief, argent; a crown royal, or.

Dr. Thomas Sherlock,	Bangor, —	1728	Baker, translated.
	Salisbury, —	1734	Hoadley, translated.
	London, —	1748	Gibson, deceased.

Arms.] Gules, two swords in saltier, or; the pomels, or.

Names.

Names.	Sees.	Year.	In the room of
Dr. Richard Trevor, —— { St. David's, ——		1744	Willes, tranflated.
{ Durham, ——		1752	Butler, deceafed.

Arms.] Azure, a crofs between four lions, rampant, or.

Dr. Benjamin Hoadley, { Bangor, ——		1715	Evans, tranflated.
Hereford, ——		1721	Biffe, tranflated.
Salisbury, ——		1723	Willis, tranflated.
Winchefter, ——		1734	Willis, deceafed.

Arms.] Gules, two keys indorfed in bend, the uppermoft, argent; the other, or; a fword interpofed between them in bend, finifter; of the fecond, pomels and hilts of the third.

Dr. Matthias Mawfon, —— { Landaff ——		1738	Harris, deceafed.
Chichefter, ——		1740	Hare, deceafed.
Ely, ——		1754	Gooch, deceafed.

Arms.] Gules, three ducal crowns, or.

| Dr. Edward Willes, —— { St. David's, —— | | 1742 | Clagget, tranflated. |
| Bath and Wells, —— | | 1743 | Wynn, deceafed. |

Arms.] Azure, a faltier quarterly quartered, or, and argent.

Names.

Names.	Sees.		Year.	In the room of
Dr. John Thomas,	{ St. Afaph,	—	1743	Maddox, tranflated.
	{ Lincoln,	—	1744	Reynolds, deceafed.

Arms.] Gules, two lions paffant guardant, or; in a chief, azure; our Lady fitting with her babe; crown and fceptre of the fecond.

| Rt. Hon. Lord James Beauclerck, | Hereford, | — | 1746 | Egerton, *deceafed*. |

Arms.] Gules, three leopards heads reverfed, fwallowing as many fleur-de luces, or.

| Dr. George Lavington, | Exeter, | — | 1746 | Clagget, deceafed. |

Arms.] Gules, a fword in pale, blade and hilt, proper; two keys in faltier, or.

| Dr Richard Osbaldefton, | Carlifle, | — | 1747 | Fleeming, deceafed. |

Arms.] Argent, on a crofs, fable; a mitre with labels, or.

| Dr. John Thomas, | { Peterborough, | —1747 | Clavering, deceafed. |
| | { Salifbury, | — 1757 | Gilbert, tranflated. |

Arms.] Azure, our Lady, with her babe in her right arm, and a fceptre in the left, all or.

Names.	Sees.	Year.	In the room of
Dr. Zachary Pearce,	{ Bangor,	1747	Hutton, translated.
	{ Rochester,	1756	Wilcox, deceased.
Arms.] Argent, on a saltier, gules; an escallop-shell, or.			
Hon. Dr. Robert Drummond, — St. Asaph,		1748	Lisle, translated.
Arms.] Sable, two keys in saltier, argent.			
Dr. Thomas Hayter, Norwich,		1749	Lisle, deceased.
Arms.] Azure, three mitres with their labels, or.			
Hon. Dr. Frederick Cornwallis, — { Coventry and Lich-field,		1749	Smalbroke, deceased.
Arms.] Party-per-pale, gules and argent; a cross potent and quadrat in the center, between four croslets patee, of the second, and or.			
D. Edmund Keene, — Chester, —		1752	Peploe, deceased
Arms.] Gules, three mitres, with their labels, or.			

Dr.

Names	Sees.	Year.	In the room of
James Johnſon, —	{ Glouceſter —	1752	Benſon, deceaſed.
	{ Worceſter, —	1759	Maddox, deceaſed.
Arms.] Argent ten torteauxes, or.			
Dr. Anthony Ellis, —	St. David's, —	1752	Trevor, tranſlated.
Arms.] Sable, on a croſs, or; five cinquefoils of the firſt.			
Dr. William Aſhburnham, —	Chicheſter, —	1754;	Mawſon, tranſlated.
Arms.] Azure, a preſbyter John fitting on a tomb-ſtone, in his left hand a mound, his right hand extended, or; with a linen mitre on his head, and in his mouth a ſword, all proper.			
Dr. Richard Newcomb, —	Landaff, —	1755	Creſſet, deceaſed.
Arms.] Sable, two croſiers in ſaltier, or; and argent; in a chief, azure, three mitres, with labels of the ſecond.			
Dr. John Hume, —	{ Briſtol, —	1756	Conybeare, deceaſed.
	{ Oxford, —	1758	Secker, tranſlated.
Arms.] Sable, a feſs, argent; in chief three ladies heads arrayed and veiled, argent; and crowned, or; and in baſe, an ox of the ſecond paſſing over a ford, proper.			

Dr

Names.	Sees.	Year.	In the room of
Dr. John Egerton,	Bangor,	1756	Pearce translated.

Arms.] Gules, on a bend, or; gutty-de-poix, between two mullets, argent.

| Dr. Richard Terrick, | Peterborough, | 1757 | Thomas, translated. |

Arms.] Gules, two keys in faltier, between four crofs croflets fitchy, or.

| Dr. Philip Yonge, | Briftol, | 1758 | Hume, tranflated. |

Arms.] Sable, three ducal crowns in pale, or.

| Dr. William Warburton, | Gloucester | 1759 | Johnfon tranflated |

Arms.] Azure two keys in faltire, or.

N. B. The bifhops of London, Durham, and Winchefter, always take place next to the Archbifhops, and all the reft according to priority of confecration.

THE

THE

NAMES and TITLES

OF THE

SIXTEEN PEERS

FOR

SCOTLAND.

---

1. CAMPBELL, DUKE OF ARGYLL.

THE Moſt Noble ARCHIBALD CAMPBELL, Duke Marquis and Earl of ARGYLL, Marquis of Lorn, Viſcount Lochow, keeper of the great ſeal of Scotland, lord juſtice-general, and chancellor of the univerſity of Aberdeen, and one of the lords of his Majeſty's moſt hon. privy council.

Chief Seats.] At Whitton, in Middleſex; Inverary, in the ſhire of Argyll; in Argyll-ſtreet, London.

---

2. HAY, MARQUIS OF TWEEDDALE.

THE Moſt Noble JOHN HAY, Marquis of TWEED-DALE, Lord Yeſter, a Lord Extraordinary of the ſeſſions in Scotland, governor of the bank of Edinburgh, and one of the lords of his Majeſty's privy council.

Chief Seats.] At Yeſter, in the county of Lothian; Groſvenor-ſtreet, London.

3. KERR,

3. KERR, MARQUIS of LOTHIAN.

THE Moft Noble WILLIAM KERR, Marquis of Lothian, Earl of Ancram, and knight of the ancient order of the thiftle.

Chief Seats.] At Newbottle, in the county of Lothian; Privy-Garden, London.

4. LESLEY, EARL of ROTHES.

THE Right Hon. JOHN LESLY, Earl of ROTHES, Lord Lefly, colonel of the third regiment of foot guards, lieutenant-general, governor of Duncannon fort in Ireland, and commander in chief in that kingdom.

Chief Seats.] At Caftle-Lefly in Fifeshire; Brook-ftreet, London.

5. DOUGLAS, EARL of MORTON.

THE Right Hon. JAMES DOUGLAS, Earl of MORTON, Lord Aberdour, and knight of the ancient order of the thiftle.

Chief Seats.] At Aberdour in Fifeshire; St. James's quare, London.

6. STEWART, EARL of MORAY.

THE Right Hon. JAMES STUART, Earl of MORAY, Lord Down, and knight of the thiftle.
Chief Seats.] At Dunnibriffel in Fifeshire; Caftle-Stewart and Tarnaway, in the county of Murray; Soho-fquare, London.

7. HOME, EARL OF HOME.

THE Right Hon. WILLIAM HOME, Earl of Home, Lord Coldringham, Lieut.-general, and colonel of a regiment of foot, and governor of Gibraltar.

Chief Seat.] At Home-castle in Berwickshire.

8. MAITLAND, EARL OF LAUDERDALE.

THE Right Hon. JAMES MAITLAND, Earl of LAUDERDALE, and Viscount Maitland.

Chief Seats.] At Lauder-fort in Berwickshire; and Halton, in the county of Lothian; New Bond-street, London.

9. CAMPBELL, EARL OF LOUDOUN.

THE Right Hon. JOHN CAMPBELL, Earl of LOUDOUN, Lord Moclyn, governor of Virginia, a lieut.-general, governor of Stirling-castle, and colonel of the 30th regiment of foot.

Chief Seats.] At Loudoun-Castle in Airshire; Privy-garden, London.

10. OGILVY, EARL OF FINLATER.

THE Right Hon. JAMES OGILVY, Earl of FINLATER and SEAFIELD, Lord Deskford, and lord vice-admiral in Scotland.

Chief Seats.] At Cullen in Bamff-shire; St. James's-place, London.

11. CAMP

11. CAMPBELL, EARL OF BREADALBIN.

THE Right Hon. JOHN CAMPBELL, Earl of BREADALBIN, Viscount Glenorchy, and Chief justice in Eyre, of his Majesty's forests south of Trent.

Chief Seats.] Glenorchy in Argyleshire; St. James's-street, London.

---

12. GORDON, EARL OF ABERDEEN.

THE Right Hon. WILLIAM GORDON, Earl of ABERDEEN, Lord Haddo.

Chief Seats] At Haddo-House in Aberdeenshire; Hill-street, London.

---

13. HUME, EARL OF MARCHMONT.

THE Right Hon. HUGH HUME, Earl of MARCH-MONT, Lord Polwarth, first lord commissioner of the police in Scotland, and F. R. S.

Chief Seats.] Redbraes in Berwickshire; Green-street, Grosvenor-square, London.

---

14. CARMICHAEL, EARL OF HYNDFORD.

THE Right Hon. JOHN CARMICHAEL, Earl of HYNDFORD, Lord Carmichael; a Lord of the bedchamber to his Majesty, a Knt. of the Thistle, and one of the commissioners of the Police, or Trade in Scotland.

Chie

Chief Seats.] At Wefter-hall in Lanerkfhire ; Craigan in Renfrewfhire ; and Green-ftreet, Grofvenor-fquare, London.

---

15. MURRAY, LORD VISCOUNT STORMONT.

THE Right Hon. DAVID MURRAY, Vifcount STORMONT, Baron of Scoon and Balvair, embaffador to the king of Poland.

Chief Seat.] At Keemlington-caftle, Anandale.

---

16. CATHCART, LORD CATHCART.

THE Right Hon. CHARLFS CATHCART, Lord CATHCART, his Majefty's high commiffioner to the general affembly of the church of Scotland, and adjutant-general of the forces in North-Britain.

Chief Seats.] Sundrum, Air-fhire ; Charles-ftreet, Berkley-fquare, London.

PEERS that do not sit in the House, are either Scots Peers that have been made Peers of Great-Britain, since the Union in 1707, or Roman Catholics.

Such Scots PEERS are,

1. HIS Grace CHARLES DOUGLAS, Duke of DOVER, created *Anno* 1708.
JAMES HAMILTON, Duke of BRANDON, created *Anno* 1708.

Roman Catholics that do not sit in the HOUSE.

2. EDWARD HOWARD, Duke of NORFOLK, Earl of ARUNDEL, Hereditary Earl Marshal of England.
GEORGE TALBOT, Earl of SHREWSBURY, Baron TALBOT.
JOHN PAUL STAFFORD HOWARD, Earl STAFFORD, Baron STAFFORD.
ANTHONY BROWN, Viscount MONTAGU.
WILLIAM STOURTON, Lord STOURTON.
ROBERT PETRE, Lord PETRE, of Wrettel.
HENRY ARUNDEL, Lord ARUNDEL, of Wardour.
CHARLES DORMER, Lord DORMER, of Wenge.
HENRY ROPER, Lord TEYNHAM.
MARMADUKE LANGDALE, Lord LANGDALE, of Holme.

RANKS

RANKS of the Sons and Daughters of PEERS.

Dukes eldeſt Sons	⎫	⎧ Marquiſſes.
Daughters	⎪	⎪ Marchioneſſes.
Youngeſt Sons	⎪	⎪ Earls.
Marquiſſes eldeſt Sons	Rank as youngeſt	Earls.
Daughters		Counteſſes.
Youngeſt Sons	⎬	⎨ Viſcounts.
Earls eldeſt Sons		Viſcounts.
Daughters	⎪	⎪ Viſcounteſſes.
Youngeſt Sons	⎪	⎪ Barons.
Viſcounts eldeſt Sons	⎪	Barons.
Daughters	⎭	⎩ Baroneſſes.

ORDERS of PRECEDENCE of the Nobility, &c.

Dukes.	Privy-Counſellors.
Marquiſſes.	Judges.
Dukes eldeſt Sons.	Maſters in Chancery.
Earls.	Viſcounts younger Sons.
Marquiſſes eldeſt Sons.	Barons younger Sons.
Dukes younger Sons.	Knights of the Garter.
Viſcounts.	—— Bannerets.
Earls eldeſt Sons.	—— Baronets.
Marquiſſes younger Sons.	—— of the Bath.
Biſhops.	—— Batchelors.
Barons.	Colonels.
Viſcounts eldeſt Sons.	Serjeants at Law.
Earls younger Sons.	Doctors.
Barons eldeſt Sons.	Eſquires.

Containing the Dates of the respective Creations, and the Pages referred to.

I N D E X.

	Dukes.	Barons.	Visc.	Earls	Marq	Dukes.	Eldest Sons.	Page.
15	Brandon, S. D. —	1711				1711	Marquis of Hamilton	31
16	Ancaster —	1314				1715	Marquis of Lindsey	33
17	Kingston —	1627	1627	1626	1706	1715	Marq. of Dorchester	35
18	Newcastle —	1706	1714	1628	1706	1715	Marquis of Clare	36
19	Portland —	1689	1689	1714	1715	1716	Marquis of Tichfield	38
20	Manchester —	1620		1689	1716	1719	Viscount Mandeville	42
21	Chandos —	1553	1714	1714	1719	1719	Marq. of Carnarvon	43
22	Dorset —	1567		1603		1720	Earl of Middlesex	44
23	Bridgwater —	1603	1616	1617	1720	1720	Marquis of Brackley	46

Marquis.	Barons.	Visc.	Earls	Dukes.	Eldest Sons.	Page.
Rockingham —	1644	1734	1734	1746	Earl of Malton —	48
Grey, Marchioness —	1663			1740	Baron Lucas —	269

	Earls.	Barons.	Visc.	Earls.	Eldest Sons.	Page.
1	Shrewsbury, I. E. —	1330		1442	Lord Talbot —	51
2	Derby —	1455		1485	Lord Strange —	53

O 3

	Earls.	Barons.	Visc.	Earls.	Eldest Sons.	Page.
23	Shaftesbury ———	1661		1672	Lord Ashley ———	93
24	Litchfield ———	1674	1674	1674	Viscount Quarendon ———	97
25	Berkeley ———	1295	1679	1679	Viscount Durfley ———	98
26	Abingdon ———	1572		1682	Lord Norris ———	99
27	Gainsborough ———	1616	1628	1682	Viscount Campden	101
28	Holdernesse ———	1295		1682	Lord Conyers ———	103
29	Plymouth ———	1529		1682	Lord Windsor	104
30	Stafford ———	1640	1640	1688	Viscount Stafford	105
31	Scarborough, I. V.	1681	1689	1690	Viscount Lumley	107
32	Bradford ———	1642	1674	1694	Viscount Newport	109
33	Rochford ———	1695	1695	1695	Viscount Tunbridge	110
34	Albemarle ———	1696	1696	1696	Viscount Bury	111
35	Coventry ———		1696	1697	Viscount Deerhurst	113
36	Jersey ———	1690	1690	1697	Viscount Villiers	115
37	Poulet ———	1627	1706	1706	Viscount Hinton	116
38	Godolphin ———	1694	1706	1706	Viscount Rialton	117
39	Cholmondely, I. V.	1689	1706	1706	Viscount Malpas	119
40	Oxford ———	1711		1711	Lord Harley	120
41	Ferrers ———		1711	1711	Viscount Tamworth	121
42	Strafford ———	1639	1711	1711	Viscount Wentworth	123

I N D E X.

F I N I S.

NEW CREATIONS,

Since the Publication of the Third Edition of *Salmon's Short View of the Families of the English Nobility*, 1760.

81. WEST, EARL DELAWARR.

THE Right Hon. JOHN WEST, EARL DELA-WARR, Viscount Cantalupe, Baron Delawarr, was created a Viscount and Earl, March 21, 1761, by the Titles of Viscount Cantalupe and Earl Delawarr. [*See Lord Delawarr, p.* 204.]

82. TALBOT, EARL TALBOT.

The Right Hon. WILLIAM TALBOT, EARL TAL-BOT, Lord Talbot, Baron of Hensol, was advanced to the dignity of an Earl by the Title of Earl Talbot, March 21, 1761, and in the same month was appointed lord steward, and sworn one of his Majesty's most honourable privy council. [*For an account of this noble Peer, see page* 246.]

A   VISCOUNTS.

VISCOUNTS created since 1760.

12. SPENCER, VISCOUNT SPENCER.

THE Right Hon. JOHN SPENCER, Viscount Spencer, Baron Spencer, of Althorpe, in the county of Northampton, was created a peer as above, April 4, 1761. His Lordship married, Dec. 26, 1756, Miss Poyntz, one of the daughters of the late Stephen Poyntz, Esq; governor to his Royal Highness the Duke of Cumberland, by whom he has issue sons and daughters.

His Lordship's Father, the Hon. John Spencer, was the fourth son of Charles Earl of Sunderland, by Lady Anne Churchill, second daughter and coheir of John the great Duke of Marlborough. [*See Spencer Duke of Marlborough, p. 21.*] He was married Feb. 14, 1733-4, to the Lady Georgina Carolina, third daughter to the late Earl of Granville, and by her he had issue,

John, now Lord Viscount Spencer, born Dec. 6, 1734, and a daughter who died young.

The Hon. John Spencer, dying anno 1746, his widow and relict married, in 1750, William Earl Cowper.

Arms.] Quarterly argent and gules, in the second and third, a frett, or: over all a bend sable, charged with three escallops argent.

Crest.] Out of a ducal coronet, a gryphon's head between two wings argent, collared gemelly gules.

Supporters.] On the dexter side a gryphon, per fess ermine and erminois; and on the sinister, a wyvern ermine, their wings erect, each gorged with a collar fleury, counter-fleury and chained sable, and on the collars three escallops argent.

Motto.] *Dieu defend le droit.*

Chief Seats.] Althorpe, Northamptonshire; Wimbledon, and Battersea, Surry.

13. NOEL, VISCOUNT WENTWORTH.

The Right Hon. EDWARD NOEL, Viſcount WENT-
WORTH, of Wellſborough, in the county of Leiceſter,
Baron Wentworth of Nettleſtead, and Baronet, was ad-
vanced to the dignity of a Viſcount, by the title of
Viſcount Wentworth of Wellſborough, May 4, 1762.
[*For a particular account of this noble Peer, ſee* Noel,
Lord Wentworth, *p.* 207.]

14. COURTENAY VISCOUNT COURTENAY.

The Right Hon. WILLIAM COURTENAY, Viſcount COURTENAY, of Powderham Caſtle, in the county of Devon, and Baronet, ſucceeded his father, the late Viſcount, May 16, 1762.

Sir William Courtenay, May 4, 1762, was created a Peer as above. He was married to the Lady Frances Finch, daughter to the late Earl of Aylesford, April 1741, by whom he had iſſue, William, the preſent Viſcount, born Nov. 31, 1742, and four daugbters.

This noble Lord is deſcended from Hugh Courtenay, who was created Earl of Devonſhire by King Edward I. 1295. There have been of this family ſeveral Barons of Okehampton, twelve Earls of Devonſhire, and a Marquis of Exeter; and is one of the firſt and moſt illuſtrious families in Europe, having been allied to the Emperors of Conſtantinople and the Kings of France.

Arms.] Quarterly, firſt and fourth, or, three torteaux, ſecond and third, or, a lyon rampant, azure.

Creſt.] A dolphin naiant argent.

Supporters] Two boars argent briſtled, tuſk'd and hoofed, or.

Motto.] *Ubi lapſus quid feci.*

Seat.] Powderham Caſtle, Devon.

B A R O N S.

Omitted in Page 225.

23. BOOTH, LORD DELAMERE.

The Right Hon. NATHANIEL BOOTH, Lord DELA-MERE, of Dunham Maffey, Chefhire, fucceeded to the title on the death of the late Earl of Warrington.

His Lordfhip is defcended from Henry, the fifth fon of Sir George Booth, Bart. who, in confideration of his great fervices towards the reftoration of King Charles the Second, was created Baron Delamere, of Dunham Maffey, in April 1661.

This family is of great antiquity and long ftanding, in the counties palatine of Lancafhire and Chefhire, and the name to be met with as far back as in the year 1275, 3 Edward I.

Arms.] Argent, three boars heads erect, and erazed, fable.

Creft.] On a wreath vert, a lyon paffant, argent.

Supporters.] Two boars fable, briftled and unguled, or.

Motto.] *Quod ero fpero.*

57. ROBINSON, LORD GRANTHAM.

The Right Hon. Thomas Robinson, Lord Grantham, Knight of the Bath, and one of his Majefty's moft honourable privy council; was created a peer, by the title of Lord Grantham of Grantham, Lincolnfhire, April 4, 1761.

His Lordfhip was fent envoy extraordinary to the court of Vienna in 1739; created a Knight of the Bath in 1742, the prefent Emperor of Germany performing the ceremony; appointed a commiffioner of trade and plantations in Dec. 1748; made keeper of the great wardrobe, and fworn one of his Majefty's moft honourable privy council, in Dec. 1749. In March 1754, his Lordfhip was advanced to the office of fecretary of ftate for the fouthern department, and in the month following, was named one of the regency in his Majefty's abfence to his German dominions. In Nov. 1755, he refigned the poft of fecretary of ftate, and a few days after was appointed keeper of the great wardrobe.

His Lordfhip married Frances, daughter to Thomas Worfley, Efq; of Hovingham in Lancafhire, by whom he has iffue the Hon. Thomas Robinfon, Efq; member in the prefent parliament for the borough of Chrift Church, Southampton.

His Lordfhip is the fourth fon of the late Sir William Robinfon, Bart. of Newby Hall, Yorkfhire; a family of great antiquity in that county, of whom was William Robinfon, Efq; in Queen Elizabeth's reign, who was twice Lord Mayor of York, and reprefented that city in two parliaments.

Arms.] Vert, a cheveron between three ftags, a gaze, or.

Creft.] On a crown fleur de lis, a mount vert, thereon a ftag at gaze, or,

Supporters.] On either fide a greyhound regardant, fable.

Motto.] *Qualis ab incepto.*

58. GROSVENOR, LORD GROSVENOR.

The Right Hon. RICHARD GROSVENOR, Lord GROSVENOR, and Baronet, succeeded his father Sir Robert in 1758, and was advanced to the dignity of a Peer in 1761, by the title of Lord Grosvenor of Eaton, Cheshire. His Lordship is yet unmarried.

Sir Robert Grosvenor married Jane, the only surviving child of Thomas Warre, of Sewell Court, in the county of Somerset, Esq; by whom he had issue,

1. Richard, now Lord Grosvenor.

2. Thomas, member for the city of Chester, and married to Miss Skynner of Walthamstow.

And four daughters.

This noble Lord is descended from Gilbert le Grosvenor, who was related to William the Conqueror, and followed him in his expedition to England, and whose son Robert le Grosvenor had the lordship of Over Lestock in Cheshire, given him by the Conqueror's uncle.

A 4   Arms.]

Arms.] Azure, a garb, or.

Creſt.] On a wreath, a talbot, or.

Supporters.] On either ſide, a talbot regardant or, gorged with a plain collar azure.

Motto.] *Nobilitatis virtus non ſtemma charaƈter.*

Chief Seats.] Eaton Hall, three miles from Cheſter; Helkin Hall, two miles from Flint; Sewell Court, in Somerſetſhire; Wymondeley, in Hertford; and on Milbank, Weſtminſter.

59. CURZON, LORD SCARSDALE.

The Right Hon. NATHANIEL CURZON, Lord SCARSDALE, and Baronet, was created a Peer in 1761, by the title of Lord Scarſdale of Scarſdale, Derbyſhire.

His Lordſhip, in 1750, was married to the Lady Caroline Collier, daughter to the Right Hon. the Earl of Portmore, by whom he had iſſue,

1. A ſon, born Sept. 16, 1751.
2. A daughter, born May 6, 1753.
3. Another ſon, born March 22, 1758.

The late Sir Nathaniel Curzon, married Mary, daughter of Sir Ralph Aſheton of Middleton, in Lancaſhire, Bart. By her he had iſſue,

1. John, who died an infant.
2. Nathaniel, who ſucceeded him in 1758, and is now Lord Scarſdale.

3. Aſheton,

3. Asfheton, who was married to Mifs Hanmer of Ifcoyd, Flintfhire, and is member in the prefent parliament for Clithero, Lancafhire.

This family is defcended from Giraline de Curzon, who came over with William the Conqueror, and had divers lands in the county of Berks and of Devon given him.

Arms.] Argent, on a bend fable, three popin jays, or, collared gules.

Creft.] A popin jay rifing, or, collared gules.

Supporters.] On the dexter fide, the figure of Prudence reprefented by a woman, habited argent, mantled azure, holding in her finifter hand a javelin entwined with a remora proper; and on the finifter, the figure of Liberality, reprefented by a like woman, habited argent, mantled purpure, holding a cornu-copia proper.

Motto.] *Recte & fuaviter.*

Chief Seat.] Keddlefton, near Derby.

60. IRBY, LORD BOSTON.

The Right Hon. WILLIAM IRBY, Lord BOSTON, and Baronet, and chamberlain to her Royal Highness the Princess Dowager of Wales, was advanced to the dignity of a Peer in 1761, by the title of Lord Boston of Boston, Lincolnshire.

His Lordship, in August 1736, was appointed chamberlain to the Princess of Wales. In 1735, he was chosen member for Launceston in Cornwall, and also chose again in 1741 for the same borough; his Lordship, in 1747, was elected member for Bodmin in Cornwall, as he was again in 1754. His Lordship, August 26, 1746, was married to Miss Selwyn, maid of honour to the Princess of Wales, by whom he hath had issue.

1. A daughter, born July 18, 1747.
2. A son, born June 28, 1749.
3. Another son, born August 29, 1750.

Sir Edward Irby was created a Baronet in the third year of Queen Anne, and married Dorothy, daughter of the Hon. Henry Pagett, second son of William Lord Pagett, by whom he had one daughter, and the present Lord Boston.

This family is of great antiquity in the county of Lincoln; of whom was Sir William de Irby, Knt. who flourished in the reign of Henry the Third.

Arms.] Argent, fretty sable on a canton, gules, a chaplet, or.

Crest.] A saracen's head in profile, sinister proper wreathed, argent and sable.

Supporters.] On either side an antilope, gules gorged, with a chaplet, or.

Motto.] *Honor fidelitatis præmium.*

Chief Seat.] Spalding, in Lincolnshire.

61. PERCIVAL, LORD LOVELL AND HOLLAND.

The Right Hon. JOHN PERCIVAL, Earl of EGMONT, Vifcount and Baron PERCIVAL, in the kingdom of Ireland; poftmafter general, and one of his Majefty's moft honourable privy council, was created a Peer of Great Britain in May 1762, by the title of Lord Lovell and Holland, Baron Lovell and Holland of Enmore, in the county of Somerfet. [*See Percival, Earl of Egmont, in the third volume of this work, among the Peers of Ireland.*]

62. MONTAGUE, LORD MONTAGUE.

The Right Hon. JOHN MONTAGUE, Lord MONTAGUE, fon of the Earl of Cardigan, was created a Peer by the title of Lord Montague of Boughton in Northamptonfhire, in May 1762. [*See Montague Earl of Cardigan, p.* 82.]

Arms.] Quarterly, firft and fourth, Montagu and Monthermer, quartered, viz. firft, argent within a bordure fable, three lozenges, in fefs, gules, for Montague. Second, or, an eagle difplayed, vert, for Monthermer. Third, as fecond, fourth as firft. Second and third, fable, a lion rampant, argent, on a canton of the laft,

a crofs

a crofs of St. George, for Churchill, differenced with a label of three points.

Creſt.] On a wreath, a gryphon's head couped, or, beaked and winged, ſable.

Supporters.] On the dexter ſide, a gryphon, or, beaked, winged, and legged, ſable; on the ſiniſter, a wyvern, gules, gorged with a collar, or, having an oval ſhield, pendant therefrom; upon the breaſts, azure, garniſhed gold, charged with a ſaltire of Scotland.

Motto.] Spectamur agendo.

63. DAMER, LORD MILTON.

The Right Hon. JOSEPH DAMER, Lord MILTON, of Shrone-Hill, in the kingdom of Ireland, was created a Baron of Great Britain, in May 1762, by the title of Baron Milton of Milton Abbey, Dorſetſhire. [*For a further account of this noble Peer, the reader is deſired to conſult the third volume of this work, among the Peers of Ireland.*]

64. MONTAGUE, LORD BEAULIEU.

The Right Hon. EDWARD MONTAGUE, Lord BEAU-LIEU, and Knight of the Bath, was advanced to the dignity of a Peer, and to descend to his heirs-male by her Grace Isabella, Duchess Dowager of Manchester, his present Lady, by the title of Lord Beaulieu of Beaulieu, Hants, May 1762.

His Lordship, in August 1753, was created a Knight of the Bath: He represented the borough of Tiverton, in the 11th and 12th parliaments of Great Britain. In 174—he was marrried to her Grace Isabella, Duchess of Manchester, eldest daughter and coheir of John Duke of Montague, and relict of William Duke of Manchester; by whom he hath had issue, a daughter, born August 27, 1749.

Arms.] Quarterly, first and fourth, Montague and Monthermer, quartered, viz. first, argent within a bordure, sable, three lozenges, in fess, gules, for Montagues. 2. Or, an eagle displayed, vert, for Monthermer; third as second, fourth as first. Second and third, ermine, three bars, gules ; on a canton, argent, a cross of St. George, for Hussey.

Crest.] On a wreath, a gryphon's head, couped, or, beaked and winged, sable.

Supporters.] On each side a stag, proper; collared with a ducal coronet and chain, the latter reflecting over their backs, or,

Motto.] *Spectemur agendo.*

65. VERNON, LORD VERNON.

The Right Hon. GEORGE VENABLES VERNON, Lord VERNON, and Baron of KINDERTON, Cheſhire, was ſo created May 1, 1762. 2 George III. His Lord-ſhip was repreſentative for the city of Litchfield in three parliaments, as he was alſo for the town of Derby in two. In July 1731, he was married to Mary, the daughter of Thomas Lord Effingham Howard, who died in February 1740, and left iſſue,

1. George Venables, born May 9, 1735, member of parliament for Bramber, Suſſex.

2. A daughter, born July 10, 1736.

3. A ſon, July 1737.

4. Another ſon, October 26, 1738.

His Lordſhip married, in Dec. 1741, to his ſecond Lady, the daughter of Sir Thomas Lee of Hartwell, Buckinghamſhire, who died Sept. 22, 1742.

Arms.] Quarterly, firſt and fourth, azure, two bars, argent. Second, argent, a fret, ſable. Third, or, on a feſs, azure, three garbs of the field.

Creſt.] On a wreath, a boar's head eraſed, ſable, ducally gorged, or.

Supporters.] On the dexter ſide, a lyon, gules, collared and chained, or; on the ſiniſter, a boar, ſable, ducally collared and chained, or.

Motto.] *Vernon ſemper viret.*

Chief Seat.] At Sudbury, Derbyſhire.

66. LANE, LORD BINGLEY.

The Right Hon. GEORGE LANE, Lord BINGLEY, was advanced to the dignity of a Peer in May 1762, by the title of Baron Bingley in the county of York, with limitation to his heirs male by Harriot his present Lady. His Lordship was representative for the city of York in four parliaments, and was married July 12, 1731, to the Hon. Miss Harriot Benson, daughter and heiress of Robert, the late Lord Bingley, by whom he has issue,

Robert, born Aug. 24, 1732, member for the city of York, married July 29, 1761, to the Hon. Miss Henley, daughter of Robert Lord Henley, Lord High Chancellor.

Arms.] Quarterly, first and fourth, argent, a lyon rampant, gules, within a border, sable; on a canton of the first, a harp and crown, or, for Lane. Second and third, argent, a cheveron between three foxes heads, erased, gules, for Fox.

Crest.] A gryphon, sable, issuing out of a ducal coronet, or, winged argent.

Supporters.] On either side a bear, argent.

Motto.] *Inconcussa virtus.*

Chief Seat.] Bramham Park, Yorkshire.

STUART, BARONESS MOUNT STUART.

The Right Hon. MARY STUART, Countefs of BUTE, was created a Baronefs of Great Britain, April 4, 1761, 1 George III. by the title of Baronefs Mount Stuart of Wortley, Yorkfhire, with limitation of the honour to her heirs-male, by her prefent hufband John Earl of Bute. [*We have given an account of this noble family in our view of the Scotch nobility under the title of* Earl of Bute, *to which we refer the reader.*]

PITT, BARONESS CHATHAM.

The Right Hon. Lady HESTER PITT was advanced to the dignity of a Peerefs in Oct. 1761, 1 George III. by the title of Baronefs CHATHAM of Chatham, Kent, with limitation to her heirs-male by her prefent hufband the Right Hon. WILLIAM PITT; which honour HIS MAJESTY was pleafed to grant IN CONSIDERA-TION OF THE GREAT AND IMPORTANT SERVICES OF THE SAID MR. PITT.

Her Ladyfhip was daughter to the late Right Hon. Countefs Temple, and is fifter to the prefent Earl Temple; was married Oct. 16, 1754, to the Right Hon. William Pitt, by whom fhe hath iffue,

1. John, born Oct. 10, 1756.
2. Another fon, born May 28, 1759.
3. A daughter, born April 22, 1758.

[*Arms*]

Arms.] Vert on a crofs, argent, five torteaux.

Supporters.] On the dexter fide, a lyon, guardant, charged on the breaft with a flip of oak fructed, proper; on the finifter, a ftag, proper, attired, or, gorged, with a collar and chain affixed thereto, paffing between his fore-legs, and reflected over his back, fable.

Motto.] *Benigno numine.*

FOX, BARONESS HOLLAND.

The Right Hon. Lady CAROLINE FOX, Lady Holland, Baronefs of HOLLAND, in the county of Lincoln, was thus created May 1762, with the dignity of Lord Holland to her heirs-male by her prefent hufband, the Right Hon. Henry Fox, brother to the Earl of Ilchefter.

Her Ladyfhip is fifter to Charles Duke of Richmond, and was married in May 1744 to the Right Hon. Henry Fox, now paymafter general of the forces, clerk of the pells in Ireland, and one of his Majefty's moft honourable privy council; by whom fhe hath had iffue four fons,

1. Stephen, born Feb. 20, 1745.
2. Henry Charles, who died in 1746.
3. Charles James, born Jan. 14, 1748-9.
4. Henry.

Arms.] Arms of Lenos (her father) Duke of Richmond, viz. (the fame as King Charles the IId. within a border, compone, argent, and gules; the firft charged with rofes of the fecond.)

Supporters.] On the dexter fide, a fox, argent, ears, nofe, feet, and tip of the tail, fable, gorged, with a collar, compone, argent, and gules; the firft charged with rofes of the fecond, barbed, and feeded, proper; and on the finifter, a like fox, collared as before, with a chain affixed thereto, or.

Motto] *Re E. Marito.*   ALTE-

ALTERATIONS in the State of the English Peerage, since the Publication of the Third Edition of *Salmon's Short View of the Families of the English Nobility*, 1760.

Page 1. l. 11. THE father of the late and present Duke, was not Duke of Norfolk, but only Lord Thomas Howard; for the late Duke of Norfolk succeeded his uncle William-Henry, elder brother to the above Lord Thomas Howard.

P. 6. Lord. Geo. Hen. Lenox married Lady Louisa Ker, daughter to, &c.

P. 8. The issue of Lord Augustus Fitzroy are wrongly stiled Lord Augustus, and Lord Charles, that being only the stile of the younger sons of Dukes, which title their father never arrived at.

P. 10. ———2. Lady Elizabeth, died 1760.

P. 21. The Duke of Marlborough, lord chamberlain, and married to Lady Carolina Russell, daughter to the Duke of Bedford.

P. 29. The D. of Rutland has no seat at Averham-Park in Nottinghamshire. It belongs to Lord George Sutton, who succeeded to it on the death of his brother Lord Robert Sutton.

——— The D. of Queensberry is not Viscount, but Earl of Drumlanrig.

P. 38 William, D. of Portland, dead, and succeeded by his son, William-Henry, Marq. of Tichfield.

P. 42. Robert, D. of Manchester, dead, and succeeded by his son, George, Visc. Mandeville, who, Oct. 23, 1762, married Miss Dashwood, daughter to Sir James Dashwood.

P. 65. ———8. Lady Diana, married to the Rev. Mr. Marriot, and since dead.

P. 66.

P. 66. John, E. of Weftmoreland, dead, and fucceeded as E. of Weftmoreland and B. Burgherfh, by Thomas Fane, Efq; member for Lyme in Dorfet-fhire, who is defcended from Francis, the fecond furviving fon of the firft Earl of Weftmoreland, of this family. The barony of Defpenfer being a barony in fee, devolves on Sir Francis Dafh-wood, Bart. as lineally defcended by the female line, from Vere (fourth E. of Weftmoreland) Baron Defpenfer, father of the three laft Earls. The title of Baron Catherlough in Ireland is extinct.

P. 70. ———2. John is one of the clerks comptrollers of his Majefty's board of green-cloth.

P. 72. ———2. William, is vice-chamberlain to his Majefty, and a privy counfeller; he had a fon (by his fecond wife) born Nov. 5, 1752.

——— ———3. John, is one of his Majefty's council learned in the law.

P. 77. l. 2. The late Earl of Thanet's Lady was not a Sackvile, but Saville.

P. 81. The daughter, born July 14, 1759, died the fame month, as well as the Countefs its mother.

P. 84. Richard, Earl of Anglefea, dead, and the title fuppofed to be either extinct, or in difpute.

P. 85. Ifabella, Countefs Dowager of Carlifle, married Sir William Mufgrave, Bart. 1759.

P. 97. ———5. Lady Mary is dead.

——— ———6. Lady Frances's hufband, Lord Corn-bury, is dead.

P. 100. ———10. Lady Sophia died 1760.

P. 101. ———3. Lady Juliana married Lord Car-bery, and died 1760.

P. 105. John-Paul, Earl of Stafford, dead, and the title extinct.

P. 106. Henrietta, Countefs dowager of Stafford, is married to Vifc. Farnham.

P. 108. ———11. Lady Henrietta died 1757.

P. 109, Thomas, Earl of Bradford, dead, and the title extinct.

P. 119. ———1. Vifc Malpas had a fon born 1749, and a daughter born 1755.

P. 119,

P. 119. ———2. Robert is rector of St. Andrew's in the town of Hertford, and also of Hertingfordbury in the same county.

P. 120. ———4. Lady Elizabeth's husband, Edward Warren of Poynton (not Poyton) is dead.

P. 122. ———1. Lady Elizabeth, and her husband, Joseph Gascoigne Nightingale, both dead.

P. 130. ———5. Lady Frances was not married to Sir William Carew, but Courtenay, of Powderham-Castle.

P. 131. ———3. Frederick is a clergyman, prebendary of Ely, and one of the clerks to the privy seal.

P. 133. John Earl Granville dead, and succeeded by his son John Viscount Carteret.

P. 143. l. 6. for Earl of Verney, read Earl Verney.

P. 147. l. 4. after issue, add—1. A son, born 1755.
———2. Lady Lucy, born 1751.

P. 149. ———2. John, besides what is here said of him, is also colonel of the second regiment of dragoon guards, usually stiled the Queen's.
——— ——— 3. Lady Henrietta is dead.

P. 153. l. 13. for Commissioner, read Commoner.

P. 156. William Lord Viscount Pultney, died at Madrid February 1763.

P. 166. ———1. Lord Warkworth is a captain in the 85th regiment of foot, stiled royal volunteers, and one of the representatives for the city of Westminster.

P. 175. Charles, Earl of Cornwallis, dead, and succeeded by his son, Charles, Viscount Brome.

P. 179. Darlington, l. 3. dele colonel of a company in the second regiment of foot-guards, which he resigned in 1758, and l. 6. for mayor read an alderman, for mayor is only an annual office, which he enjoyed in 1758.
——— ———2. Frederick is deputy-treasurer of Chelsea hospital.

P. 180.———6. Lady Henrietta died 1758.

P. 185. Edward, Viscount Hereford, dead, and succeeded by his son Edward, an officer in the first regiment of foot-guards.

P. 189.

P. 189. l. 4. Charlotte died 1760.

———— l. 23. this Roger died 1760.

———— l. 32. this Edward is now dean of Norwich.

P. 192. William, Viscount Hatton, dead, was succeeded by his brother, Henry.Charles, who is also dead, and the title extinct.

P. 194. Falmouth, l. 9. is said to be created by Queen Anne; but it was in 1720, by King George I.

P. 195.————6. Nicholas is also chaplain in ordinary to his Majesty.

P. 196.————2. John is a cornet in the horse-guards blue.

P. 199. Jacob, Viscount Folkeston, dead, and succeeded by his son, William.

———— ————3. Anne was married to ———— Plumer, Esq; 1760.

P. 211.————5. St. Andrew is a clergyman, and married Miss Chase, of Bromley in Kent, 1759.

———— 6. Elizabeth was married (1760) to William Bagott, Esq; member for Staffordshire, son of Sir Walter Bagott, Bart.

P. 213. Arundel of Wardour, l. 16. James Everard was married (1751) to Miss Wyndham, daughter and heir of John Wyndham, of Salisbury, Esq;

P. 215. Charles, Lord Dormer, dead, and succeeded by his brother, John.

P. 216.————8. Mary died 1753.

P. 235. Foley, l. 12. Elizabeth died 1759.

P. 236.————2. Henry's first wife, Mrs. Philips, is dead: and he married to his second (1759) Miss Triphena Scawen, of Maidwell, Northamptonshire.

———— 4. Allen, is also rector of Beverston in Gloucestershire.

P. 242. Matthew, Lord Ducie, is dead, and succeeded by his brother Charles, now Lord Ducie.

P. 245. Lewis did not marry Mr. Pelham's daughter Grace, but Frances. *See p. 37.*

———— 3. George is groom of the bed-chamber to his Majesty, Lieutenant-Colonel Commandant of the

96th

96th regiment, and member of parliament for the city of Lincoln.

P. 248.———7 Mary was married (1751) to Alexander Wright, Esq;

——— John Thynne, Lord Chedworth, dead, and succeeded by his brother, Henry-Frederick.

P. 249. Richard, Lord Edgcumbe, dead, and succeeded by his brother, George, who married Miss Gilbert, daughter to the late Archbishop of York, 1761.

P. 254. George, Lord Anson, dead, and the title extinct.

P. 263. L 7. Lord Mansfield is not brother, but uncle to Lord Viscount Stormont.

P. 265.———6. William Henry was afterwards, viz. in 1759, appointed governor of Jamaica.

P. 267. John, Lord Wycombe, dead, and succeeded by his son William.

——— Wycombe, l. 4. for Dunkerton, read Dunkerron.—L. 12. for be, read bees.

P. 276.———7. Elizabeth was married (1759) to the Rev. Mr. Briscoe.

The

The prefent State of the LORDS SPI-
RITUAL, with their refpective Promotions
and Tranflations.

NAMES.	SEES.	Anno.	In room of
His Grace	Briftol	1734	Cecil, tr.
Dr. Thomas Secker,	Oxford	1737	Potter, tr.
Primate of all England.	Canterbury	1758	Hutton. dec.
His Grace	St. Afaph	1748	Lifl-, tr.
Dr. Robert Drummond,	Salifbury	1761	Thomas, tr.
Primate of England.	York	1761	Gilbert, dec.
The Right Reverend	Carlifle	1747	Fleming, dec.
Dr. Richard Ofbaldefton,	London	1761	Hayter, dec.
Hon. Dr. Richard Trevor,	St. David's	1744	Willes, tr.
	Durham	1752	Butler, dec.
Dr. John Thomas,	Peterborough	1747	Clavering, dec
	Salifbury	1757	Gilbert, tr.
	Winchefter	1761	Hoadly, dec.
Dr. Matthias Mawfon,	Landaff	1738	Harris, dec.
	Chichefter	1740	Hare, dec
	Ely	1754	Gooch, dec.
Dr. Edward Willes,	St. David's	1742	Clagget, tr.
	Bath & Wells	1743	Wynn, dec.
Dr. John Thomas,	St. Afaph	1743	Maddox, tr.
	Lincoln	1744	Reynolds, dec.
	Salifbury	1761	Drummond, tr
Rt. Hon. Ld. James Beauclerk.	Hereford	1746	Egerton, dec.
Dr. Zachary Pearce,	Bangor	1747	Hutton, tr.
	Rochefter	1756	Wilcox, dec.
Hon. Dr. Fred. Cornwallis,	L'tch. & Cov.	1749	Smalbroke, d.
Dr. Edmund Keene,	Chefter	1752	Peploe, dec.
Dr. James Johnfon,	Gloucefter	1752	Benfon, dec.
	Worcefter	1759	Maddux, dec.
Dr. Wm. Afhburnham,	Chichefter	1754	Mawfon, tr.
Dr. Richard Newcome,	Landaff	1755	Creffet, dec.
	St. Afaph	1761	Drummond, tr.
Dr. John Hume,	Briftol	1756	Confheare, de.
	Oxford	1758	Secker tr.
Dr. John Egerton,	Bangor	1756	Pearce, tr.
Dr. Richard Terrick,	Peterborough	1757	Thomas, tr.

Dr.

NAMES.	SEES.	Anno.	In room of
Dr. Philip Yonge,	{ Briftol	1758	Hume, tr.
	{ Norwich	1761	Hayter, tr.
Dr. Wm. Warburton,	Gloucefter	1759	Johnfon, tr.
Dr. Samuel Squire,	St. David's	1761	Ellis, dec.
Dr. John Ewer,	Landaff	1761	Newcome, tr.
Dr. John Greene,	Lincoln	1761	Thomas, tr.
Dr. Tho. Newton,	Briftol	1761	Yonge, tr.
Dr. Charles Littleton,	Carlifle	1760	Ofbaldefton, tr.
Hon. Dr. Frederick Keppel,	Exeter	1762	Lavington, de.

The Sixteen PEERS for SCOTLAND.

JOHN Duke of Argyle.
  William Earl of Sutherland.
John Earl of Rothes.
James Earl of Morton.
Alexander Earl of Eglington.
James Earl of Moray.
John Earl of Hyndford.
James Earl of Abercorn.
John Earl of Loudon.
John Earl of Breadalbane.
William Earl of Dunmore.
James Earl of March.
Hugh Earl of Marchmont.
John Earl of Bute.
David Vifcount Stormont
Charles Lord Cathcart.

www.ingramcontent.com/pod-product-compliance
Lightning Source LLC
Chambersburg PA
CBHW060514030726
47498CB00004B/938